I0831671

BURIED FOR GOOD

ALEX COOMBS

First published in Great Britain in 2021 by Boldwood Books Ltd.

Cover Design by Nick Castle Design

Cover photography: Shutterstock

A CIP catalogue record for this book is available from the British Library.

Paperback ISBN 978-1-80048-834-2

Hardback ISBN 978-1-80426-156-9

Large Print ISBN 978-1-80048-833-5

Ebook ISBN 978-1-80048-836-6

Kindle ISBN 978-1-80048-835-9

Audio CD ISBN 978-1-80048-828-1

MP3 CD ISBN 978-1-80048-829-8

Digital audio download ISBN 978-1-80048-830-4

Boldwood Books Ltd
23 Bowerdean Street
London SW6 3TN
www.boldwoodbooks.com

To Archie, with love.

1

The fair had arrived in Lochgilphead, a small town on the west coast of Scotland about a two-hour drive from Glasgow, on the Thursday. By the Monday morning the fairground workers had mostly packed it up and departed. All that remained of the rides, the brightly coloured stalls and the fast-food booths that had been set up on the long strip of grass that ran along the seaside front of the town were three rides. These had now been dismantled and folded up like giant toys, metal origami, waiting to be loaded up onto lorries and trailers and taken to wherever the fair was next headed.

Left behind were marks on the grass, traces of the now vanished rides – the dodgems, the swing boats, the helter-skelter – overflowing litter bins, cans and bottles, the usual party hangover. No food waste, the gulls had seen to that.

Also left in its wake were a couple of twenty-something Glaswegian hard men, Scott and Callum, who had followed the fair eighty miles west from the city to Lochgilphead, hoping to get laid, get in a fight and make a bit of money selling cheap drugs: weed and knock-off Chinese ket.

The weekend had been and gone. It had been profitable, their drugs had sold well, both to the locals and to some hard-core bikers from Oban way. The bikers had wanted more but Scott and Callum were not retracing their steps to Glasgow. They had ended up staying for the duration of the fair. Right now, early on the Monday morning, they were coming down from the two-day drink and drug binge that had left them feeling as washed up and stranded as the detritus on the muddy beach below the sea wall.

It was 7.45 a.m. when Callum finished the dregs of the bottle of Smirnoff and he hurled the bottle in an arc over the main road, where it smashed on the pavement outside an ironmonger's shop at the bottom of the high street. An old man stopped and glared at them across the street. Callum made an obscene gesture at the stupid old twat.

What are you going to do about it, you old fart?

Scott and Callum were bored, drunk, disoriented from the comedown and irritable, spoiling for a fight.

Callum belched, tasting bile and alcohol in his mouth. He rubbed his eyes, taking stock of his surroundings. On his left, the long stretch of green grass in front of the wall that dropped down to the loch, stretching away, a gunmetal expanse of grey bordered by low hills on either side. To his right, the high street and beyond that some large houses facing the waterfront. A woman was walking along the pavement towards them. She'd do. She wasn't young, he guessed over thirty, wearing a red suede biker jacket, white tee, tight skinny black jeans and short black heeled boots. She didn't look local. She had an air of competent confidence that Callum suddenly found enraging. Who did she think she was, walking along like she fucking owned the place? He scowled and drew on his cigarette. He was feeling like shit; he wanted to share the joy.

She drew close to him. He noticed she was good-looking, good figure too.

He stepped out into the pavement, blocking her way. 'Give us a kiss, darling!'

She turned and looked at him; he expected a nervous smile, wanted to see the fear in her face. Far from it. All he could see was the contempt in her cold grey eyes. She didn't seem scared of him at all. That wasn't right. He wasn't having that; he wasn't taking that kind of shit. He wanted respect. He went to grab her, one hand reaching for her shoulder, the other for her chest.

Callum didn't see the punch coming. It slammed into his ear like being hit with a brick; he didn't have time to process it, and then, a microsecond later, a huge blow to his gut that left him on his knees, fighting for breath.

'See you later, prick,' said the woman scornfully.

'Callum!' shouted Scott, running over. Callum knelt on the kerb, holding his agonised stomach, unable to move, his head a mass of pain, wondering what the hell had happened. The woman walked away, unhurried. Scott ran over to his buddy to help him up.

'You OK, man?' Callum was bent over double, he could still hardly breathe and his ear was burning from the blow.

'Aye, fuckin' bitch...'

From across the road, behind the wheel of a white Range Rover Evoque, a pair of hard green eyes had watched the action unfold, the woman's face expressionless, impassive.

She got her phone out, scrolled through her contact list, selected a name and texted:

I've found who we're looking for.

Send.

2

Hanlon looked around her new office with satisfaction. It was her first business premises since she had set up as a private investigator. What it lacked in terms of furnishings – three chairs, a table for her laptop, a computer screen, a printer and a dog basket in the corner for her border collie, Wemyss – it made up for in the view.

Lochgilphead was at the top of a spur of Loch Fyne. It was a small, relatively prosperous town with a large secondary school, a hospital and a couple of industrial estates. The high street was broad and attractive but it wasn't pretty, like Tarbert further down the loch, or picturesque, like Inveraray further up. It was functional rather than touristy. The head of the loch here was shallow, and when the tide was in, you could see the sea stretching out before you, an unimpeded view of sky and water, bordered by the green hills on both sides.

Hanlon took her jacket off and draped it over the back of her chair while flexing the knuckles on her right hand. They were reddened but not too painful. She nodded in satisfaction at the memory of her fist crashing into the bony head of the kid who had threatened her a short while ago. Callum, that had been his name. That was a job well done, she thought. When she got into bed tonight and reviewed her day, she'd look back on that incident with satisfaction. If she'd meekly accepted it, put her head down and just walked away, his jeers ringing in her ears, it would have tormented her not just for a few days, but maybe for the rest of her days. Turning the other cheek had never worked for Hanlon.

She took the laptop from her rucksack, plugged it in, booted it up, logged into her bank account and checked the balance. A frown crossed her face; things were not looking great. She clicked on the calendar, a 9 a.m. meeting with a K. M. O'Rourke.

Well, she thought, hopefully Mr O'Rourke will unbutton his wallet.

* * *

K. M. O'Rourke was not what Hanlon had been expecting. For a start, O'Rourke was a she and Hanlon had assumed for no reason whatsoever that the potential client would be male.

O'Rourke was certainly an imposing figure: tall, wearing heels, with long red hair, which was piled upwards on her head, adding another good few centimetres. She sat down in the visitor's chair, crossed her long, elegant legs, smoothed a non-existent crease out of her short skirt and looked coolly at Hanlon. Behind Hanlon was the impressive view of the loch. O'Rourke didn't seem impressed. Or if she was, she was hiding it well.

'How may I help you?' asked Hanlon. There was a lengthy silence. 'Ms O'Rourke,' she added.

'You can call me Katherine,' the woman said. Her accent was educated southern English.

'I'm Hanlon.' She immediately felt slightly ridiculous. Of course O'Rourke would have known her name – she'd made an appointment after all.

'No first name?' O'Rourke raised an elegant, shapely eyebrow.

'No.'

O'Rourke shrugged and said, 'Oh, well. I'll come straight to the point. I'm looking for a temporary bodyguard. Do you think you could do that?'

Hanlon smiled. O'Rourke didn't look as though she needed one – she was quite intimidating.

She considered the question seriously. Was being a bodyguard really for her? The short answer was no. The only people she could think of who might want a bodyguard were people in the public eye. Money was tight, it was true, but the thought of ushering some minor celebrity that she had never heard of, and cared even less about, into a velvet roped-off area of a nightclub? And what a question: 'Do you think you could do that?'

Hanlon found herself, as she had done so often in the past, about to bite the hand that fed her.

'I could do that, yes,' she said slightly contemptuously. 'There are lots of things I could do. For example, I could do seventy-five continuous press-ups.'

'I didn't say I wanted a personal trainer,' O'Rourke said sourly. She brushed some imaginary dust off her skirt in an irritable way.

'I suppose what I'm trying to say is that I'm perfectly capable of being someone's minder, but I'm far from sure I want to do it,' Hanlon said, 'to be perfectly honest.'

As soon as the words were out of her mouth, she regretted them. She desperately needed money. Integrity was for those who could afford it, and she was broke.

'I saw you in action this morning,' O'Rourke said, 'beating that guy up.'

Hanlon looked at her with surprise. She wasn't sure if the coincidence was necessarily a good thing; she knew she had been provoked but she suddenly wondered what it might look like to a casual bystander.

O'Rourke fixed Hanlon with an evaluating look. 'Would you say that was representative of your approach to work?'

Hanlon bit back the obvious retort: 'That wasn't work, that was pleasure.' She frowned. Was getting involved in a fight representative of her work? Yes, it usually was.

'Pretty much,' Hanlon said irritably. 'I did consider disarming him with a tolerant smile...' her eyes narrowed, 'but on balance I thought a left hook would work better.' It was her turn now to favour the other woman with a hard stare. 'More effective.'

'I'm looking for someone who can be discreet.' O'Rourke leaned forward and tapped the desk to emphasise the word. 'And low-key,' she added.

Hanlon shrugged. 'He attacked me.'

'Was your response proportionate?'

Hanlon could feel herself getting angry. Today certainly wasn't working out as she had expected it to. She had consciously planned a peaceful day using tips from her anger management therapist. She had gone for a forty-minute run, showered, meditated (in reality, tried to meditate; she seemed to think even more when she was trying not to think, annoyingly). She had read some inspirational literature Dr Morgan had recommended – the Tao Te Ching. That hadn't helped either. If anything, it had put her in a worse mood.

And then what had happened? Someone had tried to assault her and now she was being given a hard time as if she were back in the police. Who the hell did O'Rourke think she was?

Hanlon was feeling far from calm now. O'Rourke's frown deepened. 'The reason I am so concerned is that my employer is very much in the public eye. We need a cool head as much as anything.' She did the finger-tapping thing again. 'We want to avoid controversy.'

Hanlon shrugged. 'Well, if someone attacks your employer maybe they would want someone to deal with it effectively rather than "with a cool head".'

O'Rourke shook her head and sighed. 'I'm not sure you're taking this entirely seriously, Hanlon.'

Hanlon leaned forward over her desk. 'Look, Katherine, I'm old-school. If someone attacks a woman, I am not concerned if they have issues, or what their background is, or their sexuality or their ethnicity or religion. I fight back. And that is the attitude I would bring to protecting someone who had hired me. I am not a diplomat, Miss O'Rourke.' She leaned back in her chair. 'I think you've got the wrong person here.'

O'Rourke stood up. 'Well, it was nice meeting you, Hanlon.' She obviously agreed. She was also obviously quick at making her mind up about things. Damn, thought Hanlon.

'Likewise,' she said politely.

'I'll be in touch if we think you're the kind of person we need.'

Hanlon nodded and O'Rourke turned and walked out of the door.

Hanlon stood up and looked out of the window at the sea view her visitor had so signally failed to appreciate.

'Are you crazy?' she said to herself. Her usual terms were three hundred pounds a day plus expenses. This promised to be an easy job: walking some pampered moron actor/celeb from her car to a table, to babysit them or pander to their ego. Easy money, and she'd just blown it.

This 'to thine own self be true' way of doing things had cost her a sore hand and at least a thousand pounds.

'How is your way of life working for you?' her therapist, Dr Morgan had asked her, what seemed like long ago but was actually just under a year. It wasn't a rhetorical question; it was very pertinent. Her anger issues had cost her a career in the police and a few months ago they had nearly cost her life. She sighed and watched the gulls wheeling around in the sky.

What a great start to the day. She glanced at the time at the bottom of the computer; it wasn't even five past nine.

* * *

O'Rourke stepped outside the front door of Hanlon's office.

She looked around at the seafront. The thugs had gone. A shame it hadn't worked out. She had liked Hanlon despite the woman's brusque manners and she'd enjoyed seeing her beat that dick up. She took her phone out and checked her messages. There was one from Camille.

She stared at the image attached. There was no doubting the intent behind it: violence and hatred. It was deeply disturbing. It looked as though the campaign against Camille was escalating.

This was here this morning.

It was a picture of the front door of the studio. 'Murdering Bitch!' had been spray-painted on the pale, varnished wood in large irregular letters.

I'm frightened, Kath!

She swore and turned on her heel.

* * *

Hanlon heard the knock on the door and as she looked round, it opened.

O'Rourke was back. Hanlon looked at her interrogatively, eyebrows raised.

'After a great deal of thought,' O'Rourke said with a certain amount of nuanced irony, 'I think you're the kind of person we need.'

3

'I work for Camille Anderson,' O'Rourke said. She noticed the lack of comprehension on Hanlon's face.

She studied her new employee attentively. Hanlon was about her age, she guessed, late thirties. She had dark, thick hair which was quite curly, strong shapely dark eyebrows and very grey eyes. Her face was attractive rather than pretty. She was of medium height and her obviously strong body was more of a gymnast's build than a weightlifter's. O'Rourke had seen her in action, the tracksuit-wearing chav with his badly dyed blond hair stepping out to intimidate her, the unbelievable speed with which she'd flattened him. O'Rourke hoped that her decision to hire her wouldn't be one she would come to regret.

'YouTube?' she said interrogatively, raising her eyebrows.

Nothing.

'OK,' she said. 'Camille Anderson is the UK equivalent of Adriene Mishler.'

Hanlon looked blank again and shook her head to signify her ignorance.

O'Rourke sighed; she hadn't been prepared for this. Camille's followers were almost exclusively Hanlon's demographic: thirty–forty years old, female, sporty. Hanlon was bucking the trend. 'You've never heard of Adriene either.'

'No,' Hanlon said. 'No, I haven't.'

'OK,' O'Rourke said, switching into educator mode. 'So Adriene is a yoga teacher, an American yoga teacher, a very successful one. She has millions of followers, mainly in the States, and Camille is the UK's foremost online yoga teacher. Her British equivalent. We're big business.'

'Who's "we"?' asked Hanlon.

'I'm Camille's business manager,' O'Rourke said.

'Why does Camille need a bodyguard?' Hanlon asked. Yoga teachers weren't usually high on the list of at-risk professions.

'Because she's been receiving death threats,' O'Rourke said. She opened her phone and showed Hanlon the message. 'Here's the latest example. She found this on her yoga studio door in Glasgow this morning.'

Hanlon studied the message. 'Murdering bitch? Who is she supposed to have killed?'

'Who knows? I'm not sure we're dealing with a rational person, Hanlon. The one before, in a letter, said, "die, bitch, die".'

Hanlon nodded. To her it looked more like abuse than a credible threat, the kind of thing a jilted ex might do.

'Tell me about the other threats,' she asked. 'When did they start?'

'It's July now, I would say about a month ago,' O'Rourke said. 'The first one arrived by post. I remember it well. I was going through the mail, the physical mail, of which, as a business, we still get quite a lot. It just said, "you evil bitch, Anderson". I remember it shook me – it seemed so much more threatening than other negative comments she'd received.'

'How do you mean?' Hanlon asked.

'So, Camille's got thirty thousand followers on Twitter, she'll get the odd shitty message, but...' O'Rourke paused. 'It's one thing to tap out a hundred-odd characters and press post compared to typing, printing and physically walking to a post box and putting an envelope inside as an insult. That takes commitment.'

* * *

'How many letters did you get?'

O'Rourke frowned, thinking back. 'Three or four, then we started to get e-mails.'

'I take it you tried to trace them?'

O'Rourke looked at her as if she were crazy. 'Doh, yes! E-mail address, domain name, IP address. I reviewed the headers and then I paid for a professional company to look into it.' She shook her head. 'They got nowhere. Someone was being very careful indeed. That made me really worried – it wasn't some knuckle-dragging moron with a room-temperature IQ. Whoever is doing this is bright.'

Hanlon nodded. She could see why O'Rourke was getting so concerned.

'Did you get the impression that the sender knew Camille? Were they personal or more general?'

'It's a good question,' O'Rourke said. 'The problem is, in a way, many people feel they know Camille. I mean, with the technology, she is there in your living room, just in front of your yoga mat, and people think of her as part of the family. However, yes, I do sense that the person sending them actually knew her, little details here and there. Personal details known only to a few.'

'And presumably the threat is escalating?' Hanlon said.

'The threats got nastier and more specific.'

'You've been to the police?'

O'Rourke nodded. 'They made sympathetic noises, but there was very little they could do about it. They also pointed out that in today's environment someone with a wide online presence would expect to receive a fair amount of hate mail. Social media being a happy haven for the disgruntled and the angry and expressing yourself is just a mouse-click away.'

'In other words,' Hanlon said, 'it comes with the turf, live with it.'

'We pointed out there's been cranky stuff before, as well as plenty of obscene comments on her Twitter, Instagram and Facebook feeds, but this, this is different, and then recently we received information that Camille would be killed, or certainly most at risk, from the eighth to the fifteenth of July.'

That was the following week. Not long away.

'Who did this information come from?' Hanlon asked.

O'Rourke hesitated, then shook her head. 'I can't really say, that's confidential, for now anyway…' Hanlon looked at her quizzically, 'but a trusted source. We'll leave it at that.'

'And you told the police this?'

'Yes, they were very polite but it's a question of resources. They're not going to provide a bodyguard.' She nodded at Hanlon. 'That's where you come in. We thought that getting out of town would be advisable.'

Hanlon asked, 'Where were you thinking of?'

'She's recently bought a property near Oban.'

Hanlon nodded. She knew the town well; it was about an hour's drive north.

'It's built on its own island.' O'Rourke played idly with a loose strand of hair that had come astray from her topknot. 'Ten bedrooms. It was formerly a hotel, and so next week she's got five paying guests staying there. Five-day stay.'

'How long ago was this planned?' Hanlon asked.

'A while ago, but we brought it forward. Since the numbers are so small we could contact them all personally. Camille is going to lead a retreat on the island during this time. The only people there will be staff and the guests, all of whom we know…' she paused, 'and you.'

Hanlon nodded. She thought the plan seemed to make a good deal of sense. Presumably the threat to Camille came from some crazy person, no matter how good their IT skills, rather than, say, organised crime. Even if they somehow discovered her whereabouts, the logistics of getting to a remote Scottish island could well be enough to deter them.

'OK,' Hanlon said, 'I'll just recap what you've told me. Camille's been getting threats for about a month now. The severity level of these has been increasing. The person making the threats is probably known to Camille and the next couple of weeks could well see Camille attacked.' She looked enquiringly at O'Rourke.

'Correct,' she said.

'Can you give me some background on Camille, how things operate?' Hanlon asked.

'The actual yoga classes in the studio are just a small part of what she does,' O'Rourke explained. 'Camille gets the bulk of her revenue from YouTube, mainly from people buying advertising, from sponsorship, from corporates, motivational speaking, which is very lucrative, and private classes.' She had used her fingers to enumerate these points, ticking them off one by one.

Hanlon nodded. 'OK, so what exactly do you want me to do?'

O'Rourke said, 'We want you to accompany Camille to the island for a week and keep her alive, keep her safe. So, just a week of your time.'

Hanlon thought for a moment. It all seemed simple enough. Five days in a hotel up the road, very little to do.

'OK,' Hanlon said. 'I charge three hundred pounds a day plus expenses.'

O'Rourke nodded. 'That sounds fine.' She undid her handbag and handed her a manilla envelope. 'There's information in here. I'll also e-mail you links to Camille's various sites and social-media platforms. Just to recapitulate, the danger period is July eighth to the fifteenth, a week today, so you can start on, say, Wednesday? The day after tomorrow?'

'That sounds fine.'

'Good, send me your bank details and I'll pay you in advance for ten days. You'll officially start then. I'll send you the address of Camille's yoga studio in Glasgow and I'll see you there Wednesday morning, bright and early.' O'Rourke stood up and they shook hands.

'Well, I think that's just about everything. I'll say goodbye.'

'Until then,' Hanlon said. O'Rourke closed the door behind her. Hanlon stood up and looked out of the window at Loch Fyne and the seagulls wheeling in the breeze. Good, she thought, that will keep the wolf from the door for a while. Monday was looking up.

She opened the envelope and pulled out the list of Camille's social media. She turned to her laptop and looked at what she could find on her new employer.

Instagram first, to give an idea of what she looked like. Camille Anderson was slim and blonde with shoulder-length hair. She had the right kind of face for a yoga guru, attractive but not too much so, with a hint of other-worldly. Kind of girl-next-doorsy. The type of face and body that you might admire but wouldn't make you green with envy.

Hanlon put her at about forty, approximately her own age. The pictures were the usual suspects, Camille doing mega-flexy poses with a serene look upon her face in a variety of stock locations: beaches, mountain tops and a waterfall.

Her website gave a short biography: born in London, Scottish-French and a gifted athlete. Following an injury that needed surgery and curtailed her running career, she studied yoga for a year in Benares in India before returning to the UK and setting up her practice in Oxford. She relocated to Glasgow and set up Nelumbo Yoga.

Hanlon frowned. Nelumbo? A quick search revealed that it was the Latin name for the lotus flower. She guessed that there would be quite a few sites with lotus in their names, hence the linguistic sidestep. The website gave details on her retreats. They were billed as 'a foretaste of Eternal Bliss'. And, 'a rare opportunity to experience a state of Samadhi or oneness with the object of meditation'. And, 'a chance to experience Drishti, focus on an aim or goal, free from the distractions of modern life.'

Five days of yoga and meditation. The website also promised exquisite plant-based food and spiritual growth.

There were downloadable courses available on the site and the option of booking one-to-one sessions with Camille. A further box enabled you to contact Camille for corporate bookings or inspirational team talks. It was very professionally done.

As well as an online presence, as O'Rourke had mentioned, Camille had a physical, bricks and mortar one too. She had a yoga studio in Glasgow and one in Edinburgh. Both of these had small vegetarian café/restaurants attached and these ran outside catering and cookery classes. Camille's younger sister, Siobhan, had worked in catering. Hanlon idly glanced at her short CV that was appended to the yoga-centre information. Amongst the places she had worked, Hanlon noticed she had done a spell at The Sleeket Mouse, a Glasgow restaurant that had recently won a Michelin star. Hanlon vaguely knew the owner. Siobhan Anderson must be good, she thought.

Her computer signalled she had mail. She went to her inbox. O'Rourke had just e-mailed her the property details of the place that Camille had bought where the retreat was going to be held. It was from an estate agents' website specialising in commercial property.

Duachy House was its name.

She looked at the pictures. It was a gothic, Victorian manor house with mock turrets on each of the four corners and ten bedrooms, all with their own bathrooms, built on a small island that was approximately a mile from both the mainland and the island of Seil, about a two- to three-hour drive west of Glasgow.

O'Rourke had added a short history of the place. It had been constructed for a Scottish mine owner who was known as much for his fanatical religiosity – it had its own private chapel – as his reclusiveness. He was a misanthrope, he disliked the company of others, and lived there alone for many years, dying in his nineties in the nineteen thirties. It had then been abandoned and subsequently bought in the early seventies by a rock star, Shane Gowrie, who had spent a small fortune restoring it. It had soon gathered rumours as a place of drug-fuelled parties, the chapel being used for sex ceremonies.

All good things came to an end. The rock star was now in an old people's home with dementia; the property had been modernised and made into a hotel for a few years but the last owners couldn't make it pay. Camille had bought it for a very good price.

Hanlon thought to herself that if anyone could make it work, it would be Camille. Her clientele would not be concerned about the weather, always an issue in Scotland as Hanlon well knew. If it were sunny, they could do yoga outside; if not, the studio would be fine. Nor did they demand entertainment. Well, other than spiritual enlightenment.

Also, Camille wasn't dependent on a short holiday season; the search for sacred wisdom and a healthy body lasted all year round.

Hanlon stood up, walked back to the window and stared out at the water, dark blue in the morning light. She loved the fact that her new office had a view. She wondered why anyone would want to kill Camille Anderson. The most likely candidate, she thought, looking at the slim, attractive woman in leggings and a Lycra top, was a deranged fan. Well, she felt herself perfectly capable of dealing with that threat, particularly on a relatively hard-to-get-to island.

The last thing that Hanlon noticed on her online search was a site that purported to give well-known people's net worth. She was sceptical about these claims but she clicked on it anyway. It claimed that Camille was worth several million pounds. Even allowing for exaggeration, it was obvious she was doing very well for herself. Fair enough, thought Hanlon.

But it did make her revise her earlier question of why someone might wish her harm. Money provided a good enough motive for malice, and millions a good enough motive for murder.

4

Hanlon drove home, a couple of miles north of Lochgilphead and then west along the narrow, picturesque Crinan Canal. The waterway had been built so that boats could use it to cut off the long Argyll peninsula if they wanted to access the west coast of Scotland. A mile or so short of Crinan she turned off the narrow road and up a forestry track into the hills. Home these days was a tumble-down cottage with stone white-washed walls and a small garden enclosed by a dry-stone wall that lay a mile or so from the road.

One of its main attractions, aside from its solitude – she wasn't keen on the idea of neighbours – was that it had a beautiful view. On one side it overlooked a small loch nestled in the hills and on the other you could see, far below, through the pine-trees, the line of the Crinan Canal and the flat, treeless expanse of the brown grassland known as the Crinan Moss before the dark-green, far off hills rose again to the north.

Another was the old lady who lived in a small house at the bottom of the track and who, for a small fee, was happy to dog-sit Wemyss, Hanlon's border collie, when she had to meet clients or go into Glasgow.

She collected the dog, drank tea and talked to Effie, who was always desperate for company, and went home. She suspected that the old woman would probably look after the dog for nothing. If she didn't speak to Hanlon she probably wouldn't speak to anyone. Effie needed to talk; Hanlon wasn't so sure she herself needed to.

Back home, Hanlon pulled her clothes off, changed into running gear and headed off with the dog at her heels on a ten-kilometre run on the forestry trails that surrounded the croft. The first couple of kilometres were hard work; she was running up into the hills and she could feel the muscles in her thighs and calves protesting. The sun was hot today and her top was soon soaked with sweat.

After about twenty minutes she hit her stride, and her body, now warmed up, forgave her, and she started to relax into the run and enjoy it. The iron muscles in her legs carried her effortlessly along the trails. Now she could actually notice her surroundings: the endless pine-trees, the tarry smell of their needles, the grey of the rocks, the medicinal scent of ferns, the countless small streams that were such a feature of Scotland, the peaty soil. She was able to put aside all thought and just be. Running mindlessly, without thought, Wemyss keeping her company, in these circumstances, brought her as close to happiness as she could ever be.

An hour later, showered and changed, she lay on her bed, the dog by her side. Hanlon's cottage, a bothy as it was called here, was a rudimentary stone building – more or less one large room. This one had been fitted with some modern amenities – she had electricity, a fridge, a cooker. There was a fireplace, her bed was in the corner. The toilet was outside and there was a basic shower room next to it. There was no mains water, that came courtesy of the nearby loch in the hills via some kind of filtration system. It was brown and peaty, and, after a lifetime of London water, she loved it. There was a heater for the shower, but it never got really hot; that was a minor inconvenience. The only downside to living here was the midges, tiny mosquitoes that plagued the west coast. Individually they weren't that bad; the trouble lay in their numbers. Hanlon had known them get so bad that the blue sleeve of a running top had turned black with them settling on it.

They were particularly virulent at dusk. She would have loved to be able to sit outside in the summer and enjoy the view in the evening, but it wasn't an option. Not if you wanted to avoid being eaten alive.

Hanlon had installed some gym equipment in the bothy, a squat rack that she could also do pull-ups on, a weight bench for bench press that had handles for dips. There were various dumb-bells and barbells in the corner. A heavy punchbag hung from a hook in a massive beam in the ceiling. It wasn't exactly cosy or stylish. Her house wasn't going to feature in *Homes & Gardens* or *Escape to the Country*.

Hanlon lay back on her bed, stroking the dog's silky ears, looking at some of Camille's free yoga content online. Some phone company or other had built a huge mast half a mile or so from her isolated cottage and out here, in the middle of nowhere, she got an amazingly clear signal.

Camille Anderson was beautiful to watch when she moved, lithe, graceful as the runner she had once been. She also had an engaging personality, the kind of person that you wanted to spend time with. It was no wonder, Hanlon thought, that Camille was so popular. It seemed strange that someone would want to do her any harm at all, much less issue death threats, particularly towards someone who seemed so essentially gentle and good-natured.

Hanlon had done yoga ages ago but hadn't liked it. She frowned and got off the bed; she stretched upwards, leaned forward and placed her palms on the floor. She'd always been flexible and now she recreated some of Camille's poses just to see if she could. During Downward Dog, appropriately enough, Wemyss got off the bed and poked her face with his nose, checking to see that she was OK, a faint look of concern on his intelligent face, wondering what the hell she was doing. He obviously didn't like the look of yoga.

Hanlon got back on the bed flushed and with a faint sense of triumph.

She took her phone out and texted O'Rourke, who replied almost immediately asking her if she could be in Glasgow for 8 a.m. on the Wednesday to meet Camille. Camille had thought it would be a good idea if she went along to one of her classes.

She would be there, Hanlon replied. An early start suited her.

She put the phone down. The dog looked at her expectantly. 'Yes, you can come. You'll have to wait in the car though.' She shook her head in irritation at herself for speaking to the dog as though he knew what she was saying. Perhaps I am spending too much time on my own, she thought. Perhaps I'll end up like Effie, living on my own, desperate for company, baking drop scones for people who never come.

I'll never bake, she promised herself.

She stroked the dog's head and looked at the brochure for the retreat; the words 'eternal silence' stood out. It sounded uncomfortably like a euphemism for the grave.

5

'Now, stand in Tadasana... Mountain pose.' Taking her cue from her fellow classmates, fifteen of them, thirteen women and two men, Hanlon obediently stood upright, watching Camille intently. 'And now, down to Chair pose... feel that stretch...'

She was enjoying her yoga class far more than she thought she would have done. She'd arrived at the yoga studio at quarter to eight. It was in the university part of Glasgow, Hillhead, which was an area fairly central and easy to find, just off the main road that led into the city from the west. The university area was like all such places, plenty of bars, cheap restaurants, shops selling the kind of stuff that students went for. A vibrant place, but quiet and just coming to life at this time in the morning. Not with students though; they were still asleep.

She had parked her car and walked to the studio. Wemyss had settled down in the back with obvious resignation for a wait. The yoga studio was situated in a typical street tenement block in a row of shops of the honey-coloured stone that was prevalent in Hillhead. She'd glanced at the doors as she'd walked in; the wood that had been spray-gunned with the death threat had been freshly painted. She'd nodded to herself. O'Rourke would have seen to that.

O'Rourke had met her at reception, elegant in another tailored suit.

'Hi, Hanlon. The changing room is over there, the studios are upstairs – it's Studio A. Camille knows you're coming; she'll know who you are.'

The ground floor had a couple of changing rooms, a reception desk and a café/restaurant through a glass and wood door. Everything was bright and airy, Scandinavian style, light pine and uplifting. Hanlon had gone into the changing room, put Lycra on and walked upstairs to the studio.

She'd recognised Camille immediately. She was smaller than Hanlon had thought, just over five feet and slender. The atmosphere in the class could have been described as ecstatic. Camille was a kind of goddess to these people; it was more like being at a religious ceremony than an exercise class.

There was even a Camille lookalike amongst the people in the class, an attractive woman in her forties who had a Camille haircut, shoulder length, the same honey-coloured hair, the exact same yoga clothes as Camille and an expression of dazed happiness that her hero was walking amongst the mortals.

The session was focussed and intense and Hanlon soon realised how stiff her body was getting as she stretched it in ways that she didn't normally. Not only that, she began to feel mentally more relaxed. Perhaps I shouldn't be so dismissive of things, she thought as she stared towards the ceiling during Cobra pose.

Camille walked around the class, correcting poses, offering warm words of encouragement. During Child's pose, she sat on Hanlon's lower back, pushing her hips closer to the ground with the weight of her body.

'You're very tense, Hanlon,' she said. 'I think you're storing a lot of emotion in these hips...'

The class ended with five minutes of Corpse pose, Savasana. Hanlon had been up since 5 a.m. and nearly fell asleep.

The class ended and Camille came over to her.

'How was that for you?' she asked. She pushed her blonde hair out of her face and looked intensely into Hanlon's eyes as if her opinion was of crucial importance. Camille had a kind of Roman nose, which Hanlon found very endearing. It was slightly too big for her face and added a huge amount of character. Without it she'd have been almost too pretty.

'I really enjoyed that, actually,' she said.

'I'll see you downstairs in the café in twenty minutes. We can have breakfast together.'

'That sounds great,' Hanlon said. They were interrupted by the lookalike.

'Excuse me.' She flashed an insincere smile at Hanlon, before turning to Camille. Hanlon noticed that, not only had she dyed her hair Camille's colour, she had also painted her toenails the same colour as Camille's. It was a bit creepy, this kind of tribute act.

'Camille, that was just amazing,' the woman said. 'I'm going to be on the retreat next week, so looking forward to it.'

Camille smiled. 'Thank you, Suki, I'm looking forward to it too... super-excited...'

Suki looked ecstatic. 'Super-excited too!'

That'll be her new word, Hanlon thought, now that she's heard Camille use it.

She namasted and turned and left the studio.

'See you in a minute,' Hanlon said to Camille, and followed Suki down the stairs. The stairs were steep; she had a good view of the top of Suki's head and the dark roots where her hair was growing through.

She showered and changed. Suki was nearby in the changing room. She had a much fuller figure than Camille and a pierced navel, a thing that never failed to make Hanlon wince. Suki had a very toned body and a distinctive body tattoo, a cobra whose head appeared above her pubis and whose body snaked round her hip, disappearing down between her buttocks. It looked very well executed.

Hanlon was no clothes expert, but Suki's clothes looked expensive from the labels: Louboutin on the shoes, a Versace jacket. She glimpsed the name of Suki's handbag: Hermès.

As Suki was slipping her shoes on and studying herself in the mirror, she said to Hanlon in her soft Scottish accent, 'I haven't seen you at the class before.'

'No,' Hanlon said, 'I'm new. I'll be at the retreat too,' she added.

Suki looked her up and down with what Hanlon took to be disapproval. The kind of look that translated as, 'How come they're letting the riff-raff in?'

'Oh, that's nice,' Suki said insincerely. 'What do you do?'

Hanlon searched frantically for a reply. She could hardly say that she was a private investigator.

'Self-employed,' she said finally. 'And you?'

'Well,' Suki said, 'I'm an interior designer. Hang on.' She opened her handbag and took out a business card: Suki Bly – Interiors. 'Where do you live?'

'In the countryside,' Hanlon muttered evasively. Suki was looking at her as if she expected a more detailed answer. 'Out west,' she added, gesturing vaguely at one of the walls.

'Nice,' Suki said in a tone that implied it probably wasn't. She had wanted a specific area so she could pigeonhole Hanlon, not a geographical direction.

'If ever you need advice or a consultation,' Suki said, 'call me...'

She nodded politely to Hanlon and left the changing room. Hanlon smiled grimly at the thought of what Suki would make of her one-room bothy. Perhaps she should invite her out for some tips on how to redecorate. Maybe make more of a feature of the squat rack, which was taking centre stage in the room. Idly, she took her phone out and typed in Hermès handbags on a search engine. Her dark eyebrows arched in amazement at the price. Suki was obviously not short of cash. Interior design must be bringing in a lot of money.

She pulled her own clothes on and left the changing room.

* * *

The café was large and airy, with maybe two dozen tables, and full of greenery. It had a pleasantly relaxed atmosphere. A large statue of a slim Thai-style Buddha on a plinth dominated the room.

Camille was sitting alone at a table. She stood up as Hanlon walked in.

'Hi... come and meet my sister.'

She led Hanlon across the restaurant to the open-plan kitchen. There were two chefs working, a tall, good-looking, slim, dark-haired woman and a younger blonde. Both were younger than Camille and Hanlon by a generation. There was a metal pass with lights to keep food warm that separated the kitchen from the dining area.

'Mind if we come round?' Camille asked the blonde.

'Be my guest.'

Camille escorted Hanlon into the kitchen via a swing door. Hanlon glanced around. There was the usual panoply of equipment you saw in a commercial kitchen rendered in shiny brushed steel. Everything seemed surgically clean.

'My sister, Siobhan...' Camille said. Hanlon looked at her with interest.

If Camille looked like a yoga teacher, slender, wholesome, 'nice', then Siobhan looked like the kind of girl mothers warned their sons about. She was very good-looking in a Waggy way, she had blonde hair like Camille, tied back, and honey-coloured eyebrows. Unlike her elder sister, she was into body piercing. She had the same thin, Roman nose as Camille but hers was pierced, as was her eyebrow. She had a dermal in her cheek and multiple piercings in her ears. Her mouth was full and generous, and she had the same brown eyes as her sister. But where Camille's were kindly, Siobhan's seemed slightly aggressive and calculating. She looked hard as nails.

'Hello,' she said. 'Camille told me about you.'

'So you're the chef,' Hanlon said.

She nodded. 'That's right, you'll be eating a lot of my cooking next week... Oh, this is Jenny by the way.'

The dark-haired girl nodded politely. 'Hi.' She turned to Siobhan. 'I'd better go out the back and finish those quiches, Chef, if you'll excuse me...'

Siobhan nodded and as Jenny disappeared into a prep room out back she said to Hanlon, her voice low, 'The sooner we get Camille onto Duachy Island, the better... Don't want anything happening to my big sister.'

Camille smiled. 'Don't make a fuss. It'll all be fine.'

They were interrupted by a young waiter who leaned over the pass with an order.

'Check on, Chef...'

Siobhan, with a hint of impatience, looked at Camille, who took the hint.

'We'll leave you to it.'

'See you later,' Siobhan said. She took the check glanced at it, hung it above the pass and reached for a frying pan.

They returned to their table. There were now about half a dozen customers in the restaurant.

'It's not just for yoginis,' Camille said. 'The café is open to all. Siobhan is a great cook. I'm so proud of what she's achieved... There's been a huge upsurge in interest in vegetarian food of late and people are actually prepared to spend money on it.'

She looked up. 'Oh, good, here's Katherine.'

O'Rourke came and sat down. She was wearing black skinny jeans, which made her legs appear endless, a plain cream silk blouse and a red paisley scarf. She looked incredible. 'So, what do you make of our set-up here?' she asked Hanlon.

The young waiter came over and asked if they were ready to order. A croissant for Hanlon and Camille said, 'We'll have the usual, please, Tom.' Tom nodded, smiled and disappeared.

Hanlon answered O'Rourke's earlier question. 'It's very impressive,' she said. She looked around her; there was no one sitting in earshot. 'But now you're both here I'd like to discuss the threats.'

'Fine by me,' Camille said. O'Rourke nodded.

'OK,' Hanlon said, 'when did they begin?'

'We've covered this, Hanlon,' O'Rourke said with a hint of impatience.

'I know,' Hanlon said. 'I'm interested in what Camille has to say.'

'About a month ago,' Camille said. She frowned. 'Maybe a bit longer.'

'And what form did they take?'

Camille answered, 'They were text messages, the caller withholding their ID. We didn't take them seriously at first, but then we had a couple that were written, pushed through my letter box at home.'

'That was very distressing,' O'Rourke said. 'They knew where she lived...'

'I can imagine,' Hanlon said. 'Did you contact the police?'

'No,' O'Rourke said. Hanlon raised a questioning eyebrow.

Camille explained, 'We didn't think that there was much they could do.'

Hanlon thought they were probably right.

'And the messages were?' she asked.

'All more along the lines of, "die, bitch",' Camille said. She tried to smile but it was obvious that she was deeply upset.

'A couple of them said, "you deserve it for what you've done..."' she added, her face falling. Hanlon could hear the tightness in her throat; she was obviously fighting back tears. 'But I haven't done anything, to anyone... ever!'

Hanlon thought that was unlikely. We all upset people, she wanted to say, me more than most, admittedly, but even the most mild-mannered, gentlest of people can make enemies.

'So what prompted you to act, to bring me in?' she asked.

'It came from my spirit guide,' Camille said, matter-of-factly.

Hanlon blinked in surprise. 'Your spirit guide?'

O'Rourke spoke. 'Camille uses an astrologer...'

'More of a shaman really,' demurred Camille.

O'Rourke ignored her. 'Paul Strom, he has an office not far from here.' She stressed the word 'office' as if that established Paul Strom as a man who should be listened to.

Hanlon looked at the two women sitting opposite her. They were both intelligent, she suspected O'Rourke was extremely so, and they were both making important decisions on the say-so of a shaman.

If Hanlon was correct, a shaman was some kind of tribal wizard who, to Hanlon's way of thinking, would be at best deluded, at worst a con man.

She hesitated for a moment. It wasn't for her to criticise the way they did things.

'What exactly did Strom say?' she asked.

Camille frowned. 'He was alerted by his spirit guide, who had seen a threat to me materialising around about the end of this week. A severe threat.'

Hanlon raised a sceptical eyebrow. 'Really? Anything more specific?'

'He told me that there would probably be more than one attempt, that I should beware of sharp objects.' Camille said this with the utmost sincerity and gravity. The shaman's warnings obviously held a great deal of substance for her.

'Did he mention any likely suspects, male, female, young or old?' she asked sceptically.

O'Rourke had noticed the look on her face and cut in. 'I dare say all this will seem a bit strange to you, Hanlon, but Paul has been advising Camille for over a year now and he's been amazingly helpful, not just with lifestyle issues but also finance.'

I'm sure he has, thought Hanlon cynically. If you spend a lot of money on someone you remember the good times when it went right, not the bad times when it went wrong. Look, she told herself, there was no point knocking Strom – in Camille's eyes he was obviously wonderful. Nothing she could say would change that.

'Exactly. This, for example.' Camille indicated the café. She was determined that Hanlon be converted to the Strom cause. 'Paul said that the stars were right for a move into catering. He even suggested that we employ Siobhan. The whole thing's been wildly successful.'

Hanlon decided to tactfully move the conversation into safer waters and said, 'Well, I'm glad he's got your interests at heart… Now, moving back to next week.'

They looked at her expectantly. 'I was talking to Suki. She wanted to know who I was. It's a perfectly reasonable question. What shall I say to your clients who ask what I'm doing there on the island? I need a cover story.'

Camille frowned. Hanlon continued, 'I could either make up a career or you could say I was part of the staff, maybe a trainee or something.'

Camille looked at O'Rourke. 'I don't know really. What do you think, Katherine?'

O'Rourke said, 'She's made a good point. The other guests are successful and rich, they'd know really quickly that she wasn't one of them.'

I guess I must look poor, Hanlon thought, not to mention unsuccessful. She wondered if the dig was O'Rourke getting her own back for her doubting Strom. O'Rourke looked at Hanlon in an evaluating way. 'I've seen you in action – how about self-assertiveness coach?' She put her head back and laughed soundlessly.

'So, you're pretty fit, physically fit,' Camille said thoughtfully. 'We could say you were a fitness coach. You wouldn't mind taking them for an hour's exercise class once or twice a day, would you?' She warmed to her theme. 'It'd be mixing things up with the yoga in a fun way.' She looked at O'Rourke. 'We can offer it as a pre-breakfast option, a 5K run?'

'Is the island that big?' asked Hanlon.

'It's probably well over a mile from top to bottom,' O'Rourke said, 'but it has a perimeter walk, all the way round, that's in good condition. It could be used as a running trail. You could just do it twice.'

'That sounds fine,' Hanlon said.

'Settled, then,' Camille said. 'You'll lead a 5K run, 7 to 8 a.m., pre-breakfast. They'll enjoy it, the air is amazing and the gardens are lovely. It'll be invigorating. Then let's say an evening run after my afternoon yoga class.'

'It'll obviously be optional,' O'Rourke said, adding a warning note. 'You might only get one or two takers. You might want to mix it up with a bit of general fitness training. It's entirely up to you.'

Hanlon said confidently, 'I'll put something together. Can you give me a list of the attendees and your staff members who are going to be on the island?'

O'Rourke nodded. 'I've done it already. I'll e-mail it to you later.'

'Thanks.'

Hanlon noticed Suki walking into the café and being led to a table by a waiter. 'So Suki's going to be there,' she said, nodding in her direction. 'Her interior-design firm must be doing well.' Suki saw Hanlon sitting with Camille; she gave her a filthy look.

O'Rourke shook her head. 'It kind of exists on paper only. Suki's ex pays for everything,' she said. 'He is loaded. She did very well from the divorce. He's a nasty piece of work by all accounts.' She checked herself. 'Well, by Suki's account. He's seemingly quite a violent guy – people are scared of him.'

'You seem to know a lot about her,' Hanlon said.

O'Rourke smiled. 'Suki is not one for holding back, Hanlon, believe you me.'

Hanlon nodded. 'OK, so her ex is a thug and people are afraid of him. Including Suki?'

'I don't know. I think they're still on speaking terms.'

'She seems very fond of you,' Hanlon said to Camille.

'She's a little too fond of Camille in my opinion,' said O'Rourke darkly.

'She's harmless,' said Camille.

'She's obsessive,' O'Rourke countered.

She was about to say something more but was interrupted by Tom bringing their food.

'Here we are, Camille.'

He put the tray down and handed Camille an earthenware bowl of muesli topped with yoghurt, fruit and nuts and then a plate with a mix of black beans, avocado, feta, fried eggs and tomatoes. It was very well presented, Hanlon thought, a work of art.

'Muesli for you and Huevos Rancheros for you, Katherine,' Tom said. 'And a croissant for you.' He handed a small plate to Hanlon.

Camille smiled her thanks and Tom left them with a vague, 'Enjoy.'

'That woman's got a major-league crush on you, Camille,' warned O'Rourke, resuming their conversation.

Camille smiled. 'Don't be silly, Suki's not like that...' She stared eagerly at O'Rourke's food. 'Those look really good...'

'Oh, go on, then.' O'Rourke sighed. 'We'll swap.'

'If you're sure that's OK.' Camille smiled winningly at O'Rourke, who caught Hanlon's eye and rolled her own upwards in a kind of 'see what I have to put up with' gesture. It suddenly occurred to Hanlon that the two women were probably very close; this was almost married-couple behaviour.

O'Rourke moved the plates; Camille put a fork into the eggs. It did look really good, thought Hanlon. Siobhan certainly knew how to present food.

'What's in it?' asked Hanlon curiously.

Camille raised her eyebrows. 'It's a tortilla with black beans, salsa and fried eggs... and—' she suddenly stared at O'Rourke '—it's... oh, my God, Kath.'

Startled, Hanlon looked up. O'Rourke's eyes were wide with fright. She pushed her chair away from the table and put a napkin to her mouth. Her eyes were now bulging and she suddenly coughed and spluttered into the paper. Hanlon jumped to her feet. Had she choked on something? Then she covered her mouth again, retched and, with horrible suddenness, vivid red blood poured from O'Rourke's mouth.

'Jesus.' O'Rourke spat something out and whispered, 'Look at that...'

In the napkin was a shard of glass, about a centimetre long. More blood ran out of her mouth; she staunched it with a napkin, which rapidly turned crimson. Camille handed her a tissue, with which she replaced the cloth.

'God, it's glass!' Camille said, horrified.

'I bit into it – it was bigger... I must...'

Hanlon was on her phone, beginning to stab in 999. O'Rourke stopped her. She shook her head angrily. The paper of the tissue against her mouth was turning a deeper red. She looked around the restaurant. Amazingly, nobody had noticed anything amiss. Suki was buried in her phone, the other people were either talking to each other or, like Suki, immersed in electronic devices.

'No, we keep this quiet, OK?' More blood from her mouth. She winced with the pain. 'The Royal Infirmary's only five minutes away. I'll get a taxi.'

She stood up; she looked ashen. Camille got up and put her arm around her. Suki stood up and came over. O'Rourke hastily stuffed the bloodied paper napkins in her handbag and pulled her scarf up over her chin. 'Is everything all right?' Suki asked, concerned.

'Bit my tongue,' O'Rourke mumbled from behind the silk of the scarf. 'I'm fine.' Suki went back to her seat, obviously unconvinced.

O'Rourke said to Hanlon, 'Deal with this, please.'

Hanlon nodded.

O'Rourke and Camille, her arm round her, left the café. A couple of diners looked up, but that was all. Suki went back to her table. Hanlon stood up and went over to the pass; she put her head through into the kitchen.

'You two... come here,' she ordered Siobhan and Jenny. Immersed in their work, they had noticed nothing.

The two chefs exchanged glances.

'What?' Siobhan said irritably. 'What do you want?' She strode over angrily. 'This is a work area!' Jenny, working by the stove, pulled the frying pan she had off the burner and looked over her shoulder enquiringly.

'Close the café,' Hanlon ordered Siobhan.

'What? Have you gone crazy?' Siobhan looked furious.

'Do it!' said Hanlon. 'O'Rourke's just eaten a mouthful of glass.'

'What?' said Siobhan.

'There was glass in the muesli,' Hanlon said. 'Who knows where it came from or if it's in some other food? You'll have to shut the kitchen down.'

'Jesus!' Siobhan said. She looked suitably shocked. 'O'Rourke!' She sounded incredulous. 'Are you sure?'

'Camille has taken her off to A&E. We don't want any more injuries.'

Siobhan gave her another angry look but saw the inescapable logic of Hanlon's point. They could hardly continue serving food knowing that it had been contaminated somewhere in the kitchen with a potentially lethal substance. After a moment of impotent rage, she angrily went over to the stove and turned off the burners.

'Tom.' She leaned over the pass and called the waiter. Hanlon quickly filled him in on what had happened. Tom grasped the gravity of the situation; he immediately walked over to the first of the tables and started moving people out of the restaurant.

Hanlon went into the kitchen. Jenny had joined Siobhan; she was looking aghast.

'So what exactly happened?' Siobhan asked.

Hanlon had picked up the piece of glass that O'Rourke had spat out.

One side had a jagged edge. Hanlon guessed that it had sheared off there when she had bitten down on it, mistaking it for something hard but edible. It looked as if it might have come originally from a wine glass. It was razor sharp and had lacerated her mouth or tongue. Hopefully she hadn't swallowed any more.

'This was in Camille's muesli,' Hanlon said.

'Oh my God!' Jenny clamped her hand to her mouth in horror. 'How did that get there?'

'It wasn't my fault!' Siobhan looked both worried and annoyed in equal measure, then she said, 'But that was Camille's muesli, not O'Rourke's. I don't understand...'

'They swapped.'

'Oh...'

'No one is blaming you,' Hanlon said soothingly. There was no point getting into a shouting match with the chef, which was where she could see the conversation heading.

Jenny continued to look stricken. 'God, this is awful. We could have killed her.'

Siobhan glared at her to shut her up.

'How could this have happened?' Hanlon asked. 'Show me where the muesli's kept.'

She glanced over the pass. The restaurant was now clear and Tom was locking the doors. Jenny led her to a table at the end of the kitchen where there was a trolley with several metal canisters with plastic tops.

'The cereals and the muesli, we have three different kinds, are kept on this trolley, then after breakfast service we wheel it back round that corner into a storage room. So I used that scoop—' she pointed to a cylindrical metal measure '—then added the yoghurt. That's kept in that fridge over there,' she said, pointing to a small stainless-steel locker fridge under a work surface, 'together with the juices and butter and jam.'

Hanlon went over to it, opened it. Inside it was spotlessly clean and contained exactly what Jenny had described. She looked around the kitchen. She'd been in a few commercial kitchens in her life, most had been clean, one or two filthy. In those ones it would have been credible that glass had got into food, not so here. Accident could be ruled out.

'Do you use glass much?' she asked.

Jenny shook her head. 'We try and keep glass out of the kitchen for obvious reasons, but we serve drinks, fruit juices for example, and mint and herbal tea in glasses. I can't even begin to guess how it somehow ended up in the muesli container.'

She shook her head. 'I'll have to go through the high-risk stuff now and chuck it. Thank God Katherine's OK.'

That remains to be seen, thought Hanlon. It all depends on if she's actually swallowed any glass. She suddenly thought back to the conversation about the shaman.

Siobhan said, 'What should we do?'

'Well,' Hanlon said, 'if it was up to me, I would get the police and the Environmental Health involved. But it's not up to me. Your sister won't want any of this made public and, more importantly, neither does O'Rourke. Don't reopen until you've finished your safety checks, and make sure they are thorough, and you've spoken to Camille.'

'OK,' Siobhan said. 'Well, Jenny, could you go and speak to the other members of staff, Olivia at reception too, and let them know what's been happening?'

'Sure, Chef,' she said and took her apron off and left the kitchen.

Siobhan looked at Hanlon. 'Well, it looks as if Paul Strom got it right.'

'I'm sorry?' Hanlon said.

'"Beware of sharp objects", that's one of the warnings that Strom gave, wasn't it?' Siobhan said. She had obviously been thinking along the same lines as Hanlon, although the conclusion that Hanlon reached was probably very different.

'So it was...' Suspicion flared up in her mind. Had Strom maybe been in the kitchen, making sure that his predictions were going to come true? I think I'll pay him a visit after I leave here, she thought. 'Shame he gave the warning to Camille, not Katherine. He could have been a bit more specific. Or warned them about food. Could you pass me that roll of cling film?'

Siobhan did so and Hanlon spread a generous length of cling film out over one of the steel work surfaces. She picked up the jar of muesli and tipped it out over the plastic. The dun-coloured oatmeal with its pieces of dried fruit lay there harmlessly. Hanlon brushed it gently. Here and there shards and pieces of glass glinted, revealing their unwelcome, deadly presence.

'Well, someone's been busy,' Hanlon commented.

Siobhan stared at it in horror. 'Oh, my God, and Katherine ate that!'

'She did indeed,' Hanlon said grimly. 'Who besides you and Jenny had access to this kitchen yesterday?'

'Well, Jenny and I get here at about eight and we work through usually until around four.' She frowned. 'But the cafeteria doors are kept open for clients who arrive early for a class, even though the kitchen's closed. They can use it like a waiting area. The last class is seven-thirty until nine. So it's not uncommon for, say, a woman meeting a friend who's doing a class to be in here with her laptop. In fact, someone told me Suki was in here last night. She was waiting for her niece who comes to the Tuesday night Flow class. Reception is always staffed, the lights are on in here and, although those swing doors are locked, it's an open kitchen. You could climb over the pass easily enough.'

So, thought Hanlon, in other words, just about anyone could have had a quick look around, accessed the kitchen and adulterated the muesli with glass. She glanced through the metal shelving of the pass. She could see Suki on the other side of the glass-panelled door looking through at them. Probably not her though. Hanlon could imagine Suki breaking in to discover what kind of muesli Camille favoured so she could buy it herself, not to put glass in it.

'I think the sooner my sister gets on to Duachy Island, the better,' Siobhan said with feeling. 'If anything happened to her this whole place would fall apart. She's the glue that holds everything together.'

Hanlon nodded; what she said was obviously true.

'Anyway, she is OK, that's the main thing,' said Siobhan with a sigh. 'I'd better make a start on chucking stuff out. Who knows what else has got glass in it?'

'Are you going to lose a lot?' Hanlon said.

Siobhan nodded, obviously irritated. 'I don't mind telling you I am royally pissed off. Yeah, anything that's not sealed will have to go. So essentially all our prepped stuff…' She sighed. 'What a bloody nightmare.

We'll be here till midnight recooking everything for tomorrow. Soup, quiches, dals, veg tagine... all the mise en place...' Her shoulders slumped at the enormity of the task ahead.

'Well, I'll leave you to it,' said Hanlon, somewhat unsympathetically. She liked Camille; she was not so sure about her sister.

She went back into the restaurant and out into reception. She looked back through the doors to see Siobhan standing there dejectedly, then stiffen, throw her chest forward and get to work opening a fridge to begin the long and tedious job of beginning again from scratch.

Hanlon walked down the stone steps of the yoga centre into the street. It was nine forty-five. Time to go and pay a visit to the shaman.

Undoubtedly, Paul Strom would have predicted she was on her way.

6

Hanlon walked back to where she had parked her car and let Wemyss out. They walked along to Kelvingrove Park, which was quiet at this time of the morning. Hanlon sat on a bench with her dog at her feet and searched for Paul Strom on her phone.

His consulting room was not far away, in Partick. You could book a physical session online and there was a slot available at eleven. She reserved it under the name of Ishbel Campbell. She had a feeling that the spirits (in the form of Camille) might have informed him of her name and who she was.

Hanlon didn't believe in people's ability to predict the future, but she did believe in people's ability to influence it.

She read with interest about Paul Strom on his website. He had led an eventful life. He had studied with shamans in countries as diverse as Finland, Mongolia and Mexico. His home page informed her that the tradition of the shaman was common to most cultures, that the shaman was an intermediary between this world and the world of spirits. For the spirits, seemingly time did not exist, so the shaman would be able to ask them about the likely outcomes of actions or be able to foresee events and warn people accordingly.

Sure, thought Hanlon cynically. Shame they didn't mention broken glass in muesli.

Strom would also be able to connect people to their own spirit guides and offer advice on spirit animals.

Hanlon shook her head in disbelief. Camille actually believed this nonsense, and possibly O'Rourke too, although maybe that was just her being diplomatic. She ruffled Wemyss's soft fur and the collie nuzzled her. 'You're my spirit guide, Wemyss,' she said. The dog licked her hand.

She thought about what Siobhan had said to her. Paul Strom had indeed got it right, but Hanlon was sure that it was no thanks to the spirit world. From what she had learned about the threat to Camille it seemed likely it was someone who knew her. Strom fitted the bill as a potential suspect. His choice of career marked him in her mind as a con man and this glass incident seemed very neatly timed to add to his reputation as a soothsayer. In her view there was a distinct possibility he was somehow involved. Either way, she wanted to take a good look at him.

'Come on,' she said to the dog and headed back to her car.

* * *

The entrance to Paul Strom's consulting room in Partick in Glasgow was between a betting shop and a café. Hanlon mentally compared it to her own office entrance. It was remarkably similar, the same narrow wooden stairs creaking under the client's weight as they ascended, the same sensation as you went upwards in the secure knowledge that whatever you were going to find would be underwhelming.

The stairs ended on a small landing with a dark blue door. There was a small table by the door, with a joss stick smouldering in a holder on a bamboo tray with rocks and gravel and a small, ornamental indoor fountain, about the size of her hand. She guessed that it represented the four elements of earth, air, fire and water. It was surprisingly nice to look at, somehow mesmerising. Someone had a good eye for design; she wondered if it was Paul Strom.

She knocked on the door and a man opened it.

'Do come in.'

Paul Strom looked to be in his forties or fifties. He had high cheekbones and piercing eyes; he was certainly striking. In build he was tall and slim with very short dark brown hair. It looked less like hair than the kind of animal fur on, say, a mouse. She had a strong desire to touch it, to feel its texture. He was wearing a white shirt over blue cotton trousers; the shirt was large and baggy and hung down rather like a tunic. He was intelligent-looking, professorial, slightly intimidating.

He wasn't what she had been expecting. She had assumed he would be sleazier-looking and, not to put too fine a point on it, stupid. She felt quite disconcerted. He looked at her in a shrewdly knowing way, as if he had read her mind, and she nearly blushed. Things had not got off to a good start. One person seemed very much in charge and it wasn't her.

'Please, take a seat.'

There were two low blue sofas facing each other and a low coffee table between them. She sat down and he took the sofa opposite, kicking off the espadrilles that he was wearing and sitting fluidly cross-legged on the sofa. She looked around the room. It looked like Strom's flat doubled as his consulting room. Pale blue walls, white ceiling. There was art on the walls, a mandala-style tapestry and a large intricate, semi-abstract picture. Golds, browns and blues that seemed feverishly alive swirled around within it. Another painting in a very different vein, jagged mountains and desert, simplistic, that reminded Hanlon of a seventies prog-rock band's album cover.

'So, you're Ishbel Campbell.' He had a gentle Scottish accent.

He was looking at her with what seemed polite scepticism.

'That's correct.' She was eager to move the conversation away from herself. She had used Ishbel's name as an alternative to her own in case Camille had mentioned her, she didn't want to be inventing a fictitious back-story on the hoof as well. She suddenly thought, God, I hope Strom's not a foodie and recognises Ishbel Campbell as the name of the owner of one of Glasgow's premier restauranteurs.

'I like your art,' she said.

'Thank you.' He pointed to the pictures. 'That's a Huichol yarn painting, from Mexico.' He smiled. 'It's where I first encountered the concepts of shamanism. I'm assuming you're new to shamanism, Ishbel?'

'That's correct,' she said. 'I am.'

'Well, so was I in those days. I suppose too that it was the first time I was initiated into a sacred ritual… over there in Mexico.' He indicated the mountain picture. 'And then much later when I was learning more, I did further developmental work in Mongolia, which is where that is from… but we're not here to talk about me, are we?'

Well, thought Hanlon, in one sense we are. She wondered how she was going to move the conversation on to Camille when he did it for her.

'There's no need to look so uncomfortable,' he said, looking deeply into her eyes. He had quite startling eyes, very brown with flecks of gold. She stared at them almost with fascination; it was hard to look away. 'I know you have someone else's interests at the forefront of your mind.' She frowned and he said soothingly, 'You can relax, there's no need to be so defensive… I know that you're a tough cookie or like to present that side of yourself to people, but it can be exhausting, maintaining that level of aggression.'

She felt irritation rise within her; he knew nothing about her at all. You can drop the psycho-babble sales pitch, she felt like saying.

His eyes bored into her. He was quite disconcerting; she had the uncomfortable feeling that she was transparent before his penetrating gaze. Don't be stupid, she told herself. Strom is a con man, nothing more.

He smiled at her. 'I can't blame you for being sceptical. I didn't believe in any of this until I experienced it myself.' He rubbed the bridge of his nose with a finger thoughtfully. 'I was doing a PhD in Indigenous Healing Ceremonies – my degree was in Social Anthropology. To be honest I only chose Mexico because I was sick of the weather in Glasgow. I knew Mexico was sunny, that was about all… well, that's what I thought anyway.'

Hanlon smiled, despite herself. He was curiously engaging, but then, she reminded herself, con men often were.

'The spirits have a curious way of working,' he said. 'They contacted me via my desire to see some sun… Did you know that your spirit animal is a wolf?'

'No, I didn't,' she said.

'Well, it is…' He resumed his thread. 'You obviously won't believe me, but it will come in useful one day, maybe sooner rather than later.' He smiled. 'Anyway, that's by the by. I was warned... well, that's a wee bit of a loaded word, I was informed that you were coming last night. The wolf is a suspicious animal, is it not, and you have trust issues, don't you?' He grinned and made inverted comma signs with his fingers. '"Ishbel"...'

Hanlon frowned. Who told you I was coming? she wondered. I didn't know myself until half an hour ago.

He continued, 'It might help if you told me your real name, for a start.'

'My name's Hanlon,' she said. She was so startled he had seen through her pretence that she made no effort to deny it. There was something about Strom that made her want to seek his approval. If anything, she was glad to be able to drop the pretence.

He nodded. 'My real name is McEwan, like the beer. Strom is German for "current", like electrical current. It's a good analogy for the spirit world. You can't see the energy, per se, but you can see the effects every time you turn a light on.'

'Why did you change your name?' she asked.

'Commercial reasons.' He laughed. 'I felt that nobody was going to take a shaman called McEwan seriously. I wanted something more mysterious.' She looked at him with something approaching astonishment. He had an uncanny knack for wrong-footing her.

He shifted his weight slightly on the sofa. 'So, why are you here?'

She decided to get straight to the point. 'Someone put glass in Camille Anderson's muesli this morning.'

Strom nodded. 'Makes sense.'

You don't look surprised or shocked, she thought. Is that because you know something about it?

He continued, 'I warned her about sharp objects. To be honest, I hadn't thought about glass. I was thinking it probably meant a knife. Is she OK?'

'O'Rourke took the bullet,' Hanlon said. 'She's in hospital. What else have the spirits been telling you?'

'As Camille doubtless told you, I can see grave danger coming her way.' He raised a hand as if to forestall a question. 'Sometimes you can't avoid destiny, Hanlon, if it's meant to be it will be, but sometimes you can see trouble coming, like when it's about to rain and you bring an umbrella or you take shelter. You haven't stopped the rain, but you haven't got wet. That's the idea behind my warning to her. Her danger is very real. She can't change her fate, no one can, but it doesn't have to be fatal. It can be deflected. I guess you're there to do that.'

'I guess,' she said.

He smiled. 'See? And here you are, already doing your job, checking me out, Mr Suspicious, wondering if I had something to do with it. I congratulate you. I'd do exactly the same.'

Hanlon ignored his patter and said, 'Do you have any idea as to by whom or why she is being threatened?'

Strom said, 'Only that it's someone with a great deal of rage and hate.'

No shit, Sherlock, thought Hanlon.

Strom smiled faintly. 'I appreciate that is unhelpful, but there is no rationality behind the killer, only that he or she hates Camille, who, let's face it, is a hard woman to hate. My guess, and this is me, not the spirits, is that it's a deranged fan, or someone who feels that Camille has let her down somehow. That's what I think.'

'Now...' he uncoiled himself from the sofa and stood up, 'that's us done. You've seen me, I've seen you. That'll do for today. I have real clients to see, rather than people who think I'm a charlatan or a potential murderer. I won't charge you, since I haven't helped you, but I will just say a couple of things that I know about you.'

'I'm all ears,' said Hanlon sarcastically.

Strom gave a 'be like that' kind of shrug. 'OK, here goes. You're behaving quite unpleasantly to someone who loves you, that's the first thing, even though you might not know it.'

Hanlon immediately started thinking of who that might be; nobody sprang to mind, other than her dog.

Strom continued. 'And secondly, someone you have a deep respect for will reappear quite soon in your life.'

God, she thought, with a sudden feeling of guilt, that must be Dr Morgan... Then she felt irritated. Why am I taking any of this seriously?

These are just vague generalisations. I'm not falling for any of this shit. I'm not Camille, she thought.

Strom smiled, as if reading her mind. 'Oh, and aggression is not the answer you think it is. You're fighting yourself, not the enemy. I'll leave it there. I could go on, but you're not a client and you still think I'm a fraud so I would be wasting my breath.'

She got up off the sofa. 'Well, thanks for your time and your insights...' Her tone was brusque.

'They're not mine,' he replied politely.

'Whatever,' she said, with a show of indifference although she was secretly quite impressed. And annoyed with herself for being so.

He stood up and opened the door. 'Oh, by the way, I really didn't put the glass in her muesli.' He smiled; it was a slightly sinister smile. 'If I wanted to kill Camille I'd do a better job, I can assure you.'

She blinked despite herself. 'Thank you.'

'Say hi to your dog from me.'

She nodded coldly and left the office.

* * *

Back to the car, another quick walk with Wemyss. She thought about Paul Strom, and shook her head with rueful admiration. He was very good at what he did, she could see that. It was no wonder he had got Camille eating out of his hand.

The main question in her mind was this. What was he gaining from all of this? It was, of course, possible that he believed his own hype. Hanlon was quite prepared to accept that if she dropped a tab of acid or drank mushroom tea, she would hallucinate and see visions too. But she'd put them down to tripping her head off rather than cosmic revelations or messages from the spirit world. He could well be absolutely misguided, but genuine.

She thought his guess that the person who had put the glass in the muesli was a crazed fan made a great deal of sense. She wondered about Suki. She had sensed the woman's jealousy when she had seen that Camille had wanted to talk to her, and her irritation that she was coming to Duachy Island, and that was towards someone that Suki knew nothing about. What did she make of O'Rourke, who did seem intensely close to Camille? If, for example, she had thought that O'Rourke was in the habit of eating muesli first thing then she could well imagine Suki adding glass to the container. One way of getting rid of a major rival in Camille's affections.

She looked down at Wemyss, who was sniffing a tree trunk with an expression of serious concentration before deciding that, yes, it was worthwhile leaving his mark.

She took Wemyss back to the car and checked her phone. A message from Camille: O'Rourke was out of danger, she'd been X-rayed and there didn't appear to be any life-threatening injuries. It also looked as if she hadn't swallowed any glass. They were keeping her in for now, but she was expected to be discharged the following day.

Well, thought Hanlon, thank God for that.

She stroked the dog, settled him. 'I'll be back soon,' she said. She had one more call to make in Glasgow and then they could go back home.

* * *

It was twelve o'clock when Hanlon walked into the restaurant in Glasgow's smart West End. It had been over a year since she had last been in the Sleeket Mouse. It still had the same blue façade with a small, stylised drawing of a scampering mouse that she remembered. Back then, they were smarting from having missed out on a star, but in the October that had been rectified and Ishbel Campbell, the woman whose name she had temporarily borrowed earlier, was currently the proud owner of a Michelin-starred eatery.

The grey and brown décor was as she remembered it, cool and classic, timeless.

'Good morning, madam, do you have a reservation?' asked the maître d'.

'No, but I was wondering if it would be possible to speak with Ishbel, if she's in,' asked Hanlon.

'Yes,' said the ornately bearded maître d'. He managed to make just the single word sound classy. Hanlon recognised him from her previous visit. 'I'll just go and fetch her. What name, please?'

'Hanlon.'

He returned with Ishbel. She too was unchanged since Hanlon had last seen her: short, efficient-looking, dark hair cut in a bob. She didn't look much like her brother although she shared the same green eyes. There was a restless aggression in her manner that Murdo didn't have. He was also good-humoured, again, a quality that Ishbel didn't share.

'Hello,' she said coolly. 'Come through to my office.'

She led Hanlon to a narrow flight of stairs at the back of the restaurant. At the top were two changing areas for the staff, male and female, and another door, which she opened and gestured Hanlon inside.

Her office was small and cramped, functional. They sat looking at each other for a while. It was only the second time that they had met, and Hanlon had the distinct impression that she didn't like her.

'So, what brings you here?' Ishbel asked. The tone of her voice implied she wished that Hanlon hadn't bothered.

At least she still remembers me, Hanlon thought.

'I'm here on business. Do you know Camille Anderson?'

'Yes, I do.' Ishbel looked surprised. 'Why?'

'Somebody has been threatening her and I'm looking into it,' Hanlon said.

Ishbel nodded then she leaned forward over her desk. 'I only see you when you want something, don't I?' Her tone of voice was that shade of exceptionally polite that was used when the speaker wanted to be anything but.

Hanlon felt anger rising in her. She knew it was irrational – well, up to a point, she thought, none of us likes being disliked – and that she shouldn't antagonise Ishbel, but she couldn't stop herself.

'I can't afford your prices, you're too expensive.'

Ishbel ignored the criticism. It happened to be true; even if Hanlon had been in the habit of eating out in expensive restaurants, The Sleeket Mouse was way beyond her means.

'Camille's a good customer. She eats here a lot with her lookalike friend.'

'Suki Bly?' queried Hanlon.

'Aye, that's the one,' she smiled smugly at Hanlon. 'I'm very good at remembering names and faces, it goes with the turf. She wears a lot of high-end fashion, very good tipper. She always pays. Camille's nice enough. Her sister used to work here, Siobhan.'

'I'd heard that,' Hanlon said. Ishbel was being far more forthcoming than she had imagined. 'What was she like?'

Ishbel frowned. 'As far as I know, she was good at her job, exceptionally hard-working and that means hard-working if you work in my kitchen, but she upset a couple of the waitresses. She's got a vicious tongue.' That didn't surprise Hanlon. Siobhan looked as if she was more than capable of being unpleasant. 'Quite frankly, when she left I breathed a sigh of relief. We all did, I think.'

'So she was a bit of a handful?'

'You could say that, but certainly on the technical side she was very good, and she functioned well under pressure. As I said, our kitchen is not an easy gig. We get through a fair few stagiaires here because they can't take the pressure.'

'Stagiaires?' queried Hanlon.

'Chefs working unpaid internships because it will enhance their CVs,' Ishbel explained. 'That's why Siobhan was here. We'd have offered her a job if it weren't for her personality. And that is saying a lot about her ability. Very few chefs can work, or would want to work, at this level. When you make the leap to Michelin standards, the stakes go up and work that would be acceptable at a lower level no longer is. But Siobhan took it in her stride.'

'So, a good worker but not so nice as a human being.'

'That would be a fair assessment.' Ishbel scratched her head thoughtfully. 'And when she left she took one of the commis chefs with her, Jenny McKendrick. I was glad to see the back of her too. So she unwittingly did me a favour.'

'Why?' Hanlon asked.

Ishbel gave a wintry smile. 'Jenny was keen on sleeping her way to the top. She wasn't a grafter like Siobhan. She had an affair with the sous-chef to try and get promoted and then she made a play for my business partner who co-owns the Mouse. I was going to sack her, but luckily, I didn't have to. She'll have to knuckle down and do some work vertically instead of horizontally now – I hear that Camille has an all-woman organisation.'

She seemed unusually well informed on the movements of her kitchen staff. Hanlon commented on this. Ishbel Campbell's eyes narrowed combatively.

'I run a very successful restaurant.' She tapped her desk forcefully with a fingernail; the gesture reminded Hanlon of O'Rourke. 'The Sleeket Mouse, Hanlon, is the best place to eat in Glasgow, if not Scotland – you bet your arse I'm well-informed. And unlike some people I could mention...' she leaned forward over her desk, her eyes hard, 'that's you I'm talking about, I care about people.'

Hanlon blinked in surprise. She hadn't expected that assault on her character. She guessed it was true. She had enough self-awareness to know that Ishbel's remark, although cutting, was quite accurate.

With one or two exceptions, she didn't care that much about individuals. Wemyss was by far the most beloved thing in her life. She was unsure, though, why Ishbel was so concerned about it.

'Well, I think that's a tad harsh...'

'Oh, really. Is it?' Ishbel raised an eyebrow. 'What about my brother?'

Ishbel Campbell's brother was Murdo Campbell, a DI in the police, based in Dumbarton to the west of Glasgow. Hanlon drove past his police station every time she came into the city.

'Continually messing him around.'

Hanlon looked at her in astonishment. The last she had seen of Murdo was on a kind of a disastrous date a few months ago. He'd taken her to an art exhibition here in Glasgow. She liked the guy; he was good company, good-looking too. It was why she had gone to the Picasso show when she didn't even like Picasso. She could fake it well enough when she chose to. They'd gone for a meal. Hanlon remembered she'd wondered if anything else was going to happen. She wouldn't have said no – Campbell, slim, muscular, handsome, irritatingly well informed on Cubist art, well dressed, had been looking hot. But the evening had ended inconsequentially, awkwardly. Like an expensive firework rocket that launched upwards confidently enough before fizzling out without exploding.

She'd felt puzzled at the time, she remembered, and slightly hurt. Since then, she'd heard nothing from him. She'd given him her new address, politely acknowledged; none of this qualified, as far as she could see, as 'messing him around'.

If anything, she was the injured party.

She put this to Ishbel, not that she felt it was any of her business. Murdo was thirty-five, not eighteen.

Ishbel frowned. 'Well, he's in love with you, I'll tell you that for nothing.' She added darkly, 'I know the signs.'

Hanlon scratched her head; she didn't know what to make of this. She suddenly thought of Strom: *You're behaving quite unpleasantly to someone who loves you.* She pushed the thought away.

'I don't know what to say,' she said helplessly.

'Do you want to go out with my brother or not?' asked Ishbel, drumming her fingers on the polished surface of the desk. She had nice fingers, thought Hanlon, long and slim, the nails cut short and lacquered with clear varnish. She cocked her head to one side and looked at Hanlon impatiently. It was like being interviewed for a job.

However, strangely, despite herself, she liked Ishbel and was prepared to make allowances she wouldn't normally. There had obviously been some sort of misunderstanding and she had been thinking about Murdo Campbell with a frequency that surprised her.

'Well?' said Ishbel impatiently. A woman whose time was valuable and who had no patience with ditherers.

'I thought Murdo was quite...' She didn't know how to put it tactfully. She'd been told he was a womaniser, whereas Ishbel was implying that he was actually nervous around them. 'I thought he was, well... popular with women.'

'Murdo?' Ishbel said with surprise. 'He's no womaniser. He's had the odd girlfriend but he's essentially quite shy. God knows where he gets it from – I'm not, neither are our parents, but he is. Who told you otherwise?'

Oh, God, thought Hanlon, McCleod. 'Just some woman, a long time ago,' she said.

'Well, she was wrong,' said Ishbel flatly.

'Oh.'

'So, do you want to go out with him?'

'Do you know something?' Hanlon said, if only to get Ishbel off her back. 'I think I do.' She also decided that she had had quite enough of discussing Murdo Campbell with his sister. She was forty-one, not sixteen. She stood up. Strangely, she didn't feel irritated that Ishbel had hijacked the conversation and brought it round to Murdo. Maybe, she thought, I've been softened up by Strom.

Ishbel stood up too. 'Shall I arrange something?' She glanced at her laptop.

Hanlon thought, I do not want Ishbel Campbell pencilling me in on Microsoft Calendar for a hot date with her brother as if I'm a dinner booking.

'No, it's OK.' She smiled at Ishbel. 'We'll let the universe decide.'

It was a very Camille answer.

She nodded politely and left the office.

7

'Thirty-five thousand pounds?' said DI Murdo Campbell, trying not to sound too incredulous.

He looked at the man sitting across the table from him. Hugh Kennedy, fifty-seven, head of English at a big secondary school in Govan, tall and almost painfully thin with wire-rimmed glasses. A competent, no-nonsense looking guy. Well, thought Campbell, you'd have to be, to survive what he guessed would be a 'challenging' working environment. Teaching in Govan would almost certainly not be for the faint-hearted. Kennedy was understandably angry with himself for having been scammed.

'Try not to sound so surprised, Inspector,' Kennedy said acidly. 'It was extremely professionally done.'

Campbell felt a twinge of irritation at himself for having so obviously shown his incredulity.

From what he had just learned, Kennedy had been the victim of fraud. Six months previously he had received an e-mail: 'What's Your Money Doing for You?' It was subtitled, 'You worked hard for it, isn't it about time it reciprocated?'

Ordinarily he would have ignored it and deleted it, but at the time he had been feeling annoyed with his regular bank and he'd taken the time to read it.

'I think it was "reciprocated" that did it for me, Inspector,' Kennedy said, shaking his head ruefully. 'You know, I get tired of simplistic jargon and people telling me, in my job I hear it a lot—' he put on a kind of mimsy, nagging voice '—"You can't use words like that, it's elitist." I guess I was a victim of my own linguistic snobbery.' He shook his head admiringly. 'Whoever wrote that was a smart cookie.'

The e-mail had directed him to a website that had lots of nice charts. Longwell Brothers Ltd were (or so it said) a small investment group specialising in FinTech companies and the apps that the young use to track and move money.

Interested, Kennedy had asked for more details and had ended up talking to a guy, David Piper, on the phone. He'd said that he had set up the investment company whilst on gardening leave from an Edinburgh investment company. Kennedy said, 'I can more or less remember his exact words to me.' He paused.

'Please go on, Mr Kennedy,' Campbell said.

'"Basically, Mr Kennedy, if you'd invested £1,000 with me two years ago, it would now be worth £1,500, which is a 25 per cent return per annum."' Kennedy looked at Campbell. 'I was getting about 1 per cent from my bank at the time. I was interested. I asked him how come he was getting it so right. He said that he had two advantages: he was small and could move quickly without going through cumbersome policy meetings, and he had good intelligence. He told me that we were all trying to predict the future, particularly investment advisors, but the reality is, in most cases you might as well go to an astrologer or a shaman or throw darts at a FTSE 100 listing and pick companies that way. He hesitated after he told me this, which, at the time I guessed meant he didn't want to incriminate himself. Then he said, "I invest in companies I know about... that's as much as I want to say. The figures in the prospectus speak for themselves."'

Campbell frowned. 'That sounds suspiciously like insider trading.'

Kennedy gave a wry smile. 'That's exactly what I thought. It's what made the whole thing so plausible, so inviting.' He shifted in his chair and carried on his story. 'Anyway, then he told me that he had to keep his pool of investors small. He implied that it was an exclusive club and he didn't want to make it too big. I asked him how he had got my name. He said that I had been recommended by someone who knew me, but who would remain anonymous.'

Campbell made some notes then asked, 'And the address of this company?'

'It was in George Street in Edinburgh.'

Campbell nodded. The wide street in the New Town of Edinburgh with its grey neo-classical buildings was popular with financial institutions.

'I later discovered it was just a generic mailing address.'

'A brass plate company?' asked Campbell.

'Exactly,' Kennedy said. 'It shared that address with about fifty other dodgy businesses.' He sighed. 'Anyway, I was fooled at the time.'

'This would have been...?'

'About twelve months ago. I transferred a thousand pounds to him as an initial investment and six months later that money had grown by three hundred.'

'According to the statements that he sent you.'

'Exactly, but I was happy and eager for more. So I invested another five K. That went well too.'

Campbell nodded. 'Did you attempt to withdraw any of your money at the time?'

Kennedy shook his head. Campbell made another note. So there was no way Kennedy could have known if Longwell Brothers had actually made him any money or not. The profits were entirely at their say-so.

Kennedy continued, 'Then, a month ago I got an e-mail. He said, "Obviously I don't know what your assets are, but I've got a fantastic chance for a seven hundred K share buy in from a tech start-up that is going to be taken over by one of the major banks. When this happens, its stock value is going to at least double, at a minimum It could even triple. I'm only offering this to certain customers, people whose discretion I can rely on. People like you, Mr Kennedy. The buy in for you is thirty-five K. I'll give you twenty-four hours to think about it."' He laughed mirthlessly. 'I thought about it, then went ahead. I sent him the money.'

'Thirty-five thousand.'

'Thirty-five thousand,' Kennedy said, in a dejected tone, his shoulders slumped. He suddenly looked ten years older, defeated and careworn. 'Sent to the Lothian Road branch of the Deeside Bank in Edinburgh. Then nothing. No reply to e-mails or calls to his mobile and a week ago the website disappeared. It had been taken down. The rest you know.'

The rest Campbell did know. The reason he was interviewing Kennedy was as part of the ongoing investigation into Longwell Brothers. Due to staff shortages in Fraud, he'd been drafted in to help. The bulk of the victims were from the south-east of England, but Campbell was interviewing the nine Scottish investors who had been victims. There had been forty people in total who had lost money to the fraud. Ten of them had been duped out of seventy thousand. The total was one-point-seven-five million.

Campbell read back Kennedy's statement to him. The teacher nodded. 'Yes, that's as it happened.'

As they put the finishing touches to things, he asked Campbell, 'What do you think the chances of me getting my money back are?'

'I'll be honest with you, Mr Kennedy, I would say, not good. This is a crime that's been very professionally executed. Even if we catch the perpetrators, I would imagine the money will be well concealed, but that's speculation on my part.'

'But isn't there the Proceeds of Crime Act?'

'There is, indeed, yet I suspect the money will be hard to trace. But you never know.'

'What about the banks?' Kennedy asked desperately. 'Surely they must be liable for something? This couldn't have happened without their involvement?'

Campbell thought back to his meeting with the woman from Deeside Bank, Cara Edwards, their fraud investigator. He had been looking into placement for his colleague in London, the first stage of money laundering when illegally gained funds were moved from their source into the financial system. She had been very helpful, well, to the extent that she had called up the account details and given him the details of the account of the bank in Manila in the Philippines that the money had been transferred to.

She had been adamant, however, that the Deeside Bank had done all the due diligence required by law and that they, most certainly, were not liable for anything. No red flags had been raised and nothing had been picked up by their anti-money-laundering systems.

Campbell had passed this on to the investigators in London; they were not especially optimistic about getting a result.

'I'm sorry, Mr Kennedy,' Campbell said. 'The bank says they did everything required.'

'Why does that not surprise me?' Kennedy's voice was bitter. Rain rattled on the windows, the outlier of Storm Cedric that was due to reach the west of Scotland on the coming Sunday.

He zipped his anorak up.

'So, I guess I've seen the back of my money.' He stood up. 'You know what, Inspector, I'm a Christian, I go to church on Sundays, but I really do hope that something horrible happens to this bastard. I shouldn't, but I do. Something biblically horrible. It's not so much the money, it's the abuse of trust that's so hard to take.'

Campbell stood up and shook his hand.

'Thank you for coming, Mr Kennedy. I'll be in touch.'

Kennedy left the office.

Campbell went to the window and stared out at the threatening skies. He looked down and saw the tall, spare figure of Kennedy making his way across the car park to his Corsa. The car made him think of Hanlon. He wondered if she still had her old version of Kennedy's car; it had been a total wreck. He smiled sadly. He thought back to their one and only date. It hadn't been disastrous, she'd just seemed uninterested in him. Bored, even.

It was funny really, he thought. He had never thought of himself as someone easily intimidated by a woman, but he'd suffered a kind of acute failure of nerve with her, almost like a panic attack.

He had tried not thinking of her, unsuccessfully. Little things would suddenly remind him of her. Vauxhall Corsas. Border collies. Women runners. And he would see again her shaggy dark hair, her toned figure, her eyes.

And what was really bugging him was that he wondered, deep down, if he was frightened that she would reject him and so he'd struck first, out of cowardice. You couldn't miss what you'd never had. And now he was stuck with the torment of regret, of what ifs…

His phone signalled an incoming message. He glanced at it. His sister. He wondered what she wanted; whatever it was could wait. He didn't feel like talking to anyone right now; he felt depressed and discouraged. David Piper would probably get away with it. He disconnected his laptop and stood up and stretched. He left the interview room and walked back along the corridor towards his office.

8

Hanlon turned off the single-track road that led to a small village called Ellenabeich on Seil and onto a private road, in reality more of a rutted track, that was signposted Duachy House and Island. The hills of Mull were a dark mass in the distance, under a dark sky, threatening and indistinct. She bounced along the untarmacked road in her battered old Volvo estate. She had traded her Corsa in when she had taken the lease on the bothy in the hills where she now lived. The Volvo was four-wheeled drive and altogether more suited to the mile-long track that led up from the narrow road that bordered the Crinan Canal to her new house. It was ten years old, about half the age of the Corsa, and she thought of it fondly as her new car.

The skies above were cloudy, heavy with the promise of rain, and a strong, gusty wind whipped the bracken and grasses on either side of the road. Storm Cedric was due to arrive the following day. Torrential downpours and hurricane-strength winds had been predicted. Right now, things didn't look too bad.

The track she was on continued for a couple of miles through the bleak fields of rock and grass, the only sign of life the occasional scattering of sheep. Eventually it finished in a fenced-in parking area at the edge of the sea, which had criss-crossed rubber matting designed so that grass could grow through the gaps. She parked her car next to a Maserati 4x4, a Porsche 911 and two Jaguar 4x4s. The old Volvo looked quite forlorn next to these immaculate showroom-condition vehicles. They themselves looked out of place, neatly parked in the middle of nowhere.

She got out of her car. The force of the wind took her by surprise, slamming into her, snatching at her dark, tousled hair. She pushed it out of her face and looked around. It was extremely desolate. The jagged rocks on the shoreline were a steely, gunmetal grey colour, as was the sea; the horizon was limitless. The grass by the foreshore was a matt green. There was a strong smell of seaweed from the beach and the tang of the ocean. The surrounding hills were mainly treeless and wherever you looked you were aware of the bones of the island; the grey granite and schist rocks were omnipresent. As if on cue it started raining heavily.

She was on Seil Island, which was about a two- to three-hour drive west of Glasgow. Very close to the coast and linked to the mainland by a small bridge with a grandiose name, 'The Bridge over the Atlantic,' it was known as a holiday and tourist destination. The picturesque town of Oban was just up the coast.

The grass of the surrounding fields had been cropped short by grazing sheep, which were now sheltering in the lee of a drystone wall. Through the driving rain she could see the dim shape of the rocky-sided island in the far distance.

She took her phone out and checked the signal. To her relief there was one, and she called the number she had been given. A gruff man's voice with the quiet lilt of the west coast answered. Hanlon said she'd arrived at the car park opposite the island.

'I'll be across in about half an hour,' he said.

'See you then.'

She retreated to the refuge of the car to wait. The wind strengthened; the rain switched from drizzle to downpour. It was dreadful for summer. A while later, through the glass of the windscreen streaked with rain, she could see the shape of a small boat bouncing through the swell of the sea. She got out of the Volvo and took her suitcase from the back seat and locked the car, immediately wondering why. She looked at its neighbours and thought that if anyone stole her car instead of one of the others, they'd have to be crazy.

She made her way down to the beach. There was a small jetty and she walked along it and waited for the boat. A few minutes later it pulled up, a small motorboat with a partially open cabin in the bows. There was an elderly man in an orange oilskin with long white hair straggling out from under a cap, sitting in the stern steering it. He brought it expertly against the wood of the jetty and held it against the side as it rocked and bucked against the concrete of the small pier while Hanlon passed him her case and then clambered into the small craft. He motioned to the bows.

'Get under the roof, lassie.' He scowled upwards at the heavens; rain ran down his face. 'It's fair dreich out here.'

She did so; the rain beat down. She shivered in her old Barbour jacket, cold and damp. It was hard to believe it was July.

He gave the engine some throttle and turned in a lazy arc towards the island that she could barely see now through the sheeting rain. The old guy squinted up at the sky,

'Keeps the midges down,' he shouted. Hanlon gave him a tight smile. The motion of the boat crashing up and down on the waves and occasionally pitching from side to side was beginning to make her feel queasy.

'I'm Charlie,' he said over the engine noise. The wind whipped his words away and she found it hard to hear what he had said.

'Have you been busy today?' she asked.

'Aye, busy enough... the five guests arrived earlier today... Miss Camille and the staff arrived yesterday. So after I drop you on the island I'm done for the day.'

'Do you live locally?' she asked. Stupid question, she thought to herself.

'Aye, well, locally enough, Ellenabeich, round the point,' he said, gesturing with a hand to Seil Island now falling away behind them in the distance, its rocky hills and green slopes indistinct now in the falling rain.

She pointed westwards. 'Is that where we're headed?'

Charlie shook his head. 'No, that's Insh island. We're going over there...' He pointed with his right hand.

In the distance she could see a dark mass. 'It's actually no very far,' he said. 'The weather's making it seem further than it is.'

He relapsed into silence. Time passed slowly, the noise and smell of the engine, the motion of the boat rising and falling through the waves. She was starting to feel really seasick now. She hoped she wasn't going to throw up. She looked forward. The island was getting much closer now, she could see its sheer sides, grey rock streaked with quartz. It looked sinister and forbidding, but then, she reflected as she looked around at the grey sea, waves crashing against the rocky flanks of the island, it could hardly look anything else in the growing savagery of the storm.

They sailed closer, the boat pitching and bouncing alarmingly in the swell. Waves occasionally broke over the bows sending sea-spray flying over the partially roofed cabin. She glanced at Charlie, who grinned reassuringly. 'Dinnae worry, the boat can handle it,' he shouted.

The boat might, she thought despairingly. I'm not sure about my stomach. Now the details of the island began to resolve themselves. Low, scrubby trees and bushes, then a glimpse of the house. The boat bucked up and down in the heavy sea.

'It'll be quieter in a minute,' Charlie bellowed over the noise of the wind and the engine, 'when we get in the lee of the island.'

God, I hope so, she thought. Her stomach heaved and she swallowed bile. Despite the cold wind she was beginning to sweat uncomfortably.

Sure enough, as they got closer the waves diminished in height and the wind lessened. Thank God, she thought as her body began to recover.

They were now just a few metres from the banks of the island, in its protective shelter. The howling wind dramatically lessened and she could hear the noise of the engine much quieter now as they chugged along.

'What do you make of the new owners?' she asked, desperate for conversation to take her mind off her body and also curious as to what the locals thought of the metropolitan O'Rourke and Camille. She couldn't imagine that the fishing and farming community had much truck with yoga.

Charlie fished a pack of cigarettes out of a breast pocket and lit one. He frowned thoughtfully, blowing smoke into the air. 'She seems a nice enough woman. I hope she makes a success of it.'

'You don't sound too convinced,' Hanlon said.

The elderly boatman slowed the craft down to a crawl so they were making hardly any headway along the coast of the island. He nodded up at the rocky sides of Duachy.

'Nobody has as yet. The guy who built the place originally went crazy.'

'What, the Victorian mine owner?'

'Aye, delusional, they had to haul him off to the nut-house. I guess now it would be diagnosed as dementia... He was very old. Raving about the Angel of Death.' He coughed, phlegmily, and spat over the side of the boat into the sea. 'Then yon rock musician, Shane Gowrie... people say he got up tae all sorts, particularly in the chapel.' He shook his head. 'It's maybe no surprise that nothing good has come of Duachy ever since.'

'What, people think it's cursed?' Hanlon laughed.

Charlie frowned. 'It's no really a laughing matter, young lady,' he said. 'God willnae be mocked.'

Hanlon kept forgetting that on the west coast people often took religion seriously. Where she was from, metropolitan London, it had never really seemed much of an issue.

'I'm sorry, I didn't mean to offend,' she apologised. 'Why do people think it's cursed?'

They rounded a curve of the island and there, facing Seil Island, was a small natural harbour with a sea wall. There was a little islet that lay between the jaws of the harbour, adding a further layer of protection from the Atlantic. Charlie nosed the boat through the narrow channel. The water here in the protection of the harbour was comparatively calm.

Charlie said, 'When Gowrie was here, his girlfriend died, threw herself off the cliffs into the sea. The last owner, the guy who had the hotel, hung himself in the chapel...' He looked meaningfully at Hanlon. 'Two suicides... these things happen in threes. The clock's ticking.'

He brought the boat up skilfully alongside the sea wall, stood up stiffly and clambered up a metal ladder that was built into the brickwork of the jetty. He secured the boat fore and aft with mooring ropes. Hanlon handed him her case then climbed up to join him. She looked around.

There was a small gazebo made of timber and stone built into the side of the hill and a couple of raised flower beds that were full of fuchsias and nasturtiums, their bright colours muted in the dull grey of the day, flower heads drooping under the lash of the rain. There was another building on the far side of the small harbour area.

'That path leads up to the house,' Charlie said, pointing at some broad steps that ran uphill through rhododendron bushes and ferns. She could see another path that ran into the trees to their right.

'Is that the coastal route?'

'Aye,' he said. 'It hugs the edge of the island, runs around in a kind of loop. There's all sorts of ornamental plants and statues. Gowrie spent a fortune on the gardens. Money he should have been saving for the taxman – that's why he had to sell up. He owed millions in back taxes. When they caught up with him finally he was scunnered. The last owner kept it well maintained, shame he didnae do the same for his morale.' He looked at her keenly. 'You're no like the others I brought over, I can tell.'

'In what respect?'

'You havenae got your heid jammed up your arse.'

He handed her a business card with his name and mobile number on.

'If you need anything, give me a call.'

She picked up her case and walked off, up the steep stairs towards the Duachy Hotel.

'Oh, Hanlon!'

She turned. Charlie lifted his arms up like an Old Testament prophet, like Elijah, and shouted, 'Remember to pray, Hanlon, for a' the lost souls... The clock is ticking...'

She gave him a thumbs up.

He looked at her and there was a rumble of distant thunder.

'Tick tock! Hanlon, tick tock!'

He turned and clambered into his boat.

* * *

Hanlon was met at reception by O'Rourke. O'Rourke looked pale, but then she always did. Today her hair was down, a curtain of glowing dark red. Hanlon thought she looked beautiful.

'Hi,' she said. 'Good to see you again.'

O'Rourke returned the smile. 'Good to see you too, Hanlon. Come into the office and I'll fill you in on things.'

They went into the hotel's back office. On the wall were ghostly rectangular patches where the former owners had hung photos or pictures. O'Rourke saw her glance. 'We've redecorated the public areas... backstage is yet to happen.'

'So where is everyone?'

'Siobhan and Jenny are in the kitchen,' O'Rourke said, 'and the guests, right now, they're in a yoga session with Camille.'

'I thought that nothing was happening until Monday.' Hanlon was surprised.

'Well, that was the original plan,' O'Rourke said. 'The guests were to have arrived tomorrow, but we brought things forward to the Sunday with guests arriving today. The plan had been for them to wander around the island – the gardens are lovely – maybe have a swim down in the harbour, but...' she looked pointedly out of the window at the terrible weather, 'bearing Storm Cedric in mind, we decided to throw in a class today.'

Hanlon nodded. It certainly wasn't a day for admiring a garden. As if to reinforce that, more rain rattled on the windows.

'Remind me of the schedule?' she asked.

O'Rourke consulted a clipboard. 'This is valid as of tomorrow: 7–8 a.m. will be run with Hanlon; 8.30–10.00 a.m. breakfast/meditation time; 10–12, hatha yoga; 12–2 is lunch then 2.30–4.00 p.m. advanced yoga; 5–6 run with Hanlon... 6.45–8.00 p.m. dinner, then after dinner the bar will be open, self-service until 10 p.m.'

'So I've got two slots.'

'You have, indeed. You won't be that busy, maybe you'll only have Karen Ross running with you. Staff might join in. Camille probably will.'

'Then that will mean Suki.' Hanlon smiled.

O'Rourke rolled her eyes. 'Inevitably, but I might even come, who knows?' Hanlon eyed the tall, elegant form of O'Rourke on her high heels with scepticism. She found it hard to imagine O'Rourke running.

'Really?' she asked.

O'Rourke gave her a wintry smile. 'No, not really.'

'And there are just the five guests?' Hanlon asked.

'That's correct.'

'Bar staff, waiting staff?'

O'Rourke shook her head.

'We've got a kitchen porter who comes at 9 a.m. and leaves at four, she, or he, but it's usually a woman, is there to help Siobhan, and there's two cleaners who come with her to do the rooms and public areas while classes are going on. It's all kept to a minimum. The bar, well, alcohol is not encouraged, but people obviously drink. No smoking, no drugs.'

Hanlon nodded. So, just the five of them, Camille, Siobhan, Jenny, O'Rourke and herself. That gave her little comfort. As she understood it, they were on the island to protect Camille from external threats. But the attempt to harm Camille with broken glass had probably been made by someone who was now here on the island. It was of course possible that an unknown person had spiked the muesli mix, but the prime suspects, at least to Hanlon's way of thinking, were all assembled here. Siobhan could have put the glass in the muesli, but it was not impossible that Jenny had. Or Suki. Or even O'Rourke, come to that, and then been hoist by her own petard.

'Where are the cleaners and the KP from?' she asked.

'From Seil Island. All three of them used to work for the previous owners.'

Well, they could probably be ruled out as a threat to Camille, thought Hanlon.

'And how are you?' she asked O'Rourke.

'I'm fine,' O'Rourke said. 'I had a few stitches in my gum from the cut from the shard of glass. They X-rayed me but they couldn't see anything, no blood in my stool, which I think meant my stomach hadn't been lacerated. So that was a relief. I gather if it had been ground glass it would have been a different story, a lot worse, but as it is...' she gave a humourless smile, 'no damage done.'

'Who do you think put the glass in the muesli?' Hanlon asked.

O'Rourke shrugged. 'I don't know. All the people who could have done it almost certainly didn't. If it was to target Camille, then it could have been her sister or Jenny, but it makes no sense. Why would they do it? If not them, maybe a cleaner, accessing the kitchen, conceivably they might have a grudge? Maybe that devotional fruitcake Suki. She was in the café on her own the night before – she could have climbed over the pass and done it.'

'What, love turning to hate?'

O'Rourke nodded. She grimaced. 'Fanatics are capable of anything,' she said. 'A Stan.'

'A what?' asked Hanlon, puzzled.

'A Stan,' O'Rourke said. 'A fan who takes things to extremes, like the Eminem song. You know, the kind of weirdos who rootle through famous people's bins in search of stuff they might have handled.'

Hanlon fell silent. She found it hard to believe that Suki would be capable of harming Camille. From what she had seen of Suki and from what she had heard, Suki was simply an obsessive fan, not a deranged one. She changed the subject to one that had been constantly nagging at her since she had met him.

In her mind Strom, the intelligent, amoral con man, as she saw him, had a lot to gain by the glass incident. If he had invented or exaggerated the threats to Camille, he would cement his reputation as a psychic with Camille, leading her to place even more trust in him than before. She was a wealthy, desirable woman, after all. She had trusted him a lot before the glass incident, now his credibility would be riding sky-high. His reputation was unassailable in her eyes, maybe worth the risk of actually killing her.

'What do you think of Paul Strom?' she asked O'Rourke. In some respects they were all here at his say-so. Until the glass incident there was no evidence of any threat to Camille's life, other than the texts and letters. Strom knew her mobile number, her address. He could easily have sent them.

Hanlon did not believe in Strom's ability to predict the future but she could well believe in his ability to shape it. O'Rourke frowned.

'I'm sure you think he's a fake,' O'Rourke said. 'It's what I thought myself at first when Camille came in a year or so ago raving about him.

And he does have a kind of magic act, hypnosis, card tricks, sleight of hand, that he does in pubs in Glasgow.'

'Really?' Hanlon said. Well, there you are, she thought. This shamanism malarkey is just an extension of his stage act. O'Rourke continued, 'So, initially, I thought like you, he was a con. Either hoping to fleece Camille or maybe he was just hoping that if he got Camille as a customer more business would come his way.' She shook her head. 'Camille is an influencer. If she endorses something on her blog, then an awful lot of people will buy it.' She paused. 'And I mean a lot!'

'That sounds like the voice of experience,' Hanlon said.

O'Rourke grinned. 'Yeah, that's because it is. I monetise a lot for Camille. I literally peddle influence, but, I like to think, in a low-key, semi-ethical way. Here's one example. We get through a lot of sanitiser and we don't pay for it. We get it for free in return for having a bottle in shot on her yoga videos. It's a green product and we genuinely believe in it... the company are delighted, as are we. Her clothing, we've got a big sponsorship deal with a yoga clothes firm. Anyway, back to Strom. He'd be booked solid if she said she used him. But he told her not to. He doesn't profit financially, well, other than his consultancy fees, from his connection with Camille. Like I said, he forbade Camille from telling people she consulted with him. That must have cost him quite a few potential clients.' She shook her head in amazement at Strom's altruism.

'And he does come up with some genuinely insightful stuff.' She nodded to herself, the gaze in her eyes far away as if she were recalling some of Strom's more accurate predictions or suggestions. 'Some of which is genuinely inexplicable. So, I think he is, up to a point, the real deal.'

None of that changed Hanlon's own feelings. That Strom was a charlatan, but a very good one and certainly no fool. Well, whatever he was, he wasn't here, and her job for the next few days was simply to safeguard Camille from the people who were here, one of whom might be wanting to kill her.

'Tell me about the people on the course,' she asked.

'Well, as you know, it's limited to five people. Suki you've met.'

Hanlon nodded. Oh, how pleased Suki will be to see me, she thought.

'OK, the men first. Oliver Drummond, he's in his thirties, a financial advisor... single.' O'Rourke picked up a black buckram-bound book, which Hanlon had noticed her pick up earlier from the hall stand in the reception area as they had gone through to the office.

'Let's see what he's written in the guest book.' She opened it and looked at Hanlon. 'It's practice for the yogis and yoginis to set an intention for their stay. Ollie's written, "There's more to life than money."' She looked up at Hanlon. 'Well, he should know.'

'Who else?'

'Loyd Travers, fifty-nine.' She grimaced. 'Loyd's a bit of an old hippy,' she confided. Ponytail, she mouthed silently. Hanlon nodded understandingly.

'How much does this retreat cost again?' Hanlon asked.

'Five K for the week,' said O'Rourke.

'Well, he's a wealthy old hippy,' Hanlon said acidly. 'What does Loyd do for money?'

'He's a software designer.'

'And what's his intention statement?'

'Let me see... "Enlightenment is optional."'

Hanlon shrugged; that was opaque. 'OK, how about the women?'

'Anna Reynolds, we call her the Merry Widow. She comes to a fair few of Camille's retreats. She's forty-five. I don't think she works. And she's put, "It's the journey, not the destination."'

Hanlon rolled her eyes. Was there no cliché that wasn't going to be unearthed by this group?

'And the last one?'

'Karen Ross, she's in her thirties, she's sales director for a drugs company. She's very driven. I think it's quite a stressful job. She's here to relax, I suspect. She'll be on your run. She looks extremely fit. And she's written, "By your fruits shall ye know them."'

'OK, thanks for that, Katherine, I think that's everything. I may as well go and unpack. Where's my room?'

O'Rourke stood up. 'Follow me, it's just upstairs.'

Hanlon walked behind her, admiring O'Rourke's very long shapely legs beneath the skirt as they went up the broad stairs to a gallery that overlooked the reception area. There was a large window over the front door and a chandelier hung from the ceiling; despite the terrible weather outside, it was flooded with light.

'There are five bedrooms on this floor,' O'Rourke said, indicating the five doors in front of them that faced onto the gallery. 'These are the guests' bedrooms.' Then she nodded to where the stairs resumed at either end of the gallery. 'And five above. We'll go on up.'

They walked up another flight of stairs to a corridor. More natural light, this time from Velux windows set into the ceiling above.

'This is where we all are. This end room's mine, that end room is Siobhan's and Jenny's. That room is Camille's and you're in here, next door.'

She opened Hanlon's door with a swipe card and handed it to her.

It was a very pleasant room, a low double bed with pale, Scandi-type furnishings. Hanlon noticed that there was a door that connected with Camille's room. She pointed it out.

'Yes,' O'Rourke said, 'these two rooms, yours and hers, are a kind of family room where you can put your kids in here and have access to them easily. I thought that you and Camille might want to talk, not to mention the fact that you can get in there quickly, should you need to.'

'That's true,' Hanlon said. 'We've got a great deal to talk about.'

There was a glass door leading to a small balcony. She walked over to it and looked out. The glass was vibrating in the wind and was streaked with rainwater. She could make out a small pointed roof in the distance.

'What's that building I can see?'

O'Rourke joined her. 'That's the chapel.'

'Oh, of course.' So that was Shane Gowrie's famous room, where he would deflower groupies on the altar, bringing down the Curse of Duachy on the hotel. If Charlie was to be believed, which she didn't. Of course, Gowrie, the leather-trousered, priapic Love God, was now a senile old fool wearing a nappy, drooling away in a care home in Glasgow.

Right on cue, there was a huge flash of light, followed by a rumble of thunder; the windowpanes rattled in the wind. Storm Cedric seemed to be increasing in strength. Rain beat against the glass.

'Ugh, it's grim out there!' O'Rourke said.

'Well, I don't mind rain. I'm going to go and look at the path and judge it for running,' Hanlon said, 'if you'll excuse me...' She nodded towards her case.

'Oh, right,' O'Rourke said. She looked at the clock on the wall that read eleven-thirty. 'I'd better go and make sure that everything is ready for lunch – that'll be at quarter to one today. They finish the class at twelve, they can go and shower and change, then, like I said, there's a class from two-thirty until four. I'm going to be at that one.'

'Who's signed up for tomorrow's run?'

O'Rourke consulted her clipboard. 'In the morning, Oliver, Karen and Suki. Afternoon, Camille, Suki and Karen.'

'OK, then, Katherine, I'll see you at lunch.'

O'Rourke left her and Hanlon sat down on the bed. She stared into space. Camille was too trusting. She had once heard an expression, 'There's compassion and there's idiot compassion.' To Hanlon's way of thinking that described Camille's thought processes. Idiot compassion.

She obviously thought that the person threatening her was a stranger, one of the hundreds of thousands of people who knew her from the Internet. Not someone she knew and trusted. In her mind it was simply impossible that her yogis and yoginis were a threat.

Hanlon was more suspicious. One of these nice yoga-obsessed people was a potential killer, but which one?

9

Hanlon changed into her running clothes: shorts, a top and shoes. She had a lime dayglo waterproof jacket but hung it up in the cupboard. There was no point in wearing it. It was raining so hard she thought she might as well accept the fact that she was going to get soaked.

She pulled the door of her room to behind her and jogged down the stairs.

When she opened the front door of the hotel, she had to brace herself against the force of the wind. It had increased dramatically in the half-hour or so that she had been inside. It whipped through the trees and shrubs. The garden frontage of the hotel had, she suspected, been designed with bad weather as a constant – the sea was the Atlantic Ocean and it was the west coast of Scotland, hardly a stranger to wind and rain – but everything was visibly staggering under the lash of Cedric.

She ran lightly down the steps of the hotel and then down the wider, shallower steps that led down to the small harbour where Charlie had dropped her off earlier. She had a good look at it now from this higher vantage point. Before, she had been feeling too ill to really notice that much of her surroundings.

Now she was looking down on the small pier where she had disembarked; attached to this was a small concrete jetty. On the far side of the pier was the building she had noticed before, a boathouse that jutted out into the water so you could sail right into it. Its frontage was invisible from here, so she didn't know if the hotel kept a boat in it or not. There was a row of brightly painted bathing huts she hadn't noticed before, so you could change into a swimming costume and then swim off the jetty and around the quiet waters of the harbour or venture further out into the open sea. On a sunny, calm summer's day it would be a wonderful place for bathing. But they wouldn't be doing any of that for the foreseeable future. She looked at the waves breaking on the small island, more a very large rock, that protected the harbour from the main body of the sea. They were crashing over it, the spray rising high into the sky. The wind carried some of it as far as where she was standing; she could taste the salt water on her lips. It was exhilarating, but it would have been practically suicidal to have swum in those conditions.

She paused for a while looking out across the grey, angry sea to Seil Island, which was now just a grey smudge in the distance. The weather had undoubtedly worsened significantly in the short time she had been here on Duachy. Seil was only a mile or so away, she guessed; she found it hard to judge distance on the water and the waves seemed to meet the sky, shutting down visibility. If this carried on, she doubted that the three members of staff from the mainland, the cleaners and the kitchen assistant, would be able to make it across the following day.

She reflected that it was easy to forget when you lived in a town or a city how wild the sea could be. Even though she lived next to a loch herself she had never seen waves like these at such close range.

Then the wind suddenly and unexpectedly carried a strong smell of weed to her nose. She sniffed the air; someone was smoking it nearby. She looked around. There was nobody in sight, but it seemed to be coming from the boathouse. She walked down to the building; the smell grew stronger, definitely from here. The windows in the wooden walls were above head height so she couldn't see in. She toyed with the idea of climbing up on something and peering in but she thought, What business is it of mine if one of the guests or staff is getting high?

She shrugged and, leaving the harbour area, set off along the path at an easy jog. It was a great track to run along. It didn't simply hug the coastline. It zigzagged along, sometimes past an unexpected pond with ornamental lilies, sometimes running above the rocks and the sea, sometimes leading to a viewing point. The path led her on in enticing ways, a beautiful shrub, an exotic tree, a sudden view of the water – she always felt as if there would be something exciting to see around the corner. Hanlon felt her spirits rise as she warmed up, felt the cares of the day evaporate with the exhilaration of physical activity. Her hair bounced rhythmically in time with her stride as she effortlessly covered the ground, almost floating above it.

She'd read in the literature that Gowrie had spent a small fortune on the gardens. She was no expert, far from it, but the path went through tall, delicate clumps of bamboo, past statues of the Buddha and various Indian or Tibetan gods, again she was no expert, set in grottoes or under waterfalls. There was the occasional palm tree; she was used to seeing these on the west coast where it never got really cold because of the Gulf Stream. There were giant ferns and boulders covered with moss.

The path was broad. Good, she thought, we could run two abreast. Its surface was compacted stones and chippings so it was firm underfoot and not muddy. Some of the stones protruded upwards significantly; she made a mental note to warn the runners not to trip. If you were running and your toe hit one of these it would be easy to sprawl forward and measure your length on the ground.

Occasionally the path ran inland slightly, but generally it kept to the edge of the island. When it did so, the ground fell away steeply to the sea below, which was crashing against the grey stone of the island. She stopped and looked down. It was about a ten-metre drop, maybe less, but if you fell in, you wouldn't get out. The water slammed against the rock with terrific force, churning and boiling at the base of the short cliff, turning a kind of milky turquoise colour as it smashed against the stone. It would be hard enough to climb up the rock on a calm day, the sides of Duachy Island were quite steep, but in weather like this you'd be picked up by the sea and smashed to pieces like a piece of driftwood.

When she reached the tip of the island she checked her phone to see the distance she had covered; it was about a kilometre and a half. That was fine. She guessed that the whole loop, when you added in all the twists and turns of the path, would measure about four to five kilometres, which would be ample for a good short run. She'd add in some speed running for the fitter clients, and the slower ones could pant along in their wake. They could always put in a second lap if they so desired.

She rounded a corner and saw the chapel whose roof she had seen from her room properly for the first time. It was set back from the path by about fifty metres and she jogged up to the doors. It wasn't large, it was made of some kind of reddish stone, the walls were high and the roof was grey slate, which looked quite recent. There was a kind of mini spire that rose up into the sky. It was that which had been visible above the treeline.

A huge gust of wind hit her as she walked up to the large door, which looked to be oak studded with large round-headed nails driven into it, to give it a more antique look, she guessed. Above the door was a stone lintel with an inscription. She looked up at it. Carved in heavy Gothic script were the words:

'Do What Thou Wilt Shall Be the Whole of the Law.'

Hanlon was not particularly religious but even she recognised that this was not standard Christian teaching. She guessed it was more in keeping with Shane Gowrie's ethos than that of the original builder, the religious tycoon. She tried the handle of the door; to her surprise it opened.

She walked in and closed the door behind her.

She shivered; it was cold, bitterly cold in the chapel. There wasn't a great deal to see inside. There were three pews on either side of a central nave leading to a fenced-off altar, which was a rectangular piece of rough stone. High above were massive wooden beams that held the roof up. On one of them was carved the date of construction: '1900'.

Light filtered in through narrow arched windows that had stained glass in them, mainly red, green and blue in an abstract design, which gave a slightly eerie quality to the atmosphere inside. There were statues of what she at first thought were saints inside niches on the walls but on closer inspection turned out to be erotic works of art. There were fourteen Stations of the Cross for Catholics, here there were fourteen Stations of Fornication. Scenes from the Kama Sutra. It was, she decided, shaking her head, somewhat distasteful. She guessed that it was true then, what old Charlie had said, that Shane Gowrie, rock star, had converted the chapel from a House of God to a House of Sex. The original owner who had built this as a place of conventional worship would have been appalled. Hanlon was no prude, but she found the place profoundly depressing in the iconoclastic perversion of its original intent.

She wondered what plans Camille had for it; she'd ask her later this evening. Possibly these days there was some sort of preservation order on it from Historic Environment Scotland and Gowrie's shag pad would be protected as a historical monument.

She left the building, closing the door behind her on this shrine to Shane Gowrie's sex drive and his monumental egotism.

Back on the path and down to the end of the island. She guessed that in better weather you'd be able to see the hills up towards Oban and the island of Mull, but today the horizon was obscured by low cloud and the stinging lash of the rain. She could see the roof of the hotel rising above the treeline and then it disappeared from view as she reached the tip of the island. There was a viewing platform here and some benches that had been secured with brackets to the stone floor so they wouldn't blow away. From this vantage point you could look out to the far-away coastline. It would be a great place for some morning yoga. The sun would presumably rise up over those hills that she knew lay behind the low grey banks of cloud and rain, but the sun was invisible, a guessed-at presence somewhere in the gunmetal grey of the sky.

Ten minutes later she was back at the hotel. Altogether, including the chapel, her tour of Shane Gowrie's raging priapic libido, it had taken her about forty-five minutes, and that had been going slowly.

It was twenty past twelve by the clock on the wall. She kicked off her shoes, soaked and muddy, in the lobby and opened the interior door of the hotel. She could hear the murmur of voices from the bar and ran lightly upstairs where she had a quick shower, changed into trousers and a sweater and joined the group.

Over lunch Hanlon got to know Camille's group well enough to form thumbnail opinions. She was sitting at a table with Loyd, the software guy. He was in good shape for his years, quite large and powerfully built, with long silver hair tied back in a ponytail and a beard. He had an earring in one ear, a silver bracelet on one wrist and a couple of rings on his right hand, one of a skull design in silver, the other a blue gemstone. He was wearing a Grateful Dead T-shirt under a plaid shirt, and army trousers.

He looked like the kind of guy he was, a Comp Sci graduate from the late seventies who had done well out of tech but, although he'd obviously kept abreast of computer developments and innovations, had significantly failed to download and implement any upgrades to himself over the years. His tastes in clothes, music, politics had stalled at around nineteen seventy-eight.

He was obviously successful and wealthy – he employed twenty people who did ethical hacking, cyber security and suggested software debugging ideas – but she had the feeling that if she broke into his bedroom there would be a *Lord of the Rings* map of Middle-earth on the wall, a stereo (Linn almost certainly, he'd droned on about them for a good five minutes) with Neil Young playing, and on a Wednesday night his mates would be over for Dungeons and Dragons and to get high.

He was quite likeable. His business was more or less running itself, he was semi-retired and concentrating on what he enjoyed. He was getting limbered up for a six-month trip around India, incorporating yoga at various touristy ashrams interlinked with classic train journeys.

Anna Reynolds was a buxom woman with corkscrew black hair and a smiling face. She was enjoying playing the technophobe to Loyd's obvious knowledge of the field, and was kind of flirting with him in a relatively low-key way. Hanlon rather guessed that this was her default behaviour. Although she was considerably younger than Loyd, she and he had that kind of shared universal memory in common so they were able to relate to each other on a social history level: Margaret Thatcher, punk rock and disco.

She'd just finished a relationship with a much younger man. 'Are you a cougar, Anna?' Loyd had wondered.

'No, Loyd, I'm too old to be a cougar. I'm like a mangy old lioness...' a roar of laughter and a flash of very good teeth, 'and I don't give a toss what people think.'

As Hanlon ate her lunch, a seafood ceviche followed by a dal – fish and seafood were on the menu but no meat – she discounted Loyd and Anna as suspects for an attempt on Camille's life.

'Are either of you interested in joining any of the runs?' Hanlon asked.

'I'm afraid not,' Loyd said.

'Me neither,' Anna added.

'You should go,' Loyd said. 'Work up a sweat.'

'I can't sweat,' Anna said. Loyd looked puzzled. She tapped her forehead. 'Botox,' she explained.

Jenny cleared away their plates; the hired help from the mainland had all left early because of the storm. She returned from the kitchen and said that dessert would be served in the bar area.

There was no sign of Suki. Or Camille, for that matter. Hanlon wondered where they were.

'Come and meet Oliver and Karen,' O'Rourke said to Hanlon as they stood up and moved through into the other room.

She smiled her apologies to Loyd and Anna, who were still arguing about the role of Margaret Thatcher.

'This is Hanlon, Hanlon meet Oliver,' said O'Rourke, smiling politely at Oliver Drummond. Hanlon had taken an immediate dislike to him the moment she had seen him. He had an air of arrogance that put her back up. He had the kind of face that some women would find attractive, quite broad, very thick dark hair going a distinguished grey at the temples. He had very full lips.

'Hello,' he said. He had quite a strong Scottish accent. She wondered where he was from; it didn't sound like Glasgow.

He ran his eyes over her in an evaluating way, very noticeably mentally undressing her. Not in a million years, thought Hanlon. She'd noticed earlier that Jenny obviously didn't share her opinion. She'd spent quite a bit of time clearing away his plate, openly flirting with him in textbook fashion – playing with her hair, hanging on his every word. Anna Reynolds had noticed. Hanlon had sensed a deep disapproval there, but whether that was because she shared Hanlon's opinion of Oliver or because she thought that staff shouldn't flirt with guests, was hard to know.

Hanlon had caught O'Rourke's eye. She too had noticed Jenny's behaviour and she was not amused. Hanlon thought of the sous-chef incident and the attempted seduction of Ishbel's business partner. You'd better watch your step, Jenny, Hanlon had thought, or you'll get fired.

'So you're the fitness expert?' Oliver Drummond said. He managed to impart a faint sneer to the words fitness and expert as if they were slightly disreputable, what Hanlon's adoptive parents would have called 'common'.

'I am,' she said coolly. 'Are you joining us?'

'Yeah, I could do with losing the odd pound...' he murmured.

Now it was Hanlon's turn to examine his body. He had looked in reasonable shape, but she noticed now it was deceptive. He was quite a big guy but he had a sizeable paunch. Then she thought, I'm being a bit uncharitable. Surely the whole point of yoga was that it was inclusive, not just for the lithe and beautiful, endlessly photographing themselves in flawless, hard-to-achieve poses like standing splits against a wall or a one-legged forearm wheel, both of which Camille could do. Camille had been savvy enough to prefix these with: 'yoga's not about stuff like this...' A clever humble-brag. Hanlon had detected the hand of O'Rourke there.

Then she noticed him staring at her chest and her dislike of him swiftly returned.

'You certainly could,' she remarked. His eyes narrowed immediately. Have I annoyed you? she thought. I certainly hope so.

'All those expense-accounted lunches...' (She could read the subtext clearly – people don't buy you lunch, you insignificant bitch.) He yawned. 'Sorry, I was up early.' He ostentatiously checked the watch on his wrist; it was a sizeable Rolex. She got the impression it was more to display it for her benefit than to see what time it was. The other wrist, she noticed, had an infinity sign tattooed on it. 'I was checking the markets in New York.'

'Well,' she said, 'I'll see you in reception at five this evening. Don't worry, it won't be too severe.'

Dessert was a rich strawberry gateau. It wasn't Hanlon's kind of thing. She noticed as she moved away that Oliver was moving in for another large slice. Go on, Oliver, she thought, have another five hundred calories. He added more cream, his eyes glistening. Make that another thousand, see how much your heart can stand.

Karen Ross had no fat on her, she was as lean as an Anglepoise lamp, staring out of the large window at the wild sea below. Hanlon walked over to her. 'Hi, I'm Hanlon, personal fitness. You'll be joining us for a run later?'

Karen nodded. She had red wiry hair and pale skin. There were deep bags under her eyes; she looked exhausted. She was gaunt but she had a noticeably muscular physique.

'Do you run?' Hanlon asked.

She nodded. 'Yes, I run marathons, sub three hours, on a good day.' She spoke matter-of-factly, it wasn't a boast. She wasn't like Oliver Drummond. Karen would not see the point of bragging.

'That's impressive,' Hanlon said. It was very good. Her own personal best was a shade over three hours, and that had nearly killed her, but she hadn't run a full marathon for three years now. She'd have a lot of ground to make up.

'Well, look,' she said, 'you probably know more than me about running. Just join us, keep us company and, when you want to, just leave us.'

'How far is the path?' Karen asked.

'About four and a half K,' Hanlon said.

'I'll do it as a speed run, go twice or three times round...' She looked out of the window as a fresh flash of lightning lit up the sea and a dull rumble of thunder penetrated the building. She looked at Hanlon and smiled; it transformed her face. 'Maybe just twice.'

'I'll see you later.'

O'Rourke clapped her hands to get their attention. 'Practice starts in about twenty-five minutes, everyone... please go to your rooms to freshen up... Camille and I will see you in the studio at two-thirty.'

The guests drifted off upstairs, then the door to the bar opened and Camille appeared.

'Hi,' Hanlon said. 'You didn't join us for lunch?'

Camille shook her head. 'No, I never eat lunch, but I think they get to see enough of me anyway.'

Hanlon nodded. She guessed that explained Suki's absence. If Camille wasn't going to be there, then she wouldn't be.

Camille looked out of the window. 'I've been looking at the weather forecast. This storm's supposed to intensify overnight. I don't think anyone's going to be coming or going, in fact I know they're not. Charlie texted me – he's not going anywhere tomorrow. He's not leaving Seil, and neither is anyone else, he says the sea's going to be too rough.'

'Well,' Hanlon said, 'I think he's very wise.'

'You're still doing the run this afternoon?'

'Yeah.' Camille smiled and Hanlon said, 'Look, I need a master key to the rooms.' She would have preferred to ask O'Rourke but Camille would have had to make the decision anyway.

'Why?' Camille frowned.

'One of these guests, or one of your employees, might be someone who is out to kill you,' Hanlon said. 'I want to check out their rooms, just in case.'

'Looking for clues?' Camille said, partly sarcastically.

'I was a police officer for a good many years,' Hanlon said. 'I like to think I learned something during that time. So, yes, I will be looking for anything suspicious.'

Camille sighed and nodded. 'OK then, come on,' she said. Hanlon followed her to the office just off reception. Camille opened a drawer and took out an envelope. She handed Hanlon two rectangular pieces of plastic.

'The red one opens all the doors on the top floor, the blue one the doors below.'

'Thanks.'

Camille said, 'If anyone leaves the class, I'll call you. If you see my caller ID, leave the room.'

'OK,' Hanlon said.

'I'll see you later,' Camille smiled and, with an elegant grace that Hanlon envied, stood up and, before she left the room, turned and said, 'Don't get caught!'

10

Hanlon glanced at her watch. The afternoon session began at two-thirty and ended at four; she'd have to be quick.

She gave it five minutes then went up the stairs to the first room. You didn't have to be a detective to work out it was Loyd's; an old black leather jacket hung over the back of a chair. Loyd was obviously one of those people who saw no reason to ever change the way he dressed, or his hairdo, frozen at when he was seventeen. There was a very fancy-looking laptop set up and a copy of Hermann Hesse's *The Glass Bead Game* on the bedside table. She pulled on a pair of latex gloves and quickly went through the drawers in his dressing table and wardrobe.

Nothing of any interest, as she had suspected.

The next room was Suki's. Inside there were no fewer than three suitcases and a make-up box that was enormous. Hanlon opened the wardrobe and marvelled at the amount of clothes she had brought with her. One or two even had shop labels still attached. On the bedside table was a diary. Hanlon opened it.

Her eyes widened. O'Rourke had been right; if anything, she had underestimated the woman. Suki wasn't just a Stan, she was a super-Stan. This was borderline unhinged.

It was a diary primarily devoted to Camille. They were in July; she flicked through the first six months of the year. More than half of the book was highly detailed entries about the yoga teacher. They contained notes like:

C wearing orange nail varnish on toes, like Burnt Orange Shimmer? Buy.

Great day, spoke to C for 5 mins!

C swears by Dior Massai, saw some in her bag, get.

The cow bad-mouthed me in front of C. Ginger slut!

Hanlon wondered if that was O'Rourke. Probably.

It was very disturbing. There were various, recurring cryptic ideograms – God alone knew what they meant. It was obvious that Suki was obsessed. Some entries related to photos she'd taken on her phone; when she managed to find the make of clothes that Camille wore, e.g. yoga pants – she was ecstatic.

Sweaty Betty, I KNEW it!!!!!

It wasn't all about Camille. Some entries referred to dinner parties, some to various appointments, doctors, dentists, some entries referred to money – she seemed to have a great deal of it. For example, she'd lent someone called DH sixty thousand in January. It seemed a vast amount, but Hanlon wasn't interested in Suki's finances. The crucial thing was the bulk of it was a hymn to Camille.

The week before:

Spoke to C about retreat, C said to bring waterproof, asked her what she favoured, said she wore Endura windproof jacket, good cos you can run in it. She said she was going to sign up to bitch-face's running.

That must be me, thought Hanlon with a wry smile, 'bitch-face'.

Note to self. Get one, we'll be twinnies! C has Nike running shoes. Asked! Colour???

God, thought Hanlon, 'twinnies'.

She turned to Monday 1 July, the day of the broken glass.

C with ginger cow and bitch-face. GC ate C's b.fast and ill now, in hospital. Wish it had been C. If only C were in hospital! We cld be 2gether!!!

This was surrounded by some more of Suki's incomprehensible icons. Hanlon closed the book and put it back.

She was beginning to wonder if Suki's love of Camille might take on more sinister aspects.

She slipped out of Suki's room.

Karen Ross's belongings were as bleak and monochrome as Hanlon had expected. Her bedside reading was a self-help book for business-women. There was also a novel by a writer called Ayn Rand and, more surprisingly, *Altar of Lust* (by Kristen Fogerty, the best-selling author of *Autumn of Lust*) billed as a steamy, lesbian BDSM erotic romance. That certainly raised an eyebrow.

Anna Reynolds' room contained no surprises, except for the fact that Hanlon would have imagined an *Autumn of Lust* style book by *her* bed, but instead she found print editions of *The Economist* and *Investors' Chronicle*.

She glanced at her watch. She had half an hour left. Oliver's room was the one she was most interested in. She slipped inside and looked around.

She went into the bathroom and looked inside his washbag. There were some tablets, high-blood-pressure pills, and a small box of Viagra. Well, well, she thought. She went back into the bedroom and pulled out his suitcase from the cupboard. It was unlocked. Inside were three one-litre bottles of vodka, one of which was nearly finished. In the zip compartment of the suitcase was an envelope. She opened this and found half a dozen neatly folded wraps of paper. She opened one and looked at the contents: white powder, coke, she guessed. She refolded it and replaced it. There was also a small plastic carton, like an old-fashioned film container. She opened it: green cannabis buds. She wondered if it had been Oliver smoking in the boathouse – had he left the class early? She really didn't care. She wrinkled her nose at the smell, put the lid back on and replaced that too.

Twenty minutes. She ran upstairs and, more out of curiosity than anything, went into O'Rourke's room.

It was as neat and tidy and impersonal as she expected. She opened drawers – everything neatly aligned with military precision. O'Rourke's expensive-looking suitcase was lying on a wooden shelf in the wardrobe and Hanlon opened it. There was nothing inside it except for a framed photograph of a young girl, aged maybe about seven, a school photograph. Hanlon picked it up and looked at it carefully. It was such an odd choice to take with you on a trip that would last less than a week; it was something usually found given pride of place on a mantelpiece.

She took a photo of it on her phone. The girl looked quite a lot like O'Rourke but she had never heard her mention having a daughter, maybe she was a niece? But who would carry an actual framed portrait of a relative like that?

She turned it over. There was the name of the photographer on the back: John Curry, 221 the High Street in Biggar. She photographed that too, then checked the time. She replaced the photo and went back to her own room and lay on the bed, staring at the ceiling.

Had she learned anything of interest or use?

Suki was even more obsessed with Camille than she'd imagined. She had thought it was like a schoolgirl crush, but it was beginning to seem darkly obsessive. And the cryptic comment about the hospitalisation of O'Rourke. The fantasy of looking after a sick Camille, nursing her back to health, that could lead, perhaps had led, to alarming consequences. She could imagine Suki swooping into a Glasgow hospital and whisking Camille away to a private clinic somewhere, followed by the offer of a luxury holiday somewhere, 'just the two of us, while you recuperate'.

Oliver's drugs and booze. Should she be surprised? Probably not.

Obviously the bottles were there to tide him through the long evenings after the bar closed.

By 5 p.m., Camille, Suki, Karen and Oliver were assembled in the porch. Hanlon looked at Suki. She was dressed identically to Camille in a fluorescent blue waterproof cycle jacket and black and white patterned Lycra running tights. The shoes were identical too. Good grief, Hanlon thought. She led them through a brief series of runners' stretches, then she addressed them.

'OK, Karen will probably be doing her own thing. Don't be alarmed or discouraged if she runs past you a couple of times. The rest of us will go at a nice easy pace. It's wet but the path is a good one, needless to say, don't go too near the edge, but there's plenty of room for people to run two abreast, no more than that though. OK... off we go...'

Hanlon led the small group onto the path; they started off at an easy jog. The rain was steady and not too outrageous. After about five minutes, Karen Ross, who had been running by her side, turned to her and said, 'OK, I'm going to leave you here...' Hanlon watched as she picked up her pace and disappeared around the next bend.

She dropped back to the other three. Oliver was looking distinctly unhappy; he was noticeably gasping for breath. He was even more out of shape than she had guessed. But five minutes was a long time if you'd only ever walked for the last decade. 'I'd slow it down, Oliver,' she suggested, falling in beside him. He glared at her. He wasn't going to be told what to do by a woman, that was obvious.

'I'm fine...' he said.

'OK.' She ran next to Camille to see how she was; she was light and quick on her feet. Her blonde hair plastered to her head by the rain, she grinned happily at Hanlon. 'I'm good, I like running, I don't often get the time though.'

'Good...' She dropped back to where Suki was labouring to follow her idol. She was in an even worse state than Oliver, but Hanlon could see from the grim look of determination on her face that she was desperate to keep her eyes firmly locked on Camille's back. Suki would do or die.

'I'm going to tell you to take it easy now, Suki,' Hanlon said. 'This is a fun run.'

'No... it's... OK... honestly...' panted Suki. Her face was practically crimson. Hanlon, used to hard exercise, had forgotten quite how stressful running was for people who hadn't done it since school. The idea of a fun run for the sedentary was a real oxymoron.

'I'll walk with you a bit,' Hanlon said. 'You might pull a muscle. You don't want to injure yourself for yoga...'

That had a magical effect. Suki certainly didn't want that. She slowed to a walk, Hanlon sprinted up to Camille and told her to go on ahead, she'd be with Suki. Camille nodded and smiled and picked her pace up.

Hanlon ran back to Suki, passing Oliver, who looked triumphant at the fact that he had overtaken someone.

Idiot, thought Hanlon.

The two of them walked together for a few minutes.

'How long have you known Camille?' Hanlon asked. Suki's face had returned to a more normal colour. Her breathing had returned to normal; she no longer sounded as if she was about to die.

'About two years,' Suki said. 'My husband was leaving me and I was distraught. I was so depressed I actually thought about killing myself...' Hanlon must have looked surprised at this intimate revelation. Suki said with surprising earnestness, 'My analyst says I should share my feelings more, and be honest, so, although I don't much like you, I've got the feeling you wouldn't betray a confidence...'

'Thank you,' Hanlon said. She didn't know whether to be flattered or not. Suki had obviously embraced the honesty part of her therapy. Suki hardly knew her. Hanlon had met people before who had done assertiveness training as part of their therapy; they had been remarkably rude. At least she hadn't called her 'bitch-face'.

'Anyway,' Suki carried on, 'Camille's yoga gave me the strength I needed to go on. She taught me I wasn't worthless... I don't know what I'd do without her. Luckily she's always there for me... she's so giving.'

They walked along the path together for another few metres, buffeted by the wind and the rain, then she looked at Hanlon. 'So are you going to be working for her?'

'Quite possibly,' Hanlon said. 'We'll have to see how it goes.'

She suddenly thought that she ought to check on Camille before she got too far ahead. That was, after all, why she was here. The funny thing was, she was beginning to become quite attached to Suki, in a peculiar sort of way. She reminded her oddly enough of a jealous dog, none too bright, that had attached herself adoringly to Camille.

'I'm just going to run ahead now, Suki. I want to check that Camille's OK.'

She turned and increased her pace to a fast run. In a couple of minutes she overtook Oliver, who had been walking as well. When he became aware of Hanlon he broke into a trot. 'Just tying my lace,' he said as she ran past.

Oh, grow up, she thought.

A short while on, she caught up with Camille, who was standing at the viewing point past the entrance to the chapel, looking out at the sea. It was wild and intimidating. From here you could see Seil Island on the left, but straight ahead was nothing but the Atlantic Ocean, all the way to America.

Camille turned round and smiled, her hair blowing wild in the wind and rain, her eyes sparkling.

'Doesn't it make you feel alive?' she said.

Hanlon nodded and said, 'Just making sure everything's OK.'

'It's all good,' said Camille. 'I'll see you back at the house.'

Hanlon said, 'I'll go back and check on the other two.'

She turned round and ran back down the path. Oliver was panting along, doggedly. He gave her a thumbs up as she ran by, revealing a quick glimpse of his infinity tattoo. Hanlon found it inexplicably enraging. Who do you think you are? A physicist? she felt like shouting at him. She came round a corner and saw Suki. She was running along, very slowly, almost shuffling, her feet close to the ground.

As Hanlon ran towards her, the toe of Suki's training shoe caught on a rock embedded in the ground and tripped her up. She went down as if she'd been shot, her arm flung out to break her fall. For a heart-stopping moment Hanlon thought she was going to go over the edge and into the sea. There was no fence or parapet here, just the path running along the cliff edge. Hanlon winced. Suki measured her length on the wet stone surface and lay there, momentarily, winded and motionless.

'Are you OK?' Hanlon said, helping her to her feet.

'I'm fine,' Suki said, dusting herself down painfully. The sleeve of her jacket was covered in mud but otherwise she seemed OK. Then she must have nearly fainted; her eyes rolled and she staggered, alarmingly close to the side of the path that fell down to the sea. Hanlon grabbed hold of her.

She looked over the cliff edge. About six metres below the sea was boiling and crashing around the stone edge of the cliff. There was an outcrop of rocks below and as the water ebbed and flowed, their sleek black surfaces, whitened here and there with barnacles, were visible.

'I'm OK...' Suki said. 'That hurt and I just felt suddenly faint.' She gave a shaky laugh. 'I must be getting old.'

'You're sure you're OK?' Hanlon asked, worried.

The rain slackened off momentarily. Suki pushed the hood back on her jacket and a shaft of sunlight broke through the skies and illuminated her dyed blonde hair. She looked over the rocky edge at the angry sea below. 'Close call,' she said, grinning at Hanlon. It was the first time she had seen her smile. It lit up her face; she looked happy, carefree.

'Thank God I didn't go over,' she said, then she laughed. 'Think how pleased my ex would be. No more maintenance.'

'Is your arm OK?' asked Hanlon.

'Yeah, I'm fine, really.'

'You OK to run?'

'Absolutely.'

The wind gusted past them and the thick bushes by the side of the path shook. Hanlon gave them a searching glance. She had the peculiar sensation that someone was watching them. She even walked over to the undergrowth and peered into it, but all she could see were gigantic ferns and rhododendrons.

'OK,' Suki called, 'I'm good to go.'

The two of them set off down the track. And behind them a figure got to its feet from where it'd been hiding in a hollow behind some bog myrtle and slipped away into the interior of the island.

11

Dinner was a good-natured affair. Hanlon could see that on the whole the group had gelled as a unit; they all seemed to be getting along reasonably well.

She was seated at a table with Oliver and Anna and O'Rourke. Suki, Karen, Camille and Loyd were at the other. They had just finished their dessert course. She heard Suki saying, 'So then I nearly fell over, straight into the sea, which would have been all over for me, and then thank God Hanlon arrived because when I stood up, I was so disoriented I nearly staggered off the side of the cliff!' There were appropriate murmurs from the others – 'OMG...' 'How awful!' – and she gave Hanlon an adoring look. 'She saved my life.'

O'Rourke glanced at Hanlon and caught her eye; she gave a ghost of a grin. Hanlon knew she was signalling, She'll be worshipping you now like Camille.

Oliver, oblivious to this, was talking about St Barts. Initially, Hanlon had thought he meant the famous hospital St Barts in the City of London (why would you go there for a break? she had wondered) but no, it was an island in the Caribbean.

'I usually stay at the Baie hotel,' he said in a loud, carrying voice. 'It's pricey, but worth it. I get quite stressed in my job,' he declared. He drank some more water, which was served with dinner.

Bet you wish it were something stronger, Hanlon thought, the memory of his luggage contents still in her mind. Maybe you'll slip out to the boathouse later for some more weed.

'St Barts must be wonderful,' said O'Rourke. She couldn't have sounded less interested if she had tried.

'The Baie, that has a beach front, doesn't it?' asked Anna, suddenly interested. 'I was there last year. You can just walk out of your room into the sea.'

'Yeah, that's why I like it. Up at six, in the water two minutes later.'

'Blimey,' Anna said, 'up at six! After a night of Pascal's cocktails...' She turned to O'Rourke. 'He's the barman, he's famous, he knows every cocktail ever invented, like a kind of human drinks encyclopaedia.'

'Aye, good old Pascal,' said Oliver, chuckling. 'He's a character, but, you know, work hard, play hard.'

God, you're tiresome, Hanlon thought. I hate that work hard, play hard schtick. I never believe a word of it. It's code for – I like getting pissed.

'And what else did you like about the hotel?' Anna asked. 'I'm curious...'

'Oh, all sorts,' Oliver said. He suddenly seemed to have tired of St Barts as a topic of conversation. Maybe he had realised that O'Rourke and Hanlon were unimpressed.

He abruptly changed the subject. Leaning over the table, he said, 'Katherine, can we go over those booking dates again?'

O'Rourke looked vaguely surprised by the question. 'Of course, Oliver, my laptop's on the reception desk... if you'll excuse us...'

Anna watched sourly as they left the room. The wind howled outside and rattled the glass of the windows.

She turned to Hanlon and remarked quietly, 'That man is a total fraud.'

'How do you mean?' she asked.

Anna had a sip of water. 'The Baie isn't on the beach at all, you have to get the hotel Land Rover down to it, it's about a ten-minute drive down a track, and there may well be a Pascal in the hotel, but he sure as hell doesn't run the bar...' She laughed. 'And I bet you a hundred quid that's not a real Rolex. I saw Suki staring hard at his wrist. I think she suspects too. And all this bollocks about running an investment fund specialising in FinTech companies.'

'What does FinTech even mean?' Hanlon asked.

'Financial technology...' Anna searched for an example '... like Avant or Xero, companies that do specialist financial software like... oh, I don't know... accountancy packages, or those apps that kids use on their phones to move or track their money... Either way, he was spouting off about it earlier. I notice he was careful not to do it in front of Loyd, but he knows bugger all about it.'

'And you do?' Hanlon asked.

Anna looked at her coolly. 'When my husband died his life insurance was fifty K. I've increased that a hundredfold. People think I inherited money.' She gave a satisfied smile. 'Let me tell you, Hanlon, I made it myself.'

Hanlon was impressed. 'Are you going to whistle-blow?' she asked.

Anna shook her head. 'No, I reckon he came here trying to find some sucker to latch onto. Someone to con. Karen is too bright and Suki's not stupid – she uses an investment company that I know in Edinburgh. They're good. He wouldn't be dumb enough to try Loyd. No, he's just wasted his time and money... He's drawn a blank.'

'Did he try it on with you?' Hanlon was genuinely interested now. Oliver was the nearest thing to an obvious criminal she had yet encountered here. That put him in pole position as a threat to Camille.

Anna nodded. 'He made a play for me the moment he met me here. He let me know that he was in the investment market, let slip hints that he knew how I could make a lot of money with him, but subtly.' She laughed. 'He probably would have tried to get his leg over if he thought it would have sealed the deal.' She shook her head. 'I'm frowning now, Hanlon,' she said, pointing to her forehead. 'Not that you'd know it, not with the Botox! This blank look means acute disapproval. But people like him are scum, in my view, taking hard-working people's money and fleecing them.'

O'Rourke disappeared into the office and Jenny appeared in the hall from the kitchen. Hanlon and Anna watched through the glass door of the bar as Jenny's face lit up and she went over to Oliver.

They could see his head close to Jenny's; she put a hand on his shoulder. Hanlon and Anna exchanged glances. 'Well, he's certainly moved on from me,' Anna said contemptuously. 'Nice to see he's not heartbroken.'

Later that evening, at about half past nine, Camille stood up. 'Well, everyone, I think I'm off to bed. Can I just remind you all that there's a run tomorrow morning with our wonderful Hanlon? I'll be going on it. I think it's a fantastic way to connect with nature, to feel the breeze in our hair and the wind and the rain... What better way to feel alive?'

She namasted.

'Goodnight, all.'

She left the room to a murmur of goodnights. Hanlon stood up too.

'I'm off as well. Remember, it's a 7 a.m. meet in reception. I'll see you then.'

She left the room and ran lightly up the broad stairs to the second floor. She walked along the corridor and knocked on Camille's door.

Camille opened the door. 'Come in...'

Hanlon walked in and closed the door behind her, then pointed at the door that led to her own room.

'I think we should open that and swap rooms,' she said.

Camille looked confused.

'Sure.' She sounded doubtful.

'It's in case anyone tries to get at you during the night,' Hanlon explained. She had visions of Oliver Drummond trying the handle, slipping inside. 'Mind you, I can't think who that might be.'

Camille sat down on the bed and gestured to Hanlon to take the armchair that was in the room.

'Did you find anything of interest in any of the rooms earlier?'

'Not really,' Hanlon said. 'The main thing that I've discovered tonight is that Oliver is not who he claims to be.'

She told Camille of Anna Reynolds' suspicions and Camille shrugged.

'I can't see Oliver being much of a threat to anyone, quite frankly.'

'No, but if he's desperate for money, he could be dangerous.'

'Like a cornered rat?' Camille laughed.

'Exactly,' Hanlon said seriously. 'People will do a lot for money if they're desperate.'

Camille raised an eyebrow. 'If you were me, would you be afraid of Oliver or what he might do?'

'You've got a point,' conceded Hanlon. He was despicable, untrustworthy, sleazy, but somehow she couldn't see him as dangerous. There was a mushy core to Oliver as flabby as the spare tyre around his midriff. Talking about Oliver had made her think of Jenny. There had been something very lingering in the way Jenny had rested her hand on his shoulder. She recalled what Ishbel had said about her. Jenny's morals were as elastic as her pants. If you were happy to sleep your way into money, you might well consider other avenues of enrichment that didn't require hard work, such as putting glass in someone's food. Jenny rose higher on her list of potential suspects, way above Oliver Drummond. 'Tell me some more about Jenny.'

Camille looked surprised. 'Why Jenny?'

'Just because.'

Camille shrugged. 'OK. She's been with me about ten months,' she said. 'Siobhan brought her in some time after she agreed to take on the catering for me. She's twenty-five, from Edinburgh, worked as a chambermaid, waitress, then moved into kitchen work, that's about all I know.'

She smiled at Hanlon. Hanlon guessed that would have to do for now.

'How long has Siobhan been doing your catering?' Hanlon asked.

'About a year. My last chef left and then Siobhan stepped up to the plate. She was only going to do it temporarily, but it seems to have lasted. It's a bit limited for her, but the hours are really good, and I pay her quite well. And, of course, she's in charge, she gets to write her own menu. Interesting fact, rather oddly, Siobhan ate here once when it belonged to the last owner.'

'Really? What, in this building?'

'Yes, when it was the Duachy Hotel. She was living on Seil with her then boyfriend.' She frowned. 'God, what was his name...?' She drummed her fingers on the duvet. 'He was a drummer in a dreadful grungy -type band called My Claymore Wedding...' Camille laughed. 'Not a successful band, not like Sephiroth.'

'Who on earth are Sephiroth?' Hanlon wondered.

'Shane Gowrie's old band, you know, the rock star who used to own this place. They were huge back in the day, especially in the States. Anyway...' her face lit up, 'Dan Murray, that was his name, knew it would come to me, took her here for her birthday. When this place was famous for its food.'

'That's an interesting coincidence.'

'Oh no.' Camille shook her head. 'There are no coincidences. Paul Strom taught me that. Only unseen patterns.' She stood up. 'Goodnight now, Hanlon.'

Camille went to bed in the adjoining room, the door between the two rooms open at Hanlon's insistence. Hanlon lay awake in the darkness listening to the rain. It was extreme, even for the west coast of Scotland. How much water could the sky contain?

Hanlon had left the curtains open; it was how she was used to sleeping. She thought of Wemyss – he hated storms in general and thunder in particular. She was glad he wasn't here. He would have been whining and nudging her to do something about the weather. Periodically, lightning would flicker, illuminating the furniture in the room, followed by the rumbling of thunder. She was totally unable to sleep but with that feeling of heavy tiredness as if you were carrying some kind of massive, velvet-wrapped burden.

Now she stood up and went over to where there was a TV on a table. Next to it was her phone, which had been charging, plugged into a socket on the wall. She glanced at her screen: 1 a.m. She would have to be up in five hours. The battery sign was glowing green, fully charged. She disconnected it and took it back to bed.

She read some news headlines, but reading was the last thing she wanted to do; she wanted to sleep. She thought she'd lie in bed listening to something on her phone. She looked at the podcasts she'd stored then she realised that her earphones were in the pocket of her running jacket, which was hanging downstairs in the lobby. She needed them; she didn't want to wake Camille by playing podcasts out loud.

It was one of those hard-to-call late-night sleepless decisions. Would she have fallen asleep by the time she actually got downstairs – it was now one-thirty after all – retrieved the earphones, got back into bed, or would she still be lying there awake an hour later wishing she'd got up and gone and fetched them?

Twenty minutes later she opened her door and walked down into the lobby. The hotel downstairs was in darkness apart from a light burning in the bar. It was utterly silent. She went to her jacket, which was hanging on a peg next to the identical ones of Suki and Camille, the expensive, professional one of Karen, and Oliver's old, ratty-looking one. Now she had been tipped off by Anna she looked at his old, frayed cagoule. It was not the sort of thing that a well-to-do investment consultant would be wearing.

She found her earphones and was now at the bottom of the stairs. She could see the rooms that faced onto the landing above her. The door of one, Oliver's, opened and she could see Jenny, wearing a short nightdress, silhouetted there against a low light. She put her fingers to her lips and blew a kiss, then closed the door behind her and walked lightly along the carpet to the staircase that was on the right and disappeared upstairs.

So, Oliver, at least you've achieved something, thought Hanlon cynically. It's not all been a complete waste of time.

* * *

Seven o'clock in the morning, the pre-breakfast run. Hanlon, Suki, Camille, Jenny, Karen, and Oliver had all assembled by reception. Hanlon looked out of the front window of the hotel. The bushes were being tossed around by the wind; the trees were swaying alarmingly. Rain beat hard against the windows.

Camille said brightly, 'I'm afraid that there'll be no cleaners coming today. Charlie texted me. The seas are just too rough for boats at the moment, and there's worse to come. So, you'll have to make your own beds today.'

Hanlon noticed that the mention of the word bed had triggered a kind of complicit glance between Jenny and Oliver. Lycra suited her tall, slim figure. What a shame, Hanlon thought, that her exciting new boyfriend was not the successful businessman she took him to be, but a cheap hustler with a drink and drugs problem. Oh well, disappointment was part of growing up. She was surprised to see Jenny here; she would have thought that Siobhan would have wanted her in the kitchen. She shrugged. None of her business.

'OK,' Hanlon said, 'we'll run in two groups, a faster one led by Camille, so that's Jenny, and you, Karen, and a slower group that will run with me, that's you, Suki, and you, Oliver.' Oliver frowned at being publicly relegated to the 'slow' group. 'Shall we go?'

The six of them walked outside. Hanlon held the door wide for them. She had opened it against the force of the wind and had to practically brace it open with her back to it.

The wind did its level best to slam the heavy wood and glass shut. Hanlon managed to close it without it crashing into its frame.

The power of the wind was extraordinary. Camille turned to the others and shouted, 'Isn't it great?' She was wearing a grey beanie hat. Somehow Suki must have got wind of it, or maybe she'd packed a few just in case – she'd certainly brought enough stuff with her. She was wearing an identical one. It covered most of her hair but blew her fringe across her face. It was almost impossible to tell the two women apart, they were so similarly dressed today in fluorescent-yellow running jackets.

'It makes you feel so alive!' Camille exulted.

She ran off down the path at a fast pace, leading Karen and Jenny. Hanlon turned to Oliver and Suki. Oliver had a kind of pained, resigned look on his face, like a kid not good enough for the team sports and made to do cross-country with the other losers. 'We'll start slow,' Hanlon said. 'Once you're warmed up it'll be much easier.'

She set off at an easy, slow jog, running next to Suki, Oliver in the rear. They'd been running for about three or four minutes when Oliver shouted her name. She dropped back and looked at him questioningly. 'I'm going to run ahead,' he said. 'This is too slow!'

'Fine,' Hanlon said. He nodded grimly at her and picked his pace up, disappearing round the next bend. It was obvious he didn't want to be seen to be exiled to the back of the group, especially not in front of Jenny. Maybe he was hoping to catch her up, impress her with his athleticism.

So now she ran slowly alongside Suki, the two of them together in the pouring rain. Occasionally she would glance out at the sea. It was mountainous; the water was the same dark grey colour as the lowering sky. Sudden squalls of wind and rain would blow across the huge waves looking like smoke.

'I'm going to walk for a bit,' Suki said, or rather shouted. It was virtually impossible to carry on a normal conversation. The howling wind snatched the words away almost as soon as they left your mouth.

'You go on,' she added, 'check that the others are OK.'

Hanlon nodded, accelerated and ran ahead. She hadn't gone far when she encountered Oliver. He was walking towards her, back to the hotel.

'Are you OK, Oliver?' she asked.

'The weather's too bad,' he said sulkily, scowling at her as if it were somehow her fault.

I bet it's not that, she thought. You just can't run any more.

'I'm going back for a shower...' He started into a half-run. Hanlon shrugged and picked her pace up. There ahead of her were Camille and Jenny trotting slowly along, no sign of Karen That was hardly surprising; she'd be lapping them in a few minutes. So, all accounted for – Camille seemed OK and she wasn't alone.

Hanlon decided to turn round and keep Suki company. She ran back expecting to see her round each bend; a dull sense of worry began to spread through her body. Where was Suki? She was now at the point where she had run ahead from her. She recognised it immediately. Worry was close to turning into panic. There was the remembered sheer rock face, hewn from an enormous stone boulder, about two metres high, worn and fissured with ferns and lichen growing in the cracks.

Shit, Hanlon thought, Suki must have turned back to the hotel as Oliver had done. She stood for a moment, irresolute on the path. Should she run back to the hotel and make sure that Suki was OK or should she run back to check on Camille, who, after all, was the only reason that she was here? It was an agonising decision to have to make.

Sod it. She turned and ran back towards the hotel, fast now, arms pumping, hair bouncing, her feet flying on the path, which in places was like a stream, the water running down from the waterlogged hills that formed the spine of the island. Then suddenly there ahead of her a slow-moving figure, not the jacket of Suki, but the navy-blue of Oliver. She sprinted up to him.

'Oliver!'

He stopped and turned.

'Yeah?' His face was as surly as ever.

'Oliver, have you seen Suki?'

He nodded his head. 'Yes, I passed her a while back. She was still running along...'

Oh, God, no, thought Hanlon. *I passed her a while back* – where the hell could she be?

'Is something the matter?' He frowned; he could see she was worried.

'Go back down the path,' she ordered. 'Suki's missing. Keep walking and looking for her, OK.'

'OK,' he said. He looked suddenly worried. 'I hope she's alright.'

Hanlon turned back the way she'd come. She ran slowly down the path. It was possible that Suki had felt ill suddenly, had left the track and headed inland for privacy. An anguished knot of fear was gathering in the pit of Hanlon's stomach. As she jogged along she was staring at the surface of the path, but that was useless for clues. It was hard impacted soil and stones, there was the occasional shoe print but no way of telling whose.

On her left side was the sea, crashing against the low cliff. The path was in parts screened from the edge by the odd tree or bush, but mostly the track was only a metre or so away from the edge. There was the occasional stone parapet but often it was unprotected. The way was wide, but Hanlon was horribly aware of Suki's fall the previous day. Every time she came to a gap in the vegetation that screened the sea from the path she would slow and look over into the water, just in case.

She ran past the place where Suki had nearly fallen in the day before. Feeling sick with apprehension, she looked over the edge: nothing. Thank God. She felt as if a weight had been lifted.

Round the next bend the path ran down into a kind of dip with tall dark trees either side whose boughs interlaced high above, making a vaulting, arboreal tunnel. Hanlon emerged from this and glanced into the sea.

About five or six metres below, her worst fears were realised. She could see Suki. She was in the water, her canary-yellow cagoule bright against the slate-grey water, clinging desperately to a rock. Hanlon could see her face, turned upwards, hoping against hope for rescue. She was terrified. Hanlon, looking over the edge, didn't hesitate. Suki could be swept away any minute and that would be the end of her. Pulling off her own jacket, her T-shirt plastered to her body by rain in seconds, she screamed, 'Hang on, Suki!'

Suki nodded. Her face looked panic-stricken. She opened her mouth to say something but a wave crashed over her head. She disappeared under the canopy of seawater. Hanlon stared in horror, but Suki was OK; the water receded and she was still holding on. Below, where the rock met the sea, the water was churning and boiling like a cauldron. Suki's rock, a couple of metres out, was slightly less buffeted by the waves. Her body rose and fell with the swell.

'What's happen...? Oh, my God!'

It was Oliver. He joined Hanlon in staring down at Suki, who looked up at them. Her face was crumpled with fear.

'Take your jacket off,' she ordered Oliver. She had an idea that if they tied the cuffs together they would at least have some makeshift rope. Oliver feverishly did as she told him and she knotted the arms of the two jackets together. She leaned over the side of the cliff and looked at the surface of the stone.

There were several cracks in the rock and a couple of narrow ledges. It was slick with water but climbable. On a calm, dry day she could have done it easily, but there was wind and rain, the surface was slippery and if she fell in, she wasn't coming out again.

'You're not going over... you're crazy...'

She wondered about sending Oliver to fetch help. But who? Camille and Jenny? And what could they do anyway? Rope was what they needed; rope was what they didn't have. Nor did they have time. Suki's strength could fail at any second or a big wave could sweep her out to sea. It was a minor miracle she was still there.

'Stay there!' she barked at Oliver. 'Lower the jackets when I wave.' She dug her fingers in behind a tree root that was by the lip of the path and swung her feet over the edge, feeling with the tips of her trainers for support. She found a toehold and, holding onto the root with one hand, pushing her body close against the rock, she reached for a grip with her free hand.

Another handhold, another toehold, and again. At least it wasn't far to go. The noise of the surf smashing on the rock just below her was incredibly loud; she could taste the salt in the spray all around her. Occasionally she was drenched with seawater as a wave broke against the rock. The grip in her fingers was like iron; she didn't want to be joining Suki in the water. Now she was closer, she could hear Suki screaming for help lower down.

She turned her head away from the rock and looked down. Nearly there. Suki wasn't far from her. If she could find a good handhold on the rock, she might be able to throw the end of the jacket near enough to Suki for her to grab and, with her pulling and Suki kicking with her feet, there was a chance she could get her to relative safety.

'Hang *on*!' she shouted, but the wind whipped her words away.

She now had her toes jammed firmly in the jagged crack she'd seen from above that ran at a forty-five-degree angle to below the waterline. Her feet were secure. Her palms ran along the cold, wet rock seeking cracks or small protuberances, her body pushed hard into the cliff as if it were a lover's embrace.

Then suddenly her right foot was soaking. She looked down. She was level with the water. A wave broke over her; she felt the massive power of the sea, pushing her up as if she were weightless. But her feet, jammed in the adamantine granite, held her fast.

She looked up. She could see Oliver's head silhouetted against the sky. She beckoned – no use calling. He leaned over and dropped the jackets, knotted together.

They fell towards her and she caught the wet nylon material with a free hand.

She looked out at Suki, still hanging on for dear life to the jagged rock. Holding onto one end of the makeshift jacket-rope, she tossed it out to her. It floated on the water, about two metres short.

'Grab it, Suki,' she shouted.

Suki shook her head. Hanlon could see the terror on Suki's face clearly now. 'It's too far!' she screamed.

'You'll have to let go and swim for it!' Hanlon shouted urgently. Suki suddenly let go of the rock and struck out for the jacket sleeve. It was only a short distance. She had one arm stretched out as she kicked frantically with her legs and paddled with her free arm; her fingers reached for the sleeve. If she grabbed that they'd have won.

'Nearly there, Suki,' Hanlon screamed. Then she looked behind her and gasped.

The wave coming towards them was massive.

It tsunamied into Suki and picked her up effortlessly. Hanlon felt the water smash into her; it slammed her against the rock like a giant hand. The cold cliff face scraped against the side of her head as the irresistible force of the sea mocked her puny efforts to defy it. For a heart-beating second, she thought that the Atlantic was going to wash her away into its infinite, grey depths. To weaken now would be to die. Her powerful fingers clutched the stone with limpet-like tenacity as the seawater tore at her body but somehow she managed to cling on.

Twisting her head round she watched as Suki was flung against the cliff. Hanlon could see her with hallucinatory clarity, events started unfolding almost in slow motion as the adrenaline thundered through her body. She could see her terrified face, her hair that had been dyed the exact shade of Camille's, a glimpse of nail varnish. Suki was still conscious, but she hadn't managed to catch hold of the lifeline.

The backwash from the wave pulled her away from the sheltering cliff, and now she was a couple of metres from Hanlon, hands scrabbling wildly, her movements hampered by her shoes and clothing, and then another wave. Hanlon saw the water close over her head. Another wave broke over Hanlon and when she looked around, Suki was gone.

12

'You did everything you could.' It was Oliver who spoke. The silence only deepened. Like a stone dropped down a well.

It was before lunch. Nobody had much of an appetite; everyone was acutely aware of the absence of Suki. There was an oppressive silence. Hanlon could sense that there was an unspoken desire to go home. They had come for clarity and relaxation and that was now impossible. As, unfortunately, was leaving the island. The wind outside was almost a malignant presence, storming around outside the house, ripping branches from trees, rattling windows, jangling nerves that had been tautened to snapping point by Suki's terrible death.

Camille said quietly, 'I think, in the light of the tragedy that has just happened, I am going to have to cancel the week.' She looked around at the group. 'I will of course be giving full refunds.'

Everyone nodded. It was the only thing to do.

It had been a grim couple of hours. Hanlon had climbed back up the rock, so much easier than going down. Oliver had leaned over and helped haul her up, the dark hairs on his surprisingly muscular wrist flattened by the soaking rain, the loops of his infinity tattoo dark against his pale skin. He had started to speak but she had cut him off; she hadn't been in the mood. She kept seeing the pathetic sight of Suki being swept away by the sea, her arms flailing uselessly as she tried to keep afloat in those mountainous waves. Hanlon just hoped that she didn't suffer too much, that the struggle before the inevitable had kept the dread of her impending death away from her.

The terrible thing was that she must have run past Suki on her way back when she had been looking for her. If she had got there a few minutes earlier, there would have been maybe more of a chance to save her. She knew that it was a stupid thing to do, to torture herself with should haves and could haves, but she couldn't help it.

They had walked back in silence to the hotel. There was no need to hurry. By the time they could have alerted the coastguard Suki would be long dead. No one could survive long in that heavy sea. On the way they'd met Karen, who had been on her second lap around the island, and Hanlon had explained what had happened. Karen had been stunned by the news. As they'd approached the hotel, the three of them walking slowly back, silently with bowed heads, Hanlon had noticed that she was crying.

Then back in the lobby, slowly taking her shoes off, first Camille, then Jenny a couple of minutes later, more explanations. Bad enough that the thing had happened without reliving it again and again in inadequate, wordy explanations. Then O'Rourke had joined them, taking charge of the situation immediately with her customary efficiency, dispatching Camille to inform Loyd and Anna.

O'Rourke had called the emergency services. The coastguard had been alerted but they all knew that it was nothing more than a formality, that the most they could hope for was that Suki was washed up on the Argyll coast sooner rather than later.

After a while the police had called back to say that because of the weather conditions they were not going to interview them until the following day. If possible could they remain where they were for the time being? Hollow laughter.

After Camille's announcement that classes were cancelled, people drifted off to their rooms. Later, Hanlon went into the lobby, took Camille's jacket, pulled her sodden trainers back on and went back outside. She walked down the path towards the place from which Suki must have fallen. She had to see it again.

Had it been an accident? Hanlon didn't believe that for one moment. Someone had pushed her to her death. But why kill Suki? The most likely explanation was one of mistaken identity. Someone wanted Camille dead. With Suki in her identical clothes to Camille it was perfectly possible that someone had made a mistake.

But only if that person hadn't been on the run, hadn't known that Suki and Camille were dressed the same. Hanlon ran over positions again in her mind. Jenny and Camille had been in front of them. Karen had been behind them on her second lap. Oliver could easily have pushed her to her death, but he would not have mistaken her for Camille.

Oliver, desperate for money. Suki's husband had a lot of it and by all accounts hated Suki, his expensive, troublesome ex. He could have paid Oliver to do it. In terms of competence, far from an ideal assassin, in terms of proximity, unsurpassed. If Oliver was going to kill anyone she thought that would be his preferred method – a quick shove and that would be that. No need for bravery, if that was the word for a face-to-face killing, no need for a cool head. Yes, he could have done it.

She had assumed that he was here to look for a business opportunity, to con someone into investing their money with him, but he could have arrived with murder in mind. He was definitely a suspect.

She reached the place where Suki had gone over the edge. On her left was the sea, still writhing and smashing against the rocks. The path was about a metre and a half wide here. She looked closely at its innocuous black surface. Like the rest of it, including the place where Suki had stumbled the day before, it was made of the very dark soil of the island, which had been covered with stones and rock and machine-pounded to make a more than adequate surface. But if you were running with your feet close to the ground with very little clearance, as Suki had been, tripping over was always a danger. That was certainly what had happened the previous day. But if you'd done it once, as Suki had, you would be more wary.

This section of path looked no more problematic than any other. Now Hanlon turned her attention to the inland side of the path. There were ferns, tall sedge-style grasses and thistles as well as the stunted birches and alder that were such a feature of the west coast of Scotland.

She crouched down and looked more closely. The rain beat down around her. One or two of the thistle stems had been snapped. She moved closer. Now she could see depressions in the grass where she suspected someone's feet had been. She considered it from a crime-scene point of view. She was certain that the police would put Suki's death down as an accident. Even if you investigated this area thoroughly all you were likely to find were inconclusive traces of movement, and, even if you did find an indication that someone had been there, no certain guide as to when.

The ground held no definitive shoe imprints. Even if there were something that could link one of the group to this area it would be put down as circumstantial.

It went against the grain to compromise a potential crime scene, but she left the path anyway for a closer look.

There was a tall boulder a couple of metres from the path, about the size of a small car. She scrambled up it. From the top you had a good view of the path in both directions. It was easy to imagine someone up here, surveying the runners moving slowly towards them. The killer would have seen a slim woman in a distinctive yellow jacket, alone, jogging along, no one else in sight. They would have slipped off the rock. Hanlon did so, dropped to the ground. Next, they would have taken up a position, here. Now she bent over double, she noticed a flattened patch of grass behind some tall ferns, a couple of which had broken stems. Looking hard at the ground, she could see where the soil had been driven downwards by some force, she guessed that of a foot as the killer had sprung forward, arms outstretched like a sleepwalker, slamming into Suki and driving her over the edge of the cliff and into the fatal embrace of the sea.

Then they would have turned and headed inland. Now Hanlon did so. A few metres in, she skirted a bush and there, as she had suspected, was another path. It was broad and grassy, not surfaced like the island perimeter path. She looked left. She could just see, above the trees, the tip of the spire of the chapel. In the other direction lay the hotel, maybe a kilometre and a half between the two of them. So this track ran arrow-straight down the middle of the island, linking the hotel with the chapel. If you wanted to access it you could go directly without the meandering coastal route.

Since Karen had run ahead, she would have been able to cut straight across the island from the other side and through the trees to join the path, or run up to the hotel and then join the path there. Or anyone in the hotel would have been able to wait until the runners set off and, as soon as they were out of sight, sprint down this path – it was, after all, a shorter distance, a straight line, considerably quicker – take up position, wait until the runners ran past and then strike.

Siobhan or O'Rourke, possibly Loyd and Anna, would have been able to run down this path after they had all left, taken up a position and watched as the runners passed.

So, the way she saw it, the choices as killer for her were: Karen, if she hadn't seen Camille run past. Ditto Loyd and Anna. Those three could have killed Suki deliberately, of course. She couldn't exclude that possibility.

Oliver, Siobhan or O'Rourke if Suki were the intended victim. She couldn't imagine Camille's sister or loyal employee mistaking Suki for Camille, whereas if Loyd or Anna had glimpsed Camille in those distinctive running clothes they could easily have killed the wrong woman.

Well, someone had done it, and the field was not a large one.

She walked slowly up to the hotel. She would have to see if Siobhan, O'Rourke, Loyd or Anna had alibis.

Everything that had made the retreat desirable – the lack of external stimulus, the isolation – was now, by a reverse alchemy, making the retreat intolerable. Even the proximity to nature had become a kind of curse since nature, in the form of the sea, had taken Suki's life; and nature, in the form of the storm, was keeping them trapped here.

It was obvious from the monosyllabic conversation and suspicious glances, that the bonhomie of the group had been replaced with an atmosphere of mistrust and mutual dislike. Even though they had no reason to think it was anything other than an accident, such a seismic event had shifted the dynamic of the group from a bunch of people inconvenienced by bad weather to survivors at the mercy of malignant powers beyond their control. Hanlon recalled hearing a saying from a French writer, she had forgotten who, that hell was other people. Much more of this and she could foresee blazing rows breaking out. The inability to leave the island had created a prison-like atmosphere, which only added to the febrile tension.

Hanlon got back to the hotel and took off her wet, muddy shoes and soaking coat in the lobby. She went inside and found Camille standing disconsolately in reception. Camille looked at Hanlon and her shoulders sagged. The strain was obviously beginning to tell on her. It was hardly surprising.

'God, this is awful,' she said. 'Come and keep me company.'

They walked into the deserted bar and looked at the rain lashing down outside and running down the windows.

'Where's Katherine?' asked Hanlon.

'In the office, checking weather reports. We've got to get out of this place. It's not fair on the guests,' Camille said.

'I can't see that happening today,' Hanlon said.

'I wish I had never bought this place now,' Camille said, her voice bitter.

'Why did you?' Hanlon asked.

'Siobhan talked me into it,' was the surprising answer. It had never crossed Hanlon's mind that the younger sister would have had any input into the decision-making. Team Camille had hitherto seemed very much a two-woman affair: her and O'Rourke.

'Siobhan?'

'Yeah.' Camille nodded. 'She thought it would be a place where she could showcase her cookery skills, as well as being a sound investment, and so I ran it past Paul Strom...'

'Paul Strom?' Hanlon said. Him again, the eminence grise behind everything that Camille did.

'Mm hm, I asked him what he thought. He was incredible and so insightful.'

Hanlon thought, I bet he was.

Camille continued, 'Yeah, and he pointed out that my own history was kind of connected with the place.'

'How so?' asked Hanlon, curious.

Camille looked suddenly coy. 'I'll tell you, this is how I know Paul is truly psychic...'

Hanlon looked at her earnest, attractive face, utterly innocent of guile. He'll have studied every aspect of your life that he possibly could, she thought to herself, spoken to people who know you, and then fed it back to you – and your own knowledge would embellish it subconsciously, and you'd credit it to Strom's 'psychic' abilities.

Camille said, 'You know it used to be owned by a rock star?'

'Yeah, Shane Gowrie, that was his name, wasn't it?'

Camille nodded. 'Yes, that's right, well, back in the day, it would have been in the nineties, his band, Sephiroth, I told you their name last night, reformed for a tour. Shane had made and spent a fortune. By the early nineties he was bankrupt and, not only that, he had a hell of a heroin habit. Anyway, be that as it may, I was a fan; I listened to a lot of rock music. I went to see them play the Albert Hall.' She smiled at the memory. 'I was eighteen then – my boyfriend worked for the promoter behind the gig and we had backstage passes. It was very exciting. I met the band, met Shane... went to the after party, drink, drugs...'

Hanlon looked at her, her slim figure, still taut and youthful, her unlined attractive face – she could almost pass for eighteen now.

'And I had my one and only experience as a groupie.'

'I'm sorry?' Hanlon thought she had misheard.

Camille smiled. 'I screwed Shane... don't look so surprised! Well, when I was young... I did, y'know, put it about a bit.' Despite the earlier admonition, Hanlon blinked again in astonishment. 'I'd had a fair few boyfriends and, well, Shane was very good-looking...'

Hanlon shook her head at Camille's behaviour. It all seemed a bit sleazy.

'Anyway,' Camille said, wide-eyed, dismissing the past, 'here's the amazing thing. Paul knew that I'd had a moment with Shane. Isn't that incredible?'

'Indeed, it is,' Hanlon said. 'Incredible.'

'So, anyway,' Camille continued, 'when Siobhan told me about this place, I looked at it and fell in love with it. Shane had lavished so much care on the gardens and on the house and then the next owner had left the grounds more or less unchanged.'

'Not to mention the chapel,' Hanlon said, grimacing.

'Yes, it's quite something, isn't it? Shane liked doing girls on the altar, got quite a kick out of it seemingly.' She laughed. 'He had to make do with a hotel bed with me, the Intercontinental, must have been a bit dull.' She sighed. 'Well, that was a lifetime ago, but now I'm in his old house and he's in a home. Funny how things work out.'

'An old people's home?'

'Yeah, just outside Dumbarton. Near the crematorium. Siobhan showed me an article in the local paper.'

Hanlon took the opportunity to move the conversation on to Siobhan. 'Your sister lived round here for a bit, didn't she?'

'Yeah.' Camille nodded. 'She was living in a commune on Seil. It's how she got to hear about the hotel.'

'That was before she got into catering?'

'Yeah, she was just drifting at the time. She didn't know what to do with herself, holding down odd jobs.'

'Where does Siobhan live now?' Hanlon was curious. 'In Glasgow?'

'Oh, with me... I've got quite a big place. It's nice to share it with someone, and Siobhan's a very tidy person, so it works well.'

'There's quite an age gap between you two.'

'Yeah, Mum told me that Siobhan was a mistake.' She smiled and her face lit up. 'But a nice one.'

13

The terrible day wore endlessly on. People drifted downstairs from their rooms. Oliver sat in the bar area drinking heavily, joined by Anna and Loyd. Karen was in her room. Hanlon, feeling at a loose end, sat by herself for a while playing with her phone and surreptitiously watching the other three talking. You didn't need to be an expert in body language to notice Anna's narrowed eyes or Loyd's frequent head shakes. Oliver went to the toilet twice, both times on his return rubbing his nose; his eyes were suspiciously prominent and she noticed how animated he had become. She was so glad that she wasn't sitting with them. God alone knew what kind of coked-up shit Oliver would be coming out with.

She got up and walked into the lobby. Camille and O'Rourke were in the office. She went to join them.

'So what are your plans now?' she asked them.

O'Rourke said, 'As soon as the weather dies down and we can get the boat over we're sending everyone home. We'll reimburse the clients, then, I'm not sure. I think we'll stay on here until the end of the week.' She smiled bitterly. 'It should be safe then.'

'What about the threat level to Camille?'

O'Rourke said, 'We feel secure here. There'll be us, Jenny and Siobhan. No one's going to be able to get out here to harm Camille. Nobody would take them from the mainland in this weather, and of course Charlie won't.' She smiled. 'He dotes on Camille. He's almost like family.'

Hanlon nodded. 'OK, then. Do you have any idea when Charlie will be able to get over here to take people back?'

O'Rourke shook her head. 'Not really, certainly not today, probably not tomorrow...' She shook her head sadly. 'It's all a bit of a nightmare really.'

'Yes,' Camille said irritably. 'God, I wish Paul was here, I really could do with some advice. Poor Suki, I just feel so guilty...'

'Well, don't,' O'Rourke said abruptly. 'It's not your fault that she fell over the edge.'

There was a feeling of tension in the air, as if a major row were brewing. Hanlon found it hard to believe that Camille could get angry but there was definitely a sense of antagonism between the two women.

'Do you want me to keep working for you?' Hanlon asked. 'Until this threat business is resolved?'

'More than ever,' Camille said fervently. 'I suggest you go back home and we'll get in touch.'

O'Rourke nodded. 'We'd appreciate your input,' she said.

Hanlon nodded. 'OK, well, I'm going up to my room for a bit,' she said.

Camille stood up. 'I'd better go and join the others in the lounge. I think I'll offer them one-to-one therapy talks.' She looked doubtfully at O'Rourke. 'If you think that's a good idea.'

Hanlon thought the dynamics in their relationship were quite odd. O'Rourke was nominally the employee but Camille often seemed almost scared of her and Hanlon had the feeling that the red-headed woman was actually running the whole show.

'I think that's a great idea,' O'Rourke said with conviction. They met each other's eyes and smiled. Hanlon could feel the cloud of tension lift. 'You go through now and I'll set up that small room, the one they call the Garden Room, for you. Give me half an hour.'

Camille left and O'Rourke turned to Hanlon, her eyes narrowed. 'So, what do you think happened?'

'I think someone pushed her into the sea thinking she was Camille,'

Hanlon replied. 'There are marks in the undergrowth that look like someone had been waiting there.'

She described the scene as she saw it to O'Rourke, the killer concealed behind the bush waiting on the off chance that Camille would run by, watching the figures pass, possibly missing Camille but then seeing Suki, in her running jacket with the hood up, the beanie hat pulled down. With the rain in their face, keyed up, just a split second to act, a mistake could easily have been made. 'It would have been like American football when they take someone out,' Hanlon said, 'crouching down, then springing forward, slamming into her to knock her off balance and over the edge. Then back into the bushes, and away.'

'And who do you think the killer is?' O'Rourke asked.

'It could have been any one of a number of people. It could have been Karen,' Hanlon said, stressing the word 'could'. 'She could have easily run up that path behind the chapel and ambushed Suki. She would have known it wasn't Camille, she was running with Jenny, so she would have to have had a very strong motive for killing Suki and I find that implausible.'

'Go on,' O'Rourke said.

'It could have been Oliver Drummond, but again he would have had to have known it was Suki and, to be honest, I can't see him as a murderer.' She smiled. 'Believe me, I've tried. He's unscrupulous, I have no doubt, and Anna Reynolds thinks he's a con man.' She explained her suspicions that Reynolds had aired to her. 'But a killer? And we're back to the why again. Why would he want to kill Suki?'

'Money?'

Hanlon shrugged. 'Possibly. Then,' she carried on, 'we come to Loyd and Anna. Both of them in their bedrooms, so they said. Anna was down for an early breakfast, that alibis her and Siobhan. Loyd remains a possibility. No one can verify his whereabouts and he could have run down along that central path and pushed Suki over in a case of mistaken identity.'

O'Rourke said, 'Why would he want to kill Camille?'

Hanlon shrugged. 'Someone does, why not him? And, of course, this brings us on to Siobhan.'

'Siobhan!' O'Rourke sounded incredulous. 'I thought you just said she had an alibi... Anna.'

'The timings are vague,' Hanlon said. 'You could get there and back in under twenty minutes. It's within the realms of possibility.'

'But Siobhan!'

'Why not?' Hanlon said. 'And don't say because she's her sister... siblings have been killing each other since Cain and Abel.'

'But... come on...' O'Rourke protested.

Hanlon went on, 'Motive, I can think of several. Envy of her sister's success, maybe she thinks Camille will leave her all her money, maybe she can't stand her because Camille was her mother's favourite, and she was a "mistake".' Hanlon considered Siobhan. Tough, intelligent, and she knew from Ishbel that she had a temper. She also knew that working in a kitchen was far from glamorous, that it meant long, antisocial hours and endless stress for very little money. While Siobhan worked ten-hour days, six days a week at places like The Sleeket Mouse, Camille was earning what she did in a week for a couple of hours' work. She could imagine resentment festering. In Hanlon's view she was by far the most likely candidate.

'But she'd have known it wasn't her!' protested O'Rourke.

'Would she? Would she necessarily? Suki had a beanie hat pulled down low. She was wearing the same clothes. Siobhan wasn't necessarily to know that and she probably knew her sister's running gear. They live in the same house, after all.'

'Well, maybe,' O'Rourke grudgingly conceded the point, 'but she wouldn't get any of Camille's money.'

'Really?' Hanlon was intrigued.

'Yeah, she knows it too,' added O'Rourke.

'How come?' Hanlon asked.

'We were in a pub once and the conversation turned to rich folk leaving, or not leaving, money to their families. Someone said they wouldn't leave anything to their brother and Camille said, "Oh, I'm not leaving anything to my sister either." So you can forget that one.'

'Who would she leave it to?' Hanlon asked. 'She must have a fair amount in the bank, not to mention property. You?'

'I doubt it,' said O'Rourke drily. 'You don't think I killed her, do you?'

'No,' Hanlon said, 'I don't.'

'Thank goodness for that,' O'Rourke said in mock relief. 'Anyway, I'd better go and get that room ready for Camille.'

Hanlon watched the tall, elegant figure of O'Rourke leave the office. She didn't think that O'Rourke had killed Suki because she didn't think O'Rourke was the kind of woman to make a mistake.

14

Siobhan was in her chef's whites, prepping the food for dinner. Hanlon had been ready for her to be unwelcoming, but she was actually friendly, the friendliest that Hanlon had ever seen her. Even in the unflattering kitchen work clothes that totally hid her figure and with her blonde hair concealed under a cap, Siobhan was still a very attractive woman.

'No Jenny?' she asked, slightly surprised.

Siobhan shook her head. 'No, it's her break, she'll be back at four.' She was chopping vegetables into fine dice. The large knife in her experienced grip rocked back and forward on the board as she reduced a head of celery into tiny symmetrical cubes.

'It's vegetable lasagne,' she said. 'Hardly original, but it's good comfort food and I think we could all do with cheering up.'

'Can I do anything to help?' Hanlon asked. The chef looked at her questioningly, as if to say, haven't you got anything better to do?

'No one will be running today,' Hanlon said, 'understandably. I'm at a bit of a loose end, really.'

Siobhan nodded and opened a fridge and gave Hanlon a large bunch of parsley.

'Strip this off its stalks,' she said.

'All of it?'

'All of it.'

Hanlon started her task and asked Siobhan various anodyne questions about catering and her life in general as slowly she steered the conversation into the area that interested her. Then, 'So, I gather you lived on Seil for a bit?'

'Yeah, a while back now, I had a boyfriend who was in a band and he had a mate who was living on a kind of commune near Ellenabeich and we ended up staying there for a year.'

'What did you do on Seil?' Hanlon asked. Pulling the parsley off its long stalks was a fiddly, boring job. She had a small pile of the bright green herb in a metal bowl in front of her. There was a lot left to do.

'Drugs mainly,' Siobhan replied, slightly contemptuously, whether of her younger self or Hanlon or maybe both, it was impossible to tell, 'but one thing I did do was I came here—' she tapped the board with her knife, for emphasis '—with Dan. That was his name, the then boyfriend. He was the drummer.'

Hanlon nodded. It was what her sister had told her, but she wanted to hear Siobhan's version.

'So that's how you got to know about this place, then?'

'That's right. I came here for lunch when it was owned by a guy called Malcolm Todwell. He was doing a kind of foody thing out here, had a really good chef...' Siobhan's eyes misted over. 'I had roast halibut in a mussel and razor clam nage... Do you know, I can recall every course, six of them, almost every mouthful. It was like a revelation... that's when I knew I wanted to be a chef.'

Hanlon nodded. There was no doubting the sincerity and passion in Siobhan's voice. Then the tone changed to one of genial contempt; her eyes hardened. 'Dan just munched his way through everything. When we got back to Seil he said he was starving and fancied a curry. Did I want to drive up to Oban and fetch him one? Dick,' she said with feeling. 'I left him shortly afterwards, fucking philistine.'

'And so here you are...' Hanlon picked more leaves from the parsley; the pile of stalks to be stripped didn't seem to be getting any smaller. 'Living the dream,' she concluded.

Siobhan nodded.

'Does Jenny share your enthusiasm for cooking?'

Siobhan gave a harsh laugh of derision. 'There are two main kinds of chef, Hanlon: those who love it and those who after their GCSEs were given the booklet "career opportunities for those with no qualifications". Jenny is in the second category. She just wants to find a rich man to take care of her, end of story.'

Silence fell for a while. Siobhan finished her vegetables and started mixing double-zero flour and egg. 'Making pasta,' she said, 'for the lasagne.'

She made a dough and then called Hanlon over to the pasta machine that was bolted onto a steel table.

'When the pasta comes out, it'll be like a long ribbon. I want you to gather it on your forearm as it comes out, then give it back to me when it's finished. We do that four times for each piece, OK?'

They stood over the small square silver-coloured metal pasta machine as Siobhan carefully fed the dough through the rollers, reducing the gap between them each time as the length of pasta grew longer and thinner each and every time. Their heads were close together as they bent over the machine and Hanlon could feel Siobhan's breath on her cheek. It was a surprisingly intimate moment.

Hanlon was wondering when she could, or indeed how she could, ask Siobhan where she was when Suki went over the side of the cliffs, round about 7.30 a.m.

'So,' Siobhan said quietly, 'who do you think pushed Suki over that cliff?'

'Well...' Hanlon, half suspecting that Siobhan had maybe done it, was temporarily blindsided by the question. It was the last question she'd expected Siobhan to bring up. 'I...' She hesitated. 'Well, was she pushed?'

'Of course, she was.' Siobhan snorted. 'The only reason you're here is to protect my sister. It can hardly be a coincidence that Suki died while all dressed up like Camille.'

'You have a point,' Hanlon said.

'Too right I do,' Siobhan said. 'So, who do you think?'

'Well, it certainly wasn't your sister,' Hanlon said, more to say something while she thought of a credible suspect other than the woman standing next to her.

'Why not?' asked Siobhan. Hanlon was aware of being scrutinised as the chef watched her reaction.

The question took Hanlon by surprise. 'I know that Suki was a pain in the arse, but why would Camille want her dead?'

'For one thing, she lent my sister sixty K,' Siobhan said. With a sudden shock Hanlon recalled the diary in Suki's room. DH, 60K. Duachy House. 'At least...' She looked at Hanlon with something approaching contempt in her eyes. 'Yeah, everyone falls under Camille's spell, you too it would seem, but I know her really well, and, believe me, she is no saint. And neither is that lanky, beanpole, ginger sidekick of hers. And the finances are nowhere near as good as O'Rourke would have you believe.'

Siobhan was silent until they had finished the pasta, then, as she started unscrewing the machine to carry it over to the sink, she said, 'You know, I get so sick of people making out Camille is like some sort of fucking saint.'

'She seems pleasant enough to me,' Hanlon said. Whether this was to draw Siobhan out, annoy her or defend her employer, she couldn't really say. Maybe a combination of all three.

'That's part of her job,' Siobhan said. 'She's professionally nice as well as professionally flexible, and everyone goes...' She put on a kind of sarcastic, mimsy voice. '"Ooh, that Camille Anderson, she's so lovely... she must be a really great person."'

She was still holding the heavy pasta machine, now she threw it into the huge stainless-steel sink where it crashed loudly. Siobhan's face was murderous with rage. The hate was palpable.

'Well, let me tell you, Hanlon, I had thought you'd be level-headed enough to see through her, but it would seem not. My sister will appear all concerned by poor Suki's demise, but she won't be so concerned that she'll mention the money, or the procession of boyfriends to her bed, or her tax returns or her willingness to endorse whatever shit takes O'Rourke's fancy. She'll do a lot if you pay her, will my sister!'

So this was why Siobhan was so nice to me earlier, or at least nice by

Siobhan's standards, Hanlon thought, to get the chance to plant suspicions about Camille. Effectively so. Very effectively. Hanlon found herself wondering about Camille and, by extension, O'Rourke. They both could have done it and now they had an excellent motive. Siobhan's last words, 'At least…' How much debt had been written off as Suki hit the sea?

Siobhan looked at Hanlon with her by now familiar contemptuous expression.

'You're probably wondering what I was doing while all the shit was hitting the fan down the island.' Remembering the savage look on Siobhan's face, that was certainly very true as far as Hanlon was concerned. 'Well, Anna's an early riser. I was making her an omelette for breakfast while Suki went for her last swim, so, Hanlon, it certainly wasn't me that gave her the heave-ho.'

After this, confirming Anna's story, conversation languished, as if Siobhan was conscious that maybe she had gone too far. Or had just said enough to implicate Camille.

At four o'clock Jenny appeared, and Hanlon took the opportunity to say goodbye and head back upstairs for some serious thinking.

The evening meal was a slightly more cheerful affair. There were reports that Storm Cedric was moving westwards and that the weather would improve. Camille said she had spoken to Charlie and the police and he was confident that he would be able to start taking people back after breakfast.

Oliver Drummond was now looking significantly the worse for wear, Hanlon thought. The day's drinking and drugs were catching up with him. Anna Reynolds, who, when she stood up, was swaying a little and speaking with exaggerated care as if her face muscles were finding it hard to form words, was not far behind him. Hanlon noticed that when Jenny brought the coffees and teas after dessert her fingers noticeably brushed those of Oliver, a gesture seen by O'Rourke, who looked genuinely furious.

But it was Camille who she was really watching. Did she really think that Camille had pushed Suki to her death? She could have done, if she had darted off the coast path, sprinted up the inland track and then emerged behind Hanlon. She would have had to shake Jenny off, but that wouldn't have been hard. Suki would have been putty in her hands. 'Stand in Tadasana, Suki, Mountain pose, just here, by the edge, close your eyes, breathe deep.' Camille coming up behind her, Suki, unquestioning, totally trusting, blissfully happy with the undivided attention of the person she adored. 'Feel the power of the sea and the air...' And one swift push.

It would be like taking candy from a baby.

Or O'Rourke, emerging from the shadows by the side of the path. Grimly efficient. Balancing the books. Sixty thousand pounds' worth of debt written off. Suki wouldn't have kept records, in all probability.

Sixty thousand.

At least.

* * *

Camille went off to bed at about ten o'clock and Hanlon followed shortly afterwards.

She changed into a long T-shirt to sleep in, washed and got into bed. She heard a tap on the open door between the rooms and Camille came in.

Hanlon sat up. 'Are you OK, Camille?'

'Well, I've been better, but I have thought what we can do to find out the truth of what happened to Suki. Do you mind if I sit down?'

'Please do.'

Camille sat down on the end of Hanlon's bed. She was wearing blue and white striped pyjamas and she looked about twelve rather than forty. Anyone looking less like a killer was hard to imagine. But Camille had secrets: the one-night stand with Shane Gowrie, the undisclosed debt to Suki, and Siobhan had hinted there was more she could say.

'I'm going to ask Paul to contact Suki,' Camille said.

Oh, God, thought Hanlon. 'Paul Strom?'

'Yes, he does seances, he can speak to the dead.'

She stared in disbelief at Camille. How could she be taken in by all of this? Camille looked at her.

'Ordinarily I would never do a seance, I find the idea a bit freaky, but

Katherine has. I'm not supposed to tell anyone, but I know I can trust you.' She leaned forward and squeezed Hanlon's hand.

'Why did she ask Paul Strom to do a seance for her?' asked Hanlon. It seemed wildly out of character.

'I don't know. I got the impression she had lost a really close friend. She told me she didn't want to discuss it... Anyway, Katherine said she was amazed. That's good enough for me.' She smiled. 'I can be a little too trusting, but Katherine is hard-nosed.' She stood up. 'Thank you.'

For what? wondered Hanlon. Camille supplied the answer.

'For being here for me.' She took Hanlon's hand and held it lightly between her own two; Hanlon felt the warmth of the other woman's fingers. 'I needed to tell someone. It's a big decision, meddling with the darkness.' She sighed, pressed Hanlon's hand firmly and relinquished it. 'I know we're not supposed to lift the veil but needs must. Goodnight, Hanlon, thanks for being such a good friend.'

She turned and, graceful as ever, padded softly and silently back to bed.

* * *

Hanlon heard the faint sounds from the bed through the open door between their rooms as Camille got into bed, then she did the same and fell almost immediately asleep.

A while later she woke up from a terrible dream. She lay there bathed in sweat, staring at the ceiling, mouth dry. She had been running down a track somewhere in Scotland that she didn't recognise. It was foggy, hard to see through the drifting mist. She was running from some terrible danger, running for her life. Whatever it was, she was too frightened to look round; it was closing on her. She couldn't outrun it. In the usual fashion of nightmares her legs weren't working as they should. She veered into some bushes to hide and found herself face to face with a wolf. Its lambent yellow eyes stared into hers and it gave a low growl. Neither of them moved. She could smell its musky warm scent over the damp leaves and the omnipresent smell of the sea. Then it jerked its head as if to tell her something. She looked down and saw its leg was caught in a gin trap. The cruel, serrated metal jaws had cut the flesh down to the bone. Whispering to the agonised animal to soothe it, Hanlon pulled the metal jaws apart and the wolf bounded free.

She let go of the trap and the jaws snapped shut. But this act of mercy had cost time. She was aware of a presence behind her. She turned, still crouched, and looked up into what was behind her, towards what she knew would be the source of her own death.

Then, with a start, she woke up.

Now, fully conscious in her bedroom, she lay for a minute, profoundly glad to be awake. She reached over to the bedside table and picked up her phone; it was half past two in the morning. There was no doubt where those images came from: bloody Paul Strom and his spirit animals.

She got out of bed and walked towards the window. It was still raining; she could hear the drops against the glass. She pulled back the curtains and looked out.

The sky was dark but far away she could see that the lights were on in the chapel. She frowned. The spire was faintly visible by the light of the moon diffused through the low cloud, but the rectangular window with its stained glass gave out a sinister red glow. Someone was down there inside the building.

She stared at it for a minute or so. Part of her told her to go back to bed, but she knew that she wouldn't be able to sleep if she did for wondering what was going on down there. She also felt a superstitious fear, a result of the nightmare, warning her of hidden dangers. That decided Hanlon. She had to go now, or she would lie in bed cursing herself as a coward.

'Sod it,' she said to herself. She pulled some clothes on and quietly slipped into Camille's room to check she was OK. Camille was lying on her side, one slim arm thrown over the duvet, her blonde hair against the pillow; she looked very young, very beautiful and very vulnerable as she slept.

Hanlon thought back to the scorn and hatred, yes, that was what she had felt from Siobhan, hatred of her sister. How could anyone hate

Camille? It was almost perverse. She shook her head in incomprehension and went back to her room and then out onto the landing.

The hotel was deathly quiet as she walked down the stairs, the eerie light from the moon outside filtering through the windows. She could hear the ticking of the grandfather clock in the reception area and as she slipped out through the inside door into the lobby she could hear the roar of the sea from outside. She pulled on her jacket, still damp from earlier and hanging on a peg in the porch, unlocked the front door and went outside.

She had a small torch with her but she didn't need it; the faint light from the sky, the moon diffused through the dark clouds, was sufficient to light the central path. She could smell the sea, damp vegetation, the sharp top note of pine trees. She was aware of her heart beating with nervousness. The nightmare had been so vivid she almost expected to find someone behind her, following her. So strong was this feeling that she actually did turn around once or twice to check. But, of course, there was nothing.

She reached the chapel. She felt a twinge of superstitious fear at the sight of the gothic building rising up, dark and spectral against the moonlight, like something from a bad dream. The light shone out through the tall, slender arched windows, the stained glass glowing unhealthily in the darkness. The trees rustled in the wind and rain beat against her face. She pushed her sodden hair back out of her eyes as she approached the entrance. The massive door was closed. She shone her torch over it and read again the legend, 'Do What Thou Wilt Shall Be the Whole of the Law.'

In the darkness of the night the words seemed like a warning, minatory, an omen of ill fortune.

She walked up the steps to the door and wrinkled her nose. Someone had been smoking weed. The strong smell of skunk. She immediately thought of Oliver. She put her hand on the handle, opened the door and her eyes widened in shock as she stood, framed in the doorway.

It wasn't Oliver.

Directly above the altar, hands down by her sides, hanging from a noose at the end of a rope that had been run over a beam in the ceiling, was Jenny. She was wearing the clothes that she'd changed into after service, a short black skirt and a pale blue blouse. A massive gust of wind blew the door behind Hanlon open and the force of the wind now moved Jenny's body and it swayed gently, gracefully, in the breeze.

15

'And what did you do then?' asked Inspector Munroe.

'I lowered her down,' Hanlon said. 'The rope ran over the beam and had been tied to the end of one of the pews. I checked for a pulse...' She shook her head.

It was 11 a.m. After lowering Jenny, Hanlon had run back to the hotel and woken Camille and then O'Rourke. Grim-faced, they had called the police, who had arrived at 5 a.m. in a powerful launch. The chapel was now sealed off for forensics and all the guests had been interviewed and allowed to leave.

DI Munroe was an affable-looking man in his late forties, Hanlon guessed, with a rugby player's physique. He was carrying quite a bit of surplus flesh, but he was a big guy and looked fairly fit. He seemed genuinely upset by Jenny's death and baffled by a murder following hard on the heels of what had been logged initially as a tragic accident.

'You're ex-police, aren't you?' he said to Hanlon. She nodded. She hadn't mentioned it in case they thought she was bigging herself up at their expense, the ex-Met expert come to tell the country cousins how things should be done.

'What do you think: Suki Bly, accident or murder? Originally I would have thought accident, but now, after Jenny McKendrick...'

'I looked over the scene of her death,' Hanlon said. 'There were indications that someone had been there, but nothing definitive. Maybe your experts might find something but I rather doubt it. I'll take someone along and show them exactly where it happened and give you another statement relating to those events if you like.'

Munroe nodded. 'If you wouldn't mind. Now, do you have any idea why the deceased might have been at the chapel?'

'She was having an affair with one of the course participants, Oliver Drummond,' Hanlon said. She had no doubt that O'Rourke and probably Anna Reynolds and almost certainly Siobhan would also have provided this information.

'And how exactly did you come by this information, Ms Hanlon?'

'I saw her leaving his bedroom at about 2 a.m. on Sunday morning...' Munroe made a couple of notes.

'Right, well, I'll come with you and the DS and you can show us where the accident, if that's what it was, happened right now,' he said. 'Can you think of anything else that may be relevant?'

'Not really,' Hanlon said.

'Fine, I've finished interviewing everyone else, so let's go...'

* * *

An hour later Hanlon walked into the bar. Anna Reynolds was there. Her eyes were sparkling. She seemed very excited by the whole thing.

'What did they ask you?' She didn't wait for an answer. 'I told them about Oliver Drummond. I said they should investigate him, certainly his business dealings. He's obviously a con man, but I would never have guessed he was a murderer too!'

O'Rourke walked in. Now the police had arrived she looked a lot more composed than she had a few hours ago. 'Think of the publicity,' she had been groaning.

'Ah, there you are, Anna. The police say that everyone is free to go. Charlie will meet you down at the harbour in about an hour. I'm staying on here with Camille and Siobhan for a while until the police have finished their investigations. Do you need a hand down with your cases?'

'Yes, please,' Anna said.

'I'm fine,' said Hanlon.

Twenty minutes later, Siobhan carrying Anna's bags, O'Rourke one of Loyd's, and Karen and Hanlon managing their own, they assembled down at the jetty and they could see in the distance Charlie's boat heading towards them. There was very little small talk. Loyd was grim-faced, Karen silent and withdrawn, only Anna seemed happy. She looked around.

'No Oliver?' she said innocently.

O'Rourke replied, 'The police still have a few questions they want to ask him.'

'I bet they do,' muttered Anna darkly.

Charlie brought the boat expertly in to the side of the harbour wall and threw O'Rourke the painter. She secured it to a bollard and they handed Charlie the luggage, which he stowed away in the cabin, then they all boarded.

'I just want to thank you all for coming,' O'Rourke said, 'and I can only apologise for the terrible events of the last couple of days.' She shook her head sadly. 'Refunds will be sent as soon as possible and Camille hopes to welcome you back on the mat in Glasgow very soon.' She pressed her palms together at chest height and bowed. 'Namaste,' she said.

'Namaste,' they dutifully chorused. Charlie spat over the side of the boat and engaged the engines and they swept out to sea towards Seil.

16

Hanlon was lying on her bed with Wemyss the dog when O'Rourke called. Wemyss had gone frantic with joy when she had called in at Effie's to pick him up. She had stayed for a cup of tea, cake and now had a bag of pancakes that the old woman had pressed on her. She liked them but they puzzled her. They were not what English pancakes were at all. She was uncertain if they had an English equivalent, scones of some sort? Drop scones? Hanlon was totally ignorant when it came to cooking. She also had some tablet, a kind of tooth-rotting Scottish sweet made from condensed milk and sugar that Effie had made and insisted she take. She wasn't keen on tablet; she didn't know what to do with it. She had also been given some good advice by Effie, which, as ever, consisted of the importance of finding a good man.

Bouncing up the track in her car to the cottage, Hanlon had thought about Campbell, who certainly fitted the bill as a good man, but, then again, as she'd swerved around a pothole, would she want to live with him? She had pulled up in front of the cottage. No.

Perhaps he'd eat the tablet though.

She'd opened the door to the cottage and dropped her bag on the floor. She'd looked around her room, the gym equipment, the bed in the corner, and smiled. Home sweet home. Wemyss had barked and run around in a circle then gone to his bed and found a toy, a realistic-looking cloth pheasant, and had brought it over to her and pushed it into her hand as if he was giving her a home-coming present. She had knelt down and hugged him fiercely, burying her nose in his soft fur, inhaling his dog smell. She'd missed him.

She had showered, changed, and now, on the bed, she answered her phone.

'Hi.'

'Hi, Hanlon.' O'Rourke's tones were as cool and measured as ever. 'Camille wanted me to call you. As we discussed, she wants to keep working with you. But this time, she wants you to look into what happened on Duachy Island.'

Hanlon frowned and stroked the dog's fur. She stared up at the ceiling, which was low and made of varnished wood.

'Isn't that the job of the police?'

'From what I could gather from the inspector, Suki's death is going down as accidental and they seem to have arrested Oliver Drummond in connection with Jenny's murder.'

'What evidence do they have?' she asked. Drummond was an unpleasant lecher and almost certainly some kind of con man, but she found it hard to believe that he was a killer.

'I have no idea,' O'Rourke said, 'but we still want you to look into it. It would seem likely that the person who killed Suki is the same person that threatened Camille. There can't be two of them, surely?'

Hanlon stretched on the bed and thought, I agree. She said, 'I thought Camille was going to get Paul Strom to investigate.' Via some sort of weird shamanic seance, she thought.

O'Rourke laughed. 'I dare say she is, Hanlon, but I think Camille would like to cover all her bases and not necessarily trust everything to the spirits.'

So Camille is not quite as ditzy as she seems, Hanlon thought. She then felt, Maybe I'm being a bit harsh. Someone did threaten to kill her and now two people are dead. She's every right to be worried.

'OK, then, same fees as ever plus reasonable expenses.' Hanlon was a believer in establishing ground rules.

'That's fine,' O'Rourke said firmly. 'When can you start?'

'I'll start tomorrow,' she said.

'Thanks, I'll be in touch.' The line went dead.

Hanlon put her phone down. And I'll start with you, Katherine O'Rourke, she said to herself.

* * *

Biggar was a small, prosperous-looking market town about thirty miles south west of Edinburgh. Hanlon drove through it slowly. It had a broad, spacious high street, the shops set back a considerable distance from the wide thoroughfare, giving a relaxing sense of space to the town centre. Hanlon thought it was a very attractive place.

She parked the car and looked at the address on her phone that she had taken from the rear of the photograph she had found in O'Rourke's case. John Curry, the photographer, was still there. The shop was divided into two halves. The front of the shop sold cameras and camera equipment, the rear of the shop had a small studio and there was a sign advertising the services they offered, everything from passport photos, children's photos to weddings and 'glamour'.

Hanlon studied a black and white head-and-shoulder portrait of a girl in her twenties, looking moody; there were lots of shadows. Perhaps I ought to get a glamour shot. She laughed at the thought. I wouldn't look moody, I'd just look cross. My default setting.

'Can I help you?' A man with a bald head, white hair on the sides and shrewd blue eyes had emerged from the back room. He was wearing a cheap suit and tie and had an air of being very much in charge.

Hanlon asked, 'Are you the owner?'

He nodded. 'Yes, I'm Peter Curry, how can I help you?'

She handed over a business card. 'I'm a private investigator,' she said. He raised his eyebrows in surprise.

'How can I help?'

Hanlon showed him the photograph of the young girl, which she had on her phone. 'I believe that you took this photo, some years back now, I guess. I'm hoping it might ring some bells.'

Curry studied the image.

'Do you recognise her?'

Curry shook his head. 'That's the uniform of Dalmeny Junior School,' he said, 'and we have the contract for doing the class photos with them.' He switched his attention from the image to her. 'Do you know the surname, by any chance?'

'O'Rourke, possibly,' Hanlon said.

'O'Rourke?' repeated Curry with emphasis.

'That's right, do you know her now?'

Curry nodded. 'Aye, I do now.' He shook his head. 'It was very sad. There was a measles outbreak...'

'Measles?' Hanlon said. She thought that was a thing of the past.

'Aye,' said the photographer, 'it was linked to a group of travellers who were living in the area.'

'How come she got it?' Hanlon asked. 'Surely it's not a problem nowadays?'

'The mother, she was one of these New Agey, anti-vax mums, worried about MMR. She hadn't had the girl vaccinated and she caught measles, badly. She died. This photo would have been one of the last before she got the disease.'

'That's terrible,' Hanlon said. O'Rourke's daughter had died. Hanlon found it hard to reconcile the efficient, suit-wearing woman with being a New Age type. It didn't seem to match.

'Aye,' said the photographer, 'aye, it was. Always awful when a wee one dies. It was quite a thing locally after the bairn was buried. Kathy, I mind now that was her name, got a lot of hate mail, I believe. She moved away. Her ex is still living here. Hang on...' He walked to the back of the shop. 'Hey, George?' he shouted to an unseen man.

'Aye, what?' A kid about twenty in a Cage the Elephant T-shirt appeared, his hair in a topknot. He nodded politely to Hanlon.

'Angus Buchanan, where's he working now?' Curry asked.

'At Mrs Cameron's,' the kid said.

Curry shook his head. 'Where's that exactly?'

'Up the back road, up the brae...'

'Oh, aye... that Mrs Cameron, I mind her now...' He gave Hanlon the address and directions. She thanked them and left the shop.

A short while later, with Wemyss on the lead, enjoying what Biggar had to offer in terms of smells, Hanlon was walking up one of the back streets. At the address that Curry had given her was a large stone house with a wide red stone-chip drive. There were ornamental stone lions on plinths at the entrance. Parked in the drive were two vans, a small blue one, Dugald Blair – Plumbing and Heating Engineers, and a larger white one, Angus Buchanan – Builder, with a landline and a mobile number on the side.

Hanlon wondered if she was somehow making a huge mistake. O'Rourke, tall, elegant, worldly-wise, did not seem the kind of woman to be an anti-vaxxer. But, reflected Hanlon, you never can tell. And she had paid a terrible price for her anti-medical views.

She walked up the drive and almost immediately heard the unmistakeable sounds of a cement mixer. She shrugged to herself and rounded the corner.

* * *

'So, how is Kathy?' Angus Buchanan asked. The builder was a slim, muscular man in his forties, in cargo shorts and a T-shirt, wearing scuffed steel-toed work boots, with a good-looking face. He wore round glasses and a serious expression.

'She's fine,' Hanlon said.

'What's she up to these days?' he asked.

'She works in marketing, in the health sector,' Hanlon said. 'She's very successful.'

'Good,' he said. 'She always was bright. I'm glad she's doing well. So what's this all about?' he asked.

Hanlon showed him the photo of the girl on her phone. He shook his head sadly, just as Curry had. 'Aye, that's wee Niamh. She was Katherine's daughter from a previous man, a lovely girl. Terrible what happened.' He got his own phone out and, after a while of scrolling through images, showed

Hanlon a photo of the three of them. Hanlon blinked in surprise. O'Rourke in those days had short spiky hair and was wearing a short, tight dress, showing off her fantastic long legs, ripped tights and blue Doc Martens. She had a broad grin on her face. Niamh was hugging her waist and looking up at her with an expression of delight. It was hard to equate this young, alternative punk-looking woman with the current model, the serious businesswoman.

'She was running a whole-food store and coffee shop here in Biggar, making a very good job of it too. She was a health nut, a vegan and really into yoga and meditation. She was a huge fan of this woman who was just getting famous on the Internet.'

'Camille Anderson?'

'Aye, that's her. She had a podcast at the time and Kath was always quoting from it. She believed everything Anderson said, more's the pity.'

'In what way?'

'Camille told her followers that vaccination was bad, that it led to autism, that it was injecting babies with poison, the usual uninformed shite, and she believed it.' He sighed. 'And then there was an outbreak of measles around here and, sadly, Niamh caught it and tragically she died of it.'

'What happened then?'

'Kath was heartbroken. She withdrew into herself. The business folded, she was getting a lot of abuse, people telling her that it was her own fault.' He sighed. '"Murdering bitch!" someone painted on her shop door.'

'Murdering bitch?'

He nodded. 'Aye, murdering bitch.'

Well, well, thought Hanlon, thinking back to the message that had appeared on Camille's studio door.

'Were there a lot of messages like that?' Hanlon asked.

'Sure,' the builder said. 'Things like "die bitch" and "you deserve it". The terrible thing is, they were almost certainly written by people we knew.' He sighed. 'She was just badly informed, that's what I told her, but Niamh had paid the price.' He fell silent, then continued, 'And that was the end of us too. We split up, I met someone else. I've got two of my own now. Life goes on.'

Hanlon was silent. Then she asked, 'And did it change her opinion of Camille Anderson?'

Buchanan looked at her in astonishment. 'Er, hallo! In her view Camille had killed her daughter. Yes, her opinion had most certainly changed. She hated Camille with a passion, and Kath can hold an opinion very strongly indeed. And she's not the kind of person to forgive and forget.'

They talked some more, but Hanlon had found out far more than she had expected. O'Rourke's relationship with Camille was stranger than ever.

She walked back to her car, sat in the driver's seat and stroked Wemyss thoughtfully. She didn't have children herself but imagined that the death of her daughter would have had a hammer-blow effect on O'Rourke. And one thing she did know about bereavement: the overwhelming desire to blame someone. In O'Rourke's case, Camille. Camille had persuaded her not to get her daughter vaccinated and Niamh had died.

She thought of the photo that Buchanan had shown her. A punk-rock iconoclast version of the woman she knew now, happy, riotous, fun. Hard to reconcile that with the elegant, hard, ice-cold person that she had become.

'She's not the kind of person to forgive and forget.' O'Rourke's hard green eyes, even her way of speaking, clipped, almost slow – O'Rourke was always considering her words before she uttered them.

And the eerie echoes of the abuse and threats that O'Rourke had herself received, now transferred from her door all those years ago to Camille's.

Revenge was a dish best served cold, they said. Had O'Rourke taken that to heart, got a job with Camille so that one day she could destroy her? An eye for an eye? Hanlon could easily believe her capable of that. Had it been her that had pushed Suki to her death? O'Rourke would probably have known Camille's running outfits and would not necessarily have been aware that Suki had managed to copy the look so accurately. Then Hanlon remembered Camille's remarks about Paul Strom. *'Ordinarily I would never do a seance, but Katherine has... she was amazed...'*

No prizes, she thought, for who O'Rourke had been trying to contact. That thought led her back to Strom. If she had believed that Niamh was speaking via Strom, what message had Strom passed on to her from her daughter? Was O'Rourke dancing like a puppet at the end of Strom's strings? Strom appeared to be wielding a lot of power in the lives of these women and it was making Hanlon extremely uneasy.

She put Wemyss in the back of the car and started the engine.

Strom, she thought, time to see him again.

Maybe she could make him shed some light on all of this.

17

On the outskirts of Glasgow, just before joining the M8, Hanlon pulled off the road and got her phone out. She glanced around at her surroundings, post-industrial city suburbs, housing estates and blocks of flats, grey buildings under a grey sky. She still had Strom's number on her phone, now she called it again.

He answered immediately.

'Paul Strom.'

'This is Hanlon.' But you'll probably know that I was going to call you anyway – courtesy of the spirits, she thought.

'Hello, Hanlon, how nice to hear your friendly tones again.'

The tone was ironic rather than sarcastic. She smiled to herself. She didn't like Strom, she still thought he was a con man, but, she had to hand it to him, he was a cool con man.

'I need to see you,' she said.

'I'm free this afternoon,' he said. 'You can come round at three.'

'Can I bring my dog with me?'

'Surely, I like dogs.'

'Three o'clock.' She hung up.

An hour or so later she was in west Glasgow. She parked her car near the railway station in Partick and let the dog out of the car. She walked along the street towards Strom's flat, Wemyss staring around fascinated by the unusual walk, so different from where they lived.

The road she was walking along had shops and cafés, the occasional pub along its length, with the flats overlooking the street up above. She stopped at one point as if puzzled by something although she wasn't quite sure what that thing was. It was infuriating, the same sensation as when you walked into a room and wondered what it was you came in for. She looked around her for inspiration: an Asian greengrocer's, a large pub, an open area with hipster market stalls, a pub called the McLellan Arms, posters advertising this and that on a wall, a KFC – no, none of these helped.

She shrugged and walked on. Now she recognised the betting shop and the café that Strom's business was above. The obvious place to find a shaman, she thought to herself. She rang the bell at the bottom of the stairs and was buzzed up. At the top of the stairs, on the landing outside the flat door, a fresh joss stick was burning; there were some flowers placed artfully in a vase. Hanlon knew absolutely nothing about flower arranging but she could tell that these had been expertly done. There was something about the arrangement that caught the eye and held the attention. She wondered if someone had done it for him, some other woman acolyte like Camille. But somehow she knew it would be Strom; he was annoyingly competent.

She knocked on the door and Strom opened it. He looked down on her from his great height. His deep-set eyes regarded her with either malicious amusement or genuine pleasure, it was difficult to say which. In the shadowy light of the hall his high cheekbones were even more pronounced. He looked almost satanic.

'Do come in...'

Today Strom was wearing a long white Arab jellabiya. He pushed the wide arms back to reveal slender but muscular forearms. He had the body of an athletic swimmer – he was tall and rangy, quite lean. He was striking rather than conventionally good-looking; his hair, cut short, was a kind of thick, fuzzy dark brown. It looked amazingly soft.

He sat down, cross-legged, on one sofa and motioned to her to sit on the other. It suddenly struck her that he was a very attractive man. Hanlon wondered if he and Camille were lovers. His flat was immaculate as before. He had blinds rather than curtains on the windows and they were half closed so the light was diffuse and soothing, tiger-striping down the wall. Incense was burning in a holder in the fireplace, a thin plume of smoke lazily spiralling upwards. Barely audible music came from concealed speakers, some kind of tribal chanting over a steady drumbeat.

'So, what can I do for you?' he asked Hanlon.

'You're aware of what happened on Duachy Island?'

He nodded. 'Yes, yes, I am.'

'I was wondering if you had any input on what had happened?' Her voice was taut, clipped, she could barely restrain her irritation. People were dying and Strom was behaving as if it were a mildly diverting problem. Worse, she felt that he held the key somehow to what was happening.

She looked at him with her eyes narrowed. Strom returned her hostile stare seemingly completely untroubled; he raised a quizzical eyebrow.

'I thought you didn't believe in the spirit world, Hanlon.'

He held a hand out and Wemyss crossed over to his sofa and licked his hand enthusiastically, then sat down by him, staring up at Strom adoringly while the shaman scratched behind the dog's ears. Traitor, thought Hanlon, annoyed with her dog.

'No, I don't. I believe in rational explanations, Strom,' she said. 'You predicted an attack, or an attempt on my client's life.'

'Our client – she pays me as well, Hanlon.'

'Whatever,' she said dismissively. 'First there is an attempt to injure Camille with broken glass, maybe to scare her or hurt her, maybe to kill her. Then Suki Bly dies, almost certainly in a case of mistaken identity, then Jenny McKendrick, an employee of Camille's, is murdered.'

'Go on...' His expression was that of someone discussing what bad weather they were having in Glasgow that summer, not life and death. Hanlon continued.

'Camille told me she thinks that it would be a good idea to have a seance, for you to communicate with the ghost of Suki to discover who killed her, and Katherine O'Rourke thinks it's a good idea too. I'm curious as to what you think.'

She was interested to see what his reaction to O'Rourke's name when linked with a seance would be and wanted to know more about O'Rourke's view of Camille and the death of her daughter. Her suspicions were that O'Rourke would have dropped her guard to Strom and she wanted to know what had been revealed. Would Strom tell her anything useful? It was impossible to know with him. He had his own agenda, that was for sure.

It suddenly struck her that Strom was one of those, fortunately rare, individuals who liked playing games with people's lives, not for any discernible reason, but because they could.

Strom smiled. 'You think I'm a fraud, don't you, Hanlon?'

She nodded; she didn't see any reason to deny it. Whatever else he was, Strom was no fool. 'I do.' Now she had said that she decided to go further. 'I also think that you're mixed up in this whole sorry business for reasons I don't yet know, but I will, in the end.'

'Well,' Strom said, his tone one of an adult humouring a slightly backward child, 'those are two separate issues. First of all, am I a fraud?'

Yes, thought Hanlon, yes, you are. But she held her tongue.

'Well, it's certainly how I started out,' he said unexpectedly. 'I was doing my research with these simple, gullible Mexican tribespeople, doing my doctorate. I pretended to swallow all this...' he inscribed inverted commas in the air with his fingers, '"nonsense" that they believed in, then I started joining in with their ceremonies. Then slowly, bit by bit, I realised I was the simple, gullible fool and that they were tapped into a power greater than we could possibly imagine in our narrow, materialistic ways. The roles were reversed.' His eyes burned into Hanlon's. 'They weren't the frauds, I was. Anyway... bills had to be paid. I've always been interested in card tricks, things like that, and when I got home, I developed a magic act to pay my uni fees.'

'So,' she said, 'you believed in their "magic" but you did stage magic instead.'

He laughed, impervious to her scorn. 'Correct, Hanlon. Spirituality doesn't pay for the electricity. I was getting funding for my PhD but it was nowhere near enough to live on, and one of the things I did in my show was kind of mind-reading tricks, then gradually it dawned on me I wasn't cheating. Not always. Sometimes I was cold-reading, but a lot of the time I was getting spookily accurate.'

He pushed his sleeves up and stroked his chin. 'Sometimes uncomfortably so, frighteningly so. Sometimes there are things you don't want to know, Hanlon. Anyway, back to the tribespeople. Their magic, their abilities were beginning to underpin, to supplant my fake powers. A bit like, oh, I don't know, if you joined a gym, convinced that bodybuilding was hogwash and didn't exist, but gradually, by following the advice and lifting progressively heavy weights, you ended up strong, even though you hadn't believed it possible. Basically I began to grow...'

Hanlon suddenly realised she was feeling incredibly tired. Her limbs were heavy, her eyelids drooped. She yawned. He looked at her with his head on one side, his eyes gleaming. 'I'm sorry,' she said. It struck her that she had been up since five and she was exhausted. The drumming in the background seemed more insistent, hypnotic. She looked at Strom. His eyes seemed very dark; they glittered under his heavy brows. There was silence for a while. For a moment she wondered if she'd been asleep. She rubbed her eyes. He carried on, his voice soft.

'So, tell me why you came here today.'

'O'Rourke,' she said.

He nodded. 'Of course. Have you found out about her daughter?'

Hanlon nodded. 'Yes.' She yawned again.

Strom said, 'You're very tired, aren't you?' Hanlon nodded. He said something indistinct, she couldn't hear him, then, more clearly, he said...

'I can't go into details – she's a client and there's an issue of confidentiality. But I can tell you this – Katherine has forgiven Camille. I can see you came here wondering if she was still after revenge. Well, initially she was. It's why she took the job, as doubtless you suspected. She even had a vague idea of killing Camille, of getting even, but then she fell under Camille's spell and love replaced hate...'

Hanlon yawned and nodded. She closed her eyes; she couldn't help it.

She was dimly aware of Strom speaking to her and then she was aware of him calling her name.

She opened her eyes in alarm. 'God, I must have drifted off,' she said.

'It's four now,' Strom said quietly. 'I'd go home if I were you, get some sleep. I think you've had quite a stressful few days.'

She said, 'I guess so...'

'Katherine had nothing to do with those two deaths,' Strom said. 'I can assure you of that.'

She stood up, as did Strom. As he opened the door to let her out he said, 'Oh, by the way, I'm doing a gig on Friday, a magic show...'

'Where?' she asked.

He smiled and reached a hand into the thick, wavy hair behind her right ear. 'You've got one of my fliers here,' he said, pulling a folded piece of paper out of her curls. He handed it to her, as if by magic it had appeared.

'I'll be doing lots of stuff like that,' he said. 'Legerdemain, I'm good at that. Come along.'

She rolled her eyes. It was cheesy, but it was very cleverly done. The urge to see Strom performing was irresistible. Besides, she thought, I can invite Murdo Campbell, our second date. At least that will mollify his sister, if nothing else.

'I might well do that.'

'Please do.' He paused. 'I'm not your enemy, Hanlon, please remember that.'

That remains to be seen, she thought. 'OK,' she said, 'I'll see you then.'

'Details are on the flyer – £15.00 at the website, or £20 on the door, booking advisory! You'll enjoy it,' he said. She nodded; she would definitely go.

It was only when she was halfway to her car that she realised she hadn't asked Strom half of the questions she had meant to. She was also uneasy at the fact she had fallen asleep in his flat. Had he caused that somehow? She was very wary of Strom; equally she didn't want to be crediting him with supranormal powers as Camille did. But whatever had happened, there was no doubt that Strom had dictated their conversation effortlessly and, on top of all this, had sold her two tickets to his show.

He really was something.

She shook her head admiringly. She could hardly blame Camille and O'Rourke for moving like puppets when Strom pulled the strings. She, it seemed, was no better.

18

Murdo Campbell dialled in for his midweek video meeting with Inspector Riley from Fraud who was leading the enquiry on Longwell Brothers in London. They reviewed progress so far and then moved on to new developments and leads. Two were disappointing and a cyber-trail that had looked promising had finished in a dead end, then...

'Another name cropped up when I was chasing a lead, an individual in your neck of the woods who'd been fleeced by David Piper,' Riley said.

'What's his name?' asked Campbell.

'Her,' corrected Riley. Campbell saw his head dip as he presumably consulted a document. 'A Suki Bly, from Bearsden in Glasgow.'

Campbell scratched his head. He had heard that name before but couldn't quite place it.

'Can you e-mail me the details?' he asked.

Suki Bly...? Suki Bly...?

'Of course... done.' Riley looked back to the camera on the screen. 'She got taken down for a hundred thousand.'

'This Piper guy is very persuasive,' Campbell said.

'He is.' Riley frowned. 'Of course, he could be a woman.' He saw the look of incomprehension on Campbell's face. 'It's a new theory,' he explained.

Campbell was confused. 'How do you mean? My interviewee said he was definitely a man. Well, he had a man's voice.'

Riley shook his head. 'I'm sure he was, no, one of my colleagues has been doing a forensic psycho-linguistics course and he says that the way the prospectus is written bears all the hallmarks of having been put together by a woman, something about the choice of language, the emphasis on traditionally female values, security, protection, trust, rather than, say, more overtly masculine ones, high yield, expertise, market penetration...' He shrugged. 'I just thought I'd throw that one in... you never know. Just in case we get any women suspects.'

'Well, thanks,' Campbell said. 'Quite frankly any suspect would be a pleasant change. I'll go and see her, see if there's any kind of useful input.'

'Speak to you next week,' Riley said.

Campbell left the call and stared at his blank screen. He checked his e-mail message from Riley and looked at the address in Bearsden. Why did her name seem so familiar?

Later in the canteen he bumped into his colleague and friend, DS Michael Patterson. They sat down together. Patterson looked enviously at Campbell's doughnut.

'Do you know how many calories there are in that?' he asked.

'No, should I?' Campbell replied.

Patterson said mournfully, 'About four hundred...' He patted the stomach that bulged under his shirt. 'I'm on a diet.'

Campbell shrugged. 'I'm not.'

Patterson shook his head. Campbell was lean and strong, he ran half-marathons and walked up Munro mountains, hills in Scotland over three thousand feet, for fun. Patterson struggled with the stairs.

'How come you're so slim?' Patterson grumbled.

'Exercise,' Campbell said.

'I exercise,' protested Patterson. 'I do yoga these days...'

'Really?' Campbell said disbelievingly. He looked at Patterson in his rumpled, cheap grey suit, the fabric straining at the waist to hold in his gut, and in the arms, Patterson, an ex-semi-pro rugby player, was formidably strong. He didn't look the sort to do yoga.

'Aye,' Patterson said, 'I do it with the wife. We're signed up to Camille

Anderson's online classes.' He noted Campbell's raised eyebrow. 'Yoga's for everyone... Mind, yon Anderson woman's going to be in the news for all the wrong reasons...'

He started to fill Campbell in on the news from Duachy. So that was where he had heard Suki Bly's name, he thought, as Patterson unfolded what had happened.

* * *

The following day Campbell walked up the path to a large detached house in the Bearsden area of Glasgow. The traditional front garden had gone, to be replaced by geometrically trimmed box plants and a gravelled drive in which a Porsche, a Tesla and a muscle truck were parked. Wall-mounted CCTV cameras monitored the exterior.

He rang the smart doorbell on the front door. It was opened by a short, aggressive-looking, middle-aged man with a battered-looking face, in jeans and a tight-fitting black T-shirt and a heavy gold chain around his neck. He had very muscular biceps, like a serious bodybuilder.

'Mr John Bly?'

He produced his warrant card. 'DI Campbell, could I come in and have a quick word, please?'

Bly folded his arms aggressively. 'Like I said to the other police, I have nothing to say regarding the death of my ex-wife.'

'This isn't about her death, sir,' Campbell said politely.

Bly frowned. 'What is it about, then?'

'Fraud,' Campbell said.

Bly started in surprise and sighed. 'You'd better come in, then.'

Campbell walked into the house's marbled entrance hall; a grand staircase with a gold and glass banister swept upwards. There was a large atmospheric picture of a good-looking nineteen thirties couple in an amorous clinch on the wall.

'Jack Vettriano,' said Bly laconically. It looked like an original. Campbell upped his estimate of Bly's net worth.

A girl in a tennis skirt carrying a sports bag was walking down the stairs. She was blonde and very attractive in a hardened kind of way.

'I am off to tennis club,' she said. She had a pronounced Eastern European accent. 'I will see you later, Johnny.'

'Aye, bye, darling.' He threw her some car keys. 'Take the Porsche.'

She nodded and left, ignoring Campbell.

'Not bad, eh!' said Bly proprietorially, with a 'we're all men of the world' kind of grin. 'Half my age.'

'Indeed,' said Campbell, stony faced. There was a strong Calvinist streak that ran through Murdo Campbell like lettering in a stick of rock. He was not impressed by Bly's bragging.

Bly led him into the living room, which Campbell was pleased to see was furnished with exquisitely bad taste. There were two enormous white leather sofas with gold piping, matching wing-chairs, a gold chandelier, which looked totally out of scale in a room with a fairly low ceiling; there was a bar area with dimpled white leather fronting the copper-topped counter, an optic rack and an impressive array of bottles on mirrored shelving. A massive flat-TV screen was on the wall. The floor was laminate wood with three white fluffy rugs. Also on the wall were a couple of huge, generic photos, one of a New York street in the rain and one of a woman in a cocktail dress in a nightclub. She looked sad. It was captioned 'Heartbreak' in an art-deco-style font. Bly didn't look like the kind of man who would ever suffer from heartbreak, Murdo thought.

Bly signalled to him to sit down. 'Drink?' he asked.

Campbell shook his head. 'No, thanks.'

Bly went behind his bar and came back with a bottle of lager. He sat down opposite Campbell on the other sofa.

'So what's this about fraud?'

Campbell filled him in on Suki being taken for a hundred K by the fake investment company.

'Longwell Brothers.' Bly frowned, his face darkening. He looked very intimidating when he was angry, thought Campbell. Bly's fists had clenched and the muscles in his arms bunched. He wondered if Bly had a criminal record. He hadn't thought to check, but he did look like the kind of man who knew the criminal justice system from up close and personal.

'I know she's your ex, but I was wondering if she had maybe mentioned anything to you about them,' Campbell said.

Bly said thoughtfully, 'Do you know, I think she might have? Not in so many words, mind, but a month ago, maybe longer, maybe a month and a half, she called me to meet up for a coffee. That was kind of unusual. Our divorce was not pretty.' He drank some of his lager from the bottle and carried on, 'Mainly down tae me, I have to say. I said some things... anyway... she said that she was going to be meeting a financial advisor who had ripped her off and she was going to ask for her money back.'

'Did she mention any names?' Campbell asked hopefully.

Bly shook his head. 'No, but it has to be this one. I can't imagine there being two of them. Obviously I had no idea so much money was involved. She wanted assistance.'

'Assistance?'

Bly tilted his head to one side and examined his knuckles. 'One of my businesses is providing doormen to clubs and pubs... and bailiffs, for repossession.' He looked up at Campbell. 'That kind of thing.'

That kind of thing, thought Campbell, hired muscle. 'Did she want you to threaten this person?' Campbell asked.

Bly shrugged. 'No comment, Inspector.'

'This is off the record, Mr Bly, you're not under caution.'

Bly looked at him. 'I guess she did.'

'What did you say?'

'I said, sure.' He sighed. 'Look, Inspector, Suki took me for a lot of money when we split up, and I was fucking furious, hands up to that. But she could have gone for a lot more, and she didn't. I still had feelings for her, we went a long way back together. She was infuriating, a very clingy woman, she could be fucking tiresome, but she was quite sweet, she showed restraint... so I was more than happy to help her out.'

He looked at Campbell, his eyes narrowed, suspicious all of a sudden. 'It was an accident, wasn't it? That's what I heard. Do you think her death had something to do with this?'

'It's not an avenue we're currently pursuing,' Campbell said diplomatically. Suki Bly's death was of interest to him, but he wasn't going to share that with her ex. 'Whereabouts was this meeting going to take place?'

'I don't know the answer to that,' Bly said. 'She told me she'd got an idea where the scammer was going to be and she'd speak to him. She wanted him to know that if he didn't return her money he would be seeing the insides of one of Glasgow's many fine A&E departments.' He pointed to himself. 'Courtesy of me.'

Campbell frowned. The fraudster had been very skilled so far at covering up their tracks. How on earth had they let slip their potential whereabouts? It was a question that he put to Bly.

Bly scratched his head. 'I don't know, look, my ex was not the brightest of women, but she could be cunning.' He smiled, in a reminiscing kind of way, and added, 'Knowing Suki, I'd suspect sex was involved somehow. She could make a dead man sit up and beg if she put her mind to it.'

Campbell nodded. It seemed unlikely, but then again he had known quite a few criminals who had done unbelievably stupid things and been caught because of them. It also answered any questions as to why Bly had been so keen to meet up with his ex when she'd picked up her phone.

Bly shook his head. 'When she told me she'd been ripped off, I wasn't that surprised, to be honest. She found it hard to say no to people, she always wanted to be liked and that made her easy to exploit. Of course, when she was married to me, nobody dared, but on her own... She was the sort of person who would try to buy friends.' He sighed. 'If you want affection, Inspector, get a dog.'

'Well, thank you very much, Mr Bly,' Campbell said. 'You've been very helpful.'

He stood up, as did Bly. 'I'll keep you informed.'

'You do that, Inspector. I'll show you to the door.'

As Bly let him out, he said, 'If you find out who did it, Inspector, and they don't return the money, I'll have a word...' He put his face provocatively close to Campbell's and his hard eyes bored into his, the tone and the look of someone that people were habitually frightened of.

'People don't tend to say no to me. You be sure, now, to tell me who the cunt is.'

Campbell was not an easy man to intimidate; he moved his head closer to Bly's so their noses were nearly touching.

'No, Mr Bly. I most certainly won't.'

Then he turned away and walked off down the drive.

19

Wemyss saw the car first. It was five o'clock in the afternoon, humid and overcast, and both he and Hanlon were returning from a 10K run, Hanlon bathed in sweat, Wemyss panting, tongue hanging out as he loped along, when suddenly, as they approached the edge of the forestry plantation near the brow of the hill above her cottage, he stopped suddenly and growled, flattening his body into a crouch.

Hanlon immediately knew that she had a visitor. Wemyss had become quite territorial over the croft, which in her view was no bad thing. Quite a few people had cause to wish her harm and she viewed with suspicion any visitors who hadn't made an appointment.

'Heel,' she instructed the dog, who glanced up at her adoringly and immediately, obediently, fell behind her as she approached her home cautiously, screened by the tall bracken that lined the path. When she was about fifty metres away from the house, she crouched down and took stock of the situation.

Parked next to her Volvo was a four-wheel-drive Subaru. There was a figure behind the wheel; she couldn't make out the details. Then the door opened and a man got out. He was tall and slim, wearing a white shirt and green cords. The wind blew his short red hair back from his pale face with its dusting of freckles. He leaned against the car's bonnet and checked his phone.

She stood up and walked down the hill towards him. He must have sensed her coming; he looked up from his phone and waved. Wemyss barked and ran down the hill towards him. He had known Murdo Campbell for quite some time.

Hanlon jogged towards him, conscious of her sweat-stained top and muddy leggings. Her hair was a wet, unruly mass from perspiration and drizzle; it had been raining in the hills.

'Hello, Murdo.'

He smiled and put his phone away. He let Wemyss smell his hand, then stroked the dog's head. Wemyss's tail wagged furiously.

He looked around at the small whitewashed bothy with its slate roof and small lawn, mainly moss and weeds, enclosed by a dry-stone wall. Her old Volvo was parked in front.

'New car,' he said politely.

She nodded. 'It's their latest model.' He smiled.

'You've got a nice view,' he said, looking out over the dark green pines as the hill fell away steeply below the house. In the distance was the blue of the sea and the green and brown patchwork of the low-lying ground called the Crinan Moss before the craggy hills of north Argyll rose again in the distance.

'I know.' She indicated the cottage. 'Would you like to come in?'

'Yes, please.'

There was a certain awkwardness to the encounter. They hadn't seen each other since their last, unsuccessful date. She was pleased to see him. She wondered what had brought him here, if his sister had maybe said something. It wouldn't have surprised her – Ishbel was nothing if not direct.

Hanlon took the key out of a zippered pocket on her leggings and opened the door. She bent over and removed her muddy running shoes before entering. She was very conscious of the wet fabric of her top glued to her back, the dark perspiration stains under her arms. God, I must stink, she thought.

'Shall I...?' Campbell indicated his own old brown brogues.

'No, they'll be fine,' she said.

She led him in. Campbell looked around. She watched him as he took in the large, single room, the gym bench, its supports holding a barbell with forty kilogrammes, the collection of dumb-bells, the weight rack, the punchbag, the bed in one corner, the stove and sink in the other.

'Well, this is cosy,' he said brightly. 'I like what you've done to it.'

Hanlon grinned. 'I don't get many visitors, Murdo.'

'You amaze me,' he said drily.

'Have a seat...' she said.

There was only one chair by a table in the corner near the door. Campbell sat on it while Hanlon filled a kettle and sat on the weight bench looking at him. He seemed well, tired maybe. She had forgotten how good-looking he was. He was quite fine-featured; he had a sensitive face, but Hanlon had seen Campbell angry and that was a fearsome sight. She had also seen him naked; he had an extremely good body, proportioned, chiselled. He was not the kind of man who would be worried about stripping off should the need arise. She smiled. Perhaps she ought to tell him that, she knew he blushed easily. His face would go as scarlet as the fire extinguisher she kept in the corner for emergencies.

'So, what brings you here, Murdo?' she asked casually.

'Duachy Island,' he said. 'I read the witness statements.'

Hanlon's eyebrows rose in surprise. 'Bit off your patch, isn't it? I thought you were more Glasgow based.'

'I am,' he said. 'It's a different case but there could be a connection.'

Briefly he explained the fraud and Suki Bly's connection with it.

'Well, that's certainly something,' she commented. Interesting, she thought. All of the attendees were connected in one way or another with finance. Anna was a kind of investment guru, Loyd worked mainly in the financial service sector, Karen was involved in sales for her company and Oliver Drummond was a 'financial advisor'. Suki had just been wealthy.

'Isn't it? Could it be a coincidence that a potential victim of a fraud able to identify the perpetrator should fall to her death?' He looked at her, eyebrows raised questioningly.

'It does raise questions,' she said, 'that's for sure. It's quite a motive to kill someone.'

'Have you got any ideas?' he asked. 'One of those nice people you met could well be the brains behind the Longwell Brothers fraud.'

She smiled. Rather too many ideas maybe, she thought. She countered with a question of her own.

'So what's happening with Duachy, then?' she asked.

'Suki Bly's death is still being treated as an accident,' Campbell said. 'There's just no hard evidence to suggest otherwise, even though she was potentially on that island with a man, or woman possibly, who is behind a fraud that is worth potentially millions.'

She nodded. The appearance of a motive for Suki's death did not alter the fact that there was no evidence whatsoever that a crime had been committed. That was an unfortunate fact. No hard evidence.

'What's happening with Jenny's death?' she asked.

'Munroe arrested Oliver Drummond for murder. His prints were in the chapel. There was evidence of his DNA on her underwear.'

'Has he been charged?' Hanlon asked.

Campbell shook his head. 'Not yet, he's been released under investigation.'

Hanlon frowned. Presumably now whether or not he was going to stand trial rested with the prosecution service. 'I know that he was having sex with her, that will explain the DNA, but murder? Oliver Drummond, really?' She added a strong note of incredulity to the word 'really'.

'Why not?' asked Campbell.

'He's too ineffectual,' Hanlon said. 'He's far more likely to be involved in the fraud than the murder.' She filled him in on Anna Reynolds' claim that Drummond had lied about his FinTech expertise and his lifestyle. 'I think he certainly is a con man, whether or not he's your con man is something else. From what you've told me, the Longwell Brothers' fraud was sophisticated, and I don't think Drummond is bright enough to commit a sophisticated crime. He'd like to be able to do something like that, but would he have the ability? That's the trouble with linking him to either of these crimes. I don't think he's nasty enough to kill someone and

I don't think he's clever enough to mastermind anything. Presumably you're going to interview him?'

'I am, I just wanted your input before I did so. You really don't sound convinced this is going to fly.'

Hanlon shook her head. 'Personally I think he's as thick as pig shit and as appealing. To be honest, I would rather put my money on Anna Reynolds. She is bright, market savvy and, I suspect, utterly unscrupulous. At a pinch, Karen Ross? She's bright enough.'

'It could be. There is a theory that the person behind the scam could be a woman.' He mentioned the linguistic evidence. 'But it's tenuous. What about that other man, what was his name, Loyd Travers?'

Hanlon shrugged. 'It's possible, but I doubt he needs the money to risk a crime like that. It could be, of course, that Suki was just wrong. She can't have known who the person was or she would have been in touch with them already. Presumably she was going to pick up some kind of definitive clue from their behaviour or something.'

'Well, personally, for what it's worth, I think she was murdered. I think that if she had identified the fraudster that would provide an excellent motive for shoving her into the sea,' Campbell said.

She thought that he could well be right. It made her reconsider her belief in Drummond's innocence. Somehow revealing his identity to someone he was scamming, or giving her a major clue to it, was the kind of dumb-ass behaviour she could believe him capable of. It would be well in character. Some kind of silly machismo such as thinking that an air-headed woman like Suki would never pick up on whatever it was she had picked up on.

'I guess it could be Drummond,' she said. 'I could imagine maybe Suki accusing him of being the fraudster on the run and him panicking and shoving her into the sea. It's just about possible.'

She looked at Campbell in an evaluating way. There was a definite lull now in the conversation. So, now would be the perfect time to have a frank talk about their relationship, or more accurately the lack of one. She knew that he had come out of his way just to see her; if he had simply wished to talk about the case she had a phone that functioned perfectly well. But the last time she had been in a relationship with someone in the police it had been a disaster and, although the circumstances could hardly have been more different, she was still wary about being hurt.

She scratched her head and smiled inwardly at herself, a smile tinged with contempt. She was such a coward when it came to emotions. If it had been a question of getting in a fight or an argument or putting her life in danger, she was a risk-taker. She wouldn't need to think twice. But when it came to her heart, she applied a totally different standard. She wasn't afraid of being physically hurt, but she was terrified of being emotionally hurt. She was a hypocrite, and she knew it.

Campbell must have been aware that she was staring at him. 'Is anything the matter?' he asked.

Well, she wasn't going to tell him. But she was going to ask him out. She took a deep breath. What if he said no? It shouldn't matter if he did, but it would. She felt horribly nervous.

'I'm going to be in Glasgow for a couple of days,' she said. 'Are you doing anything on Friday?'

He shook his head. 'What, tomorrow? No. Why?'

'How would you like to go and see a magic show?' As soon as she said it she nearly burst out laughing; it sounded like the least plausible date ever. More like something you might ask a child to.

'A what?' He looked confused. 'What kind of a show?'

'A magic show.' She gestured vaguely. 'With a stage magician, rabbits and hats, that kind of thing.'

'Sure, why not, where?' He was bewildered but obviously pleased.

'In a pub, in Partick.'

'Partick!' He looked startled that she should know of such an area of Glasgow.

'Mm hm.'

'Well, if it's Partick how could I say no? It's a date.'

Relief flooded through her. There, that wasn't so bad, she told herself.

They said their goodbyes and she escorted him outside.

'I'll see you tomorrow,' she said.

'I'm looking forward to it.'

She watched as the Subaru turned and jolted down the track. Wemyss nudged her with his snout and she crouched down and put her arms around his neck. She had crossed the Rubicon. She looked into his intelligent brown eyes.

'Well, Wemyss, that was easier than expected. I wonder what's going to happen.'

20

Hanlon parked her car and studied her appearance in the mirror of the sun visor. She was wearing a blue short, sleeveless dress and gladiator-style sandals. Shoes were always a problem for her. She could never really shake off the idea that she might need to fight or run after someone or something. Part of her said, for God's sake, you're going out for a fun evening, you can wear heels. Another part of her said, with Strom around, are you kidding?

She had tied her unruly hair back, was wearing a gold necklace that contrasted well with the tanned skin of her neck, and gold earrings. She looked good.

She locked the car and walked the short distance to the bar where she had arranged to meet Campbell. He was already there, nursing a pint of bitter. He was looking good too, chinos, loafers, a hint of mankle, which he managed to carry off well because, with his athletic build and slightly hard cop's face, he didn't look overly preppy or as if he'd sprung out of an upmarket under-forties male clothes catalogue. She noticed a couple of women in the bar had been staring at Campbell in an evaluating kind of way. They looked gratifyingly disappointed when she sat down with him.

They chatted aimlessly for a while, then, 'So why are we going to see a magician?' he asked.

'Curiosity.' She told him about Strom's other job as a shaman.

'Shaman?' He sounded surprised. 'I hadn't realised that was a thing in Glasgow.'

'Don't underestimate people's stupidity. Think again,' Hanlon said. 'Online there's at least twenty listed, that's in Glasgow alone. There's probably a lot more. I just got bored scrolling through them.'

He shook his head sadly. 'What is the world coming to? I thought we Scots were supposed to be hard-headed.' Then, 'Why the interest in Strom?'

Hanlon drank some of her Diet Coke thoughtfully. 'I can't shake off the feeling that Strom might be not so much predicting the future as arranging it.'

'What?' He looked surprised. 'Arranging an attack on Camille Anderson? Or are you talking about murder?'

'Neither would surprise me. I'm certainly not ruling out the fact that he might well be involved,' she said.

Campbell raised his eyebrows. 'But he wasn't on Duachy...'

'No, he wasn't, but that doesn't mean that he is incapable of getting someone to do his dirty work for him.' She tapped a finger on the table. 'Strom is very charismatic and he's extremely intelligent, and he knows which buttons to press. I think he's probably quite a dangerous person.'

'Well,' Campbell said, 'after that ringing endorsement, I'm quite looking forward to seeing him in action.'

They finished their drinks and walked to the venue where Strom was performing. She found she was enjoying Murdo's company. He was easy to be with as well as easy on the eye. The Caledonian was a large pub with tables outside, predominantly occupied by young people in their twenties. Judging by their clothes and varied accents, Scottish, English, foreign, they were mainly students as well as the local cool twenty-somethings of Partick. A sign saying 'Live tonight! Paul McEwan, Magic and Illusion!' directed them around the corner where there was an orderly queue.

They took their places. The age of McEwan's audience was probably a decade older than the drinkers round the corner, but still the right side of fifty – Strom wasn't yet playing to the Saga brigade – and these accents were predominantly local.

Hanlon was glad she'd booked tickets online – the show was sold out. A couple in front of her were turned away. Paul McEwan was obviously a thing around here. They walked into the small theatre, up some stairs to an extremely crowded bar area and then into the venue itself. Hanlon looked around, did a swift ballpark tally – three sections of seating in a semicircle around a small stage, about a hundred and fifty seats. They took their places, a bell rang 'five minutes, ladies and gentlemen,' the rest of audience went to their seats and the lights dimmed.

'Ladies and gentlemen,' a disembodied voice said, 'for one night only, the highly talented, Glasgow's own... Mr Paul McEwan!'

A blinding flash of light and as she screwed up her eyes to clear them, there was Strom on the stage.

He was extremely professional, as she had imagined he would be. The show was fast paced, a kind of introductory session where Strom did several card tricks, caused objects to disappear, produced a frozen chicken out of a beanie hat. 'Couldnae get a dove!' he said to the audience. He'd broadened his accent. 'You ever tried buying a dove in Partick?' He levitated his assistant, a dwarf called Vimto, in a red and yellow football strip. 'He's moonlighting from his main job,' Strom told the audience, pointing at Vimto. 'He's actually...'

Hanlon missed the name. The audience didn't; it got a laugh and a cheer. Campbell leaned his head close to her ear. 'He plays for Partick Thistle,' he whispered.

Strom seasoned his act with asides about life in Glasgow in general and Partick in particular. The audience laughed and clapped. Although she didn't get any of the references, she found she was enjoying herself. At some point Campbell's knee made contact with hers. She didn't pull away, she pushed back. Campbell's head turned to hers and their eyes met in the semi-darkness. Their hands found each other and their fingers interlaced. Her fingers tightened on his.

On stage, more magic tricks, then Strom interrupted his act to announce that before he had become a magician he had been a criminal, a pickpocket, to be precise. 'I was arrested several times.' He produced a pair of handcuffs. 'Could someone come on stage and cuff me...? Aye, you, son, you look like you've had plenty of experience of this sort of thing.' Laughter from the audience.

An embarrassed-looking kid in a dark-coloured, branded tracksuit came on stage and handcuffed Strom's wrists behind his back. By the time he was walking down the stairs of the stage, the cuffs were off. Strom laughed, the audience clapped.

'I'm on the straight and narrow, but occasionally I lapse, like a recovered alcoholic going on the pish... I cannae help maself... Could all the gentlemen in the audience please check their pockets... aye, in your jaycket.' He had really thickened up his accent and now out of his pocket he produced three wallets, read out names from driving licences and credit cards, and sheepishly three men walked up to the stage to collect their stolen belongings.

'But I'm nae a sexist... I wouldnae just pick on the gentlemen, now, whose is this?' He held up a purse. A woman walked up to collect it. 'And this? Is this yours, hen?' Another woman, blushing fiercely, came onstage.

Back to the act. Some hypnosis. Unsurprisingly, efficiently, un-nerving, then Vimto wheeled on stage a board with the silhouette of a person outlined in red.

'I used to work in a circus years ago,' Strom said. 'Then, after they let me out of prison where I'd been sentenced for the pickpocketing... I learned a lot about knives in the Big Hoose.' That raised a cheer from some guy in the audience. Strom grinned. ('HMP Barlinnie,' Campbell whispered in Hanlon's ear.) Vimto reappeared holding five long knives. Strom selected one. 'I used to do this as an act. I thought I'd bring it back...' He hefted the knife, pivoted on his foot and threw it at the board where it struck the outline of the figure in the middle of where the eyes would be. 'Oops, I'm a wee bit out of practice...'

He threw another one. It thudded into the wood where the heart of the silhouette would be and vibrated with the force of the throw. There was an audible gasp from the audience. Strom pulled a comical face of dismay. 'I used to be good at this. I'm sure I'll improve... hopefully I'll improve very soon... Could I have a volunteer from the audience, please?'

He threw another knife. It landed between the figure's legs.

'Any gentlemen care to step forward?' The crowd laughed nervously. He went over to the board, put his hand on the knife and turned his face to the audience. 'Ye could save time and money on a vasectomy.'

Another ripple of laughter, no hands.

'Ach well, I guess I'll have to choose someone.' He put his hands in his pocket and pulled out some keys. 'Och, I'd forgotten I had these... They're no mine, whose are they? Could you look and see if they're yours?'

There was a general rummaging around from the audience as pockets and bags were checked and then a puzzled silence as nobody claimed them. Hanlon hadn't checked her handbag, now she did, just to reassure herself that her housekeys were there.

To her horror they weren't.

She searched again, this time almost frantically. She wanted to upend her bag in Campbell's lap but she knew it would do no good – they had to be her keys that Strom was jingling on the stage.

For a crazy moment she thought about doing nothing or telling Campbell to go and get them, but then she realised she had no choice in the matter.

She stood up. 'They're mine,' she said in a loud, clear voice. As well you know, Strom, you bastard. How the hell had he managed it? Well, that hardly mattered; he had.

'Would you like to come here to make sure?' he called down to her.

She had no choice. Grim-faced, she stood up and walked towards the stage. An appreciative murmur ran through the audience. An attractive woman possibly about to be hit with a knife – it didn't get much better.

She walked up the side of the stage, reflecting that it reminded her of being back at school to collect an athletics prize. 'A big hand for the young lady!' Strom called. The audience, now a dark abstraction behind the footlights, gave her thunderous applause. Strom gave her a big smile as she stood next to him; his eyes were sparkling with good-humoured malice.

'Welcome on stage,' he said. 'Could I ask you your name?'

'Hanlon.' She returned his smile, in a kind of sarcastic way.

'Now, Hanlon,' he said, gesturing towards the board, 'have you ever done anything like this before?'

She shook her head. 'No.'

'Don't worry, you're in safe hands. Vimto will tie you up.'

Vimto led her over to the board and she stood against it while he secured her wrists and ankles with the ties that were mounted to the board.

Vimto had taken the opportunity to peer up her skirt while he was doing this.

'Do that again, Vimto, and I'll kick you so hard in your bollocks they'll come out of your fucking nose,' hissed Hanlon, sotto voce out of the side of her mouth.

Vimto twisted his face upwards to look her in the face from where he was securing her ankle.

Fuck off, he mouthed, but kept his eyes on the floor as he finished the bow and moved on to her other foot.

Being a helpless target as an adornment to a showman throwing knives had to be one of the least enjoyable things that she had ever done in her life. She stood there, totally helpless, looking, she felt, ridiculous, two of her least favourite sensations in one – no control and a figure of fun. In public, Hanlon was a very private person, so to be the centre of attention was uncomfortable at the best of times. This was the worst of times, not helped by having a man she suspected of certainly having no scruples or morality whatsoever, and who she also suspected of potentially being involved in a murder, throw knives at her.

It really couldn't be any worse, she thought.

Silence fell. The feeling of tension in the theatre as the audience held its breath was palpable, hanging like a thundercloud, heavy, charged. Strom caught her eye and winked. He lifted his arm and threw the first knife.

Hanlon involuntarily closed her eyes and felt the board behind her shake as the blade thudded into the wood above her head. There was nothing fake about the knives. They were sharp, they were heavy and they embedded themselves deeply in the solid wood. If one hit you, it could kill you; at the very least it would inflict a terrible wound. They were obviously razor sharp and Strom was throwing them with real power. It struck her that it would be the perfect crime – all he had to do would be throw a couple of centimetres closer to her body. She would be killed in front of an audience, everyone assuming it was a tragic mistake.

Then two more to the left of her body; the board trembled with the impact. Strom lifted his arm again, the razor-sharp blades of the heavy knives glinting in the stage lights. The blades were sinking four or five centimetres into hard wood. God knew how deep they would go if they hit soft flesh. Hanlon's heart was racing. You bastard, Strom, she said to herself. He caught her eye and smiled cruelly. Despite her mounting fear, she smiled back, acidly; she wasn't going to show him how terrified she was.

The worst part was the waiting, as Strom seemed to realise as he raised his arm, aimed, then changed his mind and dropped it down again. Then suddenly, bang! Bang! Two to the right. That's it, she thought, thank God that's over, but it wasn't.

Think of something else... she thought. A sudden image of Camille, of all things, floated into her mind. She thought of Camille's hero worship of Strom; she thought of Siobhan's unpleasant remark, '*the procession of boyfriends to her bed...*' Was Strom one of those boyfriends? she suddenly wondered.

There was a drum roll from the speakers of the sound system and Strom bent forward. Vimto tied a blindfold around his eyes. Hanlon felt sick and a fresh sweat broke out on her forehead. Strom faced her, his eyes covered with a black cloth. The hateful sound of the drums loud in her ears. She thought she was going to faint. He lifted his arm; the audience were totally silent, holding their breaths, then he released his arm. A blur of movement and another thud and the vibrations of the board between her legs as the knife struck home, just below the hem of her dress.

Then, it was all over. She felt like collapsing, but of course she didn't.

'Ladies and gentlemen... a big hand for Hanlon.'

He came over to her and undid the ties that bound her and took her hand for a bow.

'You bastard, Strom,' she said through gritted teeth as she smiled at him and the applause washed over them.

His eyes met hers, shining with malicious good humour. 'I know,' he said. 'I couldn't resist. Here's your keys… come and say hi after the show.'

'Oh, I will,' Hanlon promised, her eyes glaring at him.

He did a couple more tricks, then the show was over. The house lights came up and the audience stood up.

'Well, that was something,' Campbell said.

'You don't say!' she said, rolling her eyes. 'I had a whale of a time. Come on, he's invited us backstage.'

'You looked very lovely up there…' He gestured to the stage.

'What, tied up to a board? Don't get any ideas, Murdo, we haven't reached that point in our relationship yet.'

He laughed; he looked extremely happy. He switched his phone back on and read the messages on screen; his smile immediately vanished.

'I don't believe this…'

'What's happened?' She didn't need to ask if it was bad news, his face had said as much.

'It's Oliver Drummond.'

'What's he done?'

'Not sure yet. Riley, the guy from Fraud in London, who's looking into the Longwell scam, has got "important news" regarding him. I need to get in touch with him asap.'

'Can't it wait?' she asked.

'Well,' he said grimly, 'seemingly not. My boss is very insistent we all discuss it now. Munroe's got involved too. Fuck, look, I'm sorry…'

'Murdo, don't worry,' she said soothingly. 'I've been there, I understand.'

He nodded and turned to go.

'Murdo.'

He turned around, eyebrows raised questioningly.

'Come here,' she said.

He moved close to her and she slid her arms round his body, her hands stroking the hard muscles of his back, the ridges of his spine, feeling the front of his body pressing against hers through the thin material of her dress. She pulled him close against her, tilted her head back and their mouths met.

They stayed locked together for a heartbeat then she let him go. Their eyes were still locked together, then she said, 'Call me,' and turned and walked away to find Strom.

* * *

The dressing room was a tiny cubbyhole backstage.

'Hello, Hanlon, where's your boyfriend?'

'Work,' she said.

He smiled. 'It's a hard life... Do you want to go for a drink?'

She shook her head, then asked bluntly, voicing her earlier suspicions, 'Are you having an affair with Camille?'

If she had expected Strom to be fazed by the question she would have been disappointed.

'Is that really any of your business?' he asked with a slight smile on his face.

She knew then that he was.

'Yes, it is,' she said. She was beginning to get annoyed. Her evening had just been ruined; she saw no reason not to take some of it out on Strom. 'Two women are dead, Strom, and I think you know a great deal about it but, for whatever obscure reasons of your own, you're holding back on me. I don't think you're responsible, but you know something and I want you to tell me.'

Strom's smile broadened. *'I think this, I don't think that,'* he imitated her. 'What's all this thinking, Hanlon? What's it based on?' he asked contemptuously. 'Women's intuition?' He stood up and started unbuttoning his shirt. 'Now, if you don't mind, this is a dressing room and I need to get changed.'

She shook her head with irritation. 'I'd be careful if I were you, Strom.'

It was his turn to shake his head. 'No, Hanlon, it's you that needs to be careful.' He dropped his casual tone, he looked at her and for once his expression was serious. 'You'll disregard this warning, I know, but I've put it in writing for you, just so you'll remember.'

'What are you on about, Strom?'

'You'll see,' he said, then nodded meaningfully at the door. 'Until we meet again.'

He turned his back on her and she closed the dressing-room door with restraint. She really wanted to slam it behind her with all her strength.

* * *

She walked back the way she had come, back into the theatre. The lights were up, the people had gone and it stood there revealed in its tawdry glamour, the plush red velvet seats stained and threadbare, discarded plastic cups and bottles on the floor. She walked up the aisle and through the doors into the closed bar.

The shutters were down and idly as she approached the stairs she looked at a poster on the wall advertising coming attractions. Then she saw it, the following Tuesday, live at the Caledonian for one night only.

My Claymore Wedding. Siobhan's ex-boyfriend's old band.

She stared at it entranced for some time. It was like some kind of sign, she felt, almost as if the evening had been arranged simply so she could see this. She knew that was a ridiculous idea, but she also knew that she'd go along and see them, see what Dan had to say about his ex.

She walked back along the high street in the warm air of the evening city light to where she had left her car. She walked past the KFC that she'd passed before on Tuesday on the way to Strom's. There was the wall plastered in posters; there, displayed prominently, was My Claymore Wedding. She remembered how she'd paused in this place, momentarily confused. Her subconscious awareness must have noticed the poster. This fresh sign confirmed her intention in her mind.

The car park was only a short distance away. She walked over to the Volvo. Before she got in she looked down through the window at the back seat. There was her sports bag, which she'd carefully packed before she'd left her house. It sat in the car forlornly, a reminder of what could have happened. It contained a change of clothes for the morning and her washbag. She'd been intending to spend the night with Campbell. So much for that plan, she thought. Oliver Drummond, you bastard. You've got an uncanny ability to really piss me off.

She put her hand into the pocket of her dress where she had put her car keys. She always kept them separately from her house keys. Large and heavy, they lived in her bag. Strom must have pickpocketed it somehow, she thought idly, but when? Probably in the crush round by the bar when she and Campbell had been making their way towards their seats. He was a frighteningly talented guy, she thought. What was he doing lurking around in obscurity in a flat above a shop on a street in Partick? If he wanted to, she was sure that he could have made much more of a name for himself.

As she put her hand in her pocket her fingers encountered a piece of paper. She pulled it out expecting it to be an old parking ticket or credit-card receipt, but it wasn't. It was a note from Strom, handwritten.

I dreamed about you last night. Take care just before you get home. The last few steps require the greatest vigilance.

She rolled her eyes. Typical melodramatic bullshit from Strom. *I dreamed about you last night* – a likely story. She unlocked the car and got in. As she drove out of the car park and headed towards Western Avenue she thought, Melodramatic bastard.

* * *

It was still light, a kind of almost but not quite darkness, and the fast road around Loch Lomond was practically deserted. He put his foot down, hard on the gas, pedal to the metal, assuming that Glasgow traffic police would have other things to do on a Friday night than monitor the road by the loch. He had by now left the city far behind and the scenery grew more rugged, wild and beautiful with every mile.

He was a good driver and his car was fast. He could feel his mood lightening with each passing mile. He wondered what she would be wearing when he saw her; she was a bitch, but she was a hell of an attractive woman. He knew she'd give him what he craved, what he needed.

By the time he was west of Inveraray he hardly saw another car. It was like a sign from God; the portents were good. Loch Fyne was dark silver in the strange west-coast evening light, Storm Cedric had completely passed by now and summer weather had returned at last. It wouldn't get fully dark round here until about twelve. Even then, it was usually far from pitch black.

He knew the area around here reasonably well; besides, he had a satnav and her postcode. He guessed that she lived alone – he couldn't see her living with a man. Maybe a cat for company.

North of Lochgilphead he turned off the road by the Crinan Canal. He drove down the narrow road that bordered the inland waterway at a sedate pace. He didn't want to attract any attention.

Finding her house, though, proved far from easy. He drove past the unmarked entrance to the track to her cottage a couple of times before he found it, then he turned and parked nearby in a layby. He got out and walked up the steep slope, lighting his way with the torch on his phone. Occasionally he stumbled on the rutted surface of the road, his torchlight playing wildly across the columns of brown pine tree trunks that lined the way. Once, the beam was reflected from the eyes of a fox that was hidden in the bracken, startled by his approach.

He walked up to the hunkered-down bothy, a silent dark shape in the warm, summer velvet night. There was no car visible. He knocked on the door – as he suspected, no one home. He stood there silently and felt the complete silence wash over himself like a relaxing tide.

He could smell the resinous pine of the trees, the top notes of bracken, the peaty earth, the damp of the grass wet with the evening dew.

* * *

Some time later he saw the lights of her car as she drove home. He shook himself out of his reverie and checked the time. By his reckoning he had been waiting for two hours now, sitting on a mossy boulder in the gloom, then the darkness as the shadows lengthened and night fell, waiting for her return. Now, warned by the noise of the engine and the flash of the headlights as she approached her house, he stood up and stretched, readying himself. He was crouched in the dark, invisible. In his running shoes, he would be inaudible on the hard ground in front of the house.

He watched as she stopped the car and turned the engine off. She opened the door and stood there in her thin dress that clung to her curves. He watched as she stretched and felt a sharp stab of desire. God she had a great body.

She turned her back to him, opened the back door and bent over. He could see the hem of her dress ride up, showing more of her shapely, muscular legs.

Silently, hardly daring to breathe, he moved closer. And closer.

21

As he reached out a hand to touch her, before he had realised what was happening, she spun round unbelievably quickly, too speedily for him to react. He hadn't been expecting a punch. It was so fast he didn't see it coming, and she drove a powerful left hook into his face. The power of the blow had come from her legs as she straightened upwards and from her hips as she twisted round and up. Nobody had ever hit him properly in his whole life and he was totally unprepared for it. Her fist crashed into his face as if it were made of iron and he staggered back, holding his wrecked nose, blood welling darkly through his fingers. He felt the pain but above all was the shock, yet before anything could properly register, he took another punch almost immediately from her right fist directly onto the point of his chin that rocked him further backwards, and then a huge uppercut to his jaw from her left. It was all over in probably under three seconds. He was unconscious before he hit the floor.

* * *

As she had bent over to reach inside the car, Hanlon had smelt him. It wasn't just Wemyss who had a sensitive nose; hers now detected stale alcohol and the heavy, sweet, compost-like scent of weed. Someone was behind her.

She remembered Strom's note:

Take care just before you get home. The last few steps require the greatest vigilance.

Now, breathing heavily, her face and body glowing with triumph, she stood looking down at the fallen man. Despite his face being covered in blood there was no mistaking the features of Oliver Drummond. There was no time to lose; he could wake at any minute.

She opened the boot of the Volvo – there was a roll of duct tape in there. She found it, rolled him over so he was face down and, pulling his arms behind his back, taped them together securely. She heard him moan. He must be coming round.

Quickly, she secured his ankles then turned him back over. His eyelids flickered and she pulled a last bit of tape off, cutting it with her teeth, and smoothed it over his mouth.

Much better, she thought.

Drummond would have been too heavy to lift, so she took his ankles and dragged him over the stony flat ground to her door. He was making whimpering noises through his nose, not unlike a dog. She guessed he was awake now, or beginning to come round, and that it was hurting.

Good.

She unlocked the door, turned the light on and dragged him inside.

* * *

She made herself a coffee and sat down in a chair and waited while Drummond fully came to.

His eyelids flickered then opened. She watched as his gaze darted around the room before focussing on her. His eyes bulged and she could see the muscles of his face move as he tried to speak.

'You know, I'm quite tempted to put you in the back of my car, drive you down to the sea and chuck you in as you are,' Hanlon said conversationally. She watched impassively as Drummond made alarmed noises and twitched violently, shaking his head. He looked as if he'd been done up in a cocoon, an insect waiting to hatch. Or the victim of a giant spider.

She blew on her coffee and took a sip. It was still too hot to drink. She put it down on the table and said, 'I'm going to take the tape off your mouth. If you shout, if you're abusive or if you annoy me, it goes straight back. Is that clear?'

He nodded frantically. She crouched down beside him and ripped the tape off his mouth. It removed quite a bit of skin from his lips and he ran his tongue over them, exploring the painful damage.

'I was never going to hurt you...' he said, with a kind of wheedling tone in his voice.

'I ask the questions, Oliver, you answer them,' she said firmly. 'That's how it works.'

He nodded. 'OK.'

'How did you get my address?' she asked.

'From Jenny,' he replied. 'She had the password to the Nelumbo, that's Camille's company, log-in and I copied it from a file.'

'Why?'

'It wasn't just you... I've got everyone's address. As to the why?' He frowned. 'I copied a whole bunch of stuff. I was going to go through it to see if I could sell any of it, to be honest.'

It sounded plausible; it was the kind of dumb-ass behaviour she would expect from Drummond. Hanlon said, 'Tell me all about it, what you were doing on Duachy, all of it.'

'OK,' Drummond said. He looked pathetically eager to do what she had asked. She had been toying with the idea of hurting him some more if he had shown any signs of resistance or defiance. It wasn't necessary.

Hanlon got her phone out and recorded his story. Once he started there was no stopping him. Lying on his side, staring up at her, he recounted what was, in effect, his life story. She guessed it was the relief of the confessional. All of this had been pent up inside with no outlet, and here was Hanlon as an unlikely but effective mother confessor. The relief at being able to tell the truth after years of lying was there in the eagerness she could hear in his voice, the expression almost of relief on his face. It must have been considerably cathartic.

He was thirty-five. Fifteen years ago he had been thrown out of St Andrews University for repeatedly failing his exams. He'd lied about his degree, claimed he had one, and got a job in the financial sector in Edinburgh, where he'd been doing OK.

'That's when I had this infinity tattoo done,' he said, rubbing his wrist, 'to remind myself of the infinite possibilities the universe offers. I was that excited, but then...' A girl he'd known at uni had arrived one day to start in the same office and, frightened she'd reveal he'd left under a cloud without taking a degree, he had resigned.

Typical, thought Hanlon, he'd panicked for no reason and cut and run, the pattern of his life. He'd set up as a freelance business and financial advisor but things hadn't gone too great, so he'd started playing fast and loose with clients' money.

'I targeted the wealthy ones. I put their money into high-risk ventures, or said I did, and so when they crashed and burned their money went too.'

Except most of the time the money hadn't been invested, it had gone to him, to finance his lifestyle.

'I told myself they could afford it, and they could.' But now he was running out of clients. He was desperately hard up.

'Was Suki Bly one of your financial victims?' Hanlon asked.

'Nobody on that island was,' Drummond said firmly. 'I freely admit I'd gone there looking for clients. I thought anyone with five K to blow on a yoga retreat would be able to afford to give me at least three times that, but I drew a blank...' He gave her a pleading look. 'Could you at least untie my legs?'

'No,' Hanlon said. She wasn't his friend, nor did she want to be.

He rolled his eyes in disappointment but carried on. 'Suki Bly wasn't interested, Karen Ross, I thought, would be too risk averse or want too much info. The Reynolds woman, well, I tried her, no dice. I could see she didn't like me, and there was something about Loyd I didn't like. I thought he seemed a bit shifty.'

'Why, precisely?' asked Hanlon, astonished.

'I don't really know.' Drummond frowned. 'I didn't trust him for some reason, so I left well alone. You obviously didn't have any money so, when I got off with Jenny, I thought, well, I'll at least get a fuck out of this, the journey won't have been entirely wasted.'

Charming, thought Hanlon. But Drummond was entirely credible. Everything he said had the ring of truth.

'What happened at the chapel?' she asked.

'Jenny had told me how that rocker used to fuck his girls on the altar. She was keen on the idea, God knows why, maybe she was like some sort of lapsed Catholic... Anyway, I said sure...' He looked at her in an anguished way. 'Things like that really aren't my cup of tea. I thought the whole idea was creepy, but what could I do? Anyway, when I got there, she was dead. It was like something from a horror film...' he shuddered, 'hanging there. It was like she was staring at me... I thought she might suddenly come to life. I was shit-scared. I panicked, ran away.'

'Didn't stop you having a joint, did it?' Hanlon said, remembering the smell of weed.

Drummond shook his head. 'I didn't! I don't know what you're on about.'

'Whatever,' she said. It must have been Jenny herself.

'Anyway, as you know, I got arrested by Munroe—' he grimaced '—and released. Do you think I'll be charged?' He looked at her anxiously, pleading for good news. 'Wouldn't they have done it by now?'

'Not necessarily,' Hanlon said. 'They'll await instruction from the CPS or the fiscal's office, whatever it's called up here, and they'll be hoping for some more evidence against you... You're not out of the woods, which brings us to tonight.' She finished her coffee and frowned down at him. 'What were you doing at my place?'

'Waiting for you.'

Hanlon rolled her eyes. 'That much I know. What were you trying to do? Assault me?'

Drummond shook his head. 'I don't know, certainly not attack you... I was hiding because I thought if you'd seen me, you wouldn't get out of the car, you'd drive off and call the police and I'd be in even more trouble than I am now, harassment or something...' He squirmed a bit on the floor, quite literally; he wriggled like a gigantic maggot and looked at her pleadingly.

It's your own fault you're down there, she thought mercilessly.

He carried on, plaintively, 'I was only going to tap you on the shoulder, that was meant to show you I didn't mean any harm...'

She considered what he had just said. It was vaguely plausible.

'Why did you want to see me anyway?' she asked.

He said, 'I know you don't like me...'

'That's very perceptive of you.'

He gave a weak smile and persevered. 'But, I don't know, I trust you, you're... I don't know. You didn't particularly like Suki, I could see that, and you risked your life for her. You've got integrity. I haven't, but I recognise it when I see it. It's not that common.'

'That's very flattering,' she said.

'I wanted you to help me.' He shook his head. 'I had it all worked out, and then I managed to fuck it up, like so many things in my life.'

She didn't say anything, just looked at him. If self-pity were a valuable commodity, Oliver would be rolling in it, she thought. Any moment, she thought, he'll start crying.

'Someone's out to get me,' he said. 'First there was that business with Jenny and now someone's trying to frame me.'

'Frame you? In what respect?'

'I've got three bank accounts. One of them, one I don't use much, has had three payments from a bank in the Philippines to the tune of about ten K. I found out earlier today. I don't know anything about this, but I bet I'm being set up.'

'By whom?' she asked.

'I don't know.' He seemed practically in tears. 'I've been accused of a murder I didn't commit, and now this... I don't even know why... Please can you help me?'

He looked at her beseechingly. She sighed. She had never really believed that he was a killer, nor did she believe that he was Campbell's fraudster – he was too thick to come up with anything so successful. He was more the white-collar equivalent of the dodgy tarmacker or the guy who pretended to be a roofer and 'couldn't help but notice as he was passing' that you had a few broken tiles, which he would fix for a 'reasonable price' before stinging you for hundreds, if not thousands, of pounds.

He evidently had no idea of the Longwell Brothers fraud. But whoever was behind it was obviously at the retreat, the stand-out suspects now being Karen, Anna or Loyd, with O'Rourke as an outside possibility.

She looked down at Oliver Drummond. He was a pathetic spectacle, trussed like a chicken with duct tape, his eyes were damp – now he really did look as if he was on the verge of tears. He was also quite literally snivelling, his nose running, the lower half of his face covered in dried blood. There was a wedge of fat white flesh wobbling, visible from above his belt where his shirt had ridden up. She still found him odious – he was, after all, a self-confessed swindler – but someone had killed Suki, someone had killed Jenny, and, whoever that person was, Hanlon wanted them badly.

And it wasn't Oliver Drummond.

She stood up, walked over to a cupboard in her small kitchen area and came back with a knife. She saw a flicker of unease in Oliver's face. Good, she thought. Serves you right.

She crouched down beside him and sliced through the tape holding his wrists and ankles. He sat up and stripped the tape off, wadding it up.

'There's a bin over there,' she said.

He stood up, wincing in pain, dropped the tape in the bin and sat down on the chair by the table, rubbing his wrists.

'So, what happens now? What are we going to do?' he said, looking at her hopefully.

'Oliver,' she said, standing up and walking over to the kitchen sink, 'we're not partners.' His face fell. She took several sheets of kitchen roll, soaked them under the tap and handed them to him. 'There's dried blood over your face from your nose,' she said. 'Clean yourself up.'

While he rubbed and dabbed at his face she continued, 'I believe you, Oliver, and I'll have a word with the officer investigating the case and tell him I suspect you're being set up. But that's all I can do, have a word. You'll have to go home and face the music.'

He looked disappointed, as if he'd been expecting something more.

'Where am I going to stay tonight?' he asked finally.

Hanlon stood up. 'You can sleep in my car tonight. You're not sleeping here under my roof,' she said firmly, 'and you can't get into your car. You're way over the limit.'

She led Oliver outside to her Volvo, put the rear seats down and he curled up in the back under a couple of blankets she had given him.

'You haven't got anything to drink, have you?' he asked.

She sighed, went back into the house and fetched him a bottle of mineral water from the fridge.

'Thanks. You haven't got anything, umm... a wee bit stronger?' he asked hopefully. 'I could really do with a Scotch... or lager, that would do?'

'No, Oliver, no, I haven't.'

'Wine? Sherry?'

She shook her head in disbelief and shut the hatch down on him and went back to her cottage and her own bed.

As she lay on her bed, waiting for sleep to come, she thought of the three men that she had spent time with that evening. All so very different. Strom, attractive, amoral, evil to a certain extent. Doubtless he would laugh at that. 'I'm beyond Good and Evil,' she could imagine him saying. Then Murdo, upright and honest, keen to do the right thing; and then Oliver Drummond, a fool in anyone's language. But she felt that all three held some facet of the truth that might uncover who had killed those women, and that was what she wanted more than anything else: to uncover the truth before it was buried for good.

* * *

In the morning she drove Oliver Drummond back to his car, the one that she'd noticed the night before parked in the layby.

He looked an incredible mess. His face was swollen, unshaven, he had heavy bruising round his eyes and there were still bloodstains on his face. His clothes were muddy from where he'd gone down outside her house.

'Oh, there is one thing you can do for me,' she told him, handing him a business card. 'Forward me the file you stole from Camille with the names and addresses on. I might need it.'

'Sure, anything else?'

'Yes, stay away from me in future.'

He rubbed the bridge of his nose gingerly.

'I will,' he promised, then, 'thank you,' he said.

'What for?' she asked.

'Believing me,' he said.

She watched as he drove away eastwards by the Crinan Canal towards the Oban road. Despite herself, she was beginning to feel rather sorry for him. She got back in her own car. Time to pick Wemyss up.

22

Hanlon spent the next couple of days exercising hard. She hadn't had a proper weight session for a while and it felt good to load up the barbells with muscle-straining amounts of metal. Hanlon loved lifting weight, pumping iron. The smell of the old circular iron weights, their uncompromising structure, the feel of them as she hefted them thoughtfully in her hand, the purifying effort of lifting them until failure as her body screamed with pain and her muscles quivered. The sensation of muscle-overload was tremendous. It was so much more than exercise, it was catharsis.

Wemyss watched, unimpressed, from the foot of her bed where he lay resting his chin on his paws. He didn't mind her doing weights; they would go for a run afterwards, a much better idea in his opinion.

Her muscles shaking and aching, she did ten three-minute rounds on the heavy bag, working combinations and dizzying displays of speed-work. The encounter with Oliver Drummond had reminded her just how uncertain her life could be, how precarious, and how she had often needed her fighting skills just to survive in the dangerous situations she habitually placed herself in.

Tuesday arrived, she took the dog for an extra-long run, about ten miles. Wemyss probably covered three or four times that, gleefully pursuing scents through the bracken and the black, loamy soil beneath the trees, sometimes barking for the sheer pleasure of it all. When she was finished they swam in the cold brown peaty waters of the loch above her cottage. The dog was a good swimmer. Even in the depths of winter he would find her a stick to throw into the loch so he could jump in and retrieve it. Then she took Wemyss down to Effie's house and drove west to Glasgow.

While she drove the familiar road she reviewed her progress, or the lack of it, on finding out who had killed Suki and Jenny. At least she had definitely ruled out Oliver Drummond from any involvement. That was something. But O'Rourke was very much in the frame, which presented a huge problem. Was she really still a threat to Camille, or, as Strom had said, had she forgiven her? The worst of it was, Hanlon really liked O'Rourke. She had very few friends; she would like to be able to add Katherine O'Rourke to the list.

She conjured up O'Rourke's handsome, slightly mocking, enigmatic face under her red hair and finely shaped eyebrows. She felt that O'Rourke was capable of more or less anything.

She swore irritably as a gigantic lorry laden with pine-tree trunks from where the forestry had been logging pulled out slowly from a track in front of her. Sixty miles per hour down to thirty and she knew that the road would twist and turn for about thirty miles; she'd be trapped behind him until Cairndow.

While she drove along at thirty, the stretch between Lochgilphead and Inveraray particularly irksome, the truck dropping down to twenty any time a hill appeared, which was often, she took her mind off the mind-numbing tedium with thoughts as to how best to approach her investigation. Occasionally a car with Argyll plates would zoom past, driven to suicidal recklessness by the slow pace of the lorry. What was she hoping to gain from tonight? What was her purpose in seeing the band? Certainly not enjoyment. She had listened to a couple of their albums, 'Over the Seas to Die' and 'Tartan Nightmares and Other Stories' on the Internet. Squalling guitars, thunderous drums and strangled vocals.

She had looked Dan Murray up on the Internet. He'd been a very promising jazz drummer until he'd got into rock and hard drugs. He was, by all accounts, the most accomplished musician in the band.

Mainly she was hoping for some insight into Siobhan. She was sure he would be happy to share bitchy reminiscences of his former girlfriend. There was something about Camille's sister she didn't trust.

Eventually the twisting loch road straightened out near a fish restaurant, the original one of what had become the chain, in what seemed like the middle of nowhere, next to a garden centre. She guessed that there were sound commercial reasons for them to be here but as you drove past, bare hills strewn with rocky outcrops and criss-crossed with burns, and the sea-loch stretching away as far as the eye could see, one or two houses lost in the immensity, it seemed a slightly surreal place to find a business.

She put her foot down and overtook the lorry. From then on to Glasgow it was a clear run. She thought about Campbell. Holding his firm, muscular body against hers had felt great. She decided that she definitely wanted more. But not tonight; tonight was business.

After Loch Lomond the countryside ended abruptly and she was on the borders of what would eventually become Glasgow. She drove through the city streets, the reddish stone tenements around her, only half listening to the satnav. She kind of knew where she was going now. She parked her car down the road from the Partick pub and went off in search of My Claymore Wedding.

She walked into the pub, the Caledonian. It was crowded, predominantly young people drinking and chatting. The noise level was high; it was busy for a Tuesday night. The clientele was a mix of uni students, some of them, mainly girls, still wearing their leavers' hoodies from school – she guessed they were prospective university freshers – and a harder core group of stoned-looking older kids in their mid-to-late twenties. These, she guessed, were fans of the band; one or two had band T-shirts.

They were heavily tattooed, multiply pierced, several of them were dreadlocked. They were much rougher edged than the others. There was an air of aggression about them. Hanlon's nose was attuned to the fresh air and natural odours of the west-coast outdoors; to her the MCW fans smelled of old sweat, weed and stale alcohol.

She walked up the stairs where Strom had played just four days previously. It seemed a lot longer. In the lobby area a girl, late twenties, long dyed-blue hair and pale skin in a Crass retro T-shirt, 'Banned from the Roxy', was laying out MCW T-shirts, CDs and button badges on a merch stall.

She looked up as Hanlon walked over. A welcoming smile died on her face as she evaluated the woman in front of her, hard-faced in jeans and an old Barbour jacket and Doc Martens. Too old, and certainly not the type, to be wanting to buy a post-punk T-shirt.

'Can I help you?' she asked, warily polite.

'I'm looking for Dan Murray, the drummer,' she said.

Blue Hair nodded. 'He's backstage,' she said as she took her phone out of her combat jacket pocket. 'Who are you?'

Hanlon ignored the question. 'I know the way,' she said and walked through into the theatre.

The seats from Strom's performance the other night had been removed. It would be standing room only for MCW. Probably a wise move, Hanlon thought, thinking of their troublesome-looking fans.

She walked backstage and along the dark, narrow corridor to the changing rooms, squeezing past several young people who she took to be road crew or fans. The door to the dressing room where she had met Strom was closed. She could hear music and voices inside. She banged on it with the side of her fist and it opened.

There were three men inside and two girls. The men were recognisably My Claymore Wedding as seen online the night before. They were all thin, pale skinned, tattooed, with hair that covered most of the spectrum, one long and lank, one short and shaved at the sides and one not too dissimilar to her own, dark, naturally curly and uncontrollable. Long hair had a guitar slung around his neck. The curly-haired one was the tallest and wore an unbuttoned shirt. His torso was totally fat-free; she could see every muscle of his stomach under the taut skin. His jeans were low slung below his snake hips and she could see a dark ridge of pubic hair, which, to her way of thinking, was not a good look. Possibly it drove the fans wild.

Seeing the singer with his crotch-revealing trousers made her think of Shane Gowrie. She suddenly wondered what he had looked like in his heyday, before the doors of old age and the home had slammed around him. At least he'd had his sex chapel and an island to his name. She doubted My Claymore Wedding would be buying their own island any time soon.

Curly hair was smoking weed and he looked at Hanlon aggressively. Maybe he thinks I'm management and I've come to tell him off, she thought.

He handed the joint to the guitarist.

'What do you want?' he said, blowing a cloud of smoke in her direction.

'Cheers, Nathan,' long-hair said, puffing away. Five pairs of eyes looked at her with the arrogance and intolerance of youth. She suddenly felt old and tired. She wished she weren't here; she didn't belong.

'I'm looking for Dan,' she said.

'Who are you, his mam?' said Nathan, the singer presumably, with a grin. 'Or his granny?' He had that air of wanting to be centre stage. He turned round to the other two with a grin on his face as if he'd said something clever. The guitarist, to his credit, looked embarrassed.

The short-haired one, the bass player, she guessed, said, 'He's outside in the van. When you wake him up, tell him he's on in half an hour.'

'Thanks,' Hanlon said. The singer waved goodbye to her, dismissing her, turning his back. As Hanlon closed the door, she put her head round it and said, 'Oi, Nathan...' He looked round, puzzled. Hanlon pointed at his crotch. 'I'd get your bikini line waxed before you go on stage, it's not a pretty sight.'

The guitarist spluttered with laughter and Nathan looked pleasingly furious as she turned away, pulling the door to behind her.

She followed the corridor to the end and opened a fire door that led to a zigzag metal staircase, which overlooked a yard at the back of the bar. Down below she could see a large white van and a dozen or so motorbikes that she guessed belonged to the hardcore faithful fans of the band.

The crusty ones she'd seen in the bar. She clattered down the stairs and walked over to the old Mercedes Sprinter van.

She looked in the driver's seat but no one was in the cab. She went round the back and knocked on the door. She heard a muffled voice from inside. She opened the door.

Curled up on the floor was a young guy with a beard and long hair, jeans and a long-sleeved T-shirt. He pushed himself upright and peered at her through half-closed eyes. He was painfully thin.

'Aye? Whit dae ye want?'

'Dan Murray?'

He nodded.

'My name's Hanlon, mind if I have a word?'

'Surely…' he said hospitably. He indicated the empty van with his hand.

She climbed in.

The van was carpeted and there were various items that the band hadn't needed left in it: a toolbox, mike stands, gaffer tape, electrical cabling. Dan's head sank down to his breastbone and he jerked it upright to try to focus on Hanlon. The pupils of his eyes were extremely contracted, then his eyes closed again and his head started nodding up and down, gouching as they called it. Dan was out of his box on heroin. She looked at her watch. Dan was due on stage fairly soon. She felt a twinge of sympathy for the band. He was absolutely wrecked.

'Dan?' She shook him gently to get his attention.

'Mmm?' He scratched himself lazily under the armpit, then his stomach, opened his eyes and blearily focussed on her.

'Dan, I want to ask you some questions about Siobhan.'

'Oh, aye, Siobhan, she's a guid lass, she's coming tonight, ken?'

Hanlon blinked in surprise. She wouldn't have imagined that Siobhan would have been so interested in going to see her ex play a gig in a small club in Glasgow.

Dan reached down beside him and picked up a half-smoked joint, which had gone out. He brought out a cigarette lighter from his jeans and lit it. She noticed that he had a dessert spoon in his pocket too. Momentarily she wondered why, then she thought, It'll be to cook his heroin in.

That was what he would have been doing in the van before she arrived, warming the powder in some water in the spoon to dissolve it before injecting.

'So did Camille send you?' he murmured, his eyes closed again. 'Did you bring my gear?'

He thinks I'm a dealer, Hanlon thought. God, he must be really out of it. She looked at Dan. He most certainly was.

Then she thought, Camille? Why would Camille be involved with Dan? Was he implying she was supplying him with heroin? That was wildly unlikely. Was he getting Camille mixed up with Siobhan? That seemed by far the most likely explanation.

'She's bringing it later,' she said, humouring him.

He nodded. 'Aye...'

There was silence in the van, just the sound of Dan's regular breathing. His head had fallen on his chest. The joint had gone out again; it was still held in the fingers of his right hand.

He started awake again and said, 'Tell her the price has gone up...'

For a moment she wondered what he was on about, the cost of drugs?

Then he said, 'I want ten K.' He smiled. He was missing a couple of teeth in the top row. She doubted that they had been knocked out. Dan was in terrible shape. He closed his eyes.

'Who, Dan?' She moved closer to him. He smelled quite rank, a kind of metallic sweat. 'Who should I tell?'

He opened his eyes and stared at her blearily. 'Camille.' He lifted a finger up to his lips. 'Silence is golden, eh?'

What the hell was going on? Camille?

There was a bang on the back of the van door and it opened. She turned round in irritation. There was the guitarist and a couple of the bikers that she had earlier seen in the bar, standing behind him, arms folded, in a classic bouncer style.

The guitarist looked at Hanlon, not without a trace of sympathy, a sort of 'now you see what we have to put up with' look. He was a lot friendlier than Nathan.

'Time to go,' he said. 'We need to get him in some sort of shape for the gig.'

There was no point arguing. She nodded and jumped down from the van.

'Good luck,' she said.

'Och, he'll be OK, he'll perk up, he always does, kind of miraculous really... Are you staying to see us play?' He smiled warmly at her. 'We could meet up afterwards if you want?'

I too could be a groupie! thought Hanlon with amazement.

'Some other time,' she said, 'but thanks for the offer.'

He shrugged and smiled. 'If you change your mind...'

The guitarist clambered in and as she walked away towards the gate of the car-parking area she heard one of the bikers muttering something about speed.

She walked back to her car along the quiet Paisley streets, wondering if she was going to bump into Strom.

So Camille was buying Dan's silence. That was what she'd just learnt. Well, she didn't know what that meant but it had certainly been worth coming to Glasgow for. She wondered if that was recent, since the events on Duachy, or had it been going on since he'd known Siobhan? And what did Dan know that made it worth paying to keep his mouth shut? That, of course, was the main question.

Well, she thought as she climbed into the Volvo, she'd find out soon. Tonight would be no good – he was too out of it, not to mention too busy to talk. She'd speak to him when he was a bit more with it. And when he was alone. Dan wouldn't be a hard nut to crack, that was for sure.

She started the car and headed off towards Argyll.

23

'Jab... jab... straight right... left hook to the body... right uppercut.' Hanlon's thoughts as she gave her heavy bag a good workout. The bag rocked and danced on the chains that secured it to the massive wooden beam that ran across the ceiling of her cottage.

She was practising combinations. It was the kind of thing that she used to do with her old boxing trainer in London; she really missed it. She switched to a new set incorporating a roll, so a punch aimed at her head would go over it and, as her knees snapped back up, she would translate that momentum into the power behind a punch.

Wemyss watched uneasily from his basket in the corner. He didn't like the thudding noise of Hanlon's fists in their gloves on the bag, and his eyes and muzzle tracked her fast, fluid movements with alarm.

She upped the tempo, sweat pouring down her forehead, dripping into her eyes, her hair a tangled wet mess flying up and down behind her, sweat soaking her halter top and the waistband of her shorts.

Hanlon had been lost in concentration up to now, there were no thoughts in her head other than the pre-set, pre-determined routines that she was working through. Now, as the timer on her phone signalled the last three-minute round, she thought of whoever had pushed Bly to her terrible death in the Atlantic.

This was what she wanted to be doing to whoever that was. She relived those last few terrible moments, Suki's panic-stricken, terrified face as she slid under the merciless waves. Memories of Suki bobbed up into her consciousness at the most unlikely times, when she was loading the washing machine, when she ran, at the sight of hair dye in a shop. She was surprised at the hold the woman had over her. Maybe I'm a sucker for the needy, she thought, glancing down at Wemyss, who met her eyes with adoring, blind trust. Maybe I feel I let her down.

The punches crashed into the bag with real venom now, punches with the power to break ribs and fracture jaws, and she thought about Jenny. Someone had taken her life, probably the same person, and she wanted to find them and beat them to a bloody pulp.

The last minute of her session on the bag was frenzied but still with the controlled skill that came as the result of years of practice, dozens of contests, years of fitness training and years of boxing conditioning.

'I'll...' Her left jab hit the bag, pushed through it almost, at face level. 'Get...' The knuckles of her right hand crashed into the canvas. She could feel the pain through the padding of the glove and the layers of the cotton that wrapped around her hand. 'You.' She sidestepped then slammed a left into the bag, round about the base of someone's ribs, her arm bent at ninety degrees, the power of her hips whipping it in.

'Bastard!'

The bag jangled on its chains, swinging like an enormous pendulum from the energy and power of her shots.

Enough.

Hanlon collapsed down on the floor and sat with her head buried between her knees, taking huge breaths of air. Wemyss rose from his basket and came over and licked her ear, nuzzling her as if to comfort her.

She pulled off her gloves and stared at her strong, shapely hands bandaged by the sodden cotton wraps.

Her phone rang. She stood up and walked over to it, glancing at the caller ID. It was Camille. Immediately she wondered if Dan had said something to her about her visit, tipping her off.

'Hi, how are you?' asked Camille. Hanlon tried to analyse her tone over the phone. Did she sound suspicious or hostile? No, she sounded the same as ever. Sunny, friendly.

'I'm fine,' Hanlon said warily.

'Are you free for lunch tomorrow?' Camille asked.

'Yeah,' she said. Wemyss licked her and she pushed him away. He returned with his pheasant toy and gave it to her, pushing it into her hand. 'Where do you want to meet?'

'How about at the studio? Twelve o'clock?'

'I'll be there,' Hanlon said.

'See you tomorrow, namaste!' Camille ended the call.

Hanlon threw the pheasant into the air for Wemyss to catch and slowly unwrapped her hands as she sat thinking about Camille. What could she say to her when she saw her? That O'Rourke, the pillar of her empire and her trusted friend, was high on Hanlon's list of suspects because Camille's health advice had killed her daughter? Or that she suspected that she, Camille, was involved in something that was probably illegal and was being blackmailed by her sister's ex-boyfriend? Or that one of the attendees on the island, one of Camille's clients, was a fraudster and had probably been behind the death of Bly?

She remembered an earlier thought that she'd had that Suki's death would undoubtedly benefit Camille. Suki had lent her money. There might be no official record of the loan; it need never be paid back.

The whole threat thing against her could have been seen as a long lead-up to explaining Suki's murder. Of course, people would say, mistaken identity, but Suki could have been made for that part from the outset with her penchant for dressing like the woman she was besotted with.

And the incident with the broken glass, had that been designed to deflect any suspicion away from Camille from the very beginning by casting her squarely as the intended victim? The fact that O'Rourke had eaten the adulterated muesli didn't matter, it still had been Camille who had been seen as the target. Was it all a blind? A dummy, as she had been practising in her bag-work, hard left jab, an uppercut with the same hand that was never intended to land, just get the opponent's attention, then a hard right over the top to do the damage.

And Siobhan's comment that her sister wasn't as nice as she looked, what exactly had she meant by that?

Lunch promised to be a diplomatic challenge if nothing else, and Hanlon knew she was a very poor diplomat.

Well, at least she could tell Camille that Paul Strom had thrown knives at her and she was still around to tell the tale.

Strom, she thought, you bastard, you know something, don't you?

She undressed and headed for the shower.

Later, washed and wearing clean clothes, she opened up the file that Oliver Drummond had forwarded to her with the names and addresses of people in Camille's address book. She scrolled to the M's. And there he was, a relic of Siobhan's past that wouldn't go away and his name still preserved like a fly in amber in Camille's address book.

Dan Murray, Claonnaidh Farm, Ellenabeich, Seil.

When would she visit? She was seeing Camille the following day. She decided to go there and then.

* * *

An hour later, she was on her way. She dropped the dog off at Effie's first. Seil Island was only a forty-minute-or-so drive from where she lived but before she went there, she turned right at the junction to the Oban road and headed the couple of miles south to Lochgilphead to buy some supplies.

She'd need to make sure that Dan wouldn't turn her away and that he was in an amenable mood.

Despite its relatively small size, Lochgilphead had about half a dozen churches and a fair few bars. Hanlon wasn't in search of alcohol or the opium of religion, it was a different kind of opiate she was after.

She walked into a small backstreet pub, the Rhu bar. At this time of day the place was practically empty. There were a couple of pool tables and a TV behind the bar tuned to a channel showing horse racing. She nodded to the barman, who nodded silently back. He knew her face – in a town this size most people knew each other to a greater or lesser extent. She saw the guy she was looking for sitting at the end of the bar nursing a pint of Guinness. He'd been pointed out to her as the local dealer by a local cop she knew. There was an air about him that was familiar to her from her years in the police; she could have guessed his job without being told. She went and sat next to him.

'Diet Coke,' she said to the barman, 'and a pint for Kevin.'

Kevin had been staring fixedly ahead of him, now he turned and looked at her. He was wearing jeans, a blue guernsey jumper and a green gilet. He was slightly younger than her, she guessed, mid-thirties. He was quite good-looking in a bad-boy sort of way.

'Tae whit dae I owe the honour?' he asked.

'You know who I am?' she asked.

'Aye.' He was suspicious, his brow frowning.

The barman put the drinks on the counter and Hanlon gave him a ten-pound note. 'Keep the change,' she said.

The barman nodded. 'Ta,' he said and moved away out of earshot.

'I want to buy some heroin,' she said quietly.

Kevin grinned and she could see he had nearly burst out laughing. 'Really!' he said, looking at her with raised eyebrows.

'I'm serious. It's not for me,' she said. 'It's for a client.'

He looked at her in an evaluating way. He could have said, 'What makes you think I could help you?' but most people who lived here, certainly everyone who drank in the Rhu bar, knew what Kevin did. That included the police, but maybe they felt it was better that Kevin Smith supplied the hard drugs here rather than someone else. At least he was local.

'How much?'

'Do you do twenty bags?' she asked.

He nodded.

'I'll take five,' she said, 'and twenty-five quid for your trouble.'

'Where are you parked?' he asked.

'In the car park opposite the tyre place.'

'I'll see you there in five minutes.'

He slid off his seat and walked to the pub door. 'Back in a wee while, Jamie.'

'Aye, Kev.'

She drank her Coke and said goodbye to the barman. He nodded with faint contempt. He might have to put up with Kevin, she thought as she slipped out through the door, but he obviously felt he didn't have to be polite to his clients.

She met Kevin in the car park; she had the money rolled up in her palm. They shook hands and Kevin walked away without a backward glance. She got in the car and looked at what she'd just bought. Wrapped neatly in a folded square piece of paper were five small paper wraps. A hundred pounds' worth of heroin. That should do the trick.

She texted Dan.

I'm Hanlon. We met in the van at the Caledonian gig. I've got something for you if you can answer a few questions.

She sent it and looked at the screen of her phone. Almost immediately she could see he was composing a reply.

What colour?

She frowned, puzzled, then she got it – it had to be a drug reference.

Brown.

Come soon.

She thought of Dan and his pinned eyes and nodding head; she thought of the heroin she'd just bought. The doctor will see you now, she thought. She started the car, pulled out of the car park and headed off up the back road via the small industrial estate towards Oban.

Half an hour later she drove over the small stone bridge that linked the island to the mainland – the bridge was about the size that would span a small river, far from dramatic – and she followed the road round the island towards Ellenabeich, the way she had come when she had driven to the Duachy Island car park to be picked up by Charlie.

Before she reached the village, she saw a sign pointing down a track that led to the sea, signposted Claonnaidh Farm. She drove past the sign and parked her Volvo on the grass verge a couple of hundred metres past the turning and got out. She opened the rear hatch and changed her shoes into walking boots, picked up a pair of binoculars and walked back along the road to the farm. The track sloped down towards the sea and dog-legged around a small hill. She guessed that the farm lay beyond that.

She cut across the field to the hill. Although it was sunny, the sky a vivid blue with large, dramatic white clouds, it was very windy.

She was glad that she was wearing walking boots. Although the grass had looked firm and green from the road, it was boggy and her feet sank to above the ankles in the squelchy, mossy ground underfoot. As she climbed the hill it firmed up underneath her. Approaching the brow, she dropped into a crouch so she wouldn't be seen silhouetted against the skyline and then she was lying on her stomach looking down on the farm.

Farm was a bit of a misnomer. There were a farmhouse and outbuildings, it was true, but there was also a small housing development opposite. She focussed the binoculars on the buildings.

Siobhan had said that she had lived with Dan on a kind of commune. This was obviously it. She could see half a dozen motorbikes parked up, a pick-up truck, a couple of beaten-up old cars and the large white Mercedes van that she'd seen at the gig in Glasgow. She remembered the heavily tattooed bikers she'd seen in the pub. She guessed that these bikes belonged to them.

She lifted the binoculars up slightly and looked out to sea. There were a couple of fishing boats bobbing around on the swell and then to her surprise she saw a small boat that looked very much like Charlie's, the guy who had taken them to Duachy. Then she remembered that he lived round here, just up the road, at Ellenabeich. She smiled, wondering what the old religious nut would make of the band and its followers living on the commune. If Charlie had his way, she guessed that they'd be driven out with pitchforks by irate Calvinist islanders.

She walked back to the track and then down to the houses. A couple of dogs ran out of an outbuilding, some kind of lurcher-type animal and a

Staffie cross. They barked loudly, not in an aggressive way but noisy enough to attract attention. A couple of bikers, a kid in a blue tracksuit and then a woman wandered out from a barn to find out what the commotion was about.

The woman had her straw-coloured hair in dreads and a pierced nose. She was wearing a blue dress with a man's jumper on top, unlaced steel-toe-capped boots below, and was very pregnant. One of the bikers had dreads too, short ones, the other had long dark hair tied back in a ponytail. Ponytail walked over to Hanlon. He was tall, about six three, and was wearing a cut-off denim jacket and jeans. Tattoos covered his arms.

'This is private property,' he said, pleasantly enough.

'I know,' Hanlon said. 'I'm here to see Dan Murray. Could you tell me where he lives?'

'Why do you want to see Dan?' The blonde woman was looking at her in an aggressive way.

What's it to you? Hanlon felt like saying, but decided to be tactful for a change. She heard the rattle of a sash window being pulled up; another biker was looking at them from an upstairs window. There was a definite feeling of hostility in the air.

'A friend of his asked me to give him something,' she said. She gave a deprecatory smile and shrugged. 'Y'know.'

To her relief the ponytailed biker grinned. 'I can imagine... He'll be pleased tae see you. Last house on the left,' he said, pointing to the row of wood-framed terraced houses behind her.

'Thanks,' she said and walked over to the house he had indicated. By the doorstep she turned and looked back. The biker community seemed to have lost interest in her and were now looking at a car that was driving slowly down the track to the farm.

The door was ajar. She knocked and went in.

'I'm in here,' said a voice. The hall was untidy, but not desperately so. There was a bicycle leaning against the wall at the bottom of the stairs that was currently serving as a coat rack, and some old dirty training shoes by the door. The staircase, steep and narrow, was acting as a series of shelves. There were books, clothes, some old CDs on the banister side so there was a narrow passageway to reach upstairs.

Ahead of her she could see a door that led to the kitchen; the living room was on her right. She went inside.

Dan was sitting on a threadbare sofa. He looked terrible. Maybe the gig from the night before had taken it out of him. His long hair was greasy and pushed back from his sweat-stained forehead. There were purple bruises under his eyes from lack of sleep. He was wearing a pair of jeans and an old baggy jumper and he was trembling as though he was cold, although there was an electric heater on in the room and it was unpleasantly hot.

He gave her a wan smile. 'Hi... so you're Hanlon?'

She wondered if he recognised her from the evening before.

'That's right.'

'Have a seat.'

She looked around. The lounge was sparsely furnished. There was the sofa that Dan was sitting on, a pine coffee-table with several old cups containing coffee dregs and an overflowing ashtray, and a couple of old armchairs. On the wall were several posters of bands that she had vaguely heard of: Tool, Linkin Park, Slipknot.

She sat down on a chair.

'Have you got my smack?' Dan asked, his eyes feverish. She could hear the pleading in his voice. She nodded. 'Could I have it?' he said in a wheedling tone. 'I really need it, Hanlon.'

Right now he would sell his soul for some junk, she thought. She unzipped the pocket in her jacket and brought out the folded piece of paper. Dan's body stiffened with excitement; he sat upright on the sofa. He stared at the paper she was holding in her hand as if it were the Holy Grail.

'How much...?'

'There's five twenty-pound scores in here, Dan,' she said, dangling them temptingly close. His eyes were glued to the bag, like Wemyss's when she was eating her dinner.

'Can I have it?' he whispered, almost tearfully.

'Tell me about Camille, Dan,' she said quietly.

'It's what I know about her sister.'

'About Siobhan?'

'Aye... let me have the bag and I'll tell you... it'll knock your socks aff. Please, Hanlon, please... I'm really hurting.'

'OK.' Cursing herself for being too soft-hearted, an easy touch, she handed the paper containing the bags over to Dan, who held it tenderly between his fingers.

'Come tae Daddy,' he crooned to the heroin he was holding. He looked up at Hanlon. 'Would you leave me alone for five minutes? I'm just going to have a wee...' He didn't say the word 'fix' but they both knew what he meant. Hanlon could think of nothing she'd rather not see than Dan hunting for a vein in his spindly limbs.

'I'll be back in ten,' she said, sighing with exasperation. She stood up and went into the kitchen, which connected via a door to the living room. Hopefully when she returned he'd be a bit more chatty.

She immediately wished she hadn't. The kitchen was a disgusting mess. There was an overflowing swing bin, the sink was full of dirty dishes, there was a stack of empty takeaway food containers and pizza boxes in the corner. The stove was filthy, the floor, sticky. Maybe unsurprisingly it smelled, the sweetish smell of rotting food and a back odour of drains.

I can't wait in here, she thought, I feel sick. She opened the back door and went outside into the fresh air.

If Dan had cleaned his kitchen window he would have had a superb view. The row of four terraced, wooden-framed houses, of which his was an end one, looked out over the Atlantic, which stretched away limitless in front of her. To the north she could see hills, which she guessed might be Mull, or maybe the mainland, she wasn't sure. There were some islands in the distance, which she recalled someone saying were the Slate islands, but again she couldn't swear to it. Her geography was hazy.

She walked down the steps. Below her was a small rocky beach and the rowing boat that she'd seen earlier with a fisherman in was pulled up on the shingle, its painter tied around a boulder. There was no sign of anyone at the rear of the houses.

I'll go back to the car, she thought, get some money. That'll kill ten minutes. The state he'll be in he won't be going anywhere. He's bound to pester me for some. If what he tells me about Camille is worth it, he can have it.

She didn't worry about Dan being too out of it when she got back. If he was, she'd just wait till he came round. She walked round to the front of the houses, to the large yard that separated these houses from the farmhouse with its barns and outhouses.

There was the car she had seen coming down the drive earlier, a beaten-up old BMW, now parked outside the barn with a guy wearing a tracksuit talking to the bikers. As she emerged from around the corner they stopped talking and stared at her as she walked past on the other side. She ignored them and carried on walking back up the concrete drive that led down from the road.

A short distance up the track she had the feeling that she was being followed. She stopped and turned around.

The road had taken them uphill a couple of hundred metres and the farm and the houses were out of sight behind a bend. She saw the young kid in the tracksuit who had been talking to the bikers walking up to her. He looked somehow familiar, but she couldn't quite place him.

'Can I help you?' she said politely. She felt a sense of mounting unease growing inside her.

He walked up to her, the expression on his face one of definite hostility. He stopped about a metre away from her, staring hard at her. Hanlon shifted her weight slightly, putting more on the back foot, gently rubbing her jaw with her knuckles as though she were thinking.

'Aye, it is you, you fucking auld bitch,' he said, spitting the words at her. 'I thought I kenned your face.' She looked at him, trying to place him, the blond hair cut short at the sides and long on top, a gold necklace round his neck. His eyes were slightly glazed and she could smell the weed that he'd been smoking.

Who the hell was he? she wondered, then it came to her. Lochgilphead – he was the kid who had tried to grab her, the one she had hit. Callum, that was his name.

Hanlon thought, So, he wants a rematch, does he?

He threw a sudden punch at her face. It was a fast enough punch but Hanlon had been in a boxing ring with good professionals, to her it was both obvious and woefully slow. She jerked her head sideways and his fist missed her head, then she slammed a left jab into his face.

She felt it make hard, jarring contact. It hurt her knuckles but it must have hurt the kid even more. It was one of the combinations that she had practised endlessly on the heavy bag. Hanlon didn't just throw single punches, she immediately hit him with a left hook and then slammed an uppercut into his stomach.

The kid knew how to start a fight but not how to follow through. He collapsed and went down on the distressed concrete of the road. She was tempted to kick him in the head or stamp on his right hand that lay tantalisingly available on the hard surface. But she refrained.

She looked down at him in his cheap blue nylon tracksuit with his crappy trainers.

'Don't bother me again, or I'll put you in hospital,' she said, and turned away and walked up the road.

* * *

Callum looked at the woman's back as she strode angrily away from him. He didn't waste any time in recriminations. It wasn't the first time he'd lost a fight, it wouldn't be the last. The important thing was to get even. There would be no mistakes this time.

He had severely underestimated the bitch. Well, he wouldn't make that mistake again. His head was still humming from the ket he'd taken earlier. It had slowed him up but, on the plus side, he didn't feel any pain from the beating he'd just taken.

He stood up, staggering a little. His balance was a bit fucked, maybe from drugs or maybe from the punch to the head, he didn't really care. He wiped some blood from his nose, took a couple of deep breaths and unzipped his tracksuit top pocket. He took out the knife he had in there and removed it from its sheath. It wasn't a big knife – at home he'd got a thirty-centimetre proper fuck-off zombie knife with a serrated blade – but this little mofo with its fifteen centimetres of razor-sharp steel would well do the trick. He wasn't planning anything too extreme. It wasn't as if he was going to kill her or anything. He'd slash her face, give the bitch something to remember him by. As she rounded a corner ahead of him he broke into a loose run so he'd catch her before she reached the main road.

'Ready or not, here I come, bitch,' he said to himself as he closed down the distance.

24

Murdo Campbell was looking at the website of Terrapin Solutions UK, Loyd Travers' IT company.

On their home page, Terrapin Solutions – Find, Fix, Prevent! Solutions for all Industries – he read about how Terrapin could identify systems' weaknesses, assess cyber-security protocols, prevent PII breaches, predict and prevent cyber attacks and provide a variety of other services. Unfortunately, the information that he wanted, a number to contact Loyd Travers on directly, was, of course, not to be found. Nor was there an actual physical address. With a mounting sense of frustration, he filled out the 'contact us' section of the web page and pressed send.

Well, if necessary, he could get Loyd's contact details from Camille's yoga company.

He stared out of the window. If Suki was to be believed, then one of the guests on the ill-fated island yoga retreat was the fraudster he was looking for. Hanlon had told him that she thought it was unlikely to be Oliver Drummond. That was good enough for Campbell to relegate Drummond to be the back of the pack.

He thought of Hanlon, of their evening together at Strom/McEwan's magic show. He remembered how excited he had been when their legs had met and she hadn't pulled away; it was like being a kid again. He ran over the tactile memory of holding her warm, hard body against his, the feel of the outline of her underwear through the thin material of her dress, the unfathomable look in her grey eyes, usually so hard and watchful and now not. And then being called away to some utterly unimportant 'crisis' meeting that hadn't been a crisis at all.

Oliver Drummond's suspicious bank activities had come to light and both Munroe and London were excited about it. Drummond had been hauled in again for questioning.

He sighed and opened up LinkedIn on his PC. Well, as soon as he was finished trying to track down Anna Reynolds and Karen Ross, he'd call Hanlon. He wanted a fail-safe date, one that couldn't go wrong, one where he would make sure to emphasise to all and sundry he would be uncontactable and have the intelligence to turn his phone off, not just to silent.

He found Karen Ross easily enough. He glanced through her career history and her current job; he looked at her exemplary educational career, the first in Maths from Glasgow, the marathon running, the volunteering at an animal sanctuary. Anyone less likely to be a criminal might have come across his desk, but he found it hard to think of an example.

Anna Reynolds was a slightly different prospect. He found her on LinkedIn and she had helpfully given her Instagram details. He looked at multiple images of Anna leading the high life, partying in the Caribbean and the South of France. Lobster, champagne and ice sculptures seemed to form quite a part of her life. A much more likely candidate for relieving the innocent of their savings and she had the kind of face that would tick all the boxes: hard-faced, shrewd, quite a lot of surgical cosmetic work done that would not have come cheap. (What would Karen Ross squander stolen money on, he wondered, new trainers? Repair work for the dogs' home?)

He e-mailed Anna Reynolds to arrange an interview with her regarding Duachy Island. He left it deliberately vague.

He looked at his list of reminders. He had staff appraisals that needed doing, a task he had been putting off that really had to be done by the end of day.

He'd do it in a minute. He looked out of the window again. He was trying to remember how Hanlon had smelled when he kissed her, a heavy, sensual perfume and a hint of sweat that he'd found extraordinarily erotic. He wondered what she was doing right now.

Something more interesting than staff appraisals, he guessed.

25

Hanlon heard Callum's trainers slapping on the road surface as he ran towards her. Jesus, did he never give up? She turned around, wearily.

The blue tracksuited figure with dyed-blond hair. Something in his hand. God, he's got a knife, she thought with alarm. Several thoughts flashed through her head with lightning speed. First the physical situation. They were still on the road leading down to the farm, effectively alone, no witnesses, no possibility of a car passing by to disturb him, to make him think again.

Could she run? On one side of the farm track was the green waterlogged grass field that she had struggled through earlier to climb the hill that overlooked the commune. On the other, gorse bushes and bog myrtle. There was what looked like a path that emerged close to where she was standing. She hadn't noticed it before. She guessed that it would lead down to the houses where Dan lived, a shortcut up to the main road. Hanlon was a good runner, but a good distance runner. If she turned her back on him he could possibly catch her. The thought of being knifed in the back was horrific, and, not only that, she wouldn't stand a chance afterwards.

So, no running.

Was there anything she could use as a weapon? Even a length of wood would be something, but there was nothing.

She was wearing a hoody. She pulled it off and wrapped it round her left arm as the kid stopped running. He could see that she was going to stand and fight. He glanced down meaningfully at the knife in his hand and slowly back at her. The meaning was cruelly obvious.

Light on his feet, eyes moving rapidly, he was obviously completely out of his head, she could see now as he walked towards her. Hanlon backed away slowly, eyes fixed on the sharp blade.

* * *

Murdo Campbell walked up to the large front door of the imposing Victorian house just outside the village of Cardross near Dumbarton. He rang the bell, hearing the noise echoing sonorously in the airy depths of the house.

He heard footsteps and the door opened.

Anna Reynolds, round about fiftyish he guessed and still attractive, the skin of her jaw tight against the line of the bone, well dressed in an elegant skirt and a patterned silk blouse, her make-up low-key and immaculate, stood looking at him with frank interest. Murdo felt he was being mentally undressed. He tried not to blush as he produced his warrant card.

'Do come in, Detective Inspector,' she said. He smiled and entered the house. The hallway was tiled, as carefully looked after as its owner. He looked at the floor and then at his feet. 'Don't worry about your shoes, Inspector,' Anna said. Her voice was very cool and collected. Campbell walked inside and glanced up at the staircase. He thought back to Bly and his girlfriend young enough to be his daughter. He wondered if any moment now a twenty-year-old boy would appear at the top on the landing and say he was off to play football. There was even a Porsche parked in the drive next to a Range Rover Evoque. Anna could toss him the keys – 'Take the Porsche, darling...' – then say with a leer, staring at his bum, 'Not bad, eh! Half my age.'

'Come through into the lounge,' Anna said, holding out an ushering arm.

Murdo walked into the high-ceilinged room. He looked out of the huge bay window. The view of the River Clyde, snaking its way down to the sea, very wide at this point, the far-away hills near Port Glasgow rising green in the distance, was spectacular.

'Yes, it's lovely, isn't it?' She had obviously guessed what was in his mind. 'Can I get you a drink?'

'No, thanks, I'll get straight down to business.'

'Suki Bly?'

He nodded. 'Suki Bly.'

* * *

The kid was holding the knife at just above waist height. He closed in on Hanlon, who moved sideways to her right as she would have done if she'd been in a ring. He jabbed at her with the knife. It was a clumsy motion and as she recoiled he took a step closer. He blinked, trying to focus properly.

She had all her attention on him, then she was aware of movement behind him. It was Charlie! Hope rose in her heart, although what use a man in his seventies could be against an armed young thug was anyone's guess. Callum hadn't heard him. Charlie emerged from the footpath onto the farm road and was now standing behind the kid. There was a blur of movement and a loud, solid thud, the kind of noise you heard when you dropped something onto a wooden floor from a height. The kid collapsed on the ground in front of her, blood pouring from the top of his head, turning the blond hair a deep red, his eyes closed.

Hanlon stared in disbelief and gratitude at Charlie, who stood behind the fallen boy, beard bristling, holding a long black heavy boat hook in his hand.

'Are you OK, lassie?' he asked her. 'Did this wee shite hurt you?'

'I'm fine...' she said. She didn't feel fine. Her legs were beginning to tremble and she felt horribly light-headed – shock, she guessed. There was a large boulder by the side of the road and she sat down on it heavily before her legs gave way and she collapsed.

'What...?'

What are you doing here? was what she meant to say. How did this happen?

'I deliver fish to those kids who live doon there on a Wednesday,' he said. 'I thought I recognised you, and when this wee pluke took a notion tae follow you, I thought it would not be to chase after you with a bunch of flowers, so I came up the side path.'

The kid stirred and groaned, but his eyes were still closed. Hanlon stood up. She felt a bit better now. She frowned. She was going to have to go back down to Dan's. What was she going to do with her attacker?

'Charlie, I've got to go back down there. I need to speak to someone... I don't know what to do about him.'

They both contemplated the boy. Blood was running freely from the gash in his head.

'We should take him to hospital...' she said.

'It was only a wee tap on the heid,' Charlie protested.

The top of his head looked dreadful, his hair full of blood, both fresh and matted.

'He should get looked at. His skull could be fractured.'

'The Lord will decide,' Charlie said piously. He saw the look on her face and then he said, 'OK, you can haud your wheesht. I'll take him to Oban for you.'

'Thanks,' she said.

He put his hands in the pocket of his old tweed jacket and took out a length of baling twine and secured the kid's hands behind his back, using the knife that Callum had dropped to cut it. The tough string parted effortlessly. The old man looked up at Hanlon. 'If he'd got tae using that on you, you wouldnae be going tae hospital, it'd be the morgue.'

He lashed Callum's feet together at the ankles.

'What was he doing down there?' she asked, pointing down the track.

'Selling drugs, I would imagine, what else? The devil's work.' He cut the string, stood up and threw Callum's knife away in a high arc into the bushes. He dragged the kid, still unconscious, to the side of the road.

'I'll go back and get my truck that's down there and take him to the hospital. I'll drop him near the entrance. I'm not getting involved. Someone will find him.'

'Thanks, Charlie,' Hanlon said.

'There's no need to thank anyone for doing the Lord's work,' Charlie said a little stiffly, as if slightly embarrassed at her gratitude that he had probably saved her life. 'You take care now, young lady.'

He turned and walked off down the track. Hanlon took a last look at her attacker, still unconscious by the side of the road. She shook her head in sadness. She wasn't angry any more. She'd beaten him twice, but what had she ever done to provoke him in the first place? Nothing, just been in the wrong place at the wrong time, peacefully going to work to meet O'Rourke, and the whole thing had spiralled from there. It made no sense but sometimes things didn't.

Maybe that was what had happened to Suki Bly, the wrong place at the wrong time. Sometimes things really were that simple and that tragic.

She walked back to her car and drove down the track to the commune. On the way down she pulled over to let Charlie's battered old Toyota Hilux pass her by. They waved at each other and she felt a wave of affection for the old fisherman who had stepped in to help her. For a man in his seventies he was powerfully strong. And not only that, he was prepared to act. Maybe it was his faith that made him so strong. Dan could do with some old-time religion; heroin dependency wasn't working out too well. Perhaps Charlie could take him to the kirk on Sunday. Sing a few psalms.

She parked outside Dan's house and went inside. She felt a heightened sense of excitement, expectation and curiosity about what he would reveal about Camille.

* * *

'I must have known Suki for about a year, over a year,' Anna Reynolds said. 'We became quite good friends.' She had made herself a cup of herbal tea, which smelt quite unappealing to Campbell's nose. She had a sip. 'Are you sure you don't want some?'

'Yes, thanks.'

She shrugged. 'It's very detoxing, chamomile. I grow it out the back. It's 100 per cent organic, I dry it, add some other herbs, and some tea as well. I give it to Camille as well. She swears by it.'

'I'm OK, honestly.'

Anna continued. 'Suki had changed a lot over the last year. She came to the yoga class initially because she was going through a divorce... Have you met her ex?'

'I have actually,' said Campbell.

'He's one of those Glaswegians who makes you embarrassed to be Glaswegian,' said Anna. She looked up at a framed wedding photo. 'My deceased husband was from Laurieston, the Gorbals as was. You could not have met a gentler, kinder man, but then there's folk like John Bly glamourising violence and people think, oh, aye, your typical Glaswegian hard man. I think we're well overdue a rebrand.'

'I know what you mean,' Campbell said.

'Anyway, she was very unhappy, but Suki was one of those very needy people. She fell for Camille.'

'She was in love with Camille?'

Anna frowned. 'Not sexually, no, not really. She just wanted someone to adore. I think that she and her ex had been part of some kind of wife-swapping group, swingers... Are they still called that? It sounds very dated.'

'I'm afraid I don't know,' said Campbell.

'Doesn't matter. Really, she had been little more than Bly's whore, I think. She told me as much once when we'd gone out for the evening together and she'd got hammered. I think she might have actually been a call girl before they were married. She was very boastful about her abilities sexually...'

Campbell remembered her ex confirming this.

'But recently she didn't have any ongoing troubles with men?'

Anna shook her head. 'There was no one in her life, not romantically or relationship-wise.'

'Did you know that she'd been defrauded of a lot of money recently?' Campbell asked.

'No, no, I didn't, she never mentioned it.' She shook her head firmly. 'We never discussed money.'

'She never asked you for financial advice?'

Anna looked him straight in the eyes. 'Never, Inspector.'

Campbell said, 'It's possible that one of the reasons she was on Duachy was because she was going to confront the fraudster, that she might have recognised them, does that ring any bells?'

'No.'

'And she didn't give any signs of recognition at all?' he asked.

Anna shook her head. 'No, Inspector, there was no kind of "aha!" moment at all that I was aware of, none whatsoever.'

He looked at her self-assured, composed face. He felt that if Anna wanted to lie, he would never be able to read it as such on her controlled features. Well, that was all he was going to get from her.

'Thank you very much for your time,' he said.

'You're welcome.' She stood up and smoothed her skirt. 'Let me show you out.'

They stood for a moment on the broad front steps of her house, the magnificent view stretching away in front of them. The borders of the front garden were hardly any less spectacular. They were a riot of colour, nasturtiums, geraniums and tall back-of-border plants, foxgloves.

'Your garden's beautiful,' he said.

She flushed with pleasure. 'Thank you, but I cheat a lot. Most of these plants naturally do well in Scotland, and of course the foxgloves self-seed, which is a boon. Well, I hope you catch Suki's fraudster, not to mention whoever pushed her off that cliff.'

'Thank you.' He walked away down the path back to his car.

* * *

Hanlon called out, 'Hello, Dan, it's me again,' as she walked into the house through the still-open front door. No response. She rolled her eyes; she hoped he wasn't too far gone.

She walked into the living room.

She knew he was dead immediately.

He was on the sofa, head thrown back, eyes open and mouth ajar. Unmoving.

God, no! 'Dan!' she shouted. No reaction.

Hanlon felt a jolt of alarm; surely he must be OK. He couldn't have died? She ran over to him. There was no pulse. She held his face between her hands and stared into his eyes, ridiculous she knew, but she was hoping for some reaction, for his eyelids to blink and flicker into life. But, of course, there was nothing.

She knelt down in front of him and bowed her head.

Whatever he was going to tell her about Camille would remain a mystery.

She shook her head both in sadness, although what had happened had been surely only a matter of time, and irritation. Perhaps I could get Strom to do a seance, she thought. That'll be the only way I'll ever find out.

She took her phone out and called the emergency services, explained the situation and settled down to wait.

26

The following day she drove to Hillhead where the yoga studio was and parked her car. She walked through streets that, after the quiet of Argyll, seemed amazingly busy. She wondered if she would ever live in a city again. It seemed odd after a lifetime of living in London to be living, and enjoying living, in a part of the world that held so few people, but then again, reflected Hanlon, it wasn't as if she ever made much use of London's cultural heritage. She rarely went to museums, galleries or the theatre. She didn't listen to music; she was indifferent to food. It was hardly surprising that the relatively deserted west of Scotland should feel so like home. As she walked into the yoga studio, she decided that habit rather than anything else had kept her in London, and habits were notoriously hard to break.

'Hi,' she said to the young girl behind reception, 'I'm here to see Camille – my name's Hanlon.'

'Of course... would you like to wait in the café while I find her?'

Hanlon walked into the café, the first time that she'd been in there since the attempt on Camille's life. She thought about all the events that had happened since then. It seemed an awfully long time ago now.

She looked into the kitchen behind the counter. There was a new girl in chef's whites, Jenny's replacement presumably.

A waiter she didn't recognise greeted her and led her to a table by the window where she ordered an Americano. She looked again at the kitchen. Now she saw Siobhan – the bright kitchen light glinted off the stud in her nose as she took a sauté pan off the stove and began to plate up someone's lunch. The other woman noticed her and inclined her head in greeting.

The café was half full – about twenty or so people were eating in it. It was a good advertisement for the yoga studio. The space was calm and relaxed, the food looked and smelled good, it was pleasantly civilised.

Camille walked in and conversation stopped as the faithful glimpsed the Messiah. Hanlon looked at her with deep suspicion as she walked towards her table.

Camille was wearing a long man's shirt that reached to her thighs over her leggings and Lycra top. Her blonde hair was tied back in a loose ponytail; she gleamed with health and well-being.

Seeing Camille brought back memories, vivid images of Dan.

She had sat opposite the dead musician for about half an hour whilst waiting for the police and the ambulance to arrive. She remembered how he had looked. Thank God his eyes had been closed, but the contrast between the healthy glow of Camille's radiant skin and Dan's slightly sallow pallor could not have been more marked. Yet something, some shared secret, had bound this unlikely couple together.

She'd had a quick look around upstairs at his house. More squalor. The contrast between Dan's bedroom and this bright, airy café with its green plants and Buddha statues was dramatic.

It had been more or less as she had expected: a mattress on the floor, a cheap pine chest of drawers that had seen better days, a bin bag full of dirty washing that smelled of bacterial mould and damp. She'd been wondering whether to go through his belongings looking for some kind of clue as to what he was blackmailing Camille with, but she'd thought better of it. She hadn't known what she was looking for and she really hadn't wanted to touch anything in Dan's place, it had all been so grotty.

One thing was for sure, she'd thought as she'd surveyed his sad, filthy bedroom, he hadn't been having an affair with Siobhan's elder sister.

Who now sat down brightly opposite Hanlon.

'Good to see you!' Camille said, her brown eyes warm. 'How have you been?'

'I'm fine,' Hanlon said, her voice tight. She was convinced that Dan's overdose was not self-inflicted. Junkies had a reasonably good knowledge of dosages and she doubted that Kevin's heroin was super-strength. If it was, she reasoned, he would have warned her. She felt that Dan's death was almost certainly linked somehow to Camille and here was Camille, certainly on the surface, completely untouched by his demise. It seemed unfair. Somewhere there would be a mother grieving for her son. Dan could only have been, what, mid-to-late twenties? A talented musician who would never fulfil his potential now. The mother might well be not that much older than her or Camille. Who was sitting serenely, smugly smiling at her. Hanlon felt an overwhelming desire to puncture her self-satisfied bubble.

'And you?' she asked.

'I'm OK...' She looked at Hanlon's coffee. 'Can I get you another one of those?'

'No, I'm fine.'

The waiter appeared and Camille said, 'I'll have an elderflower spritz, Michael.'

The kid nodded and walked away.

'Now,' Camille said, 'how is the investigation going?'

'Suki Bly had been defrauded of a great deal of money,' Hanlon said.

Camille's eyes widened in astonishment, a pantomime look of surprise. 'Really! Oh, my God...'

'Yes,' Hanlon said, 'really.' She looked hard at Camille. She wondered if Camille would feel alarm bells ringing at the conjoined sound of fraud, money and Suki. Was she even now thinking of Suki's loan to her? Or, like Dan's death, had that been relegated to history?

Well, she was going to find out who had killed Suki no matter where it led. If it upset Camille, so be it. Hanlon needed money, she was only too aware of that, but she needed to appease her own conscience more than she needed a healthy bank account.

'Suki had been taken for a six-figure ride,' she said. 'She suspected that the person responsible was going to be on Duachy... but then, of course, she died... Do you know anything about it?'

'Of course not!' Camille was indignant. 'What do you take me for? I'd have told you.' She looked hurt. The conversation was taking a turn she could hardly have planned for. It was probably many a year since anyone had accused her of anything.

'Well,' Hanlon said, her cold grey eyes boring into Camille's, 'you do sometimes have trouble with your memory, don't you, Camille?'

Camille's eyes widened. People simply didn't speak to her like this. She glanced around her to check that there were no eavesdroppers to their conversation. Hanlon noticed this, a sure sign, to her way of thinking, of a guilty conscience.

'What do you mean?' she asked. Hanlon carried remorselessly on.

'You forgot to tell me that Suki lent you money, didn't she...' here Hanlon went out on a limb and took a guess, 'to prop up your finances...? You should have mentioned that Camille.'

'I didn't...'

'At least sixty K, wasn't it, Camille?' Her cold grey eyes bored into the woman opposite. 'Or was it more? Poor Suki Bly, everybody's cash cow. Her death was very convenient for several people, wasn't it?'

Camille had gone very pale; she licked her lips. 'I think you should leave now, Hanlon...'

Hanlon leaned forward menacingly. She was surprised at the fury that was welling up inside her. Camille's world was all very lovely on the outside, the meditation, the yoga in expensive clothes on a pricey yoga mat in a chic area of Glasgow, the Instagrammable plant-based food, the mindfulness schtick, but inside, borrowing money from a needy friend, paying her sister's ex blackmail money, the ill-judged advice that had led to Niamh's death, the story appeared to be very different. Hanlon suddenly thought of Charlie – he'd have a phrase from the Bible ready: whitewashed tombs and sepulchres, all looking nice and pretty on the outside, the rotting bodies within.

'Well, at least you'll be saving a fortune now that Dan Murray's dead. Think of all that hush money you don't have to fork out.'

Camille glared at her, lips compressed, saying nothing.

'That's right, Camille,' she continued. 'I found Dan and he told me that you were paying him off. Would you mind coming clean and telling me why, or do I have to find that out by myself? Because I will, you know.'

Camille was on her feet now. 'Get out!' she hissed, pointed at the door. 'Get out of my building and my life, you bitch.'

'That's a no, then, I take it,' Hanlon said acidly. She stood up. Michael the waiter came over.

'Is everything OK, Camille?' he asked nervously.

Camille pointed to Hanlon. 'Get her off the premises!'

Michael looked at Hanlon in alarm. He put out a tentative hand towards her.

'If you touch me, Michael,' Hanlon said in a conversational tone, staring at him menacingly, 'I'll break your fucking nose.'

He withdrew his hand in alarm. Hanlon noticed that the other diners had all stopped eating and were staring at them. Siobhan had come to the front of the kitchen and was watching them over the shiny metal of the pass. Hanlon guessed that she would be delighted by what was going on.

'Drishti – you taught me that word, Camille.' Hanlon pointed an accusatory finger and Camille flinched. 'Drishti, focus. Well, Camille, I'm focussed on finding out who killed Suki, and, Camille, I am not going to stop!'

She turned and left the restaurant.

* * *

Hanlon walked back to her car. She felt full of unreleased anger. It was a good job that Michael had heeded her warning – in her present mood she would have flattened him.

She took several deep breaths. Then she felt a stab of guilt. She was falling back into her old ways of thinking and behaviour, a default mode of violence. The fact that it was possibly linked to the stress of recent events was no excuse. Hanlon's chosen way of life involved investigating criminality. If she couldn't stand the heat, she reasoned, she shouldn't be going into the kitchen.

Violence was fine if it was called for, if she was defending herself, for example. She felt no guilt over Callum or Oliver Drummond, but back there in the restaurant she'd realised that nothing would have given her greater pleasure than to smash Michael in the face, slap Camille and knock her off her chair and then kick over a few tables. Maybe destroy a few plates while she was at it. It was the behaviour pattern of a psychotic toddler.

She thought of her therapist, Dr Morgan. She made a mental promise to seek her help, soon.

Sitting back in the Volvo, she thought about the incident the day before on Seil. What could Dan have possibly known about that would have led Camille to have allowed herself to be blackmailed?

Could it have been something to do with the commune itself?

She typed in a search on her mobile for the Scottish land registers office, then entered the name of Claonnaidh Farm. After a short while and the payment of a fee, the name of the owner came up on the screen. Hanlon's eyes widened in astonishment. The owner of the commune was listed as Shane Gowrie, the rock star who had previously owned the Duachy Hotel.

She had been planning on returning home, but now she thought she'd have to stay on in Glasgow just a few hours longer. She needed more information on Camille and there was only one person who could help her.

* * *

There was a bar opposite the yoga studio and it had a window that overlooked the studio's entrance. There was a long, tall, narrow table that ran the length of the pub window with high stools and power points so you could plug your laptop in and work from there. Hanlon walked in at about five o'clock and sat in between two twenty-somethings who were drinking fruit juice and a smoothie. She got a Diet Coke from the bar, opened her laptop and pretended to look at her screen while she kept an eye on the door opposite.

She knew from the online timetable that Camille's last class ended at about quarter past five. Sure enough, at half past, she saw women and a couple of men leaving the building holding rolled-up yoga mats. Although there were changing rooms, most people seemed happy not to bother, to just wear their yoga clothes home. She noticed Anna Reynolds, looking carefree, leave and head up the street.

Then Camille herself appeared. She had changed. She was wearing a tan raincoat, a white blouse worn unbuttoned over a white T, blue jeans and chunky white trainers. Her long blonde hair gleamed in the evening sun. She looked very pretty, Hanlon thought, and absurdly young. She also looked worried, as well she might, Hanlon thought grimly.

What was it that Dan knew, wondered Hanlon as she stared at the innocent face across the street, that you were so desperate to keep hidden? Well, I'm going to find out.

Camille walked off, small and elegant, in the opposite direction to Anna. Next out was Siobhan. She was wearing black jeans and a grey satin blouse with chunky black boots. The afternoon sun glinted on her face piercings, the nose stud and the dermal and the rings in her ears. There was something about Siobhan that was quite frightening. A quality that was non-existent in Camille. Maybe it was the self-possession, maybe the inner hardness that the woman seemed to have. She looked around her, as if she was expecting someone, and then crossed the road heading for the bar where Hanlon was sitting.

Her heart sank. Seeing Siobhan was the last thing that she wanted to do. Although she suspected that Siobhan was long past any feelings whatsoever as far as Dan was concerned, she still did not relish the thought of having to go through Dan's last few minutes on earth with her. Nor did she want to have to explain what she was doing lurking in the bar. Siobhan seemed to be heading straight for the bar door. Hanlon bowed her head and hid behind her laptop screen, which seemed wholly inadequate, but fortunately Siobhan didn't come in, instead heading off up the road.

Hanlon breathed a sigh of relief. Ten minutes later she saw the woman she was waiting for.

O'Rourke, tall and elegant as ever, in dark, straight-leg trousers, her hair down for a change, a splash of dark red against the ivory colour of her blue dotted silk shirt, left the studio.

Hanlon quickly packed her things up, slipped off her stool and left the bar.

She followed O'Rourke through the streets of Glasgow. It was easy – she didn't look behind her once. Ten minutes later they had left the area of Hillhead and then they crossed the Great Western Road into the Botanic Gardens.

The park was quite full with groups of people enjoying the late afternoon sun. O'Rourke hadn't noticed Hanlon. Here seemed as good a place to speak to her as any. Hanlon increased her pace and caught her up.

'Hello.'

O'Rourke stopped and looked round. When she saw it was Hanlon, a guarded expression settled on her face. People never seem overjoyed to see me, Hanlon reflected ruefully.

'Hello, Hanlon.' She paused. 'Have you been following me?'

'I needed to talk to you,' Hanlon said. 'I'm not exactly welcome in the yoga studios.'

'You can say that again,' O'Rourke said. 'I've never seen Camille so upset.' She looked at Hanlon with curiosity. 'What did you say to her?'

'Well, I suggested she shouldn't lie so much,' Hanlon said, raising an eyebrow.

'How do you mean?' O'Rourke frowned.

A couple who'd been sitting on a bench by the path finished their conversation, stood up and moved away.

'Shall we?' asked Hanlon, motioning towards the bench.

O'Rourke nodded and they sat down together. O'Rourke's expression was one of scepticism.

'So, what exactly did you say to her?' she asked Hanlon.

Hanlon thought for a moment and then decided to bring up the commune first. Talk of Suki's loan might well spook O'Rourke – she almost certainly had to be involved in that herself.

'What do you know about the commune that Siobhan used to live on?' Hanlon asked.

O'Rourke thought this over and then said, 'Very little. It's on Seil, obviously. I'm guessing those houses are ex-forestry and they got sold off to someone cheap when the forestry closed that operation down. I went there a couple of times running errands for Camille. Basically she wanted to know how her sister was. She was very concerned about her at the time.'

'That's when she was living with Dan?'

'Correct.'

O'Rourke's phone went. She pulled it out of her pocket and glanced at it, then turned it to silent and put it on the arm of the bench where she could keep an eye on it.

'What sort of things was Camille concerned about?' asked Hanlon.

O'Rourke shrugged. 'Lifestyle issues, drugs, that drummer she was going out with was a total mess...'

'He's dead,' Hanlon said.

O'Rourke looked at her, startled. Hanlon explained that she'd been there more or less when it happened; she omitted the part about her buying heroin for Dan.

Now she decided to see what O'Rourke would make of the connection with Camille.

'Dan was blackmailing Camille,' she said.

O'Rourke looked confused. 'Dan?' she said incredulously. 'What on earth are you talking about?'

'At the gig I went to see Dan. He told me that Camille was paying him to keep his mouth shut.'

'Why? What reason could Camille possibly have for that? I don't believe a word of this, Hanlon.'

She pressed ahead. 'I went to visit him the following day. He died of a drugs overdose while I was absent for half an hour.'

O'Rourke looked at her quizzically. 'Do you think he killed himself? OD'd?'

'No, no, I don't.' She shook her head. 'Dan had been jacking up smack for years. It would be an amazing coincidence if the moment he took too much coincided with my visit. I was out of the house when he died. I think someone helped him on his way to that great gig in the sky.'

O'Rourke nodded. She said to Hanlon, 'I can't imagine what kind of a hold he might have over her.' Her tone was final. The look on her face made that clear.

Well, that was that avenue exhausted.

'Did you know that Claonnaidh Farm is owned by Shane Gowrie?' asked Hanlon.

'What, *the* Shane Gowrie, the old rock star?'

'I would imagine so.' The information obviously meant nothing to O'Rourke. Hanlon had been studying her face, hoping for some sort of reaction. But there was none. Well, that had got her nowhere. Now she moved the conversation on to more dangerous grounds.

'Suki Bly – how much money exactly did she lend Camille?'

Now Hanlon could see the shutters coming down.

'How do you mean, Hanlon?' O'Rourke said, picking her words carefully. Hanlon could feel anger begin to well up inside her. This was getting to be a repeat performance of the conversation with Camille. She had expected more from O'Rourke. She had thought she had integrity.

In a way she didn't mind people like Dan, or even that violent nutcase Callum, behaving badly. They were low-lifes, that was what people like them did, but when people who claimed to occupy the moral high-ground started, then she saw red. Hypocrisy, that was what really turned her stomach.

'It's a simple question.'

'Sixty thousand.'

Hanlon looked at her. O'Rourke was visibly squirming; it was a look that didn't suit her at all. She was lying.

'Why are you covering for her, Katherine?' Hanlon asked, her grey eyes boring into O'Rourke's green ones.

'What do you mean?'

'I know you're lying.' Hanlon looked at her angrily. Then she said something she immediately regretted. It was the verbal equivalent of lashing out. 'Why protect her, after what she did to you?'

The effect on O'Rourke was electric. She stiffened and as Hanlon looked at her, two red spots appeared on her high cheekbones and her face flushed crimson. The blush of rage worked its way visibly up her pale skin, from the base of her neck to the top of her cheekbones, like mercury rising in a thermometer.

'You know!' She was suddenly furious. 'How dare you bring Niamh into this? How fucking dare you?'

Hanlon was aware of having crossed a line she never should have; the damage was done now.

'I'm sorry,' she said, trying to backtrack, aware of her dreadful error of judgement.

'How did you find out? Have you been spying on me... you have, haven't you?'

'I'm a detective – you hired me,' Hanlon said flatly.

'It's not like you've ever had any children,' O'Rourke spat, 'which is probably a good thing, you nasty bitch.'

She stood up. 'Don't ever come near me again, Hanlon, OK, just don't!' She turned and marched away across the park. Hanlon watched her go. She sighed heavily. She'd handled that terribly.

She realised that she didn't care too much about what Camille thought, but she'd grown to really like O'Rourke and now she'd irrevocably destroyed their relationship.

'Shit,' she said out loud. O'Rourke had been so furious, so eager to storm off that she'd left her phone on the bench. Hanlon picked it up; she was still visible in the distance. Hanlon stood up and, moving in an easy jog, set off after her.

O'Rourke had reached the gate on the north side of the gardens. She turned and saw Hanlon, who waved, holding her phone aloft. O'Rourke ignored her and walked through the gate. Hanlon quickened her pace to a sprint and reached the gate just as O'Rourke crossed the road ahead.

'Hey, Katherine... your phone!' shouted Hanlon.

O'Rourke turned and looked back at her, her right hand went to her bag to check, and then, quite suddenly, she staggered backwards as though an invisible hand had punched her, her legs buckling, and she collapsed, almost in slow motion, onto the pavement.

Hanlon had heard the noise, a car backfiring, she'd thought; she had ignored it. Now she ran across the road to O'Rourke. As soon as she reached her and saw the blood she realised it hadn't been a car she'd heard. O'Rourke had been shot. She looked around the empty street, no one visible. What to do? Try and chase down the shooter? Run for cover? Help O'Rourke? She turned her attention to the injured woman.

O'Rourke was half lying on the pavement, her hand pressed to just under her ribs, blood pouring out between her fingers. Not trickling, pouring. Oh, God, thought Hanlon. She ripped off her denim jacket, wadding it up, pressing it to the wound, in a futile attempt to stem the bleeding.

O'Rourke looked up at her, her face chalk white... 'Oh, God, it hurts, Hanlon...'

'You'll be OK,' Hanlon said, with an authority and an assurance she didn't feel. She pulled her phone out of her back pocket and pressed nine nine nine with her bloody fingers, gave details. Cars drove by but no one stopped.

O'Rourke smiled. 'I'm sorry.' Her eyes closed and Hanlon suddenly felt her body relax as she exhaled her last breath. Hanlon looked down at O'Rourke's face, beautiful in death, and felt tears fill her eyes. In the distance she could hear sirens.

'Goodbye, Katherine,' she whispered. She leaned forward and gently kissed her forehead.

27

Two days later, Hanlon sat in bed and balanced her laptop on her knees. She had scheduled a Zoom call with Dr Morgan; this was it.

She had spent the previous forty-eight hours grieving. An unaccustomed black depression had taken her over. Over and over in her head, replaying those final moments with O'Rourke. Walking for miles with Wemyss in the hills above where she lived to try and exorcise the misery with exercise. Eventually she did what she should have done from the very start: sought help.

Now the familiar feelings of unaccustomed worry were rising up inside her. Hanlon really disliked talking about herself. It made her feel uncomfortable and exposed, a kind of emotional nakedness that she hated.

She followed the prompts on her screen. Dr Morgan's consulting room appeared on the screen.

'Hello, Hanlon,' she said. 'How are you?'

Hanlon studied the therapist and her background while she marshalled her thoughts. The large, spacious, airy room had been redecorated since she had seen it last. It was now a pale grey, on the walls were some paintings she didn't recognise, abstract art.

'I'm fine,' she said. 'Actually, no, I'm not... I feel terrible...'

'Tell me,' the therapist said.

Hanlon did so and for the next half-hour she poured her heart out to Dr Morgan, who listened, occasionally commenting on issues that Hanlon raised. The terrible moments in the sea with Suki, watching her be swept away in front of her. The ghastly sight of Jenny hanging from the ceiling of the chapel like a human pendulum, her helplessness with the dying O'Rourke. She was beginning to wonder how much more of this she could actually take.

After they had finished talking about the death of Katherine, Duachy Island and Camille, she felt emotionally drained but far better than she had expected. It was as if she had had a painful swelling lanced, a kind of spiritual abscess drained. She felt more relaxed now. She shifted the conversation to a neutral topic.

'Are those paintings new?'

'New to this room,' Dr Morgan said, looking over her shoulder. 'They're by Roland Penrose and those two are by Desmond Morris. Do you like them?'

Hanlon studied them. They looked as if someone had taken a dream and framed it. She said as much to Dr Morgan, who brightened like a teacher with a clever student.

'They're surrealist paintings... those artists are considerably influenced by ideas of the unconscious mind.'

'They're not my cup of tea,' Hanlon said. Dr Morgan's eyebrows rose; she was clearly not interested in Hanlon's contribution to art criticism.

'And I'm sure your subconscious mind is not a lot of people's cup of tea, your own included, but you're stuck with it,' said the doctor, slightly combatively, Hanlon thought. She frowned. Dr Morgan noticed.

'I'm not here to flatter you, Hanlon,' she remarked with asperity. 'Why has it taken so long to get in touch with me?'

She looked at the therapist while she tried to come up with a credible excuse. Dr Morgan was elegant as ever, in a dark blouse, a string of pearls at her throat; her short white hair was immaculate, her face tanned and fit-looking. But it was the eyes that were her stand-out feature. They seemed to have an alarming intensity, like a painter's blowtorch, able to strip away lies and deceit to reveal the soul underneath.

Dr Morgan coughed gently to get her attention.

'I guess things had been going well I felt I didn't need you,' she admitted candidly.

'Until they weren't,' said Dr Morgan. She sighed. 'Hanlon, we've been through this. You need a bridge to normalcy. Just because things go well for a while doesn't mean you can take your foot off the gas.'

'I'm not disagreeing with you,' Hanlon said, slightly irritably. 'I'm here now.' She was immediately aware of how ungracious that sounded. It was as if she were doing Dr Morgan a favour; the reality was very much the other way round. Dr Morgan was much sought after and very expensive. She was treating Hanlon as a pro bono patient, a charity case basically.

'Indeed you are, and about time too,' said Dr Morgan drily, 'and where is "here", by the way?'

Hanlon stood up and wandered around her room with her laptop, giving Dr Morgan a guided tour of her room.

She sat down at the table. 'So this is where I'm living.' Wemyss wandered over and put his front paws on her thigh and peered at the screen. 'I'm not alone, as you can see.'

'So you've still got Wemyss?'

'Of course,' she said.

'I guess that's your longest relationship ever?'

Hanlon frowned, then did some mental arithmetic. 'Yes, that's actually true,' she admitted.

Dr Morgan smiled. 'Are you in a relationship with anyone at the moment?'

Hanlon found herself telling her about Murdo Campbell. Now she had told her about Katherine, talking was hard to stop. The parallel with what had happened the other night with Oliver Drummond was uncomfortable. He hadn't been able to shut up either, for very similar reasons. She found herself sharing this insight with Dr Morgan.

'Well, I can't fault your honesty, Hanlon. Not many people would admit to similarities with a man like him. What conclusions can you draw from that?'

'That I have a lack of friends... I think that's why I've been so shaken by Katherine's death.'

'Did you see her as a potential friend?'

Hanlon nodded. 'I liked her. I liked her a lot... It's not a common feeling. I felt I had something in common with her – we were both outsiders.' She stood up restlessly. 'I'll be frank with you, Doctor... most people bore me rigid and if I'm with them I think, Jesus, what's the point? What am I getting out of this? This is such a waste of my time. I'm just looking at my watch thinking when can I go...'

'And you don't find Murdo Campbell boring?' asked Dr Morgan.

'I don't think so... To be honest, I wasn't planning on doing much talking with him.'

Dr Morgan rolled her eyes. 'That's not a healthy recipe for happiness, Hanlon.'

She fell silent. She'd enjoyed their drink, their chat before the show with Strom. She shared that with Dr Morgan.

She nodded. 'So Strom doesn't bore you, then?' she said with evident interest.

'No, far from it. I think he's one of the most interesting people I've met in a long time.'

'But you wouldn't go out with him?'

Hanlon blinked in surprise. 'Strom, God, no way...'

'Why not? He's intelligent, entertaining, he doesn't bore you... He's ticking a lot of boxes.'

'He's also untrustworthy, quite possibly evil.'

'So, it's not just a question of being "interesting", then,' Dr Morgan said. 'You want friends with high moral fibre as well. Maybe you should think about compromise in your relationships, Hanlon, settle for "mildly interesting".'

'Maybe you're right.' She thought about Strom. He was certainly charismatic enough, certainly attractive enough, but he was just too sinister.

'Tell me more about this case you're working on.'

Briefly, Hanlon described the events that had unfolded over the previous two weeks. At the mention of Duachy Island and Shane Gowrie, Dr Morgan's eyes widened,

'I used to know him,' she said. 'Well, I met him a few times in the mid-seventies.'

For a horrible moment Hanlon thought that she was going to say that she'd been his lover, as Camille had. She said as much and Dr Morgan laughed. 'I'm sure he probably tried… I was a second-year medic back then. I knew quite a few people in the rock business – my mother worked for RCA.'

'What was he like?' asked Hanlon.

'Very good-looking, very exotic. He was an early adopter of tattoos. Usually only criminals or merchant seamen had them way back then. He had an eagle tattooed on his left chest, round about here.' She circled the area around her left breast with an elegant hand. 'He was really crazy as well, not in a good sense either. He'd taken a lot of acid, which I doubt helped. I think it was him who got me into psychiatry. I think, in retrospect, he was paranoid schizophrenic. Is he still alive?'

'Seemingly,' Hanlon said, 'he's got dementia. He's in a home.'

'Sad,' Dr Morgan said. 'He had a son, I remember, he'd given him one of those stupid names like rock stars did in those days, Horus, that was it… Horus Gowrie.' She laughed. 'I'm sure he's changed it to something a bit more normal now.' She looked hard into the eye of the camera. 'Now,' she said, 'let's wrap this up for today.'

Then all too soon, their time was over. The screen went blank as the therapist terminated the call. Hanlon slumped in her chair, emotionally drained.

She went to the door, pulled on her training shoes. There was no need to call Wemyss, he was there immediately, wagging his tail, excited to go out.

She closed and locked the door behind her. The sky above was dark and threatening and she could feel a cold wind shaking the pines. Maybe the rain will hold off, she thought. They headed upwards, into the hills that stretched away for miles behind the house. Hanlon felt light on her feet, purged spiritually, cleansed by the therapy session. As she ran, Wemyss scurrying ahead of her, zigzag fashion, in his usual search for interesting smells, occasionally looking over his shoulder to check on her, she thought about what the doctor had said about Shane Gowrie. He'd had a son. In the mid-seventies, making him in his mid-forties now. She came to a steep slope and changed down a gear in her stride. She was good at running up hills. Some sort of metaphor there, she thought.

Horus, that had been the kid's name. Doubtless he'd changed it to something more normal... Paul, for example. But with showbiz in his blood, the desire to have a more unusual name had returned... Strom.

He was a good fit for the son of a rock-star. The choice of studies at university, ethnology, the experimentation with drugs to expand his consciousness. Shane Gowrie had been a fan of LSD, Dr Morgan had said. The apple didn't fall far from the bough. His father was famous for chasing women too – she could well imagine Strom being highly successful there. And was that what had attracted him to Camille, some kind of sick one-upmanship, screwing his father's one-night stand? Some variant of the Oedipus complex.

She vaulted across a drainage channel that had been cut across the path. In fairness to Strom, he probably didn't know about that. Just one of those cosmic coincidences that the hippies had been so fond of.

She heard Camille's voice echoing in her memory: *There are no coincidences. Paul Strom taught me that...*

She reached the top of the hill and stood for a moment, drinking in the view, the tops of the green pines swaying in the cool, fresh wind, the grey of the rock, mottled with lichen, streaked with quartz. Far away was the Atlantic, today a very blue colour under the sun, the sky to the west a much lighter blue than here where the heavens were dark with dramatic grey-black clouds heavy with the threat of rain.

Stop getting carried away, she told herself sternly. You don't actually know that Strom is Gowrie's son... but if he was, the old rock star now an incontinent, helpless, mindless mess in an old people's home, Horus Gowrie would have power of attorney over his father's affairs, he would have control over the farm where Gowrie had allowed the commune with its hippy ideals to settle and take root. Of course, now it had morphed into a kind of biker-cum-low-level-criminal hangout. But Strom would be their landlord, and Camille had been paying Dan to keep his mouth shut over something. And she and Strom were an item.

There had to be a connection.

Had it been he who had watched Hanlon arrive, possibly sent Callum after her, probably paid a visit to Dan and made damn sure he wouldn't trouble Camille any more?

She could easily imagine Strom dispassionately noting her arrival from an upstairs window of the farmhouse. Sending Callum after her. It would have suited his control freakery, the puppet-master pulling the strings.

There was a sudden rumble of thunder and Wemyss's tail drooped. He looked stricken and ran over to her for comfort. He hated thunder. She crouched down and put an arm around him to reassure him. There was another crack of thunder and far away, over the sea, she saw a fork of lightning. She felt Wemyss's warm body tremble with fear. She clipped a lead onto the ring on his collar. She was concerned that he might just bolt with terror, losing all sense of direction. If he did run off into these woods it would be impossible to find him without a great deal of luck.

She stood up. She could see the rain in the distance drifting towards her like smoke. 'Come on, dog,' she said, turning for home, and the first fat drops of rain started to land around them.

The run back was increasingly unpleasant. The wind had risen and what had been a warm afternoon was now feeling bitterly cold as she ran into the headwind, her T-shirt soaking and plastered to her body. The rain was blowing into her eyes, stinging them.

They ran up to the house, more thunder, the dog whimpering, and she threw the door open. Wemyss scurried inside, still trailing his lead, shook himself vigorously and ran to his basket to hide from the terrifying noise. Hanlon unlaced her soaking trail shoes, closing the door behind her, kicked the shoes off, took the lead off Wemyss and walked over to the kitchen area to make some coffee, pulling her wet clothes off as she went.

Her phone rang as she switched the kettle on, looking at the rain running down the outside of the window. Another roll of thunder. The ID of the caller was unknown.

'Hello?' she said.

'Hello, Hanlon.'

It was Strom.

28

'Hello, Strom...' She looked out of the window. Rain was streaming down the glass. 'What do you want?'

Strom laughed. 'That's not a very pleasant thing to say to someone.'

Hanlon said unapologetically, 'No, I suppose it's not.'

She couldn't help but feel that Strom was somehow playing with her in a kind of malicious way. It was as if he knew what was going on, like in the child's party game 'pin the tail on the donkey' where the person wearing the blindfold is guessing wildly, to the amusement of the sighted spectators. Her and Strom.

Her recent thoughts returned to her in a rush. If her Strom/Gowrie thesis was true, then he owned the commune where Dan had died; he was the bikers' landlord. Someone had given Dan a fatal overdose. It was very easy to imagine Strom watching as Callum had followed her up the hill, then slipping across the yard, entering through the door that she had left open and injecting the drugged-up Dan with another syringe of heroin. Or even – she'd seen his skill on stage, hypnotising men into believing they were contestants and presenters on *Strictly Come Dancing* – handing Dan a syringe and telling him to inject again. And she could imagine his cruel, mocking smile while he did it.

'I'll get to the point,' Strom said. There was an echoing quality from her phone when he spoke.

'Are you in your car?' she asked.

'I haven't got a car,' he said impatiently. 'I'm worried about Camille.'

'I don't work for Camille any more,' Hanlon said abruptly.

'I think whoever killed Katherine is coming after Camille,' Strom said, 'and tomorrow night she's going to be extremely vulnerable.'

'I don't care. It's nothing to do with me any more,' she said with finality.

There was a momentary silence, then, 'It has everything to do with you, Hanlon. You're caught up in all of this, and I know you want to find Katherine's killer. There was a bond between you two.'

Hanlon frowned; he was right. Damn Strom, he was just so irritatingly intuitive. She thought about what he had said about Camille – vulnerable. She caught a glimpse of herself in just her pants in the mirror on her wall; she suddenly imagined Strom staring at her. Vulnerable. She walked over to the cupboard she kept clothes in and pulled a pair of jeans on and a jumper. She felt marginally better.

He carried on. 'It's not like you've got anything better to do, pounding the trails around the hills, moping about your house all alone...'

It was uncannily accurate. Now she really couldn't shake the thought that Strom was in his car somehow observing her.

'OK, Strom, you win...' She went to the window and glanced out.

'Come round to my place tomorrow about 6 p.m. Make sure you've got the night free,' he said.

'OK, I'll be there.'

'Good.' There was a pause then he said, 'Well, I'd better go, see you tomorrow.'

He hung up.

The thunder was dying away, moving further up the coast. She could still see lightning flicker through the low grey clouds, but the silence between the flashes was growing longer and she could see the dog in his basket start to visibly relax. She, however, couldn't. The call from Strom had needled her, reminding her of what she considered to be her duty: to avenge the deaths of O'Rourke and Suki. And it wasn't some abstract idea of the righteousness of justice that motivated her. She wanted revenge.

Her feelings towards Camille had shifted. Camille had now become a suspect in her investigation – even if she was not definitely involved she was somehow complicit. She had lied to Hanlon by omission, and that was something she found hard to forgive.

And at the back of her mind, she heard Dr Morgan's sceptical voice saying, 'Is that because you're only too happy to lie yourself, except you justify it by saying the ends justify the means? And I'm sure in her own mind Camille has a perfectly valid reason for not telling you everything.'

Shut up, Doctor.

She paced up and down her small living space and tore her thoughts away from this useless introspection. The feeling that she was being watched grew on her. She went to the window again – nothing. She pulled on her old Barbour jacket and went to the back door. She unbolted it. Wemyss, alerted by the noise, sprang out of his basket. 'No, stay,' Hanlon said. The collie looked at her accusingly and grumpily went back to his basket, his tail low, signalling his disapproval.

She slid her feet into her wellingtons and, keeping low, walked into the conifers that ran down to the edge of her garden. Keeping hidden behind the first couple of rows of trees, she walked along parallel to the track that led to the bothy.

As she had suspected there was a vehicle parked up a couple of hundred metres from her cottage, an old Land Rover. The car was parked on a passing place cut high up on a bank; from there her cottage front door would be visible. From its vantage point it would have a perfect view of her coming and going. She immediately thought of Strom. It had sounded as if he was speaking from a car. It would be a very Strom-like thing for him to do – he would enjoy the sensation of hidden power, observing her from here.

Well, he's not getting away with that, she thought. She moved closer to the road through the trees. His attention would be on her cottage; she would move unseen down under cover of the trees and emerge behind him, yank the door open and confront him.

She was nearly by the road when suddenly, filling the air with their metallic, panic-stricken two-note alarm calls, half a dozen pheasants that she'd disturbed, escapees from the local shoot, ran ahead of her, out of the trees, flapping their wings loudly. One took off, narrowly skimming the bonnet of the stationary Land Rover, the others ran past it, shouting their loud warning cries. She saw movement from inside, heard the engine starting.

So much for that idea, she thought. She strode out through the trees, visible now to the driver. He'd have to do a three-point turn to drive back down towards the road. She'd confront him then.

But the Land Rover driver had other ideas.

Strom, if it were Strom, didn't turn the car round, but reversed down the track at speed. She felt a wave of fury, bent down, picked up a sizeable stone from the dirt at her feet and flung it at the Land Rover. She felt a savage stab of joy as she heard it hit the windscreen. It didn't shatter but the loud crack made her think she'd probably damaged it enough so it would need replacement. Serves you right, Strom, she thought, watching the boxy shape of the vehicle disappear round the corner through the falling rain.

It was an impressive piece of driving, Hanlon ruefully acknowledged as the vehicle roared backwards at speed, the driver a shapeless, faceless figure behind the rain-soaked glass of the windscreen.

She clambered down the steep, sodden muddy bank to the stony track that was like a small stream now from the rain pouring down off the hills.

She stood looking down the road to where the vehicle had disappeared.

'Strom, you bastard,' she said with feeling and turned and walked back towards her cottage.

* * *

Back inside, in the warmth, she looked up on the Internet the names and numbers of all the old people's homes in a fifty mile radius.

To her relief there weren't that many of them. It was only when you got inside Glasgow itself that the number of homes multiplied. There were about seventy; she hoped it wasn't going to be necessary to call her way through these. She had a feeling that if Strom was indeed the son of Shane Gowrie, he wouldn't be one for visiting much, if at all. He certainly wouldn't want his father parked right on the doorstep.

She called the first one. 'Hi, I wonder if you can help me...'

No, unfortunately they did not have a patient of that name listed. Three calls later she got lucky. Yes, they did have a resident of that name, Gowrie, Shane Gowrie, and by all means come and visit.

The home was in a small village just outside Dumbarton, which was on her way in to Glasgow. Hanlon thanked the nurse from the home and ended the call.

She idly looked Shane Gowrie up on the Internet. There were quite a few entries. She read a short biography. He was from Glasgow, born in 1950. His future was decided when he was fifteen and won a talent contest as a rock and roll singer at a holiday camp in Largs. The entry informed her that he had sung 'That'll Be the Day' by Buddy Holly. He had left school at sixteen and worked as an apprentice welder in the Govan shipyards but left a year later and formed a band called The Scarecrows, who had a minor hit in 1967 with a song called 'Playtime for Jane'. In 1968 he left The Scarecrows and formed Sephiroth, who released their first album in 1969. Their second album, 'Emanation' released in 1971, was a top-ten US Billboard hit.

She looked at an image of Gowrie from Madison Square Garden in 1972. Three sold-out nights. He was standing, arms outstretched as if he were being crucified. There was the famous tattoo mentioned by Dr Morgan. His head was bowed, long hair hanging down. His body was impressively muscled; he was wearing a pair of very low-cut leather trousers, his lower ab muscles sharply defined. See, Mr My Claymore Wedding singer, thought Hanlon, no pubes on show there. And by all accounts, unrestrained crotch thatch was all the rage then, but Gowrie was ahead of the curve.

She read the rest of the article. He'd had an interest in the occult, purchased Duachy Island in 1972, retired from music in 1977. She noted his comeback tour when he reformed Sephiroth in 1995, culminating in a sold-out performance at the Royal Albert Hall that was recorded and released as a critically acclaimed live album.

She looked at the images of Shane Gowrie. He was very good-looking. From snake-hipped sixties icon in a tight-fitting paisley shirt and drainpipe trousers, to cheesecloth, long hair and studded loons garnished with magical signs and sigils in the early seventies, Gowrie exuded the heady testosterone-heavy, musky odour of rock star.

There was nothing about him having a son.

She looked again at the article. The Royal Albert Hall gig, she remembered Camille talking about that. She frowned, then she checked the Internet entry for Camille Anderson, born 1980. So Camille would have been fifteen, not eighteen when she had slept with Shane Gowrie.

Did that make any difference to anything? People were a lot more tolerant of underage sex in those days, but if Camille chose to make a fuss about it, it could still have consequences. It would be hard to imagine her wanting to make something like that public. Gowrie, now safely effectively under lock and key in the old people's home, was scarcely a threat to anyone and obviously unfit for any kind of trial. Arguably he was now being punished far more severely and cruelly than any prison sentence or public shaming over paedophilia could have done.

Had this maybe been the hold that Dan had over Camille? It was perfectly possible that Camille had confided her fling with Gowrie to her sister, who could have worked out she was underage, and Siobhan had told him. But was this something you would bother to pay money over to keep secret?

She was going to speak to Siobhan anyway about O'Rourke's death. As Strom had correctly pointed out, she desperately wanted to find her killer, and he had been right that she had felt a strong affinity with the dead woman. She shook her head in frustration.

Strom, he was such an infuriating mix.

He was genuinely empathetic. Strom had a genius for penetrating the veil that separated the surface from the feelings concealed within.

Well, all that could wait until tomorrow. She would leave in the morning, visit the home and satisfy her curiosity as to what Shane Gowrie looked like these days, and there was a slim possibility that he might say something of value. Dementia was an odd thing – the sun might briefly rise above the clouds for a moment. She doubted it, but it was worth a shot. Then Siobhan, then Strom.

Her phone rang and she glanced at the screen: Murdo Campbell.

'Hi, how are you?' he asked. She was pleased to hear from him.

'Fine, and you?'

'I'm well...' There was an awkward silence on the other end of the phone. This could go on for ages, thought Hanlon. She was aware that she was impatient by nature but sometimes she felt this could occasionally be useful, as it was now.

Maybe it was the Zoom call with Dr Morgan, maybe it was hurling the rock at Strom that did it. She said, surprising herself with her directness, 'Murdo, I miss you, can you come over tonight?'

I really do miss you, she thought. God, how long is it since I've said that to anyone? There was a pause. She rolled her eyes. Murdo dragging his feet as per usual.

'Hello?' she said. It would be an eighty-mile drive for Murdo but, she decided, it would be well worth it.

'I'd love to,' he said, warily, as if there was going to be some catch.

'I don't cook, Murdo,' she warned.

He laughed. 'I really don't mind. I'll get something from the canteen before I leave. I'll be round about eight, if that's OK?'

'Perfect, see you then.'

She put the phone down and looked at Wemyss. The dog looked up at her suspiciously as if he knew something was going on. There was no way on earth that Murdo could stay the night under the accusing gaze of Wemyss.

'Dog hotel for you tonight, Wemyss,' she said apologetically.

29

'Where's Wemyss?' asked Murdo Campbell, taking off his shoes by the door – it was still raining heavily outside – and looking around Hanlon's cottage.

'He's out, on a sleepover,' Hanlon said. She'd cleaned the bothy thoroughly, not that it had needed that much doing to it, she was a naturally tidy person anyway, but she'd made it almost forensically clean – well, as much as someone who lived with a dog could realistically achieve.

Seeing Dr Morgan's consulting room had made her aware of how unhomely her place looked, dominated as it was by all the exercise equipment. She'd done what she could to minimise the effect. Hardest to tidy away had been the weights that fitted onto the barbells. She'd stacked them in order of size on top of the gym bench she used for bench press. That looked fine; at least it was symmetrical. The dumb-bells were a problem. They took up a lot of floor space, more than their fair share. She had initially placed them on top of the weights. That had looked dangerous, in her opinion, and she had moved them back to the floor.

Now, with her guest inside, she looked around her house, following his gaze, wondering what Murdo made of it. It certainly couldn't be described as cosy. The bench with its collection of dull black metal weights balanced neatly on top of it, the bar heavy on its rests with two twenty-kilo discs on either end, a replica of which was sitting on a squat rack bolted to the floor near her kitchen area, the heavy bag hanging down from the hook in the ceiling, the bare walls devoid of decoration – unlike Dr Morgan, she didn't own any pictures. There were no bookshelves or books. She couldn't really see the point of fiction. You could call it minimalist, but bleak might be more accurate.

'Would you like a drink?' she asked. 'Have a seat.' She indicated the chair by the table in the corner. Murdo smiled and sat down. He was wearing a pair of dark blue cotton trousers and highly polished black boots. He took his coat off, a dark blue wool jacket, and hung it over the back of his chair. He was always elegant-looking, Hanlon thought, his pale face with the well-shaped red eyebrows and red hair, serious. Damn, thought Hanlon, I should have taken his jacket. She was a bit rusty at entertaining.

'What have you got?' he asked.

'Scotch? Wine? Coffee?' she said.

'I'll have a whisky,' Murdo said. 'Just a splash of water.'

Hanlon went over to the cupboard in the kitchen area and found a bottle of Jura whisky that had been given to her. She put the kettle on to make herself a coffee and found a whisky glass in a cupboard. She poured Murdo a generous measure and added a splash of water.

She handed it to him, suddenly realising she had nowhere to sit other than the bed, which was on the other side of the room. That would look weird. I must get another chair, she thought.

'Thanks.' He took it and had a sip. 'I spoke to the officer who's in charge of the O'Rourke investigation,' he said.

Hanlon leaned against the work surface while she waited for the kettle to boil.

'What did he say?'

'She,' Murdo said, 'DI Annabel Strachan. O'Rourke was hit with a single bullet from a .22 rifle. The shot was fired from behind a bush in the park – someone was obviously waiting for her. The murder weapon hasn't been recovered.'

The kettle boiled and Hanlon added coffee to a cafetiere. 'I just don't understand it,' she said. 'Why kill her? It makes no sense at all.'

Murdo had another mouthful of malt whisky. I should have bought some crisps or nuts or something, Hanlon thought suddenly. I'm such a shit hostess.

'Strachan interviewed Siobhan Anderson first. She lives with her sister, Camille, north of the park. Siobhan said that she wasn't expecting her.'

'Did she have an alibi?' asked Hanlon. If anyone had killed O'Rourke that she knew, Hanlon would have guessed Siobhan.

'Yes, a cast-iron alibi,' Murdo said. 'She was on a Zoom call with the catering manager and chef at the Edinburgh branch of the yoga studios when the murder happened. She couldn't possibly have done it.'

Hanlon poured herself a cup of coffee. Milk, she thought, something else she had forgotten to buy. I could have bought breadsticks, she suddenly thought, wildly. Or maybe olives. Murdo looks like the kind of man who would enjoy an olive.

'And Camille?'

'At home with her sister. No alibi as such, they didn't see each other until later, but Strachan couldn't imagine her doing it.'

Hanlon shook her head. 'Me neither. Even if I could, I can't imagine Camille being able to cross the Botanic Gardens carrying a .22 rifle without anyone noticing. I mean, it would be noticeable enough at the best of times, even if she weren't so well known, a slim pretty blonde woman with a firearm.'

She imagined Camille wandering through a crowded Botanical Gardens in her jeans and light raincoat. She supposed it was possible that she was concealing a rifle under the coat in some kind of shoulder harness, but Camille was a yoga teacher, not a trained assassin.

'Where exactly was the shot fired from?' she asked. Or crostini, they'd have gone with the olives... would he have preferred black or green?

'We think from a clump of bushes just opposite where she was hit. That's our best estimate anyway. We put word out on local media but no one seems to have seen anything.'

He shook his head. 'It's strange that nobody noticed a man with a rifle. I suppose you could have hidden it there the night before, but it seems unlikely, and, anyway, how would you know where O'Rourke would be at that point in time? Plus, of course, someone might have found it, or there could have been people sitting around by those bushes.' He shrugged. 'All we can do is to hope for a break.'

The conversation stopped and they looked at each other. She had been going to tell him about the incident with Strom and the Land Rover but she decided against it. Murdo was a worrier, in her opinion, and he would start fretting about the suitability of her living in such an isolated place. She suspected she would never hear the end of it.

Hanlon put her cup down. The atmosphere in the bothy felt heavy and charged, like before a storm. Murdo stood up and they moved towards each other. They held each other, momentarily, hands resting on elbows, then kissed, at first almost nervously, then, both reassured, passionately, and they locked together in an embrace. They ran their hands over each other's bodies. She felt hard, defined muscle under the cotton of his shirt and slipped a hand beneath it, caressing his smooth skin. Their mouths met again hungrily and, bodies pressed together, almost as if they were slow dancing, she gently steered Murdo backwards as she moved him towards the corner where the bed was.

Murdo's heel encountered one of Hanlon's barbells with a small five K weight at each end that had rolled out from under the bench. The weight rolled backwards under the pressure and, startled, he lost his balance. He grabbed the end of the barbell resting on its support on the bench to steady himself. The bench didn't move much, but enough to dislodge a ten-kilo metal disc from one of the neat stacks of weights on its top.

It slid off and fell, landing on Murdo's right foot, just above his toes.

'Fuck! Jesus...' An agonised expression flickered across his face, pain and disbelief equally represented.

'Murdo, are you OK?' Hanlon was aghast.

Murdo hopped towards the bed keeping the injured foot off the floor and sat down heavily. He gave a kind of a rueful laugh. 'I'm fine...' The look on his face suggested that wasn't true at all.

Hanlon moved forward, knelt down by his foot and gently pulled Murdo's sock off. He had a very shapely foot, but as she watched it was starting to swell.

She looked up at him. 'Murdo, we're going to have to go to A&E.'

'No, honestly, I'll be fine...' He patted the bed beside him. 'Where were we, Hanlon?'

'No, Murdo, it will not be fine...' she said. The expression on his face was one of almost pantomime woe.

'Hanlon, I've longed for this moment for months...' He winced and gasped in pain, trying to disguise it as a cough. 'Can't we just at least make love and then go to the hospital?'

She laughed. 'It's very flattering of you to ask...'

'It won't take long...' He smiled through his pain. 'I'll lie on my back, my foot'll be fine, please!'

She grinned back. God he was desperate. 'No is the answer, Murdo... We'll get you X-rayed then strapped up, then we'll consider our options, but right now, quite frankly, Murdo, the moment's gone. Come on, we'll get you to my car.'

He nodded glumly, accepting the situation, then he winced. 'Have you got any pain killers?'

'Yes.'

She fetched him a couple of Co-codamol and some water and then, putting his arm around her shoulder, she helped him upright. They stood looking at each other. He looked incredibly attractive, she thought, and their mouths met as Murdo slid a free hand under her blouse.

For a moment she closed her eyes as she felt her body respond and she considered his earlier request seriously, but then common sense reasserted itself.

'Come on...' she whispered. 'The quicker we get to A&E, the quicker we'll be together, OK.'

'OK,' he sighed, and together they limped out to her Volvo.

30

After she had driven him to the hospital at Lochgilphead, he was triaged, they waited an hour or so, then he was called through to the X-ray room, which was like every other X-ray room she'd been in: spacious, a feeling of silent tranquillity, a kind of dim bluish light, the padded bench for lying on with its paper cover.

Then a further wait for a couple of hours and then a tired-looking doctor – by now it was 1 a.m. – who informed them wearily that there were a couple of fractures in Murdo's foot and they'd have to plaster it. A follow-up appointment would be arranged to check on the foot and remove the cast.

Afterwards, as he limped alongside her back to the car, his foot in a boot cast, leaning on his new crutches, she said, 'I'm going to take you back to your place. You'll be more comfortable there.'

'Thanks...' He looked down. 'I look ridiculous...'

He was wearing a borrowed pair of Hanlon's tracksuit bottoms. She'd brought them along with them in case they'd needed to strap his foot up and he wouldn't be able to get his trousers back on, which was what had happened. But she only reached his shoulders, height wise, and the pants were correspondingly short.

She thought that it was an indication of how much it was hurting that he made no attempt to disagree with her.

On the drive to Glasgow they talked for a while and then Murdo fell asleep. She was glad of that as she drove through the pale light of an early Scottish dawn, her eyes as grey and as cold as the waters of Loch Lomond on her left as she left Argyll behind. Her thoughts turned restlessly back to O'Rourke. Who had killed Katherine? It couldn't have been Siobhan, not with her irritatingly watertight alibi, and the idea that it might have been Camille was simply preposterous. Strom, well, he was certainly capable of it, and if anyone could spirit a .22 rifle through a crowded park then her money would be on him. But why?

As she drove past Dumbarton, the grotty-looking concrete walls of the distillery and the quarry that always served as a landmark that she was nearly in Glasgow, Murdo woke up. She followed his instructions when they got into the city. She didn't know Glasgow well at all. At this time of the morning there was hardly anybody around. They pulled up outside a tenement block somewhere near the city centre.

'I'll come up with you,' she said.

Murdo lived on the top floor of the three-storey building. He hobbled awkwardly up the stairs. He unlocked the door, the sound of the key echoing around the empty stone stairwell.

They walked into the living room, Murdo turning lights on as they went.

It was more or less everything her own home was not. He escorted her into the living room. It was a beautiful room. The floor had been restored to its original wooden boards, which gleamed from being lovingly polished. Bookshelves lined one wall; there was an expensive-looking sound system with a high-tech record turntable. There were framed pictures on the wall. It was a far cry from Hanlon's utilitarian cottage. It breathed sophisticated culture. Hanlon found it deeply unsettling. The flat made her feel horribly inadequate. She doubted she would ever have invited him home if she had seen his place first. Murdo certainly wouldn't be banging a hook into a supporting beam of his high-ceilinged living room with restored original cornicing and a central moulded decorative relief where the light fitting was, to hang a punchbag from; nor would he be pushing the massive grey sofa into a corner to make way for a bench-press station.

'It's a lovely flat, Murdo,' she said wistfully.

'Thanks...' He smiled at her.

'Come on, let's get you to bed. I'll give you a hand. We don't want to fall over again.'

'It's more or less opposite,' he said.

She nodded, left the living room and went into his room, turned the light on and looked around.

Murdo's bedroom was kitted out in pale oak furniture, a large double bed, some abstract art prints on the wall. It was utilitarian. She felt obscurely relieved. It would have been terrible if it had been some kind of sex-temple – unlikely, she knew, but you never could tell – or alternatively some kind of slobby man-pit. And, of course, few places could equal Dan's horror show. But no, it was as spotless and elegant as Murdo himself.

She went back into the living room and helped Murdo off the sofa. They walked into his bedroom and he sat down heavily on the bed, staring mournfully at his foot strapped up in the cast. She sat next to him.

'I'd often dreamed of you in my bedroom,' Murdo said, 'but never like this...'

He looked sadly down at his bandaged foot.

Hanlon stroked his face with her fingers – he had quite prominent cheekbones; the pale skin had a dusting of freckles – and tilted his head towards hers by his strong chin.

'It'll mend, Murdo, and when it does you can sweep me off my feet...' She put her mouth to his and they kissed. 'Meantime...'

She stood up.

'Are you sure you won't sleep here?' he said, patting the mattress hopefully.

Hanlon shook her head. 'When we go to bed, Murdo, I'm expecting fireworks, not a yelp every time your foot nudges the sheet.' She walked to the door. 'Get some sleep. I'm heading out about eight. I'll be in touch.'

'Hanlon...' their eyes met, 'thanks.'

'Sweet dreams, Murdo.'

She closed his bedroom door and went into his kitchen to make a cup of coffee. The room was, like everything in his flat, sizeable.

She looked around. It was very well equipped. She suspected the hand of Ishbel, Murdo's interfering restaurateur sister. She stared at the Gaggia coffee machine in perplexity. How would that even work? There was a large Hobart stainless-steel food mixer, a five-burner stove with the double oven, his enormous fridge next to a stand-up freezer. She reflected that the kitchen and its contents probably cost more than her cottage.

On the wall by the door were a couple of framed menus, one from some hotel in Berlin, the other she recognised as being from a famous London restaurant, signed by its famous chef/owner.

She thought of her small kitchen corner, the old-fashioned electric cooker, dating from the sixties, she guessed. Her empty fridge. She opened his, stared at the neatly organised shelves. Just as she had suspected: olives. Two kinds. She closed the door.

She had absolutely no idea of the unfathomable coffee machine. She filled the kettle from the tap and found some teabags in a cupboard – that would have to do.

She went back into the lounge with her tea and looked at the time. It was 4 a.m. It was completely light outside now. She sat on the sofa with her tea feeling unusually depressed and flat.

Maybe I'm just tired, she thought, maybe that's all it is. She stretched out on his sofa and set the alarm on her phone to 7 a.m.

Lying down on the sofa brought the large bookcase across the room into her field of vision. The spines on the jackets of Murdo's books, in more than one language, seemed to mock her. She had often sneered at people who read a lot, now it seemed literature and the arts in general were getting their own back. Payback time, proclaimed Jean-Paul Sartre's *La Mort dans L'Âme*. This time it's personal, said Camus' *L'Étranger*. Boot's on the other foot now, said Dürrenmatt's *Justiz*. Fuck, she thought miserably, and closed her eyes.

I can't compete with the kitchen and the books, she thought unhappily. The face of Dr Morgan swam up through her consciousness: it's not a competition, you dimwit.

As she drifted off, she seemed to see the face of Strom, laughing at her.

Her alarm woke her up what felt like seconds later: 7 a.m. She got up, stretched and went into Murdo's room to check on him. He was sound asleep, lying on his back, his injured foot poking out of the duvet. His fine red hair was tousled over his pale forehead, one muscular arm, more freckles, on top of the bedclothes. He looked incredibly attractive and she felt a sharp pang of desire, a crazy urge to undress and slip into bed with him. There was really nothing stopping her, nothing except her own pride; in other words, everything.

She gently closed the door behind her and left the flat. She walked down to where she had left her car, texted that she would be in touch soon and went in search of food and where someone could work a coffee-machine.

After an expensive breakfast in a hipster-style café in central Glasgow, Hanlon pulled into the sweeping drive that led up to the old people's home in the village outside Dumbarton, the final resting place for Shane Gowrie.

Like so many of these places, it had obviously once been a grand house that had belonged to some wealthy local in mid-Victorian times. It was quite a handsome building, devoid of the mock Gothic castle ornamentation that was such a feature of the style of the time up here in Scotland.

She parked in the car park. She had a panoramic view of the Clyde below her and the far side opposite. It was still before nine, which was when visiting hours started, so she got out her tablet and called Dr Morgan.

She answered almost immediately. Hanlon looked at her calm face with relief.

'Hanlon, twice in two days, I am honoured. How can I help you?'

She felt a great sense of reluctance suddenly to speak. 'I'm sorry to bother you, it's not all that important...'

Dr Morgan raised a wrist so Hanlon could see the black rubber strap of her fitness watch. 'I've got twenty-five minutes before my first patient, off you go...'

Hanlon found herself pouring her heart out about the night before to the impassive-faced Dr Morgan, who listened without interruptions.

'So, as far as I can gather,' she said, 'with Murdo Campbell, you don't feel worthy of his love. You also suspect that he's just amusing himself with you, he'll soon tire of you, is that more or less it?'

She nodded. 'I just don't see how it can work.' She shook her head despondently. 'All those books... Sartre, for fuck's sake.'

'Language, Hanlon.'

'Sorry, Doctor, but really!'

'They're only books, Hanlon...'

'No, they're not.' She shook her head obstinately. 'They're a metaphor.'

Dr Morgan shook her head in exasperation. 'Do you really think that Murdo Campbell cares whether or not you know anything about literature?'

'No,' Hanlon said truthfully.

'And do you think that Murdo Campbell is essentially a trustworthy, decent person?'

'Yes,' Hanlon said. Dr Morgan made a pantomime-like gesture of exasperation.

'Well, then, I really think you should give him a chance. I think he's attracted to you by your toughness mixed with your vulnerability, your bravery and general incorruptibility, both of which, by the way, are quite rare in people.'

'Thank you.'

'You're welcome. Time for you to take a risk.' She shook her head wonderingly. 'I never thought I'd need to say that to you, given your addiction to danger... Anyway, do you know what Sartre said about literature?'

'No.'

'Of course not. It was a rhetorical question,' snapped Dr Morgan. 'He said that literature was a bourgeois substitute for commitment in the real world. So, be more Sartre, Hanlon, go and find out who killed Suki Bly and Katherine O'Rourke. That's my professional advice to you. Enough with the moping around, it doesn't suit you...' She looked at her wrist. 'I've got to go now. Stop trying to analyse things, that's my job. Go and do what you know best.'

'OK.'

'Oh, and don't hurt anyone, OK.'

'I promise.'

'Call me in a week.'

Her screen went blank.

Hanlon breathed a deep sigh of relief. That went better than she'd hoped. What the hell is wrong with me? she thought angrily. I shouldn't need to call a therapist because I feel unhappy.

No, she heard Dr Morgan say, that's what friends are for. Is that why you're so upset by O'Rourke's death – you saw her as a friend?

Yes, that's right, she was my friend, we liked each other, and I'm going to avenge her, thought Hanlon.

She got out of the car, walked up to the door of the home and rang the bell. A young girl in a blue uniform opened it. She was overweight with short hair dyed candyfloss pink and tattooed arms. She had an open, friendly expression.

'Hi, can I help you?'

'My name's Hanlon. I spoke to someone here about visiting Shane Gowrie. They said to come any time after 9 a.m.?'

'Oh, sure, I remember you now. I'm Natalie. That'll be fine, do come in.'

She did so. The entrance hall had a warm, stale smell of old food, predominantly cabbage, a faint hint of urine and disinfectant.

'Come with me...'

Natalie led her down a corridor. There were grab handles attached to the wall every half-metre and she walked past bedrooms with open doors. She saw one figure, immobile on a bed, staring at the ceiling, another, an old lady in a wheelchair, looking blankly out of the window.

'Have all the patients got dementia?' Hanlon asked.

'Aye, some more so than others, but yes,' Natalie said. 'We're a specialist home in that respect. Shane's pretty bad. Are you a relation?'

'No,' Hanlon said, 'I'm a family friend.'

'Well, it's nice that someone's come to visit,' said the carer.

They walked past some more doors. 'Does he get many visitors?' Hanlon asked.

The carer shook her head. 'Nobody in all the time I've been here,' she said.

You bastard, Strom, Hanlon thought.

'And how long's that?' she asked.

'Two years.'

They walked into a living room where about fifteen old people were arranged in a semicircle facing a large TV that was showing some daytime-presenter woman talking to a fashion expert about what to wear this coming autumn.

Several heads looked up hopefully as the two of them walked in, just in case they were hoped-for relatives. Disappointed, they dropped their gaze. None of them would be wearing this autumn's fashions, that was for sure.

Natalie led Hanlon to a man at the end of the circle. He was in a wheelchair. Age had robbed him of mobility but it hadn't softened him. He had a hard, violent-looking face. His hair was long and grey and swept back from his forehead. He looked like Hanlon would imagine a retired violent criminal, an armed robber, who had got old and lost his mind. There was little trace of the young rock star he'd been.

'Shane, sweetheart, look, you've got a visitor!'

Shane looked up at Hanlon. He frowned.

'Who are you?' he muttered suspiciously.

'My name's Hanlon.'

He frowned again and pointed at her handbag she was holding in her left hand. 'That bag...'

'Yes,' she said.

'That's my bag.' He nodded emphatically. 'Give it me!'

Natalie whispered, 'He always says that.'

'The bag!' whimpered Shane, stretching out his hands imploringly.

'There's a room through there you can go to if you want to be alone,' Natalie said.

'Sure,' Hanlon said.

She walked behind the wheelchair, took the handles and gently pushed Shane through the doorway that Natalie had pointed to.

The room was obviously the activity room. It had an upright piano and plastic boxes with beanbags and balloons and other simple toys in bright primary colours, suitable for the demented.

It was airy and bright and light streamed in through the large floor-to-ceiling windows. She sat down on a chair opposite him and they looked at each other. Shane seemed faintly puzzled. At least he realises he doesn't know me, she thought. He pointed at the piano.

'That's mine... my piano.'

'Of course it is,' Hanlon said. She was at a bit of a loss as to what to do now.

'I was on Seil Island,' she said. 'Claonnaidh Farm.'

'No,' said Shane, shaking his head irritably. 'Not Claonnaidh Farm, no, no.'

'Yes, it was,' Hanlon said.

Shane looked at her with contempt. 'No, my farm, Corranbuie Farm. That's my farm, not Claonnaidh Farm... Corranbuie Farm, my farm.'

'What about Strom?' Hanlon asked. 'Paul Strom?'

'I can't remember,' Shane said, shaking his head, dismissing Strom. 'Give me the bag...' He pointed at her handbag again. 'Give it me.' He started to cry. 'It's my bag.'

Hanlon tried asking him about Camille, Duachy Island, Paul McEwan. Nothing provoked a coherent response.

She wheeled him back to the TV room. Natalie was giving an old lady a couple of custard creams. Shane swivelled his head.

'My biscuits...' shouted Shane. 'Give me my biscuits...'

Natalie came over to Hanlon. 'I'll let you out,' she said.

As Natalie keyed in the code to let her out of the front door a voice came floating down the corridor. 'They're my biscuits...' she heard Shane wail despairingly, then, 'Corranbuie Farm!'

'Do come again and visit him,' Natalie said. 'I know he really enjoyed your visit.' She shook her head. 'He hasn't been so animated for ages.'

Hanlon thought, Poor old sod. From the adulation of thousands at huge events, Madison Square Garden and Knebworth, to the activity room of an old folks' home. Natalie looked at her enquiringly. Hanlon thought she had a lovely face, her eyes, intelligent, kind and compassionate. Shane was lucky to have her.

'I'll be back to see him.'

'Thank you,' said Natalie, 'that means a lot.'

The door opened and Hanlon escaped outside.

* * *

She sat in her car with the windows down, breathing in great lungfuls of air. Well, that was utterly pointless, she thought. She had been hoping for some kind of miracle, for Shane to have produced some sort of revelation. She realised now what a long shot it had been. The chances had been slim, but she guessed at least she had done it. It had achieved something; she could tick that off her list. She need never go back.

Strom, you bastard, she thought, then this was followed by, don't get over-excited, Hanlon, it is only a theory that he's Strom's father. It might not be so. But deep down she thought it probably was the case.

She looked up at the big brick building that was now home to Shane Gowrie, a man who had prowled the stage at Wembley, the Bath Festival, Madison Square Garden, the Isle of Wight Festival and the Fillmore East, a sex god in the same mould as Jim Morrison, now confined to a wheelchair, wearing not skin-tight leather trousers but Tena pants.

What a waste, she thought.

She shook her head sadly and started her car.

There was a text on her phone from Murdo.

Miss you.

She smiled and replied.

You too.

As she drove back towards Glasgow she wondered if she was going to tell Paul Strom where she had been. She decided not. So far it had been Strom who had held all the cards, who had been pulling the strings, who had known all the secrets.

It was her turn for a change.

31

'Thank you for coming,' Strom said. She sat down on the sofa and he took a place opposite her.

Strom was dressed formally in a dark, casual two-piece suit and a white shirt. The clothes emphasised his tall, slim body and his angular, handsome face. She thought of Dr Morgan's comment about him. Not in a million years, Doctor. She thought of Shane Gowrie – was he really Strom's father? Had she just made up a convenient story, playing fast and loose with sketchy facts? Just because Strom was the kind of son a rock star might have, it didn't mean he was. They didn't look the same, although there was a hint of cruelty in Strom's face that echoed the faded arrogance of the old man, an arrogance and selfishness that still lived on in the ruins of his brain like a reflex twitch. '*Mine... it's mine...*'

'You mentioned something about a threat to Camille?' Hanlon said.

He nodded. 'Camille's distraught at the death of Katherine,' he said. 'We all are...'

Are you? she thought. You don't look it.

'But Katherine and Camille had a special bond.'

'Well, that's true,' Hanlon said. She was in no mood to defend Camille. 'Her stupid advice killed her daughter, for one thing.'

'I told you, she had forgiven Camille.'

Hanlon shrugged. 'So you say.' Part of her still wondered if O'Rourke really had forgiven Camille.

Strom said, 'Anyway, Camille is going to try to summon Katherine's spirit tonight.'

'Fat lot of good that will do,' Hanlon said contemptuously. She was not in the mood for Strom and Camille's mystic bullshit. 'Look, Strom, someone shot Katherine from behind some bushes. Even if Camille managed to summon her from the spirit world and she appeared, which, face it, she's not going to, she wouldn't have any more idea who pulled that trigger than I do.'

Her contempt bounced off Strom; he just smiled. 'You're such a sceptic, Hanlon.'

'Too right,' she said, 'and you know what? I'm rarely disappointed, Strom. Anyway, why didn't she ask you to do it? I thought that was your job, that sort of thing.'

Strom ignored her question and said, 'I told her not to, but she didn't listen. She's going to go ahead with the ceremony. Right now she's spending the afternoon at Anna Reynolds' doing spiritual exercises and purification meditations, then her plan is to return to the yoga centre alone, where she won't be disturbed and she'll be in a secure place to begin the sacred rites.'

'So, I don't understand what the problem is,' Hanlon said. It sounded stupidly New Age but if Camille wanted to do that, so what? She was slightly surprised that Anna, who seemed quite sensible and hard-headed, should be part of this nonsense, but if she'd learned one thing it was that the most unlikely people believed this kind of stuff.

'The ceremony involves drugs,' Strom explained. 'In Mexico it would be peyote, in the rainforest ayahuasca, on the steppe, amanita mushrooms.'

'And in Glasgow?' Hanlon asked. Give me strength, she thought, what year are we living in?

'I make my own sacred drink,' Strom said. 'Psilocybin mushrooms and ayahuasca, but I know what I'm doing.'

'I still don't get what the problem is,' Hanlon said.

'Well, here's the thing.' He suddenly looked unusually embarrassed.

'Camille has got her hands on my preparation and she's going to take it tonight.' He paused. 'Unsupervised, alone... it's a very bad idea.'

Hanlon looked at Strom suspiciously. 'How exactly do you mean, "got her hands on" some?'

Strom sighed. 'Come on, I'll show you.'

He led her through a door in his living room into the flat's kitchen. It was very clean and neat, although lacking the impressive array of equipment that Murdo Campbell's place had.

There were two fridges, one a conventional fridge freezer, the other a small, portable one about the size of an average microwave. He opened this. Inside were a number of small transparent plastic screw-topped containers such as you might find in a lab. They had calibrations on the side measuring the amount of liquid. Each contained 50 ml of clear liquid.

'This is it,' he said. 'These are the tinctures of the sacred herbs and fungi used in the ceremony. I calibrate the dosage according to the needs of the seeker of truth, according to physical factors, age, weight, fitness and so on, and psychic factors, mental stability, resilience and experience of such ceremonies. The tincture is very strong. Its effects can be alarming, terrifying even.' He picked up a small notebook that was on top of the fridge. 'This is my inventory. There should be eight of these, there are six. Half of one of these, 25 ml, is quite a strong dose. That's the amount I take. For someone like Camille I would only give about 5 ml, maybe less. More could be dangerous.'

'And you suspect Camille took it?'

'Yes.'

So you two have almost certainly been having an affair, thought Hanlon. Otherwise how could Camille possibly know where to steal things from?

'Why are you telling me all of this?' she asked.

'Camille is going to take this tonight,' he said. 'If she takes too much, it could really affect her badly.'

That's probably an understatement, Hanlon thought. She'll probably be hallucinating wildly.

Strom continued, 'And if you're inexperienced, then you need to have someone who is unaffected keeping a close eye on you. If I engage in a ceremony with a client, then I guide them through what they are experiencing, protecting them mentally and, of course, I make sure that they are not getting up and moving around, protecting them physically.'

He looked at Hanlon. 'So that's one worry I have. I don't know what precautions, if any, she's taken, but there is another worry, specific to Camille.'

'There's more than that to worry about?' Hanlon asked. She could obviously see the force of Strom's arguments. She had a vision of Camille stumbling around her studio, the mirrored walls full of writhing monsters trying to seize her while she headed inexorably towards the steep staircase by the studio door.

'You do realise that what you've been doing is highly illegal?' Hanlon said.

Strom shrugged. 'I'm hoping that times will change. Different countries have different rules. For example, they charge a couple of thousand US dollars in Peru for an ayahuasca experience over there.'

'I wouldn't hold your breath,' Hanlon said, 'and we're not in Peru, we're in Partick, but go on, you were saying about another threat to Camille.'

'I was.' Strom's face was grim in the bright light of the kitchen. 'I think that with the deaths of Suki and Katherine there's been a danger of forgetting why you were employed in the first place, which was to protect Camille, and that threat has not gone away. It's still there. Camille will be totally and utterly helpless. If someone were to get into that yoga centre tonight and shove Camille down the stairs, or out of a window, it would be put down to a regrettable accident due to drug misuse.'

She nodded. Camille would obviously be hopelessly incapacitated if anyone tried to hurt her. Hanlon had always believed that the threat to Camille came from someone who knew her, so there was a very real chance that person might know what Camille was going to be doing and act accordingly.

'Well, in that case, if you're so worried, why aren't you going to be with her tonight, babysitting her?' she asked. 'Or guiding her through the astral realm, come to that?' she added as a sarcastic afterthought.

'Because she told me that she never wanted to see me again,' Strom said simply.

'Why's that?' Hanlon asked. She was inwardly pleased that her feeling they had been having an affair had been confirmed.

Strom sighed. 'Because I slept with her sister.'

'You did what?' Hanlon said, scarcely able to believe her ears. He'd screwed Siobhan! 'Why did you do that?'

Strom smiled. 'Because she's a very attractive woman, that's why.' He sighed. 'I thought I'd get away with it. Siobhan obviously told Camille and she went berserk.'

'Berserk?'

Strom shrugged. 'I'm exaggerating, no, she didn't. But she was most certainly furious. And she told me that she never wanted to see me again, amongst other reflections on my character.'

'Well, there's a surprise. I always knew you were unscrupulous, Strom, but I didn't realise you were stupid.'

Strom waved a dismissive hand. 'Look, Hanlon, I am the way I am. Sometimes I do bad things, sometimes I do good things. I admit I am quite amoral, but I never claimed to be otherwise.'

Hanlon shook her head irritably. 'Am I expected to applaud your honesty?'

'No, Hanlon.' He stopped smiling. 'But I do expect you to save Camille's life though, or at least protect it. I can't. If I turn up there she won't be best pleased to see me.'

'She probably won't be able to recognise you, Strom. She'll be tripping her arse off.'

Strom said, 'It's impossible to know what effects the drug will have on her. It varies from individual to individual. It could be auditory visions, or tactile as well as visual. But it will distort reality and if you have strong feelings about someone it will amplify them. That's why you need someone to be with you that you can trust, and, unfortunately, I don't fit that bill.' He pulled a face. 'She would probably think I was there to kill her. It'll have to be you.'

'Really?' said Hanlon. 'She fired me, remember?'

'Probably because you had backed her into a corner and she felt she had no option. But she trusts you, Hanlon. We all do. O'Rourke certainly did.'

She thought to herself, He really does know what buttons to press.

He pressed some more. 'There's been enough death already, hasn't there?'

She shook her head in irritation.

'And how do you expect me to protect her? How do I even get in?'

Strom handed her a piece of paper with three numbers written on it.

'These are the codes for the keypads of the yoga centre: outside door, alarm, internal door. These will get you through, then you go up to the upstairs studio, which is where she'll be. You'll be able to get fairly close. Camille's internal world will be quite vibrant, overly so, I suspect. She won't see or hear you if you're quiet. Don't make any loud noise or try to communicate with her unless she initiates it.'

'So what do I do, then?' she asked.

'Stay close, make sure she doesn't try to move around. Her geography may well be very different from where she actually is. You can gently restrain her if she does. By midnight she should be re-entering reality. She'll need a friendly face.'

Hanlon glared at Strom, who smiled sweetly back. Her evening could scarcely be worse, spending it in the company of a woman out of her head on hallucinogens, a woman who, despite Strom's claims, probably thoroughly disliked her and had certainly fired her. And worst of all, Strom knew she would do everything he had asked her to.

'Anything else I should know?'

Strom scratched his head. 'Before she found out about Siobhan, she had brought the subject up. That's when I said I wasn't going to help. She wanted to speak to Katherine's spirit to find out who had killed both her and Suki.' He shook his head. 'That was a bad idea.'

'Why?' Hanlon asked.

'Without me there, there is too much, well... Let's call it psychic noise. The astral realm is a confusing place, Hanlon. As well as that there are malicious spirits who can mislead you, or your own suspicions that the drug will take and build on. You need to have assistance to find your spirit guide. That guide will help you through the maze of the otherworld. And that realm doesn't like trespassers, Hanlon. It throws up barriers and obstacles to prevent you reaching it… Anyway, she found out from me that round about 7 p.m. would be the best time. It's still light for four or five hours, by which time the drugs will be wearing off. It can be a frightening experience – it's less so when you're not in darkness. So, if you go up about seven-thirty, she'll be well on her way, and you can watch over her, make sure she's OK.'

'Did you try and talk her out of this idea?' Hanlon asked.

'Of course I did, but I don't think you realise quite how strong-willed Camille is. How many competent yoga teachers are there in this country? Quite a few. And how many yoga-teacher millionaires? Camille didn't get where she is today without a huge amount of determination.'

'So she can't be talked out of it?'

'She's determined to go ahead,' Strom said.

'And when she comes round?' Hanlon asked.

'She'll be disoriented, cold, frightened. Take her home. She'll want you to stay with her.' He looked at her with a kind of strange compassion. 'That's your burden, Hanlon. Like I said before, you are trustworthy. It's why people fall for you. You're not very likeable, quite frankly you're often rude, you certainly are to me, but you are a compelling person.'

'Thank you, Strom,' she said acidly.

'And you've got a great ass, Hanlon.'

She stood up. 'Don't push your luck. I'll let you know how we get on.'

'Call me any time,' he said. 'Oh, Hanlon, one more thing. I know you don't believe in my shamanic abilities…'

'No, Strom, I don't, save it for the gullible.'

'Don't go back to Seil Island until this is all over,' he said matter-of-factly.

'Why not?'

'At the risk of sounding melodramatic, Hanlon, death awaits you there.'

'Save your bullshit, Strom, for people that believe it.'

She walked out of his flat into the bright evening streets of Partick.

32

The yoga centre was shut. Hanlon rattled the door experimentally then keyed in the first number that Strom had given her. She checked her watch: quarter past seven.

The evening was bright and sunny, the street was full of young people, predominantly students, she guessed. They seemed happy and carefree, more or less the opposite of her, worried, guilt-ridden, confused. Hanlon looked at them enviously and she heard the door latch pop open. She was in.

She closed the door behind her and looked around. She could hear the insistent warning buzzing of the alarm; she went over to it and tapped in the code. A green light flashed and it stopped.

Once she was inside, the building had that peculiar air that such public places had when they were deserted, almost as if they were holding their breath. The windows were slightly tinted and the glass was double glazed so no sound from the busy street outside penetrated and the light in the lobby was diffuse and calmly dim. There was a faint hum of air conditioning.

Hanlon looked into the deserted cafeteria. It seemed an age since O'Rourke had bitten into the glass concealed in the breakfast muesli; since then three people had died, four if you included Dan. Until about three weeks ago she had never heard of any of these people. She knew none of this was her fault, but she nonetheless felt a deep stab of irrational guilt.

She went over to the internal door and keyed in the number. It clicked, a green light came on and she opened it. The staircase rose steeply before her and she slowly went up it, putting her weight on the handrail to try to minimise any creaking noises from the stairs. At the top she paused on the landing and looked through the glass panel set in the light oak door.

It was a very peaceful-looking scene.

Camille was lying on her back in the centre of the enormous room. She had spread out her yoga mat and a couple of cushions; she had lit a couple of joss sticks and Hanlon could see the spirals of fragrant smoke rising up into the still air of the large, tranquil, spacious room.

She frowned, and looked more closely – something felt wrong. Camille was not so much lying there as sprawled, as if she had been sitting upright and had fallen backwards. Hanlon quietly opened the door and slipped inside. Camille didn't move.

Hardly daring to breathe, she moved closer. Camille's eyes were closed and her breathing was loud and erratic. Hanlon could see her chest rise and fall as if she had been running a race. As she got closer she could see that she'd been sick; traces of vomit were on her T-shirt and yoga mat. Her forehead was slick with sweat.

'Camille!' Hanlon said, kneeling beside her and gently shaking her. No answer. It looked as if she'd lost consciousness.

'Shit,' Hanlon muttered. Whatever was happening to Camille wasn't good. Strom, you cretin, she thought. You've poisoned her. God knew what had been in those containers that Camille had stolen from his fridge or indeed how much she'd taken.

She took her phone out and called 999.

'Hang on, Camille,' she said, squeezing her hand as she ended the call. 'I'll be back soon with help...'

Camille moaned and then retched. Hanlon put her in the recovery position and ran downstairs to let the paramedics in.

She just hoped they would be in time.

* * *

Two hours later Hanlon was back at Murdo Campbell's flat, telling him what had happened.

'So, is she going to be all right?' he asked.

Hanlon paced up and down on his rugs and polished floorboards. She felt stressed out and irritable. It had been so close.

'Who knows?' she said. 'Seemingly she's in no immediate danger but, from what I can gather from the doctor treating her, there could be permanent damage to her kidneys and liver.'

The doctor had assumed that Hanlon was one of Camille's followers and had delivered a stern lecture on the downsides of DIY herbal treatments.

'Then I explained that it was nothing to do with me and he relented a bit.' She ran her fingers through her hair, which was tousled and stiff. It felt dreadful, like Medusa's.

'He told me that regardless of the mushrooms and the ayahuasca there was evidence that she'd ingested digitalis. He'd seen a couple of cases before from naturopaths who'd used it to self-treat and poisoned themselves.'

'Why would Strom add digitalis to the mix?' asked Campbell, puzzled.

'God alone knows,' Hanlon said. 'Maybe you can get high on it, maybe the spirits told him to? Maybe he picked the wrong mushrooms?'

'Did you tell the police where she got the drugs from?' Murdo asked.

'No, I didn't need to. Siobhan arrived when I was at the hospital. I was talking to one of the policemen and she started kicking off about Strom...'

Siobhan had interrupted their conversation, furiously wanting to know if the police were going to arrest the man responsible for poisoning her sister. Whatever affection Siobhan had felt for Strom, if indeed any had ever existed, had obviously vanished.

On balance, thought Hanlon, there probably never had been any anyway. She guessed Siobhan had slept with him with the express intention of telling Camille, just to spite her.

At least her intervention had saved Hanlon any worries she had been harbouring about whether or not to disclose to the police Strom's drug hoard. Siobhan had been doing this loud and clear, the policeman noting down the details.

She'd wandered off to get a coffee and returned to the waiting area. Siobhan had been there, waiting for her, grim-faced.

'So how come you were there in the studio?' she'd said in an accusing voice. 'Were you part of Strom's little plan?'

Hanlon had felt herself getting angry.

'Me! Part of a plan? You've got a nerve... I was the one who found her and called an ambulance, Siobhan. If it weren't for me Camille would be dead, so lose the snotty tone, OK.'

Far from losing her snotty tone, Siobhan had cranked it up another couple of notches. 'Yeah, you find quite a lot of dead people, don't you, Hanlon? Suki, Jenny, Dan, Katherine... you're the common denominator.'

'Are you saying I had something to do with their deaths?' Hanlon had said incredulously.

Siobhan had been breathing hard, her brown eyes narrowed; she obviously had a hell of a temper. Hanlon had never realised this before; she had then. Siobhan had squared up to Hanlon as if for a fight. Go on, Hanlon had thought, make my day...

She'd replied quietly, 'I'm getting sick of people abusing and threatening me, Siobhan. If you try and lay a hand on me, I swear to God you won't be leaving this hospital tonight.'

Siobhan must have seen the look in her eyes. 'I'm just saying... OK?' she'd said, sulkily.

'How did you get into the centre?' she'd demanded.

'I'll answer to Camille, not to you, Siobhan,' Hanlon had said. She'd turned on her heel and walked away.

* * *

Murdo looked at her inquisitively. 'So what do you think?'

'Well, I think Strom's innocent of trying to kill Camille,' Hanlon said.

'I think she either took an overdose by mistake or someone poisoned her, maybe both.'

'Digitalis, eh?'

Hanlon nodded. 'That's what the doctor thought, why?'

Murdo told her about the foxgloves in Anna's garden. 'She was there this afternoon too, getting ready for this ceremony.'

Hanlon shrugged. 'So what? I've got foxgloves in my garden. They grow wild all over the country. They're not exactly rare, Murdo.'

'No, but you're not the one with an interest in medicinal plants and herbal infusions. And you didn't spend the afternoon alone with Anna. I think that it would be very easy for Anna to persuade Camille to drink a glass of herbal tea, don't you? And if she died as a result the chances are that it could well be put down to whatever weird concoction she took from Strom, which might well contain digitalis anyway, who knows?'

Hanlon fell silent.

'Why would Anna poison Camille?' she wondered.

'Who knows? Maybe it's something to do with Suki's death, or Jenny's. But I'm still looking into that fraud and for all we know Anna may be the one who committed it and killed Suki. Maybe Camille knew or suspected something.' He made an open-handed gesture. 'I'm only putting this forward as a hypothesis.'

'Well, I guess it's possible,' Hanlon said sceptically. 'Have you seen Loyd yet?'

Murdo shook his head. 'I'm seeing him tomorrow. DS Patterson's swinging by to drive me. We'll see what he's got to say.' Murdo looked at her.

'Cheer up. Camille would be dead if it weren't for you.'

She gave a wan smile. 'I know.'

Murdo asked casually, 'Would you like to stay the night? I could always make a bed in the spare room. It's ten o'clock, after all.'

Hanlon smiled. 'No, thank you all the same. I think after all the excitement I just want to go home.' She stood up and stretched. 'As you say, Murdo, it's gone ten. I'm going to head off back to Argyll.'

'What are you doing tomorrow?'

She thought of Strom's melodramatic warning. Sod you, Strom.

'I think I'm going back to Seil Island.'

'Seil?' Murdo looked surprised. 'Why?'

'Just because,' Hanlon said, picking up her handbag. 'Just because.'

33

'Can I sign it?' Patterson said, pointing to Murdo Campbell's cast.

'No, no, you can't,' he said irritably. 'We're not at school, we're grown men.' He glanced over at his colleague. It did cross his mind that, although Patterson was a large, overweight, balding man in his late thirties, there was something strangely schoolboyish about him, as if he'd never quite grown up. Patterson pulled a disappointed face. An unlikely Peter Pan.

They walked down the stairs to the street and got inside Patterson's car. Murdo Campbell restrained himself from saying anything, but the car interior was a disgrace. The rear was full of junk, empty soft-drink cans, bottles and old food wrappers. It was as if someone had emptied the office wastepaper bin out in the car. And then some.

'Where to?'

'Bearsden, we're off to see Suki Bly's ex.'

* * *

John Bly answered the door to Campbell's ring. He glanced down at his foot.

'Sporting injury,' Campbell said, forestalling the inevitable question.

'Do come in,' Bly said. He led the way across the hall, into the gangster-style living room. There was no sign of his girlfriend today.

Patterson looked around appreciatively. 'Lovely place you've got here, Mr Bly.' Campbell looked at his colleague with surprise. Patterson wasn't being sarcastic; he genuinely was enthusiastic.

'Cheers,' Bly said.

'You said you'd got something to show me?' Campbell said.

Bly nodded. 'Aye. It may be nothing,' he said. 'The police returned Suki's stuff to me from the hotel at Duachy. I'm still listed as next of kin. Her phone was included. She still had the old code on it, so I unlocked it and looked through it.' He took out Suki's phone in its hot-pink case from a pocket in his shirt.

Campbell stared at the short muscular figure with growing interest. Bly was not the kind of guy who would have called him for nothing. He smiled at Campbell; he knew he'd got his interest now.

'What did you find?' he asked.

'I'll show you.' Bly turned the phone on and his fingers moved swiftly over the keypad. 'Where are we...? It's different from mine... ah, here we go, photos...' He looked up at Campbell.

'This,' said Bly and handed the phone over.

Campbell took it and his eyes widened in surprise.

* * *

Hanlon returned from a ten-kilometre run with Wemyss. Both of them were exhausted. She'd incorporated quite a lot of speed work into the run, choosing the steepest and hardest hills to open up on. There were also parts of the run that she used as a kind of open-air gym. The forestry commission, or whatever they were called these days, had at one part of the track, for unknown reasons, created a kind of large cairn of varied-sized boulders. Hanlon had a small selection of rocks she'd picked out from the heap a few weeks previously and had lined them up to create a kind of outdoor gym. She held the large stones goblet-style and used them to do squats and overhead raises with. There was also a convenient tree branch for pull-ups, an exercise at which she excelled. She varied this with sit-ups and push-ups, a couple of hundred of the former and about a hundred of the latter in four punishing slow sets. There were other stomach exercises to add to the fun – holding a straight-arm plank until her abs screamed in agony. Hanlon could take it. Pushing through the pain was how she lived her life, spiritually and physically.

Wemyss had lain under a tree, watching her sceptically.

Now, back home, she'd showered, she'd washed the dog as well, who wasn't keen but accepted it with good enough grace, and she was lying on the floor next to him, playing with his ears, scratching behind them, something Wemyss loved, and staring at the ceiling.

Did she really want to drive up the coast to Seil?

Part of her said no. She'd called the hospital. Camille was making good progress seemingly.

She stared some more at the ceiling. She thought back to her first meeting with O'Rourke. It seemed so long ago now, so long ago and so many deaths. She couldn't really blame Camille for taking Strom's hallucinogenic cocktail in an effort to discover the truth. If she had thought it might have worked she'd have been tempted. What she was going to be doing on Seil would not be so very different, a kind of desperate attempt to find out what had been going on and why.

'Come on, Wemyss,' she said, standing up. The dog jumped up enthusiastically.

'Let's go.'

* * *

Forty minutes later she was driving over the bridge and through the scattering of buildings that was the village of Balvicar and took a right, following the road to Ellenabeich. North of Ardfern, mist from the hills had rolled in, cold and clammy. Maybe it was just very low cloud. Whatever it was, visibility was not good and the journey had taken longer than she thought.

She was driving slowly along the twisting single-track road, wisps of fog obscuring her view, when suddenly, without warning, a huge tractor appeared from round a corner, forcing her to swerve into the verge. The tractor rumbled past, the huge wheels nearly scraping her car, the high-sided steel trailer swaying and jolting alarmingly, deafeningly noisy. The container absolutely reeked, slurry of some sorts.

'Cretin!' she shouted at the driver. She shook her head in annoyance; she'd nearly ended up in the ditch. Then she saw it. She rubbed her eyes in disbelief.

* * *

'What do you make of that, then?' John Bly asked, grinning.

'I don't know what to say,' Murdo Campbell said.

'Well, you can't say you've never seen one,' Bly said.

'Not looking like that, I haven't.'

He was looking at one of three pictures of an erect penis on Suki Bly's phone. He wondered what to make of it. It was certainly sizeable, veiny and bulbous. What made it so hard for him to look at was the piercing at the tip. He looked at Bly. 'What do you think?'

'I'm wondering if it belongs to the guy who took that money off her.' He scratched his head. 'I can't imagine why else she would have it there. It's hardly a thing of beauty, ken?

Patterson looked at it. 'Well, it'll make a line-up fun,' he said. 'Nice Prince Albert going on there.' He grinned. 'Wish we could do it old-style, with actual men lined up in a row with their knobs out.'

Murdo Campbell privately wondered what on earth possessed people to mutilate themselves like that.

'What makes you think that it belongs to the fraudster, Mr Bly?' he said.

'Suki used to do phone sex before we were married, Inspector, for...' he paused, 'for professional reasons. She wouldn't keep this sort of thing on her phone for fun, believe me.' He looked at Campbell. 'I'm wondering if she flirted with him on the phone, tried to get him to send her a pic of his face, which he obviously didn't want to do, but maybe...' he put on a kind of coquettish voice, '"well, if ye willnae send me a photo of your lovely face, send me one of your cock, it'd really turn me on, and I'll send you a photo of me... Aye, you show me yours, I'll show you mine...” Just like that. Then she’d have something, better than nothing.’ He shrugged. ‘That’s my guess. I can tell you now she wouldnae be turned on by dick pics.’

Campbell looked again at the photo. If you disregarded the obvious, the hand and wrist that were visible did give something to go on.

‘Can you send me those images?’ he said.

‘Of course,’ Bly said. ‘Do you think they’ll be useful?’

‘Yes,’ said Campbell, thoughtfully. ‘Yes, I do.’

* * *

‘Corranbuie Farm,’ the sign she was looking at said. It was half obscured by a gorse bush that had grown over it. There was a rough, rutted track leading down the slope that ran inland. She would never have seen it if she hadn’t been forced to stop by the tractor. She started the car and pulled into the top of the drive and parked in the mouth of the track where it met the road.

She thought of Shane Gowrie raving away in the home, the frazzled, decayed parts of what was left of his mind firing away at random. Corranbuie, well, he had mentioned it – here she was. She drummed her fingers on the steering wheel. She might as well visit the farm or the house or whatever lay at the bottom of the track.

She got out of the car. Wemyss whined hopefully and swished his tail.

‘No, boy, stay!’ She could see sheep in the fields beyond the gate that blocked the track a little further down. Wemyss was fine with sheep but she knew that any farm owner would get antsy at the sight of a dog with a stranger walking through their land and she didn’t want an angry confrontation. Part of her was hoping the people who owned the farm would be connected to Gowrie somehow, that maybe she could talk them into visiting. It had depressed her that you might live out your final years in a care home visited by nobody. Even mass murderers in high-security prisons got visitors. And unlikely proposals of marriage. No one these days would be doing that to Shane Gowrie; all the groupies had gone.

She walked down the track for about a kilometre and a half. The fields stretched away on either side. The weather had been getting progressively worse as she'd driven north. It was cold and blustery and it felt more like October than July. As she neared the house, low cloud from the hills inland was beginning to roll onto the island. It was the weather she had driven through earlier, now reaching Seil.

A few minutes later she arrived at the farmhouse. The mist or freezing cloud was really closing in now and the slopes around were indistinct shapes, nearly lost in the ghostly light. The place looked a mess, forlorn, decayed. The gate to the farmyard was rusted and sagging on its hinges. In an open barn opposite she could see a couple of vehicles and an old tractor parked. On its wooden lintel a macabre decoration: about a dozen deer skulls had been nailed up in a row, their bleached white bone in contrast to the dark of the rotting wood of the building.

The house was two-storey and stone-built, painted an off white. Paint was flaking away from the windows and weeds grew in the courtyard in front of the door. There was a depressing air of dereliction about the whole place.

Hanlon walked up to the front door and knocked.

The door opened and a man stood there looking at her. She blinked in surprise.

'Do come in, Hanlon,' he said.

34

Loyd Travers lived in a large house set in a couple of acres of ground in the countryside north of Glasgow on the road to Cumbernauld. Patterson parked in the driveway outside the front door next to a Porsche Carrera. He looked at his colleague. The DI's attention had been firmly fixed on his tablet for the duration of the journey. Now he closed the iPad and nodded at Patterson.

'Find what you wanted?'

'Yes, Sergeant, I rather think I did.'

Both men got out and looked at the imposing Georgian-style building with its large symmetrical windows overlooking the surrounding hills.

'Well, this is very nice,' Patterson said. 'Wonder how much it cost.'

Murdo Campbell shrugged. 'A lot less than John Bly's place, that's for sure.' He looked at Patterson. 'Are you coming inside?'

The DS shook his head. 'No, I'll wait in the car if that's OK with you. I don't really know anything about this fraud case. I'll catch up on some paperwork.'

'OK, I shan't be that long.'

'Don't forget to get a good look at his cock, sir,' Patterson suggested. Campbell shook his head sadly.

He got out of the car and walked up to the front door of the house and rang the bell. He heard footsteps and the door opened.

'Please come in, Detective Inspector,' Loyd Travers said.

He followed Travers into the house. The hall was painted pale gold and there were a couple of very large, tall brass Indian vases decorated with relief work of various Hindu gods. A faint smell of incense perfumed the air.

'Come through into the lounge.'

Campbell did so, limping in on his crutches. The lounge was enormous. Indian tapestries hung on the walls and there were framed posters of bands from the psychedelic era, mainly San Franciscan bands like the Grateful Dead and Jefferson Airplane. His eye was caught by a large painting of a skeleton against a blue background; bright crimson roses crowned his skull and floated around in the foreground. It was a beautiful picture, playful and macabre all at the same time.

'It's by Mouse and Kelley,' Loyd Travers said, seeing his interest. 'It's a signed print. They did lots of album art covers in the sixties and seventies, mostly for the Dead.'

'It's very good,' commented Campbell. 'Food for thought.' Smouldering in a holder in the fireplace were three joss-sticks. Across the room a huge bright green statue of Ganesh stared down at them.

Campbell looked at Loyd Travers. The businessman was a fit-looking guy who looked to be in his sixties. He had a neatly trimmed white beard and a full head of white hair brushed back and secured in a kind of rudimentary pigtail. One ear was pierced. He was wearing a plaid shirt, jeans and a Crosby, Stills & Nash T-shirt. He had Converse sneakers on his feet. Rock music rumbled quietly through a couple of enormous speakers at opposite ends of the room.

'So, how can I help you?' he asked pleasantly.

'Suki Bly,' Campbell said.

'Yes,' Loyd said, 'that was a terrible accident, the poor girl.' He shook his head sadly.

'I'm not here about her death,' Campbell said.

'No?' Loyd looked surprised. 'Why are you here, then?'

'Suki Bly was defrauded of a lot of money by a person claiming to be from an investment company.'

'That's terrible,' Loyd said.

'It was a lot of money,' Campbell said, 'a six-figure sum.'

'What can I say?' Loyd was looking distinctly uncomfortable.

'Yes, we're having trouble locating the paper trail,' Campbell said. 'That's normally not a problem in fraud cases, but the money went from Edinburgh to the Philippines and from there it was finally paid into a bank account in Mumbai... You like India, don't you, Mr Travers?'

'What's that supposed to mean?' Loyd asked guardedly.

'It's simply an observation.'

'You don't think I had anything to do with it, do you?' Loyd tried for an incredulous laugh. It really did not work.

'Terrapin Solutions...'

'Is the name of my company, yes.'

'I've been looking at your records at Companies House.'

'I think you'll find everything's in order.'

Campbell frowned. 'It's red-flagged that your accounts for this year are overdue. Is there a reason for that?'

Loyd shrugged. 'I'll have to speak to my finance guy about that. I can't really answer your question.'

'Perhaps you should – maybe he could tell you why your full accounts haven't been made up for two years.'

'I'm sure there's a reason...' Loyd was looking distinctly uncomfortable.

'I'm sure there is,' Campbell said politely. He allowed the silence to deepen while he studied his tablet closely.

Campbell looked up from his screen and again at the picture. 'Mouse and Kelley?'

'That's correct.'

'Could you give me some more detail about M&K Holdings?'

'Umm, I'm not sure...'

'They're listed as having significant control over your company Terrapin Solutions. Coincidentally, not only do they share the initials of your favourite artists...' he nodded at the painting of the skeleton, 'but they're based in Mumbai too, which is of course where a lot of the stolen money wound up.' He looked hard at Loyd, who stared at him defiantly.

'I've got no idea.'

Campbell nodded. 'Really? Well, here's another question, a simpler one since you're not doing well on these tricky financial ones.' He winced with pain; his foot was aching.

'Can you explain why Suki Bly named you as the man who defrauded her of her money?'

'That's a lie, she can't have...'

'She has a photo that you sent her, Mr Travers, not just one, three of them. They are highly distinctive. When you sent the photo you were claiming to be someone else. David Piper. That's the name of the man who is the salesman for—'

'She's lying, she's a dirty lying bitch...'

Loyd was on his feet now, red-faced and furious. 'I never... it was digitally altered,' he added wildly.

'What was digitally altered?'

'The dick pic.'

Murdo Campbell stood up. 'Loyd Travers, I'm arresting you—'

For a man of his age, Loyd moved with impressive speed. Murdo Campbell saw the punch coming but too late to do anything about it. It wasn't a hard blow, Loyd hit him on the side of his nose, but it knocked him off balance and he staggered and landed on the sofa.

He reached for his crutches and hauled himself to his feet as he heard the front door slam. He looked out of the window in time to see Patterson, with an athleticism that surprised him, leap out of his car and grab Loyd as he was opening the door of the Porsche. Loyd took a wild swing at the sergeant, who slipped the punch and hit Loyd with a short brutal uppercut to his midriff.

Loyd's legs buckled and he collapsed next to his car. Patterson was hauling him to his feet as Campbell walked slowly up to them. The sergeant, grinning all over his face, spun Loyd around and cuffed him. Patterson was enjoying his day out hugely.

'As I was saying, Loyd Travers, I am arresting you on suspicion of Fraud, you do not have to say anything but it may harm your defence if you do not mention when questioned something you later rely on in court, anything you do say may be given in evidence.'

Campbell looked at the tell-tale jewellery on Loyd Travers' right hand, the silver skull-design ring, and the ring with the blue gemstone. Loyd turned around angrily. He had a miniature silver Buddha hanging on a necklace that had been concealed by his T-shirt but was now visible.

'Put him in the car, Sergeant,' Campbell said. 'Careful of his penis.'

Loyd was looking furious. 'You bastard, Campbell!'

Murdo Campbell smiled at him and nodded at the Buddha.

'Om Shantih, Loyd.'

35

'Do come in,' Charlie said.

Hanlon stared at him in surprise. She knew he lived on Seil but she had always imagined, just because he had a boat, he would live on the coast rather than inland.

She didn't know what she had been expecting but certainly not him – then again, why not? He had to live somewhere. And, to be honest, if she had been asked to guess the kind of place he would live she might well have come up with a place like this. An unhygienic, ruinous dump. She nodded and stepped into the dark, gloomy hallway.

The old farmhouse reeked of smoke and soot. The wallpaper in the hall was coming off in places; the paste had long ago disappeared and strips of it wafted gently in the draught from the front door like a gossamer-thin tapestry. A bare wooden staircase led upstairs. She noticed beneath the smell of soot and smoke that was coming from a doorway she guessed was the lounge – she could see the back of a sofa – a pervasive smell of damp. It seemed colder in the house than outside, a bone-aching chill perhaps compounded by its depressing nature.

'Come through into the kitchen, lassie,' he said.

She followed him into the room at the end of the hall. It was at least warm. There was a battered old Aga in the corner. Hanging from the ceiling was an old-fashioned wooden drying rack – Hanlon seemed to remember that it was called a pulley. Charlie's stained underwear was hanging from it, a grim sight. Charlie himself was wearing an old zip-up tracksuit top over a string vest, and a pair of old tweed trousers. The top was half undone and she could see wisps of white chest hair poking through the holes in the vest. He moved a walking stick from out of the way and sat down in a battered leather armchair in the corner, He waved a hand at the big wooden farmhouse table that dominated the room.

'Take a seat. Would you like a tea or a coffee, maybe a wee dram?'

'No, I'm fine...' Charlie looked disappointed; his face fell. Hanlon thought, He'll be like Effie, the poor old sod probably gets zero visitors. 'Actually, second thoughts, I'll have a coffee.'

'Aye...' He stood up, crossed the kitchen, opened a cupboard and got out a jar of instant coffee.

Oh, well, thought Hanlon, what did you expect? 'No milk,' she said.

Charlie got an old-fashioned kettle, the sort that sat on a stove, and carried it over to the fridge. He opened it, crouched down and took out a glass bottle. 'Well water,' he said to Hanlon, filling the kettle. 'Better for you than that muck you get oot the taps.'

He put the kettle on top of the stove and looked out of the window into the yard.

'Where's your car?' he asked.

'Parked at the top of your lane,' she said.

'I hope you closed all the gates behind you,' he said suspiciously. 'Dinnae want the yows tae escape.'

'I closed the gates,' she said. 'The sheep are just fine.'

'So, Hanlon,' he said, sitting down, 'what brings you to Corranbuie Farm?'

She told him of her visit to Shane Gowrie at the home. She didn't want to make it sound too grim; surely Charlie couldn't be far off ending up there himself. If he ever went into hospital, for whatever reason, and social services inspected this place, he would in all probability not be allowed back. Ever.

'Shane Gowrie,' he said, 'a puir sinner. I shall pray for his soul tonight. I shall add it tae my tally when I go tae bed tonight.'

Well, she thought, that was an image to conjure with, Charlie kneeling at the foot of the bed, hands folded.

'Do you pray for every sinner you meet?' she asked.

'Aye. Regardless. I pray for the Quick and the Deid. I prayed for the lassies on Duachy,' he said sonorously. 'I prayed for that wee shite who attacked you and I prayed for the dead yin at the commune.'

'Don't forget to pray for me.' She smiled.

'I willnae forget, lassie, rest assured.' She knew he would be true to his word. God knew what would have happened to her if he hadn't flattened Callum. Maybe dead. Certainly still in hospital.

Charlie spooned coffee into a cup for her, added water. He stared at it. 'That looks a wee bit hot,' he muttered. 'One minute.' He wandered over to the fridge and added a splash of water from a smaller bottle and handed it to her. 'That's better, you'll no scald yourself now.'

She took it from him. 'Did you know Shane Gowrie?' she asked, curious.

'In a manner of speaking,' he said.

'What was he like?' She drank some of her coffee. It wasn't as bad as she feared.

'He was a lost soul,' Charlie said, 'more to be pitied than scorned. He had lost his way long ago.'

'Why do you think he was raving away about this place, Charlie?' Hanlon asked. 'He kept shouting about it. Did it mean anything to him?'

Charlie shrugged. 'Who knows what's going on in his head? Dementia's a terrible thing, terrible.'

Well, that was true, she thought. It had certainly condemned Shane Gowrie to an awful zombie-like existence. Hanlon yawned. She was tired; she'd have to be heading home soon. She was glad she'd come though. It was nice to see Charlie.

'Thank you for saving my life the other day,' she said.

Charlie smiled. 'Always a pleasure to do the Lord's work. I couldnae pass by on the other side like the Priest and the Levite.'

She smiled at him, blew on her coffee and drank some more.

'Do you mind if I use your toilet before I go?' she asked.

'Surely, it's in the barn. The one in the house is broken.'

God, she thought, an outside privy. Charlie nodded to the kitchen door. Hanlon stood up and went outside. The fog or cloud had really rolled in. You could see across the farmyard, but only just.

She walked into the barn. There was Charlie's pick-up truck and an equally old Land Rover parked on the far side. The rear of the barn had a couple of old grease- and dirt-stained workbenches running along the back, bits of incomprehensible rusted machinery sitting next to a jumble of tools. She could see a door ajar at the far side, probably the toilet, she thought.

After she'd finished – the toilet hadn't been as bad as she had feared, not that her expectations had been high – she walked round by the side of the Land Rover and stopped abruptly. There on the windscreen was a small starred crack in the glass, just as if a rock had hit it. She ran her fingers over it thoughtfully. The paint on the edge of the bonnet was chipped just below the damaged glass. She recalled the heavy weight of the rock in her hand as she'd hurled it at what she'd thought had been Strom's vehicle. Had it been Charlie who'd been parked outside her house? Surely not?

She was thoroughly confused now. Charlie had saved her life when Callum had come at her with a knife, he'd also seemed like a beacon of normality at Duachy Island. This had to be some sort of coincidence? But if so, it was stretching the bounds of credulity.

She walked to the back of the barn and along by the bench. There was a back door to the barn and impulsively she opened it. She stepped through into the yard at the rear.

The area behind the barn was a mess of tangled old farm machinery, rusted heaps of metal, a burnt-out car and the skeleton of a prehistoric tractor. There was a shed next to it and Hanlon went over to it. There was a strong and unpleasant smell of rotting meat from behind the door. She thought it could just be old rubbish, but she knew it wasn't.

She opened the door. It was far worse than she could ever have imagined. She stepped back, gagging.

36

Callum's body was propped up in a folding deckchair, his eyes staring sightlessly at Hanlon. It was horrible. The blue nylon of his tracksuit top was obscured with a huge black stain from top to bottom, which she assumed was dried blood. His throat had been cut. She guessed he must have been dead for about four days. Flies were buzzing noisily around him, some crawling over his dead flesh. Tossed on the floor by his feet, like an afterthought, was an old hand sickle, its curved, razor-sharp edge stained with dried blood.

She closed the door behind her and went back inside the barn. She pulled out her phone – no signal out here. She thought frantically. There was no reason to suspect that Charlie meant her any harm, but if she didn't reappear, he'd guess why. Charlie almost certainly would own a shotgun or a rifle, most farmers did. She didn't want to be hunted down like a fox or a deer.

She walked back to the kitchen, determined to act as if nothing had happened. Even if trouble kicked off, she could handle it. He was an old man; she was hard as nails. She went inside, back to where she had been sitting. Charlie was still at the table. He was examining the walking stick that she had noticed earlier. As she moved towards her chair, he unscrewed the ferrule at the end and put it on the table. He squinted down at it.

'Found it all right?'

She sat down and picked up her coffee cup. It was still a third full. Charlie was fiddling with the handle of the stick, then he twisted it and slid it down a little. It must be adjustable, she thought. She finished her coffee and put the cup down.

She thought again of Callum and her gorge rose. His decaying corpse, its smell, the colour of his skin. A fly had been crawling across one of his eyes. For a second she felt light-headed and thought she was going to faint.

'Yeah, thanks.'

She yawned, feigning nonchalance, and stretched.

'Well, I'd better be going... It was good seeing you again, Charlie.'

'Aye, it was guid tae see you.' He took something small and shiny out of his pocket.

She wondered, Why is he holding a lipstick? Then she realised her mistake. It wasn't a lipstick. God, my mind's slow, she thought. He slid the bullet into the chamber in the walking stick and slid it shut. It closed with an audible click.

She stared at Charlie blankly. She couldn't really understand what she was seeing. Momentarily she couldn't work out where she was; things had lost their meaning. That's a table, she thought without really comprehending its function. She stared at it, four legs and a rectangle. Then, what's it for? she wondered. She looked around the room. Things were beginning to change, to go in and out of focus. She made a major effort to look at him. The ceiling gently pulsed and changed colour to a pale gold. It was entrancing.

'It's called a cane gun,' he said. 'It belonged to my granddad. It's Victorian, it takes one cartridge...'

What was he on about? She smiled vaguely at him. She could see the gun, but it was writhing in his hands as if it were a snake. She wondered what Charlie was doing with it. Some kind of pet, perhaps?

She had a sudden burst of clarity. I've been drugged! Then her mind drifted away from that thought like a boat drifting away from land on a loch.

She looked down at her hands. How amazing they seemed. She had never really noticed before how beautiful they were. She flexed her fingers experimentally. She looked over at Charlie.

'Can you hear what I'm saying?' he said.

She smiled. She tried to stand up, but her hands sank into the arms of the chair. She frowned. That had never happened before. They had literally disappeared so only her wrists were visible, as if the old, scuffed leather were liquid.

She tried again.

'Stay where you are, Hanlon,' Charlie said. 'I hit that woman you were with, O'Rourke, from thirty yards, I can hit you from here with my eyes closed.'

It took time for her to process what he had just said, as if she were translating from a foreign language. Then the meaning of the words hit her. This evil old man opposite her had murdered O'Rourke.

She fought to regain control of her mind through the coils and snares of the chemicals racing through her system.

She returned to her moment of clarity. I've been drugged, she thought. Charlie's drugged me and he's going to kill me, like he did Callum. Callum's throat had been cut. She had a sudden vision of Charlie with the sickle in his hand as he stood behind her as she sat, like Callum, helpless and immobile in a folding chair, his old man's bony knuckles pale white, clutching her by her thick, curly hair as he pulled her head back, exposing her throat.

She felt a floating sensation, as if she was leaving her body; she wondered if she was actually dying right now. Charlie had drugged her, had he poisoned her too?

Everything went dark, momentarily. Then her vision was restored. But by some trick of whatever he had given her in her coffee, she felt she was standing behind herself, looking down on her body. She had heard about out-of-body experiences, now she was actually having one.

She could see her bent head, her back, she was wearing a thin Fair

Isle jumper that was slightly too small for her. The wool clung to her muscular shoulders and she could see the clearly defined trapezius muscle running from the rear of her neck downwards. Her sleeves were pushed up and she could see her tanned, muscled forearms as her fingers grasped the chair.

The kitchen door opened and Siobhan walked in. Hanlon felt a sense of vindication. It was her behind all this. I never liked you, she thought. Bitch.

Charlie looked at her and smiled. 'There you are, darling. You're just in time.'

Darling! thought Hanlon almost with a sense of horror. Surely to God she's not his lover, the elderly man in his stained tracksuit top, trousers and string vest, the faded, baggy Y-fronts hanging from the pulley above their heads.

'Yeah, lucky for you I was coming over today.'

'I'd have managed,' Charlie said sniffily.

'Of course you would.' Her tone was contemptuous. 'Anyway, how's she doing?' asked Siobhan with a glance over at Hanlon in the chair.

'I think she's well out of it, tripping her wee arse off,' Charlie said. 'What was in that stuff?'

'God alone knows,' Siobhan said. 'It's Strom's shit that I nicked, magic mushrooms and some South American shite. She seems to be enjoying it.' She walked over to where Hanlon was sitting and lifted her head up by her hair, staring down into her face.

'Not so scary hard now, are you, you interfering bitch?'

She pulled Hanlon forward by her hair and Hanlon toppled off the chair like a life-sized rag doll and thudded down on the filthy, cracked lino of the kitchen floor. Hanlon watched this happen to herself with impotent rage. She lay there immobile, face down, motionless, her left arm pressed against the Aga, her right arm stretched in front of her.

'Bet it's not as good as the acid I used to take,' Charlie said, in a reminiscing tone of voice. 'I mind one time when we were on tour in San Francisco, we were staying at the Marriott and I thought I was being—'

'Chased by a Chinese dragon around the dining room, aye, I know,' Siobhan said irritably. 'You've told me about twenty times, Dad.'

Dad, Hanlon thought. He's Shane Gowrie. Her mind went back to Camille's one-night stand with the rock singer all those years ago at the Royal Albert Hall. Siobhan was the product of that night of lust. Camille's been passing her off as her sister all these years when in reality she's her daughter!

'So what's the plan?' Charlie asked. It was hard to think of him as Shane.

'You've still got a boat on Loch Caithlim?' asked Siobhan.

'Aye, the *Dooker*. You ken the boat, you've been in her before.'

'Yeah, still with the Yamaha outboard?'

'Aye, the petrol can's in the barn together with the oars and the other stuff.'

'We'll get her into the Land Rover, take her down to the boat, then out to sea, then overboard. She'll wash up somewhere eventually. We'll let the police puzzle over it. I doubt she told anyone she was coming here. That's not Hanlon's style.' She frowned. 'How did she know you were here?'

'She didn't. She went to visit Shane Gowrie in the home. Charlie must have given her the farm's name. It's the only explanation.' He looked almost pleadingly at Siobhan. 'As soon as she arrived I knew I had to deal with her. She's trouble. I knew that from the second I clapped eyes on her.' He motioned towards Hanlon with a powerful, mottled hand. 'I had to do this.'

'OK,' Siobhan said, 'come on, let's go and get the Land Rover ready.'

They stood up. Charlie, as Hanlon still thought of him, looked over to her. 'Shall we kill her now?'

Hanlon's heart raced. Oh, God, no, she thought. She remembered the blood-stained sickle. She tried to move but her body refused. It was a total dead weight.

'No,' Siobhan said, 'I want her alive when she goes in the sea. We want cause of death to be drowning, that's the whole point... Jesus Christ! Come on.'

'Shall we tie her up?'

Siobhan looked down at Hanlon. 'She's not capable of going anywhere.'

The two of them left the kitchen.

Hanlon was alone with her thoughts.

37

Strom drove over the small stone bridge that spanned the narrow strip of sea separating Seil Island from the mainland, and parked his rental car. He rubbed his jaw thoughtfully. He had an unusual sense of things slipping away from him. He looked through the windscreen. The thick mist that had obscured the road since he had been north of Lochgilphead seemed even more opaque.

He suddenly felt a burning sensation in his left arm. He thought of Hanlon again. Something was happening, he thought, something bad. The pain was increasing now, as if his forearm were on fire; it drove him on like a goad. He had a sudden terrible feeling of doom hanging over him. He guessed that he didn't have much time left.

He had woken up that morning thinking of Hanlon with an uneasy feeling of worry. Ever since she had turned up at his flat, she had exercised a strange influence on him. He found her disturbingly physically attractive. When he'd seen her in her revealingly short blue dress in the company of the red-headed guy he'd been plagued by feelings of envy. He wasn't used to that. But it wasn't just that, it was the force of her personality pulling him like a magnet. He was well aware of her dislike towards him. Strom didn't care particularly. He didn't give a toss what other people thought about him, even her. He knew there was some kind of connection to her and that was enough. The whats and the whys had never bothered him in the past and they didn't now.

He had walked around his flat restlessly. He had told her not to go to Seil and he strongly suspected that she had, if only to spite him, even though he would not necessarily ever know. At about 11 a.m. the feeling of impending disaster had got too strong to ignore.

Strom, as he had told Hanlon, had initially viewed all forms of mystical experience with rationalist scorn, but spending time with the shamans in South America and Mongolia had, he felt, opened his mind. Hanlon had been wrong about him. He wasn't a con man, he was a believer.

He still was unsure as to what underpinned all this. Maybe it was some kind of Jungian collective consciousness, some kind of unseen neural network; maybe there really was a spirit universe or maybe he was simply a man with unusually heightened sensitivity. Maybe he was crazy or completely wrong, he neither knew nor cared. He didn't have to justify anything. Results were what mattered and Strom knew deep down that Hanlon was heading for trouble.

Now he had arrived on Seil, he thought, What do I do now? His options were limited by lack of choice. There was one road that led to Cuan Ferry via a tiny village called Balvicar and a spur road from that that led to Ellenabeich. He put the car in gear and headed for Cuan Ferry. The mist was drifting across the single-track road like smoke and he was driving very slowly along when he saw the blue Volvo parked at the top of a farmyard track. Somehow he immediately knew it was her car. He stopped and pulled in next to it. He got out and looked inside.

There was a sizeable black and white border collie inside that he recognised as Hanlon's. He tried the hatch; it was open. He lifted it and Wemyss sprang out. He let the dog sniff his hand.

'Where's Hanlon?' Strom asked.

Wemyss looked at him questioningly, his ears moving backwards and forwards in perplexity. Strom opened the driver's door and glanced inside. In the door compartment was a black beanie hat. Next to it was a lead. Strom took them out, clipped the lead on the dog's collar and gave the hat to Wemyss to examine. The dog sniffed it and looked expectantly at Strom.

'Find!'

Wemyss barked joyfully and snuffled the ground, then he moved forward purposefully, pulling Strom with him.

38

Hanlon lay on the kitchen floor trying unsuccessfully to get her drugged body to move. Her head was still a riot of exploding colour, fireworks, tracer fire, and the room spun around her as if she were on an out-of-control carousel.

Somehow, slowly, painstakingly, she managed to fathom a coherent narrative. Charlie, she thought, he's the man I saw in the home. This is his farm. 'My farm,' she heard him say, 'Corranbuie Farm, my farm.' And indeed it was. Gowrie must have swapped identities with Charlie, the poor old sod had been taken to the home under Shane Gowrie's name and Gowrie/Charlie had stayed on at the farm. Presumably Charlie, like Effie, had no close relatives to notice his disappearance.

Then, all too soon, although by now she had lost track of time, she heard voices and the kitchen door opened. Shane resumed his place at the table and Siobhan sat down opposite. Father and daughter relaxing together before having to go and do some dull chore. They ignored Hanlon as if she were part of the furniture.

Shane took his tracksuit top off. Hanlon could see his tattoo under the vest, as Dr Morgan had described it, faded slightly, but still recognisable, covering his left breast and shoulder. He took a pack of cigarettes, some

Rizla papers and a small bag of weed out of his pocket and started to roll a joint. He asked Siobhan, 'How's your mother?'

'Annoyingly, Camille's going to pull through,' Siobhan said. 'If it hadn't been for that fucking cow—' she prodded Hanlon's inert body with the toe of her training shoe '—she'd be dead by now, and I'd have my inheritance.'

So that's what this is all about, Hanlon thought. Money. She remembered O'Rourke telling her that Camille had said she wasn't leaving any money to her sister. Now she understood, it was her private joke. She never had a sister anyway; she was going to leave it to Siobhan, her daughter.

Who now looked down at her speculatively, as if gauging her weight, and took a pair of leather gloves out of her jacket pocket and pulled them on.

'And I'd have Duachy back,' Charlie said.

So, that was the plan: with Camille gone, Siobhan would get the bulk of the money and the old man's reward was to get his beloved house back. Siobhan could install him as 'caretaker' and he'd be free to relive the glory days. Now she could understand why Siobhan had persuaded Camille to buy the place, the perfect carrot to dangle in front of her homicidal father.

Who now said, 'You should have given her more of yon digitalis I brewed up for you.'

Siobhan turned round, her face suddenly filled with rage. 'I should,' she shouted. '*I should*, you stupid auld twat – if you'd pushed Camille off that path and not Suki Bly we wouldn't be in this mess, would we?'

So it was you, Charlie, who killed her, Hanlon realised. It was all a genuine mix-up after all.

Siobhan pointed a black-gloved finger at Shane accusingly. 'All that hard work just to make sure Camille would be on Duachy Island and then you fuck it up!'

All that hard work... So Siobhan had been behind the threats to Camille all along. The threats, the e-mails, the texts, the message painted on the wall, that was probably done by Charlie. It was she who had put the glass in the muesli, the final push to ensure that Camille would be on the island ostensibly for her own safety, but in reality so she could be killed by Shane Gowrie, who everyone thought was in a home in Glasgow.

'I did not fuck it up!' he said resentfully.

'Well, what about Jenny?'

'How was I to know she'd find me sleeping in the chapel? I wasn't supposed to be on the island, remember!'

'You were supposed to be sleeping in the boat in the boathouse!'

So it wasn't Oliver smoking weed that I smelt, Hanlon thought. It was Charlie. He never returned to the mainland. He just sailed out of the harbour, waited until I was out of sight and then came back and hid his boat in the boathouse. He was on the island all the time.

'Have you ever tried to sleep in a boat like that?' he complained. 'It's so uncomfortable and freezing cold!'

'Well, whatever.'

Shane puffed away on his joint. 'Calm down, and don't make it sound like I was incompetent. I dealt with that junkie pluke Dan for you.' He frowned. 'I don't get why you wanted him deid anyway?'

'Because,' Siobhan said, 'I'm supposed to be in the dark about Camille being my mother, that's why. I told Dan one night when I was fucked on drugs and he knew that Camille didn't know I knew my parentage. And I didn't want it out there. So when she died and left me all the money, I could act surprised and not get suspected, that's why.'

Charlie said, 'So, to get this straight, Dan told Camille he was going to tell you the truth, that you weren't her sister but her daughter, and she was too ashamed to admit that, so she paid him to stop him telling you what you already knew anyway.'

Siobhan nodded. 'Exactly, Dad. Camille's a coward at heart, she didn't know how I would have reacted. So she paid Dan to keep his trap shut... She's pathetic, she'd rather lie to me than acknowledge her own daughter. I always knew something was fishy, that's why I did the DNA test, but I think I'd known forever.'

She fell silent and stared at the floor. Lost in memories.

Hanlon felt a burning sensation in her left arm. She looked at herself on the floor, her arm by the Aga was pressed against the hot metal of the base. She felt a kind of pull. An irresistible force that was dragging her back to her body.

Everything went black for a moment. And then she was back inside herself. Half of her was her usual rational self, the other half was fighting the damage that the drugs were doing to her brain. Flashes of colour like sheet lightning, a feeling of total disconnect between her body and her mind. But one thing was a constant and that was the agonising pain from her arm, from the burning metal of the stove. She pushed down into the floor and felt it move like a sponge beneath her fingers, but she persevered and managed to shift her body a few centimetres away from the heat. Her face was resting on the filthy floor, which configured and reconfigured itself in a series of spiral mazes and weird Escher-like landscapes.

She closed her eyes. That was worse – it was like a bonfire in a firework factory. She concentrated, thinking of Strom; he had done this sort of thing for years, no wonder he was so fucked up.

She tried to remember what Strom had said to her. Wild flickering images of Strom appeared in her conscious in quick succession and then, suddenly, all the noise and the colours disappeared and she could see him clearly, sitting on his sofa and saying to her very distinctly, '*...the otherworld. It doesn't like trespassers, Hanlon. It throws up barriers and obstacles to prevent you reaching it...*'

'Is this what this is, Strom?' she said. 'Is this chaos what you meant by barriers?'

He nodded and stood up. She knew that in reality she was lying on the filthy kitchen floor of the farmhouse, but the vision she was having, the hallucination, was unbelievably real. She was in his lounge talking to him. Her mind had recreated his flat perfectly. She could make out the smallest details in the pictures hanging on Strom's walls; she could smell his aftershave.

He said to her, '*You must find your spirit guide to help you through the maze... do it now...*'

She knew that he'd told her it was an animal... what kind? The image of Strom dissolved and she was back in the maelstrom of whirling colours, memories, like being caught in a tornado, a vortex of fragments of dreams and snatches of events. It was hopeless. Memories swirled around her like autumn leaves in a gale.

Then she felt it. Its coarse fur that she clung to, its heady, comforting animal smell.

The wolf.

She opened her eyes. The kitchen was still a disconcerting jumble of images, but it was manageable. She turned her head, Shane was smoking his joint, Siobhan was sitting on a chair near him and examining the cane gun. It was incredibly realistic; it did look so much like a walking stick. You would never suspect what it really was.

'So there's no safety?' she asked, frowning at the cane gun.

'No, why do you ask?' he said.

She shrugged. 'So if I put the end here...' She picked it up and rested the tip under Shane's chin and pushed gently. His head tilted back, the end of the gun's barrel digging into the wrinkled flesh under his chin.

'Please don't do that, darling,' he said, with a placating grin. 'You're alarming your old dad.'

Siobhan smiled and pulled the trigger.

39

Siobhan stared thoughtfully at her handiwork. The force of the shot had knocked Shane Gowrie off his chair. He was now lying on the floor, his dead eyes staring sightlessly into Hanlon's. She looked upwards; blood and gore spattered the dirty ceiling of the kitchen.

'You gullible fuckwit, Shane, like you were ever my father,' muttered Siobhan. She pulled the gloves off her hands, crouched down and started sliding them onto Shane's dead fingers. Hanlon usually had a strong stomach, but the sight of the blood, bone and brain, magnified and distorted by the drugs, was more than she could take. She started to retch.

'Oh, for God's sake,' Siobhan said, irritably, turning her attention away from the corpse. 'Not over the floor...'

She bent over Hanlon, hauling her up by the collar of her jumper. Hanlon stood up, her legs feeling like jelly. She tried to speak but all that came out were inarticulate sounds. Siobhan steered her towards the kitchen door and she stumbled outside, the floor bucking beneath her like a ship on a rough sea. The walls of the kitchen billowed like sails in a breeze.

The two of them staggered outside into the farmyard. The cool, fresh air rallied Hanlon slightly. As she stood there, swaying on her feet, she closed her eyes and had a moment of acute clarity.

It was similar to the experience in the kitchen, a kind of out-of-body experience. It was as if she was looking down at the two of them. Hanlon's arm flung around Siobhan's neck as she supported her weight as they made their way to the Land Rover parked in the barn. Her vision was so acute she could even see the dark roots of the other woman's hair. She's going to kill you, she's going to take you out to sea and drown you, just as she worked out with Shane. Nobody would ever know she had been here. Siobhan will hope the police think it's murder, suicide when they find the bodies. Doubtless she'll volunteer that Charlie was starting to lose his mind, dementia. So sad. And in another couple of months, Camille will meet with another accident. And Siobhan would have it all, the money, the business, Duachy Island, and the one woman who might suspect something was wrong, O'Rourke, was dead.

And Hanlon was helpless, unable to do anything about it. An impotent observer as Siobhan tipped her unresponsive body over the side of Shane's boat into the cold, dark waters of the fog-bound loch.

Then, as hope started to fade, she felt the presence of the wolf. Whether or not it had any intrinsic reality or was simply part of the crazily firing neurons in her drug-frazzled brain, she neither knew nor cared.

It was there, real, solid, menacing. She felt its hot breath on her face, looked into its yellow, sinister eyes and then, quite suddenly, she was back in her body. She could smell Siobhan's perfume overlying her sweat as she struggled under Hanlon's weight. She could smell the sour tang of her own vomit on her jumper. She felt in control of her body for the first time since the drug had taken hold of her. She was still weak and shaky, but she felt capable of trying to escape.

'God, you're heavy, you fucking bitch,' she heard Siobhan mutter. Hanlon let herself go limp, sagging to the left, Siobhan turned her head slightly and Hanlon suddenly swivelled and hit her in the face with a left hook.

If Hanlon had done this an hour or so ago, Siobhan would have been unconscious before she hit the floor. But she was very disoriented. Even in her terribly weakened state, Hanlon could still land a powerful punch. Twenty years of practice, two decades of relentless physical training lay behind the blow. Siobhan staggered backwards, blood pouring from her nose.

'Jesus... you bitch.' Pain and incredulity equally mixed in her voice.

Hanlon staggered away from her across the farmyard in what felt like a drunken run. She reached the gate and fumbled with the latch.

Siobhan disappeared through the kitchen door and, as Hanlon struggled to make her fingers work, she reappeared with a large club hammer in her hand.

'I'm coming, Hanlon,' she called and started jogging towards her.

Desperately, Hanlon managed to get the gate open and she started to run up the drive, staggering in a zigzag fashion. She fell over and picked herself up. Despite the head start, Siobhan was catching her up with ease. Hanlon tried to sprint, but her legs obstinately refused to go faster.

'Give up, Hanlon,' she heard the mocking voice of Siobhan. 'Look at you, you can't run, you're pathetic.'

She veered off the rutted track onto the grass and heather. She hoped against hope that the fog might disguise her flight, that Siobhan might somehow lose the trail. There were some gorse bushes ahead. To Hanlon's skewed vision they were something out of a Grimms' fairy-tale illustration, similar to the impenetrable thorns around Snow White's castle. Their spiky branches were like jagged barbed wire, their yellow flowers exploding like suns going nova.

She fell over again before she reached the shelter of the bushes. It felt as if she had been standing upright and the ground had suddenly slammed upwards into her face. She lay there, unable to move. She heard Siobhan.

'I can see you, Hanlon. Here I come, ready or not...'

She turned herself over slowly so she was lying on her back and raised herself up onto her elbows. A gust of wind blew through her hair and she could see Siobhan now, just a few metres away. In her hand was the long-handled, heavy-headed hammer.

There was nothing more that she could do. She watched as Siobhan drew nearer, like an executioner approaching the block, her face implacable. Hanlon stared in fascination as she swung the hammer back. It was as if there were a succession of hammers describing a perfect arc, maybe twenty or so – as if her eyes were like the camera on her phone taking a multiplicity of shots in a single rapid burst. Then, at the top of her swing, Siobhan paused; she stood like a statue, arm upraised, and then slowly sank down to her knees. Hanlon saw an expression of surprise and pain and astonishment flicker across her face, as if she couldn't understand what had happened. She dropped the hammer and twisted her right hand round behind her back as if to scratch it, then she suddenly pitched face forward on the ground.

Silence. The wind sighing across the fields. Siobhan lying face down.

There was a slight slope from where she had fallen that led down to where Hanlon was sitting. Sticking out of Siobhan's back were two slim long knives with red handles. She'd seen them before. She had felt the solid wood she had been strapped against shake with the force with which they had embedded themselves deep in the hard surface of the board. They were Strom's throwing knives.

Unable to stand up, she lay there immobile, staring in astonishment at the fallen woman. The wind blew Siobhan's blonde hair over her face and her brown eyes stared unseeingly ahead.

There was a joyous bark and Wemyss appeared at the top of the slope and ran down to her, leaping on her and licking her face. She threw her arms around her dog, feeling his fur, inhaling its familiar, biscuity smell. For a moment she actually wondered if she were dead, then she raised her head and saw Strom walking slowly down the slope over the grass, towards her.

40

'So, what happened?' Murdo Campbell asked her. It was three days later. Hanlon had been discharged from hospital the day before. She'd spent a day at home and today she'd driven to Glasgow and Campbell's flat.

She gave Murdo an accurate account of what had happened up until Siobhan's arrival.

'Then I was out of my mind, Murdo, until I came to in the hospital in Glasgow, in the Tox ward. I say, "came to", I mean until those hallucinogens had worn off. It was pretty unpleasant. It was the weirdest thing that I've ever experienced.'

She cast her mind back to the moments after Siobhan's death. Strom had calmly retrieved his knives, then he'd knelt down beside her. 'I'm going to call the police in twenty minutes. I'll put Wemyss back in the car. I wasn't here.'

'You weren't here,' she repeated.

'I was never here.'

'Thank you, Strom.'

He said nothing, but smiled. He clipped the lead back on the collie, who, much to Hanlon's amazement, followed him without complaint.

'I've got no recollection of the police,' she said quietly, 'no recollection of the ambulance to Glasgow. It was all one huge, weird trip. What do your colleagues think happened? Maybe it will all come back to me, one day, but right now, it's just a void.'

'Well,' Campbell said, 'you were found about five hundred metres from the farm. Siobhan was lying there dead. She'd been stabbed in the back, twice, deeply. The body you discovered in the outbuilding was a kid from Nitshill in Glasgow, Callum Fergusson. He's got a record for drugs, possession and supply and petty violence. Quite a lot of drugs were found in the farmhouse.'

'But what happened?' Hanlon asked. 'Charlie drugged me, that much I know, and then?'

'We're working on the hypothesis that Siobhan rescued you and Charlie pursued both of you, stabbed her, realised he was going to be caught and killed himself.'

'Why didn't he kill me too?'

Campbell shrugged. 'Who knows? We'll never know for certain, but Charlie certainly killed Callum, there's no doubt about that. His fingerprints were all over the murder weapon. It looks like Siobhan saved you from being killed by him, somehow.'

'Yes,' Hanlon said, 'I can see that.'

'He also murdered Katherine O'Rourke,' Campbell said. 'The bullet that killed her was fired from that antique disguised gun of his.'

'So that's how he was able to smuggle it into the park.'

Campbell nodded. 'Exactly. An old man, leaning on a stick. And if someone had seen him shuffling into a bush, or emerging out of it, well, an old man caught short.' He shrugged. 'He was invisible. Nobody notices the elderly.'

'So, the drugs?'

'Yeah, we think he was dealing, maybe to Callum, or vice versa. Anyway, it's plain Charlie killed him for whatever reason, as he did O'Rourke.

Hanlon said, 'I wonder why he killed O'Rourke.'

'Munroe thinks maybe he was going crazy with pre-onset dementia. Unfortunately there was so much damage done to his head by that shot, nobody really wants to say.'

'Well, at least we know who did it now.'

'That's true,' Campbell said.

'How come the police arrived so soon?' Hanlon asked.

Campbell frowned. 'Someone called the emergency services, a man. He said they'd heard a shot from Corranbuie Farm and, as an elderly man lived there, they were concerned.'

'Did they get the number?'

'No, pay as you go phone. We think that it was probably an associate of Callum's. Munroe suspects Charlie was dealing and that's why Callum was there. Charlie killed Callum for whatever reason and someone from Glasgow turned up to investigate and discovered the bodies. As to why Siobhan was there, who knows? Maybe simply on business, arranging transport for the Duachy Hotel, and she stumbled on Charlie and you.'

'Some things remain a mystery, I guess,' Hanlon said.

'Yeah.' Campbell nodded.

'And how's Camille taking it?' she asked.

'Heartbroken. She asked me to apologise to you, she says she wants to see you as a friend. She says she's proud of her sister for having rescued you.'

'Thank goodness for Siobhan,' Hanlon said, hiding the sarcasm in her voice. Siobhan might as well be remembered as a hero. It would be some consolation for Camille; she wasn't going to shatter the illusion.

'Anyway, that's that.' Campbell smiled at her. 'How's your arm?'

'It's fine. I'm going to have quite a scar where the burn was, but otherwise OK. How's the foot?'

'Fine, the cast is coming off soon.'

They fell silent. She looked at him. 'Murdo?'

'Yes.'

'Could you stand up, please?'

He did so, she walked over to him and looked into his eyes. Their mouths met.

'It's all over now, Murdo...' She pulled him close to her, rested her hand on the small of his back and pushed herself hard against him, felt him respond.

'We've got unfinished business.' Her voice was a whisper. He looked into her grey eyes. 'Let's go to bed.'

* * *

The following day, over the kitchen table – Murdo, unsurprisingly, had cooked a great breakfast – he asked her, 'What are your plans for the day?'

'I'm going to see someone, then I'm going back to Argyll.'

'Strom?'

She shook her head. 'No, not Strom.' She smiled. Not yet, but she would. She owed him an apology.

* * *

Hanlon got out of her car outside the old people's home, holding the small paper bag she'd brought from her house. She rang the bell and the door was opened by Natalie.

'Oh, it's you again.' She looked delighted to see her. 'Have you come to see Shane? He'll be so happy.'

'Yeah, I've brought him a present.'

Natalie led her to the communal room. Charlie/Shane was sitting in his wheelchair in the same spot as last time.

Hanlon had spent some time agonising over whether to come clean about the deception the real Shane had committed. On balance she thought that, whatever she did, the man in the home wouldn't really know what was happening and, now that he'd had several years of being called Shane, she might as well let sleeping dogs lie.

She drew up a chair and sat next to him. He stared at her.

'Hello,' she said.

He smiled; he seemed pleased to see her. He pointed to her handbag. 'Aye, you've brought my bag?'

'I've brought you a present.'

'In my bag?'

'Well, I brought you your own bag,' she said.

She opened her handbag and brought out the bag that Effie had given her. Effie's home-made tablet. It somehow seemed fitting that at last she had found a good home for it.

'Tablet.'

His eyes lit up. 'My tablet?' He stretched out a hand trembling with hope.

'That's right, Shane.' She smiled, handing it over. 'Your tablet.'

MORE FROM ALEX COOMBS

We hope you enjoyed reading *Buried For Good*. If you did, please leave a review.

If you'd like to gift a copy, this book is also available as an ebook, digital audio download and audiobook CD.

Sign up to Alex Coombs' mailing list below for news, competitions and updates on future books.

http://bit.ly/AlexCoombsNewsletter

ALSO BY ALEX COOMBS

The DCI Hanlon series

The Stolen Child

The Innocent Girl

The Missing Husband

The Silent Victims

Private Investigator Hanlon

Silenced For Good

Missing For Good

Buried For Good

ABOUT THE AUTHOR

Alex Coombs studied Arabic at Oxford and Edinburgh Universities and went on to work in adult education and then retrained to be a chef. He has written four well reviewed crime novels as Alex Howard.

Visit Alex's website: www.alexcoombs.co.uk

Follow Alex on social media:

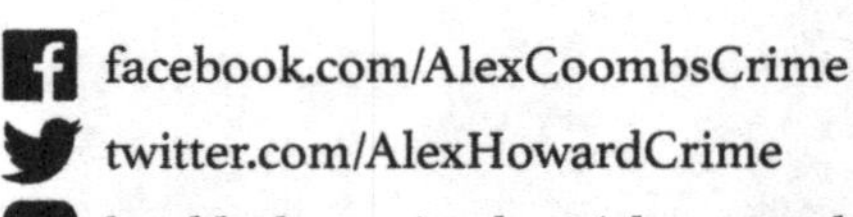

ABOUT BOLDWOOD BOOKS

Boldwood Books is a fiction publishing company seeking out the best stories from around the world.

Find out more at www.boldwoodbooks.com

Sign up to the Book and Tonic newsletter for news, offers and competitions from Boldwood Books!

http://www.bit.ly/bookandtonic

We'd love to hear from you, follow us on social media:

facebook.com/BookandTonic
twitter.com/BoldwoodBooks
instagram.com/BookandTonic

www.ingramcontent.com/pod-product-compliance
Lightning Source LLC
Chambersburg PA
CBHW010746310726
48980CB00004B/385